I0692712

ALSO, BY R.W. MARCUS

The Fate of Tomorrow: Tales of the Annigan Cycle
Book One

Shadow of the Twilight Lands: Tales of the Annigan Cycle
Book Two

R.W. Marcus

WHISPERS *from* NOCTURN

*A Tale of the Annigan Cycle
in Three Acts*

BOOK THREE

R.W. MARCUS

LAUGHING BIRD PUBLISHING
GALAX, VA USA

Copyright © 2020 by Jeff Morris

All rights reserved under the Pan-American and International Copyright Conventions. No part of this publication may be reproduced, distributed, or transmitted in any form or by any means, including photocopying, recording, or other electronic or mechanical methods, without the prior written permission of the publisher, except in the case of brief quotations embodied in critical reviews and certain other noncommerical uses permitted by copyright law.

Published by Laughing Bird Publications,
Galax, Virginia USA

Visit us on the web!
https://AnniganCycle.com

Front and back cover design by SelfPubBookCovers
https://SelfPubBookCovers.com

Laughing Bird Publications® is a registered trademark of Mark W. Phillips

Manufactured in the United States of America
10 9 8 7 6 5 4 3 2

First Printing, 2020
Revised Second Printing, 2023
ISBN 979-8-9877180-1-8

R.W. Marcus

Dedicated to
Edgar Rice Burroughs,
with a wink and a nod to
Philip José Farmer,
and Quentin Tarantino.

CONTENTS

ACKNOWLEDGEMENTS

Writing a novel is never a solitary effort. Behind the author's name is always a small army of support. It is to these people I am eternally thankful.

To my partner in crime, Cheryl Pepper, who puts up with my ramblings on plots, characters and all my writer's insecurities.

My critique partner, Mark "The Muse" Phillips, whose brainstorming sessions have gotten me out of many a corner I'd painted myself into.

Not to be left out are my awesome beta readers: Dave "I Wanna be Sedated" Holman, Lynn Marie Firehammer, Max Yrik Valentonis, Tom Landcraft, Doug Dewitt, Tristan Shuler & Chris Breton.

Special thanks to cover artist Viergacht for the cool artwork in keeping with my theme.

As always, a big thank you to the folks over at Mr. Media Books for believing in this project. The passing of my good friend and publisher Bob Andleman leaves me with a heavy heart but makes way for my new publisher, Laughing Bird Publishing.

WELCOME TO THE ANNIGAN

This mostly aquatic planet travels in a geosynchronous orbit around a small yellow sun. It's set far enough back in the solar system's Goldilocks Zone it maintains an atmosphere conducive to a wide variety of life.

Sentient creatures, terrestrial, marine or amphibious, share a hyper-fertility devoid of genetic boundaries. Any sentient creature may mate with any other and produce offspring.

Lumina basks in perpetual sunlight on one side of the Annigan. Humans dwell alongside many other sentient races thriving across its various continents and island chains. The fertility enriching rays of the sun, and the warmth of the Shallow Sea, support a vibrant and rich ecosystem.

Although life is abundant there, Lumina is hardly a serene place as you will see. Millennia of feuds, ruthless ambition and individual hatreds forged a fragile peace, barely sustained under the rule of the Great Houses.

Because of the incredible diversity of sentient creatures, all races, genders and hybrids in Lumina enjoy social equality, judging each as an individual based upon their own merits. Beneath the veneer of peace, however, dwells a hotbed of totalitarian torture, raider uprisings and a constant escalating cold war between the Great Houses.

Nocturn, languishes in constant darkness on the other side of the Annigan. Only moonlight, starlight and bioluminescence illuminate the land of endless night. Without the warming rays of the sun, Nocturn's oceans froze over, but constant geothermal activity heats the land masses, creating a temperate and misty terrain teeming with exotic and predatory sentient races.

Imperialistic cat people rule aboveground and hive nations of humanoid mantises swarm beneath the surface. In the Ocean Deep, a race of sentient octopoids dwell in vast underwater cities worshiping the ancient ones of the abyss. You are predator or prey in Nocturn's despotic societies.

The Twilight Lands reside at the fringes of the Annigan and remain in a constant gloaming. Here, warm and cold air currents clash, generating a perpetually stormy climate.

Ruled by the amphibian Bailian race, the Twilight Lands serve as a neutral zone for cultures from every corner of the Annigan. Many encounter the other races for the first time, and like the weather, their clashes can prove tempestuous.

Only the sun of Lumina keeps back the nocturnal predators of the dark side. Legends tell of a prophesied great eclipse stripping away all boundaries and igniting an apocalyptic war. Until then…

…these are the tales from the Annigan Cycle.

R.W. Marcus

The Annigan whispers,
Down through the ages
Myth and rumor,
Story and song
Always present, for those who will listen
A menacing reminder,
When the balance is gone

ACT ONE

Shun-Dra Rising

The mutual defense alliance was little more than two quinte old and already being tested. Sheea Calden bowed deeply before Queen Omaris Atona of the Free Amarenian Sisterhood. Her curly mane of thick black hair swayed gracefully in front of her as she righted herself. Her bright blue eyes flashed.

"Your Majesty, I'm afraid my news is dire."

Queen Atona studied the Calden ambassador's apprehensive demeanor. The black streaked makeup which swept outward from her eyelids contrasted against her golden skin and grim expression.

"I should think so," the Armarenian sovereign said, "seeing you requested a full council."

The Calden ambassador found the central throne room in Mostas small by comparison to the other royal receiving areas across the Annigan and nautically rustic. As with all Amarenian structures, it was round with a seating area running along one half and three sets of beaded doors along the other. Shea glanced at the Mahaila city guards standing at relaxed attention at each of its secure openings, each adorned in traditional red crop pants and decorated lurah bolo stretched between their bare breasts.

"Your Majesty, I'm sure you're aware of the hijacking of the three ships House Calden were returning to you?"

"Of course."

"The Rayth left one sailor alive, mutilated, but alive. They let him live to deliver a message. It was a declaration that they were now a sovereign nation."

The queen's wrinkled face soured as the Calden Ambassador continued, "Your Majesty, this egregious action against our people and in our very waters constitutes a declaration of war against House Calden."

A nervous murmur passed through the seven regional governesses who sat directly behind their leader. The queen uneasily inspected her red traditional Amarenian court dress. Smoothing it, she looked back up at Sheea.

"I suppose House Calden will be invoking the mutual defense pact?"

"Your Majesty," Sheea defended, "it is in both our mutual interests that this dangerous movement be dealt with."

The queen sat forward aggressively. "Young lady, do not presume to dictate the best interests of my people to me!"

Sheea bowed and stepped back slightly. "I'm sorry Your Majesty. I meant no disrespect."

A middle-aged woman with long greying brown hair rose behind the queen. "Anointed Sister," she interrupted.

Queen Omaris broke her intense gaze on the reprimanded Calden Ambassador and turned. "You have something to offer Lideri Fink?"

"Yes, Anointed Sister. A short while ago, in rapid succession the prison farms of my Dor, Durik and my neighbor Rakam-Dor were attacked. The Rayth killed the guards and any prisoner who would not join them."

The sister sitting next to her rose and gestured in confirmation. "It's true. I lost dozens of sisters in the assault. All those killed were beheaded and buried upside down. Only their legs stuck out of the ground."

The queen's features remained taunt. "Why am I just now hearing of this?!"

Both Lideris' expressions turned apologetic. "Anointed, we travelled as quickly as possible."

Spinning back to Sheea the queen's mood was sober. "It appears these actions are more than random banditry from a disgruntled faction. When you combine this with the other reported incidents, it appears we've a full revolution on our hands. Very well young lady, I agree with your assessment. This is in both our interests. Exactly what do you propose?"

Sheea inched forward. "Your Majesty my father already has a force in place. Out of respect, he has been delaying the attack based on the outcome of this meeting."

After several moments of reflection, the queen nodded her appreciation.

Sheea continued, "Your only involvement would be making sure none escape into the country."

The sisters standing behind the queen glanced at each other, then spoke up. "We can assure that."

From behind the Calden ambassador, a squeaky but firm voice joined the conversation. "House Valdur offers assistance."

Sheea glanced back to Winny Valdur. Her freckled, almost childlike appearance was balanced by a determined expression. "There is an air-caravan arriving upon the next moonrise. It's being escorted by three Resistance Class cruisers. We can assure support from the air."

The queen sat back and sighed deeply as she stared off into space. "This must be dealt with," she said grimly. Her gaze finally settled on the raven-haired Calden ambassador. "Very well. If they want to be treated as a sovereign nation, then they can be crushed like one!"

Commander Benteen de Voria scowled as he fixed his gaze upon the small flotilla bobbing about the turbulent sea. The winter winds were definitely upon them, making any nautical operation all the more difficult.

Stretched out behind the Calden Man-O-War *Jeonham* were two defense/support ships and a military transport which sported four away boats on either side. In the hold, itching for a fight, were fifty battle hardened marines of the elite Calden Maritime Legion and two EEtahs of Garf Sunal.

The commander gave a sad chuckle of recognition as he spied three legionnaires throwing up over the side of the transport. Even the ukko wood hulls couldn't control the pitch of ocean waves. Directly below the heaving marines, two giant seahorses undulated back and forth in the sea below the falling vomit. Their riders vainly attempted to curb their mounts as they greedily sucked up the delicacy the second it hit the water. Once the discharge was consumed, the Nyanja riders gained control of their aquatic colts.

Nothing wasted, the commander noted watching the sea cavalry as they joined the twenty others circling the ships.

The naval force had been in this location, one hundred miles off the northern coast of Amarenia for two full cycles, enduring less than ideal conditions, awaiting orders.

Benteen bit down hard on the well-chewed end of the carbana, severing the shriveled tip from the tightly rolled tobacco tube. Spitting the separated end over the side he placed the fresh tip back between brownish yellow teeth.

"I tell ya, the longer we sit out here the harder it is on my boys," he stated to the two cadre facing him on the quarterdeck.

Admiral Lasia stood formally behind the helmsman, her hands clasped behind her back. As always, her pale blue naval uniform was meticulously tailored. The haggard marine commander had always thought her hairstyle of clean-shaven temples and mushroom crown looked 'ridiculous. What was not to be ignored was her reputation;

Brightstar qualified, as all Calden naval captains were now required to be and tough. She had seen and overseen many a naval operation.

Standing next to her, was a thin young man in a black and grey sealskin wetsuit. Suvari, the Nyanja commander had removed his fish-skin mask, revealing his bald head and troubled expression. Benteen always appreciated true strength and these wiry kids were some of the toughest he ever served with. Each of these Calden sea cavalry had to bond with their mount. There was no other way to join. Once accepted, mount and rider were inseparable. A common joke among legionnaires was that the only time Nyanja were aroused was around their seahorses.

"We wait!" Admiral Lasia authoritatively proclaimed. "Your men will see action soon enough."

The lead marine pulled the carbana out of his mouth and scratched the stubble on his cheek and nodded toward Suvari. "How are your people holding up?"

The young man absent-mindedly adjusted the trident on his back. "A little restless…"

His statement was cut short by a lone gull's squawking as it descended toward the bridge. All squinted up at the approaching bird, then at each other. Circling twice, it navigated the high winds and landed on the deck railing.

Without a word the Calden Admiral retrieved the rolled paper attached to its leg. Opening it, she silently read the message, then recognized her two commanders. "It's on," she solemnly said. "House Valdur has committed to air support and the Amarenians will ensure none escape by land."

"That's more like it," Benteen said. "My boys are gonna be very happy!"

"Prepare your men," Lasia dispassionately ordered the two. "Helmsman take us to just below the horizon line of Durik."

"Aye, Admiral," came the reply as Benteen started for an away boat back to the transport while Suvari slipped over the side to his waiting mount.

With a massive crackle of energy and a brilliant blue flash the *Haraka* burst from the Middle Realms. A collective cry of surprise rang throughout the cabin upon viewing their destination. A faint omnipresent orange glow revealed a perfectly cut empty rectangular tunnel. It was easily thirty feet across and twenty feet high leading out to infinity.

The ship rapidly careened off three walls before a frantic Orich could even attempt to gain control of the wheel.

"One of this craft's greatest assets, is now a bit of a challenge," the Bailian calmly said as he cut the engines.

When the *Haraka* bounced four more times, Mal spun in her chair. "Okay, you can quit this shit anytime!"

"Sorry captain," the albino said as he avoided another collision. "Our hull's composition, keeps us from directly colliding against these walls." He deftly maneuvered alongside another partition only to collide ellipses later. "However," he amended, still intent on the ship's trajectory, "it does make us an effective projectile."

With the next clash, the bags of gems broke loose. They plunged to the deck popping open, allowing a cascade of brightly colored rocks to bounce wildly, peppering the craft's interior.

"Perfect!" Shom groaned as he ducked, covering his head from the multi-colored avalanche which bounced about with every violent lurch of the ship.

Time seemed to move in slow motion as everyone swayed back and forth. All gripped their seats as the *Haraka* travelled another hundred yards then finally settled in the center of the barren passageway.

Peering through the dim light, Mal made out an intersection ten feet away. "Where in the name of the goddess are we?"

Orich looked over Mal's shoulder. "Unclear. However, the architecture appears strikingly similar to the structures in Immor-Onn."

"What's with the burn marks all over the walls?" Mal said as Shom stepped up beside her.

Alto's complexion had become pale and he rubbed his stomach. "I think I'm going to be sick."

"Out!" Mal snapped. "Do not barf in my ship!"

Taa immediately lowered the side door and the swordmaster hastily bolted from the craft, his hand covering his mouth. Immediately upon the hatch being lowered everyone inside the airship was inundated by a blast of hot, humid air.

Shom reeled at the waves of heat and humidity that permeated the craft. "Good gods Maluria! Have you brought us to a furnace?"

Mal ignored the royal's whine as she observed Alto round the corner of the intersection. "Alright," she said addressing the group as she stared at the gems littering the floor. "Let's get this mess cleaned up, then we'll try and figure out where the fuck we are."

Alto hated being sick. He feared throwing up even more than being struck in combat. The thought of becoming sick in front of others was utterly humiliating. Luckily, he made it around the corner just in time as the remnants of his last meal were hurled into a disgusting pile of vomit. When the last spasms passed, the stricken swordmaster stood up and realized he was sweating profusely. *Why was it so hot?* He was standing beside one of several smaller passageways which dotted the wall on his right. Fifty feet beyond, the tunnel — with exacting precision — opened even larger with another intersection. As with the shaft they had landed in, it appeared empty and the walls were badly scorched.

Wiping the sweat off his brow Alto considered returning to the ship when he heard the rumbling. It was low, rhythmic and making its way to the massive juncture. Cautiously, the swordmaster flattened himself against the wall. The approaching reverberation now had the definite cadence of foot falls. Something very large was approaching.

Alto froze in position when he saw the intersection become bathed in light. The rumbling footsteps gave way to a massive creature easily as large as the biggest Sunal EEtahs. The fifteen-foot-tall biped for the most part had no discernable detailed features. Its lumbering form of superheated rock glowed as it radiated waves of intense heat.

Following close behind, were four beasts that resembled the Do-Tarr bug sentients he had seen back in Immor-Onn. These however had scaly plates covering their insectoid bodies. Where the plates met, Alto could see the same type of heat generated glow as the scales shifted with their movement. Behind each was a long supple tail with a tip that resembled both a barb and penis combined.

The swordmaster swallowed hard when one stopped and scrutinized his direction. It appeared to be sniffing. Rivers of perspiration soaked his clothes as he resigned himself that he may be obliged to fight these deadly looking monstrosities. The sniffing insect turned to the others and began a series of high-pitched clacking.

The instant it glanced away, a large furry hand reached out from the smaller tunnel to his right and seized Alto's upper arm. By the time the insectoid started to approach the fighter was snatched through the opening with a force he had never experienced. Pinned to the wall, Alto stared up into the maned face of a mature male man-lion. His scarred, slightly greying features were devoid of hostility. Alto peeked about and saw two other cat beings of mixed lineage. All bore concerned expressions. The humanoid lion looked at Alto and raised a forefinger to his lips. Nodding he understood, everyone froze listening to the clacking on the stone of the approaching fire bug.

The swordmaster felt the muscles tense in the man-lion as the insect sniffed at Alto's pool of vomit. It lingered suspiciously, smelling along the walls. Finally sensing no movement or odor, it returned down the corridor to join its companions.

Heaving a large sigh of relief, the man-lion stepped back freeing Alto. "Human," he said in shocked recognition. "I've met your kind before."

"I sincerely hope the experience was a pleasant one," the swordmaster said apprehensively.

"Not really," he scowled. "War is never pleasant. But the few I encountered fought valiantly and were completely loyal to our cause. Now, what are you called?"

Alto straightened a bit, then gave a brief, shallow bow. "Alto de Gom, at your service. You saved my life sir. I am in your debt. And whom may I inquire have I the pleasure of speaking with?"

The lion's mane shook as he chuckled. "I am Lazio. General Lazio of the Chenakan Resistance Front. And I've never had anybody in my debt before."

"What's he doing here?" One of the mongrels moved forward aggressively. The other fell in behind him. "He could be a spy! How is it he speaks our language so fluently?!"

Reaching in his pocket, Alto retrieved the crude piece of larimar and casually held it up. Scrutinizing the white stone with blue striations the mongrels frowned in defeat. As Alto pocketed the etheria crystal, Lazio laughed at the two young mongrels. "Lads, did either of you bother to get a look at the man's swords?"

The two stared at Alto's sash, then back up with confused expressions.

The haggard general shook his head. "Lesson one cubs: No one with blades like that is to be taken lightly. And I can't afford to lose two of my newest lieutenants."

"So," Alto interrupted. "Exactly what was that we just avoided?"

"Na-Kab patrol, this one had a magma golem. Nasty stuff. No way we could've won," Lazio said nonchalantly.

"They smelled your vomit," one of the lieutenants said in an accusatory tone.

Alto was genuinely confused. "If they smelled my vomit, and they were that close, why couldn't they smell me?"

"We all possess Tiikeri pheromones. To the bugs, we're invisible," Lazio explained.

Alto's eyes widened in recognition. "The reason you pinned me to the wall with your body!"

Lazio grinned. "Well it sure wasn't your looks."

"Then I am truly in your debt sir!"

The general stroked the long tuft of hair on his chin and stared at the swordmaster. "We need another blade on our side. Especially if you're as good as I think you are."

Alto blushed slightly. "I am travelling with others, and we are already attempting to fulfill a prior obligation. However, perhaps our respective causes may be of mutual benefit to each other."

All of the mawls looked at each other in confusion at the translation. Then slowly, awareness set in. "Yes," Lazio concurred. "Do you always talk like that?"

Alto grinned. "Alas, yes."

Lazio scratched the top of his mane. "You say you are not alone?"

Alto pointed to the nearby corner. "Our ship is over there."

The lion general stopped scratching and froze, his gaze locked on Alto. "Ship?"

How can you be uncomfortably hot and cold at the same time? To Stryder Aramos, ever since travelling eastward from his home islands, the conditions went from bad to worse. It had been three miserable lunas since the caravan left the port city of Ka-Beer. The ground's warmth when combined with the cold air produced a thick, damp fog that sometimes surpassed the Kan back home. The bad part was, this fog never receded. *The Land of Mists, aptly named,* he thought as he noted the triple canopy jungle of multi-colored leaves go by. The trees had been cut back a substantial distance from the wide, well-travelled road.

The procession he journeyed in stretched out almost half a mile behind Ma-Tah's lead wagon. The cavalcade of carts and mongrel slaves on foot reached back until they disappeared into the misty darkness. Stryder so far was impressed with the Tiikeri hospitality. The massive royal wagon they travelled in was almost as wide as the road itself. Many times, since their journey began, other travellers had to step aside to let the colossal rolling platform pass. It was covered and easily contained the EEtah as well as a mongrel service staff. Flanking the column were Tiikeri foot soldiers. The orange and black man-tigers in grey robes were armed with both sword and bow. They grimly surveyed the forest beyond.

"It appears you've tamed the wilderness," Stryder said commenting on the seemingly excessive military presence. "You expecting any problems?"

The Tiikeri royal was reclining on a cushioned bench. A fresh batch of Maudo Grass had just been served to him. Stripping a stalk in his mouth, he cast a casual glance off the side of the slow-moving vehicle.

"Nothing we can't handle," he said nonchalantly.

"I can see that," Stryder replied.

The white tiger gave a condescending smirk. "Besides my presence, there is a sizeable gem collection, slaves, and a large supply of sheet glass from the glassworks in the Twilight Lands. We want to make sure everything arrives safely in Shun-Dra."

"The same glassworks we saw from your ship?"

Ma-Tah stripped another stalk of the blue grass and discarded the stem over the side. "Exactly."

"You still didn't answer my question," Stryder pressed.

Swallowing the dissolved petals, the Tiikeri finance minister gave a small ominous snicker. "Please forgive me. I forget who I'm involved with. You humans are a naturally curious lot. The answer is no, I don't expect any trouble. The various criminal groups that find sanctuary in the jungle rarely prey on caravans of this size."

Stryder gave a skeptical grimace.

Ma-Tah waved his hand dismissively. "The Kusars are predators of opportunity. Because of their spies they knew what we were carrying before we set out. These bandit clans have no use of glass. The rest of our cargo isn't enough to warrant such a blatant and costly attack."

From the rear of the caravan a commotion caused all to turn and glare. A barrage of arrows was flying from the jungle on their right, pelting the last two wagons.

"You were saying?" Stryder said with a slight mocking tone.

From their vantage point they saw Tiikeri soldiers charging into the forest and the sound of combat reverberated from the trees. Instinctively, Rootah stood and unsheathed his yudon harpoon.

The fighting was over quickly and the tiger soldiers led two mongrel prisoners out to the caravan. Ma-Tah stood as the prisoners were led over to his wagon. He examined them with a condescending sneer.

12

"You're in for a treat," the Tiikeri said as they approached. "We'll impale them along the road to serve as a warning to others."

"Well," Stryder began in a superior tone. "That is an amusingly normal tradition, and it will take care of the immediate problem. It may even dissuade them for a time. May I suggest pulling up this weed by the roots."

Ma-Tah stopped and regarded his human guest. "I'm intrigued."

Stryder gave an evil grin. "Seerd, get my kit."

The young aide reached inside his travel bag and pulled out a rolled-up leather satchel.

"I'll need you to translate," the quartermaster said to the Tiikeri.

"With pleasure," Ma-Tah enthusiastically responded as they made their way off the wagon.

The two brown and grey mongrel prisoners struggled against their larger Tiikeri captors, their faces a mixture of rage and fear. Both were equally startled to see the humans and EEtah.

The prisoners hissed defiantly as they were brought forward. Stryder chuckled at the bravado as Seerd unrolled the satchel and held it open. The smooth, worn leather was lined with ominous looking hooks, blades and other various torture implements.

The two mongrels reeled in shock at the glistening instruments of pain. Stryder lovingly ran his hand over them with a wicked twinkle in his eyes.

"There's a reason I attained the position I now hold," he said confidently to Ma-Tah who nodded appreciatively at the kit.

"Hand!" he snapped to Rootah.

The EEtah yanked the arm of the closest mongrel bandit out in front of him. Using his powerful grip, the man shark pried apart the mongrel's hand and held it open.

Reflecting on his choices, the quartermaster selected a three-inch-long flat metal shim and a pair of pliers. Both mongrels glared in silent horror as he held them up.

"Alright, we'll start with some easy questions." He began in a friendly voice as Ma-Tah translated. "Who was your informant in Ka-Beer and where are the rest of your friends?"

The mongrel's demeanor went from fearful to defiant and they remained silent.

Shrugging, Stryder slowly moved the shard of metal toward the mawl's outstretched hand.

"I must thank you," the quartermaster commented with a sadistic smirk. "It's been ages since I brought my toys out to play."

The captured duo remained silent.

With gruesome precision Stryder plunged the sharpened tip of the shim an inch into the soft flesh under the nail. The mongrel screamed out in pain and doubled over. The Tiikeri standing behind him roughly pulled him back up by the scruff of his neck.

The prisoner was breathing heavily as Stryder repeated the question.

Giving a thick guttural sound, the prisoner spit out a hairball. It struck Stryder directly on the cheek with a wet plop.

The quartermaster retained his malevolent grin as he calmly wiped away the viscous object. Using the tip of the pliers he rapped the protruding edge of the shard. The mawl screeched out in pain once more but said nothing.

"So silly," Stryder commented, as he gripped the edge of the shard with the pliers. "This could all be over so quickly if you would just cooperate."

Once again, he was greeted with panting and silence.

"Suit yourself," he nonchalantly said as he gave a savage twist with the tool.

The man-cat screamed once more then passed out. A stinging slap to the side of the head from Stryder brought the unfortunate mawl back to consciousness.

Yanking the bloody shard out he examined it as he addressed his Tiikeri host. "You see, the trick is to keep the pain level uncomfortable. Occasionally you let it spike to get their attention. Then of course, dead sufferers give no information, so, care must be given."

Ma-Tah eyed the tense scene with malicious interest as Stryder placed the bleeding claw directly in the pliers' jaws.

The quartermaster frowned directly into the mongrel's glazed expression. "My reluctant friend, there is a practice in my part of the Annigan in dealing with the destructive habits of our domesticated felines. Can you guess what it entails? No?"

With slow, systematic meticulousness and a sickening tearing sound, he pulled the nail off the finger. The man-cat howled even louder and thrashed about in vain against his captor's hold. The surrounding Tiikeri winced at the vicious act. Some shuddered and turned away.

As the mawl began a mournful sob, Stryder put his hand gently beneath the mongrel's chin, raising it so their gazes met.

"And think, we've got nineteen more to go. Then, I get to start on your friend over there."

With a panicked yelp and the sudden smell of bowels being released, the other mawl babbled and cried as fecal material streamed down his legs. Stryder didn't understand anything he was saying but by Ma-Tah's satisfied leer he was certain the interrogation had worked.

After a brief grilling, Ma-Tah glanced confidently over at Stryder. "I do believe we have all we need. Thank you."

Nonchalantly wiping the shard on the mongrel's tunic, Stryder returned the implements to their case. "Excellent. Now, I was promised an impaling."

The rest of the trip was uneventful. Slowly, the thick jungle gave way to rolling hills which ascended southward to a massive mountain range. Gazing out with the moonrise, the quartermaster distinguished a fairly large settlement in the distance.

"The Unaligned City of Shun-Dra," Ma-Tah stated proudly as he stepped up beside him.

Stryder shook his head. "Seems like an awfully long way to travel to meet with these, Chenoans did you call them? Then there's the location. Rather remote don't you think?"

"In this instance it is the only place acceptable," the Tiikeri said.

Stryder curiously studied his host. "Oh?"

"There is no more secure city in all the Annigan. You shall see."

A wide river cut across the landscape. The caravan flanked and followed it as the rushing water led them to the city beyond. The anticipation could be felt all along the parade of wagons as they slowly approached the settlement. For Stryder and his human aide Seerd, the permeating odor of cat spray was the first thing to assault their senses. The humans had been subject to it with every mawl community they had passed through and it never got better. The thing that bothered Stryder the most, was that he now found himself able to discern the subtle differences in the mawls' signature scents. All were still equally revolting.

The procession arrived at the outskirts of the city just as the moon was dipping below the hills in the west. On the side of the road immediately in front of the first buildings, a large monolith loomed.

Ma-Tah pointed to the two simple lines in Tiikeri which were carved on its smooth surface. "This is the whole of the law in Shun-Dra. Violence is not tolerated," he stated firmly before pointing to the second line. "Stealing is not tolerated."

"Simple enough," Stryder said as he and his entourage followed Ma-Tah out of the wagon. "Because as you stated this is a secure city, I imagine there's a suitable armed presence to back up those rules?"

"No," the Tiikeri answered. He stopped, pointing at the buildings and the thinning crowds of mawls and other sentients. His gaze settled on the mist which was only ankle high. "There is only the mist. No one knows where it came from or how it works. Some say it's bug magic from below. No matter. Those are the laws, undeniable and inescapable."

Stryder continued to gaze at the monolith. "I'm not sure I follow you."

The white tiger pointed to the fog as it swirled tumultuously around Rootah's ankles. "Your bodyguard's naturally aggressive nature draws the mist to him. Best keep your protector under control or the mist will take him."

"You're telling me..."

"Violence is not tolerated," he repeated, his tone serious. "The mist will take him."

"Shommy, get your ass over here and give us a hand!" Mal snapped as she placed several palm-sized raw gems into the canvas bag.

The prodigal was staring out the windshield as the others moved about the deck of the *Haraka* retrieving their scattered cargo. He had observed Alto sprint toward the corner, hand over his mouth. The swordmaster had yet to return and the royal was growing concerned.

"I was not the one who improperly secured them," he said condescendingly. "Besides, I'm keeping watch for Alto."

"Taa can do that! Come on, we can use the help."

The royal scoffed as he resumed his scrutiny out the window. "Oh, I prefer the personal touch when it comes to a vigil."

Mal was about to comment when Orich stood and called out. "Captain, I've found something very strange." The albino approached his commander while examining a small box in his hands.

Mal stared curiously. "What ya got?"

"Unknown captain," Orich confessed, as he held it up for inspection. "But it was mixed in among the gems."

"Looks like ukko wood," Mal said as she examined the five by seven-inch oblong box.

The Bailian indicated the box's unique binding. "It is, however, these chains are the fascinating part."

The Spice Rat carefully examined the delicate black bindings which held it closed. "These chains aren't metal."

Orich's fingertips traced the links. "There is no lock and the one that circles it horizontally actually fuses with the vertical when they cross each other on the top and bottom."

Both pilot and captain exchanged confused glances.

"Another thing captain," Orich scrutinized the box. "The minute I touch any of the gems I can tell you it's story. I'm getting no reading from this."

"What do you think it means?"

"I'm not sure, but with your permission I would like to study it."

Shom found himself heaving a sigh of relief as he saw his friend turning the corner making his way back to the ship. Relief quickly changed to confusion. The swordmaster was flanked by a humanoid male lion as tall as Zaad on one side and by two mongrel man-cats roughly his size.

Mal was still staring at the mysterious box. "Sure Orich, now ya got me wondering."

"Uhhh..." the tone of Shom's voice caused Mal to spin in his direction. "Don't tell me Alto's pulled another disappearing act?!"

"No, no, he's here…"

"Well?!"

"It would appear that he's found some friends."

The table in Fia's quarters creaked loudly as the two Rayth shifted nervously.

Morax's tone was serious. "Mark my words. The Annigan grows smaller by the luna! Your remote location in Amarenia will not shroud you for long."

Almost on cue a cold gust of north wind swept through the empty streets of Durik and rattled the door against its frame. Fia stared attentively at her Chenakan guest but remained silent.

The tentacles on top of the sentient's head undulated restlessly as he sat forward. "As we speak, to the east in Immor-Onn, the Tiikeri already established an embassy."

"Tiikeri?" Blenda questioned.

"Tiger people from the Land of Mists," Morax replied. "They bring with them a powerfully nefarious god. They've already begun seducing the western houses too."

"Besides buying horses from the Bailians, what has Immor-Onn got to do with us?" Fia asked.

"May I speak frankly?"

"I thought that's why you were here," Fia's tone was dry and matter of fact.

Morax sighed. "You will be running out of room very quickly. Considering the mutual defense pact your former sisters signed with the western houses, the new raiding corridor you hoped to exploit between the Twilight Lands and the west is rapidly shrinking." He paused briefly to let the statement sink in. Blenda's face was taunt while Fia's was totally unreadable. "House Calden and Valdur have a substantial presence on this continent. There is a triumvirate rising in the Annigan which spells the destruction of both of our peoples."

Once again Fia's reaction was cold and dispassionate. "For someone from Nocturn you seem to know an awful lot about the goings on here in Lumina."

"We watch. We listen." Morax fixed his gaze on the pirate queen. "The fact that you in Lumina are blissfully ignorant of the goings on in Nocturn is what makes this situation truly frightening and very dangerous."

"Who the fuck are they!?" Mal blurted as she stared out the windshield over Shom's shoulder.

"They appear to be friendly," Shom said as he assessed the approaching group. "Alto does not appear to be under duress."

"Well I guess we're gonna find out. Zaad be ready just in case."

"Yes captain," the EEtah replied, as he secured one of the bags to the winch in the ceiling. Reaching over, he made sure Bowbreaker was within his grasp.

"Taa, drop the side hatch."

Once again, the oppressive heat swept through the hatch the instant the door opened. Mal and Shom stepped out onto the ramp observing the four figures approach, as Zaad stood imposingly in the hatchway.

The quartet came to a halt at the bottom of the ramp. With a suspicious grin she placed her hands on her hips and stared at Alto. "Well you're full of surprises, aren't you?"

Lazio smiled at Mal while his two lieutenants stood mesmerized by the *Haraka* and Zaad standing in the doorway.

Coming to attention, Alto did a slight bow and gestured toward the lion. "Captain Maluria, I present General Lazio of the Chenakan Resistance Front."

The man-lion did a deep formal bow. "It is my pleasure to meet you."

"Oh no, not another one of you," Mal groaned at the formal greeting.

Lazio gave the swordmaster a confused look.

Alto shook his head and chuckled. "It's alright. She grows on you."

Introductions complete, the scruffy general's gaze swept along the length of the airship as it hovered inches above the floor. "Nice ship. Never seen anything like it before." Finally, his attention settled on Zaad who's massive shark frame filled the hatch. "You're kinda puny for an EEtah aren't you?"

Zaad sneered and leaned forward ominously. "Big enough. What do you know about my people?!"

Lazio glared at Zaad directly. "I did battle with one by my side three grands ago. Dak was the bravest, most potent warrior I have ever encountered."

At the mention of the name the EEtah's expression changed instantly from anger to suspicion. "You know Dak?"

Without hesitation Lazio placed his clenched fist over his left breast in the traditional Sunal salute. "He saved my life on more than one occasion."

Zaad remained skeptical. "Was there anyone with him?"

This caused the lion general to grin. "He did indeed. An insane Avion, Lord Julius was his master. Then there was

Kai. She was a small human female, quiet and absolutely deadly with a bow. They are considered heroes in this part of the Annigan."

With that confirmation Zaad visibly relaxed.

"Do you have tidings of them?" Lazio asked.

"All three now reside in my adopted city of Immor-Onn in the Twilight Lands," the EEtah said.

Shom, who had been uncharacteristically quiet, finally spoke up. "Well, I'm certainly glad that we've got old home week going on, however it is sweltering out here wherever 'here' is?"

Lazio assessed the prodigal with an amused smirk. "You are in the tunnels of No-Zann and the reason for the heat is because this area rests between the Na-Kab fire hive and the Do-Tarr's northern hive."

Shom swept at a lock of his blond hair which was plastered to his forehead. "Hmm, well I'm not sure what most of that meant. I guess my question really is, where can we get out of this heat?"

"Sorry. For that you've gotta go topside," the lion lamented.

"Ah!" Shom raised a finger. "Now were getting somewhere. Where exactly is topside and how do we get there?"

Lazio sighed and scanned the group. "That's complicated. However, I know someone who can explain it much better than I. I'm pretty sure you both are going to want to meet each other. Is this craft operable?"

"Fully," Mal staunchly said.

"Better follow us," Lazio advised. "We don't want to get caught out here by another Na-Kab patrol."

"A what?" Shom impatiently asked.

"I'll tell you on the way," Alto said as he started up the ramp. "But he's right."

The rapidly passing storm had cleared. Now, a cloudless moonrise greeted them as they exited their recently procured room. Stryder Aramos, was a man used to the finer things in life. He detested the small, sparse accommodations that he was forced to share with a seven-foot-tall man-tiger with less than ideal hygiene. However, lodging was always in demand because of the city's reputation as a safe neutral meeting place. The recent squall had reduced the streets of Shun-Dra to a muddy mess. Thick, deep, brownish red mud, discreetly hidden by a layer of mist clung to everything, making travel anywhere difficult. With the clearing of the weather, small pockets of citizens began to congregate and pass by the front of the small boarding house to get a glimpse at Rootah. The fifteen-foot EEtah stood guard by the front door at attention. Water dripped off his snout and the yudon harpoon on his back as the city's mist swirled ominously around his legs. Word of the wonderous giant fish being, which stood as high as most roofs, spread quickly and the population made any excuse to pass by and get a look.

Ma-Tah peered out at the predominately mongrel population attempting to navigate the viscous streets and grunted in disgust. "All of these filthy creatures belong on the auction block."

Stryder chuckled in agreement as the muddy parade of mongrels sloshed about in an attempt to get the city moving again. "I imagine they congregate here to avoid that very thing."

"Slavers will get them sooner or later," the white tiger declared with a sneer of revulsion. "They can't stay in town forever." The Tiikeri Minister caught a glance of Stryder and his aide, Seerd sniffing the air then trading expressions of revulsion. "Yeah, mongrel scent makes me sick too. So, the

23

sooner we get these meetings over with, the sooner we can be done with this city."

The Unaligned City of Shun-Dra is divided where the Kel-Raku river briefly parts, forming a small island. The majority of the city at large rests on the southern banks. Sequestered on the island called Suci, are a number of large temple areas and the Agora Den.

All along the way through town the mongrel population rapidly got out of the way and gawked as the Tiikeri nobility led the small parade of strange figures down the slushy streets. Stryder could hear the rushing of the river long before it came into view. He gave a relieved sigh when he realized that, as they neared the quickly moving water, the air was getting clearer.

When they finally exited the last street, they stood at one of the two wide bridges which connected the segregated section of the city. Off to their left was a large courtyard flanking the river. It faced a small stage directly across the rushing water. The building complex was the largest in the city, with a connecting courtyard in the center. Stryder noticed that a wider range of sentients was crossing the bridge in both directions. Most he had never encountered. "The better part of town," he noted aloud with an intentionally flippant tone.

The white tiger pointed to the complex which dominated the small island. "The Agora Den is the sole reason for this city's existence. Here, warring or contentious factions can meet and broker deals and treaties. All know the mist's protection ensures a peaceful if not fruitless encounter."

As in the streets, the mawls crossing the bridge moved aside for the Tiikeri and his guests. Three Do-Tarr scurried past them, mandibles clicking, unimpressed by rank or race.

Ma-Tah scowled as they almost collided with him. "If the bugs are in town there must be a building project in the works."

"Do you use the Do-Tarr to build everything?" Stryder asked.

"We don't. Everyone else does, if they're smart."

"Oh?"

"If your building disturbs the hive below, you're dead," the Tiikeri said. "So, it's best to let them approve the project and do it."

"Why don't your people play by the same rules?"

Ma-Tah gave a broad, satisfied smirk. "That's the best part! We emit a pheromone which renders my race invisible to the bugs. They can't defeat what they can't see. We build where we wish!"

The quartermaster nodded in appreciation but concentrated on the landing they were approaching. "That's why the insects almost ran into you. They couldn't see you."

"Exactly. I normally would kill them where I find them, however our location prohibits such actions."

"Tunnels huh?"

"Those lowly, mindless bugs are milling about under the entire continent."

Stryder smiled, enjoying the Tiikeri's blatant elitism. "Tell me, are there any races you don't have disdain for?"

Ma-Tah stopped. "Yes, yours and the one we are about to meet."

"I can accept that," Stryder replied as they started off again, turning right into the courtyard of the Agora Den.

Three buildings surrounded the tiled open area. The largest was directly in front of them. Its grand entrance porch was supported by a row of thick white columns. Two smaller, less grandiose edifices flanked the main building. Groups of sentients mingled and talked all about the courtyard. A small chanting group of humanoid jaguars in robes walked in a single line from the main building to one of the smaller ones. In the far corner a group of twenty robed figures kneeled in front of a central individual. Their cloaks were bowed below the fog, apparently deep in prayer.

Ascending the wide steps, they paused on the porch. "I'm afraid your aide and bodyguard must remain out here." The Tiikeri informed. "There is a private meeting room reserved for us."

"He says you can't go in," Stryder said. "It's alright. Wait out there in the yard."

Another robed jaguar stood by the open doorway. As they passed Ma-Tah reached into his robe. Retrieving a gem, he offered it to the priest. Assessing it with satisfaction he bid them enter.

The several small docks which line the shore where the Kel-Raku River passes by Shun-Dra are all built on an angle facing upstream. Directly across, on the island side, a small solitary landing dips into the swiftly moving water. When not in use, the low access to the river is a favorite spot for the half dozen fishers who claim it first.

As usual, six mongrels stood with their feet in the water casting small weighted nets in a prescribed order so as not to get tangled. Behind each was their current catch, which was often more than just fish. Many different things washed down from the mountains to the southwest. Along with wiggling fish of different size were fruits, pieces of exotic wood and various other odd but potentially useful articles of debris.

Now, as the first net in the cycle was cast yet again, it bounced on top of the water. All gasped and backed up the ramp as a translucent dome crested. When the twelve-foot diameter bubble was halfway out of the water the mawls panicked. Dropping their nets and abandoning their catch, hissing out frightened protests all scurried to safety.

From behind the relative safety of an outcropping, suspicious eyes followed the translucent globe as it was moved onto the ramp. Through the skin, they could make out that it was filled with fluid and there was something moving inside. The ball was being pushed up the ramp by three scaly bipeds about as tall as them. The minions had large fish heads with mouths full of sharpened teeth. Their hands and feet were webbed and made wet flopping noise as they muscled the bubble up the ramp. Exiting the water right behind them were six significantly smaller globes of the same malleable material. They moved past the fish creatures and circled the large bubble under their own power.

As they passed, the fish humanoids and mawls hissed at each other. Getting a closer inspection of the sphere they could make out long thick tentacles and large claw-like hands resembling crustacean legs moving in the murky liquid.

Waiting until the aquatic procession moved onto the road heading for the Agora Den, the frightened mawls grabbed their catch and hurried away.

They weren't supposed to be there. The two mongrel fishers had promised their mates that since the drownings two grands ago they would not fish from under the bridge leading to Suci Island. However, the temptation was too much. The location was secluded and the fishing was great. Already, both were ecstatic they had caught quite a few exceptionally large fish.

One cackled. "Dinner tonight is gonna taste even better cuz I know where it came from."

"Yeah, we better get outta here soon. We've got enough for…"

The companion's suggestion was interrupted as a pale blue humanoid rose from the water under the bridge on the other side. The short, stocky middle-aged Yupik raised his hand and pointed it directly at them.

A sudden violent pull on the lines snatched them from their mesmerized stares. Looking out at their nets they saw no fish in them, yet the lanyards were pulled taught. Suddenly, the lines crossed and both were yanked savagely into the rushing water and pulled under. Briefly hands and feet thrashed about in a panic before both fishers disappeared beneath the surface.

Raising his arm at a ninety-degree angle he now pointed it upriver. Closing his eyes, he started to chant softly. Slowly, the speed of the swiftly flowing water slowed and the level dropped. Upstream, the river quickly ascended into a wall of agitated churning water held in place by an invisible dam.

When the Yupik ice clansman dropped his arm, the pent-up river rushed back into the almost dry bed in a torrent of watery destruction. It flowed around the strange blue man sweeping the two mongrel bodies along with its destructive path downstream.

As always, Rootah stood by the bottom of the stairs of the Agora Den waiting for his master. Seerd, sat on the steps and watched the prayer group stand and begin to walk toward the den's entrance. As they passed, he got a peek under one of the hoods. These were beings he had never seen before. They had a conical mouth with small teeth. He also noted short tentacles covering the tops of their heads, undulating below the cowl. He was about to mention it to the EEtah when everyone heard the screams coming from the riverbank. It was immediately followed by a foot-deep inundation of water as it rushed across the tiled courtyard. The swiftly flowing deluge swept the mawls in the area off their feet. It tossed Seerd to the floor of the porch as it swept up the stairs crashing into the wall sending currents of water spinning and crashing in every direction.

Under the bridge the Yupik remained stationary and submerged up to his waist as the waters rushed around him. Extending both arms in front of him he opened his hands, palms out as he continued his low chant.

Rootah, who had managed to keep his footing, focused up onto the porch. Seerd was on his back gaping at the prayer group as it rushed through the doorway along with the water. Most of the group had entered and now the water quickly rose in a thick sheet in front of the door and windows, blocking any passage. Three of the robed figures were now trapped outside on the porch. Pulling back their cowls they produced thin bright orange wands. Seerd was still on his back. He had managed to get his bearings and was slowly crawling away.

The EEtah now saw they wore no clothing under the robes and the short tentacles on their heads undulated furiously. Hissing, they lunged for the unarmed aide. The one closest connected and plunged the blunt wand into the retreating human. As Seerd screamed in agony Rootah unsheathed his yudon harpoon and charged up the stairs bellowing at the top of his lungs. The mist had been temporarily washed away and he was free to unleash his lethal fury.

It was hard to determine which sight Stryder found the most shocking: The twelve-foot hovering orb and the six smaller orbs which randomly orbited it, or the three gruesome looking bipedal fish men who smelled like a beach during red tide. Focusing on decorum the quartermaster fought revulsion and forced a smile as Ma-Tah introduced him. "Your eminence, allow me the honor of introducing to you, Lord Stryder Aramos of House Aramos."

The murky liquid of the interior swirled. Tentacles and large crustacean claws came into view. They preceded a head that resembled a helmet with two white eyes and a jutting lower jaw with barbed teeth spiking upward. The body was mostly obscured by the liquid but Stryder could tell it stood about eight feet tall and had many swirling appendages of various shapes and sizes.

"It is indeed good to meet you lord Aramos," came a deep, friendly greeting from inside the bubble in Aramos-Ya.

Extending a hand toward the bubble Ma-Tah continued. "Lord Stryder, it is indeed my great honor to introduce Grand Ambassador of the Chenoan people, Goez Kor."

Stryder bowed deeply. By the time he finished his placation, Ma-Tah had already heard the commotion. The Tiikeri's face tightened as he spun to see water running in from under the door.

"Somethings wrong!" he warned an instant before the wooden door violently blew open.

Seeing no mist, the Tiikeri opened his robes. In one fluid motion he snapped out two throwing daggers and flung them into the first two Chenakans through the opening. They both toppled to the floor dropping their orange wands. Stryder drew his sword and stood in front of the Chenoan ambassador.

Inside the bubble a gnarled hand resembling crab legs swirled in the murky liquid. The rushing water rose rapidly, forming a barrier across the now open doorway. The next Chenakan in line tried to leap into the room, only to be severed in half by the rapidly rising wall of water. The upper torso dropped on top of his two companions, twitching violently as its lifeblood spilled onto the already wet floor.

Beside the Chenoan's bubble the smaller orbs proceeded to undulate and morph into dog-like beasts with fish tails and barracuda heads. Hunching, they growled and lunged to the other side of the watery barrier into the hall.

"Best get ready to move at a centi's notice your eminence," Stryder said over his shoulder.

The quartermaster hefted his blade in front of him and Ma-Tah readied two more knives as they witnessed the water barrier sizzle and evaporate when one of the wands touched it.

Through the steam five Chenakan warriors stormed into the room.

Rootah saw the lifeless body of his travelling companion as it lay staring upward on the wet porch. His delicate human features were permanently frozen in a contorted grimace of pain. Smoke drifted out of his nose and mouth as well as the burn hole is the front of his shirt.

The three Chenakans cringed in horror. Nervously, they readied their wands as fifteen feet of mountainous rage charged straight at them. The first died instantly as the harpoon plunged into his chest and out his back. With a savage yank to the left he embedded the barb and pulled the now dead Chenakan into the one beside him toppling both to the ground.

The third swung its orange wand wildly in a panic missing by a considerable distance. Leaning over the EEtah's jaws bit down on the extended appendage severing the entire arm and shoulder socket. The Chenakan spun from the force and squealing in pain, dropped as blood spewed like a fountain beside him.

Pulling his yudon from the corpse of the first, he spit the severed appendage onto the second Chenakan who was attempting to crawl away. The massive man-shark's breath was ragged and heavy with bloodlust as he slowly approached his terrified opponent. A long strand of drool, thick as a rope swung from the corners of his massive jaws as he raised the harpoon for the killing blow. He loved the fear and took a second to savor the terror.

With the water receding the EEtah was too distracted with bloodthirstiness to notice the mist flowing back into the square. Rootah roared with rage as he plunged the harpoon into the chest of the petrified Chenakan. Lifting the impaled enemy high in the air he stared euphorically at the dying sentient as he gave a loud victory roar.

Trembling in violent ecstasy, he didn't notice the mist swirling violently about his legs. As he shook the body, showering in its fluids, the thick vapor enveloped his waist. As it engulfed his chest and shoulders he broke from his brutal trance and looked confused. The EEtah was now totally engulfed in the cloud. As it lifted the behemoth from the ground, he dropped his victim and gave a growl of protest. Now completely obscured in the mist, snapping and breaking sounds were followed by eerie silence. Soundlessly the mysterious fog enveloped the bodies and carried them away, out of the courtyard in a willowy shroud.

After handily stabbing one of the charging Chenakans, the only thing that concerned Stryder was the orange wands they wielded. He wasn't sure what they were capable of, but he was convinced he didn't want one to touch him. Luckily, the two now challenging him were apprehensive about any attack.

The quartermaster stood between them and the Chenoan ambassador's bubble staring at his attackers' fear-laden expressions. As one lunged forward in a half-hearted strike, Stryder did a quick circling parry. The collision of steel and etheria crystal enveloped both in a shower of sparks.

Taking advantage of the distraction the human lashed out with a savage kick which catapulted the smaller sentient onto his back sending his wand sliding along the floor. A quick slash across the chest of the second one dropped him where he stood.

The remaining three ganged up on Ma-Tah and Stryder was about to intervene when three of the barracuda dogs, pale mouths bloodied, rushed back into the room. As they leapt on the attackers, one of the Chenakans managed to plunge his wand into the attacking creatures' jaws past rows of razor-sharp teeth. The beast squealed in pain as its pale smooth skin burned away and its thick, viscous life essence splattered the area.

The other two Chenakans glanced over at the attacking beasts. Ma-Tah seized the opportunity and deftly threw a dagger into the throat of one. The two barracuda dogs pounced on the remaining Chenakan tearing at his limbs.

As silence descended on the room Stryder looked over at the Chenoan's orb. "Something out there is doing this." The human pointed to the beasts who had just finished biting out the Chenakan's throat. "Can they find it?" he asked pointing at the dogs.

From inside the bubble's cloudy liquid he saw the ambassador nod yes. He then raised a claw-like hand and pointed toward the door. The barracuda dogs immediately bounded out of the room.

Reaching down, Stryder picked up one of the discarded wands. He walked into the hall in time to see the dogs bound through the water barrier which still covered the main entrance. Stepping up to the obstruction he placed the tip of the wand against it. As before, the water bubbled and evaporated in a giant cloud of steam.

When he made it out onto the porch, he noted the large pools of gore everywhere. Lying at the bottom of the steps in the courtyard was Rootah's discarded yudon harpoon. His bodyguard and aide however, were nowhere to be seen.

Something was wrong. The Yupik shaman felt the unusual vibrations in the water. When he saw the barracuda dogs charging across the surface of the water at him, he was certain of it. Lowering his hands to his sides he swiftly and silently descended below the waves narrowly avoiding two sets of gnashing jaws. The elongated fish snouts snapped ravenously at the area where he descended kicking up streams of river water. Making shallow dives they vainly attempted a pursuit only to resurface with nothing.

They circled the area briefly, it was obvious their quarry had escaped. Hissing in frustration, they then began undulating, morphing back into their original orb shapes.

Circling the area of the water once more they levitated back to shore and their master.

Fia sat back in her chair and furrowed her brow at the Chenakan seated across from her. "Alright, exactly why should I give a shit about the goings on in Nocturn?"

"Quite simply, because in a very short period of time decisions made and actions taken over there, will directly affect you and every other sentient being in Lumina. Your small fledgling nation will be crushed."

"They can try!" Fia sneered.

Morax's tentacles fluttered in frustration. "A human/Tiikeri/Chenoan triumvirate will have the power to enslave all and destroy those who oppose it. There won't be a safe place on the entire Annigan."

"I know about humans," Blenda spoke slowly, her voice laced with uncertainty. "But, about those others you mentioned?"

"Tiikeri are the tiger people from the Land of Mists. Theirs is a tyrannical government. They are already allying with the predominate race that lives below the ice floes in the Ocean Deep of Nocturn. They are an old, powerful race. Their mages are without peer using etheria crystals to manipulate water. The Chenoans bred my race to exert their influence on land. But they made us a little too smart to blindly follow. We rebelled."

The Amarenians stared silently at the Chenakan.

Fia shifted in her chair. Her entire body bore a countenance of weariness and frustration. "My people are just now getting settled. We lack the swords to aid your cause."

Morax continued his intense stare. "You misunderstand. In order for your people to survive you must disperse and go underground."

The pirate queen sat forward ; her nostrils flaring. "Never! They tried to rob us of the Rayth life, and we fought back. To sail and raid is what we live for. Fear and respect are what we demand. Anything less disgusts us."

Morax sat back. His tentacles slowed their flutters betraying a touch of sadness. "Any peoples we can ally with are dwindling as they join the oppressors. Very well. However, should you change your mind my people will welcome you. I sincerely hope it won't be too late."

The corners of Fia's mouth drew up into a doleful smile. "You are a friend to the Rayth nation."

Reaching behind his neck the Chenakan removed the only thing he wore. A solitary pendant on a chain. It was a small white crystal disc with blue striations. On one side were small intricately carved runes. He handed it to Fia. "With this you can always contact me. It also gives you the gift of tongues."

"Thank you Morax," Fia said placing the bauble around her neck and tucking it in her winter tunic.

The Chenakan stood and bowed slightly. "I must go. I've already lingered longer than I should. If my vessel is spotted it could bring unwanted attention on you."

"The most secure city in the Annigan huh?" Stryder jabbed as he watched the mist carry away the last attacker's body.

"Chenakan scum!" Goez's voice resonated from the bubble. "They did not accomplish this alone."

"They've allied with a Pagos Shaman," Ma-Tah declared confidently.

"More parlor tricks?" Stryder said in a dismissive tone.

"The oceans and ice floes of Nocturn teem with sediment from massive outcroppings of etheria crystals on the seabed. There are disciplines that can manipulate the Pagos, the living water."

Stryder's skeptical expression caused Ma-Tah to point at the door in frustration. "Did you not witness it with your own eyes?"

"I saw something," Stryder replied. "I'm not sure what it was. And I'm curious as to where my aide and bodyguard went?"

The Tiikeri shook his head. "One day you will believe. As for your companions, if they were involved in this fight, the mist took them."

The quartermaster stared out into the courtyard consumed with concern. "About those 'Chenakans?'"

"We bred them long ago," Goez said in a deep baritone. "They were to go where we couldn't, on the land. Eventually they betrayed us. I was their target. If one of those trinilic rods touched my protective bubble it would've boiled away as the door barriers did and I would be dead."

"They fancy themselves revolutionaries," Ma-Tah added. "When in fact they're nothing more than common bandits.'"

Concern faded to confusion on Stryder's features. "Why would common bandits want to target a single dignitary?"

"Because I am for uniting peoples across the Annigan," Goez said proudly. "They realize my efforts spell an end to their brutal reign of thievery."

As Stryder processed the answer the Chenoan ambassador signaled for his walking fish. "I must go. My presence is known and I've lingered too long." With that declaration the Gar-Kal fish men slowly pushed the orb in the direction of the river. "We will meet again, soon."

Shom and Alto stood behind a seated Mal. They stared out the windshield of the *Haraka* as it floated inches off the ground. On foot in front of them, the three mawls fanned out cautiously leading them down the burnt tunnels of No-Zann.

"Where again did they say they were taking us?" Shom asked.

"I don't know," Mal said not taking her attention off the tunnel before her.

The prodigal shifted his gaze to the Spice Rat. "Did he say who we were going to meet?"

"Nope," came the bored solitary response.

Sighing in frustration, Shom concentrated on Alto who continued to stare forward. Not receiving a response, his attention returned once again to Mal. "And do we know what these peoples want from us?"

"Not sure," Mal droned as she saw Lazio hold up his hand to stop, then, when satisfied nothing was amiss, resumed the pace.

"Stop me if I'm wrong here," Shom said sarcastically, "but we don't seem to know very much about the situation we find ourselves in, or the people we've just met."

Mal jerked an annoyed glance at her friend. "Dammit Shommy, are you writing a fucking book?! Right now, these are the only ones who've got any idea how to get the fuck out of here!"

Eventually, the tunnels widened revealing large rooms lining either side. Mawls and other sentients traveled lethargically about, usually in small groups. With the change in locale, Lazio and his men seemed more at ease.

One of the rooms to the right had a large opening in the tall ceiling. Moonlight through thick fog could be seen just beyond the cleft. In one corner was a large crevasse. Sitting on his haunches next to the crack in the ground, a large white gorilla ate from a crude metal bowl with an oversized spoon.

Up above, the fog began to swirl. The gorilla stopped, gazed up and calmly set the bowl down. Almost immediately, twenty bodies fell and landed in the middle of the room. There were several live mongrel mawls who stood on shaky legs, their panicked gaze darted around their new location before scampering off. The rest appeared to be fifteen humanoid fish men with tentacles on the top of their heads, a large Sunal EEtah and a young human male. All were dead, their bodies lying in a grotesquely mangled pile.

"What the fuck is an EEtah doing here?" Mal gasped.

Zaad, who was napping, sprang to his feet and rushed over to the windshield.

The man-shark gasped in disbelief. "Huh…captain, I'd like to have a look."

Mal briefly considered the request. "Put her down Orich."

"Yes captain," came the reply as the airship settled to the tunnel floor.

By the time they made it over to the bodies, the gorilla who was slightly shorter than Zaad, was on his feet and untangling the corpses. With a bored expression, he lifted each one and unceremoniously heaved them into the crevasse. As they approached, he briefly studied the group and the ship beyond out in the tunnel. He betrayed no emotion as he returned to his work.

Zaad assessed the lifeless EEtah. The top of his body had been completely twisted backwards. Jagged pieces of cartilage jutted from the mangled torso. His face was still contorted in rage as it grimaced up from its unnatural position. The human was dressed in traditional Aramos court attire. His eyes were frozen open wide in fear. The interior of his open mouth, as well as a large wound on his chest, were burnt and black.

"I know these two," Zaad declared. "The EEtah's name was Rootah and last I heard he was the personal bodyguard of Stryder Aramos.

Shom was genuinely curious. "How in the name of the gods do you know them?"

Zaad gave out something between a sneer and a chuckle. "Back in Immor-Onn. It bothered the Sunals that the Marine Commander was an outer clansman and they were required to check in with me."

"I cannot imagine anything able do that to a Sunal EEtah," Alto said as the gorilla effortlessly picked up Rootah's body and tossed it over the crevasse's lip and out of sight.

"What the fuck is this?" Mal wondered aloud as she pored over her surroundings.

"Well, with the exception of your arrival, it's one of the few ways to enter our little part of the Annigan."

All spun to see Lazio standing behind them alone. "And to answer your question, the mist did it to him." The Singa man-lion pointed at the cloudy opening. "There are only two rules in Shun-Dra and it seems like he broke the big one: Killing." He paused for a bit, acknowledging their puzzled appearances. "Come, all your questions will be answered. You might want to leave your ship in one of these empty rooms. The quarters get a little tight from here on."

Mal pointed to the opening in the ceiling. "If that's an opening why can't we just leave that way?"

"In only I'm afraid," Lazio answered ominously. "The mist is not to be trifled with."

The walk from the entrance room was short. Lazio led them from the tunnel to a large landing overlooking a huge cave complex. Below them, a sprawling ramshackle town filled the cavernous cube and contrasted against the perfectly hewed walls. Mal determined the population to be mostly mawls however several Do-Tarr were scampering about as well as Bailians and quite a few mawl hybrids. A loud roar snapped their attention to a small side street where a large humanoid bear was accosting a group of mawls outside a small hovel.

Lazio pointed toward the altercation. "Stay clear of the Ursas. They're from cold country. The heat down here keeps them permanently cranky."

Orich assessed the scene before him then gave Mal a sideways glance. "Captain, given the location and manner of arrival we witnessed, I believe this to be a penal colony."

Lazio gave a sad resolute smirk. "Your pale friend there gets the prize. Welcome to Rapscallia, located right below the Unaligned City of Shun-Dra."

"And exactly where may I inquire is that?" Shom asked in a weary voice.

"Northeastern Land of Mists." The Singa said matter-of-factly. "Come on. Like I said, you need to meet someone."

The walk through town proved uneventful. The buildings were thrown together using anything that had been confiscated. Shom reeled at the smell of body odor and waste, all made worse by the stifling heat. The inhabitants, who lethargically lounged about, briefly took notice as they passed but otherwise ignored them. Even Zaad, whose appearance formerly never failed to get a stunned reaction was greeted with apathy. In a congested town square mawls moved about engaging in the apparent bartering for food items mostly.

Lazio stopped them in front of a small square building which was fabricated entirely of dismantled wooden shipping crates. Mal immediately recognized the lettering along the side of the wooden slats. It was written in Calden-Ya. *Huh*, she mused to herself. *All the way from Lumina.* There was a simple cloth covering the door. Lazio parted it and beckoned them inside. The entrance was nowhere near large enough to accommodate the EEtah.

Mal gazed up at her friend with an apologetic frown. "Sorry big guy. Looks like ya gotta wait outside."

"It's alright," the man-shark assured. "I'm getting used to it."

There were two sentients in the sparsely furnished, dimly lit single room. A short humanoid fox in a simple brown tunic conversed with a short, stout Bailian offshoot. His skin was the same pale blue, but his head was oval and tapered at top and bottom. Their conversation abruptly ended when the group entered. Both glared over in annoyance at the interruption.

Lazio held up his hands in a placating gesture. "You're gonna want to hear this."

The fox was grim. "They're all dead."

The Singa gave a remorseful grimace. "Yeah, I know. The mist just dumped the bodies."

Shom lightly stamped his foot and huffed. "Will someone, for the love of the gods tell me what is going on?!"

The fox sneered contemptuously as he defiantly crowded the royal. He only came up chest high, but his intense gaze made Shom shift anxiously. "Yeah, who are you?"

Shom sighed. "I am someone who is desperately attempting to leave this place that by all appearances has been completely forsaken by the gods!"

This caused the fox to chuckle as his left eye quivered slightly. "Well you're right about the location. And we all wouldn't mind getting out of here."

Mal put her hand on Shom's shoulder and stepped forward. "My friends and I were being chased by a shitload of irate wolfmen through the Barrens when we hit a portal and well, here we are."

"Me and a couple of the boys found their ship in the tunnels," Lazio said as the fox walked back to the Yupik. "They almost ran smack into a Na-Kab patrol."

"Did they have a golem?"

Lazio gave a relieved sigh. "Oh yeah."

"That could've been bad." The fox hopped up on a crate, crossed his legs and pointed at Mal. "Northern coast, outside the Darwan village of Mawaena?"

Mal slowly nodded in confusion.

"Two blue trees?"

The Spice Rat was now extremely puzzled. "Yeah, but how?"

The fox held up a finger. "I got a similar story; except I was on foot trying to make it to an ice boat...something about rustling. Those Onay, they got no sense of humor."

This caused both to laugh. "Ain't that the fucking truth," the Spice Rat agreed. "I'm Mal by the way."

"Twitch," the fox said, then pointed over to the Yupik. "That's Voda. He's our resident shaman."

"I believe you are an Akina," Orich deduced. "It's strange we never ran into any of you in the Barrens. That is your native land, is it not?"

"Yeah, well we like to keep a low profile, for obvious reasons. So, what's your group's story?" he asked Mal.

The airship captain gave a frustrated sigh. "We're tryin' to finish up a run."

Twitch's eye involuntarily fluttered as he jumped off the crate. "That's the story of almost everyone down here."

Under a moonless sky the Rayth raiders *Korsan* and *Hurley* steered a slow but steady course toward the faint sun on the far western horizon and home.

The raid had technically been a success. The Calden merchant ship under tow behind the *Korsan* was evidence of that. However, the ship did not surrender without a fight and her broken main mast would need replacing once they reached Durik. Still, the captive ship's hold was filled with exotic spices and liquors as well as sheets of glass, all from the Twilight Lands to the east. Up in the rigging the heads of the merchant crew swayed in the wind. Captain Giana Roko was feeling proud of herself and the sisters under her command.

The solitary mariner on the towed merchant ship stood watch on its stern. She didn't hear the three large seahorses and riders as they surfaced by the ship's rudder and easily kept pace. She did feel a slight bump as the Nyanja riders leapt from their mounts onto the side of the ship's stern. Peering cautiously over the railing she gasped in shock to see three hideous fish heads staring up at her. Before she could cry out, a trident barb caught her in the back of the neck puncturing her spinal cord. A violent yank pulled her paralyzed body over the railing and into the dark sea below.

Three figures rapidly shimmied up to the deck. Removing their masks revealed two young men and one female. All, in direct contrast to their fish head breathing masks, were stunningly attractive. One of the men brandished a heavy short sword while the other two readied compact bows. Quickly scanning around and finding no further threats, they moved surreptitiously toward the bow.

Staying low on the merchant ship's bow, the young man with the sword positioned himself by the tow rope. The other two studied the capabilities of the twin raiders thirty feet in front of them. Both were the same: Night watch commander and driver on the quarterdeck with two armed mariners on the main deck.

In rapid succession each let four arrows fly with lethal results. Silently the Rayth dropped to the deck gripping the projectiles imbedded in them. The Nyanja with the sword raised his hand and struck his forefinger and thumb together causing a single spark to flicker then disappear.

On cue, five of the Calden sea cavalry slipped over the sides of both raiders as the two Calden support ships swiftly approached. Their ukko wood hulls silently and effortlessly slipped across the waves toward the unsuspecting Rayth ships. Once on the deck, the Nyanja rushed over to the hatches leading below barring them with thick planks.

The Calden support ships now slid quietly past on either side of the raiders in opposite directions. The sea horse riders bolted for the railing, diving off just as the Calden war ships fired several rounds of ballista chain shot at the masts. As the rounds sailed through the air the Nyanja on the merchant ship severed the tow line.

The Rayth below deck and awake on the *Korsan* realized something was amiss as their speed briefly increased. It was followed immediately by the crashing sound of mast, sail and rigging smashing onto the deck.

The Calden war ships circled out of sight as the Man-O-War *Jeonham* loomed out of the dusk. Both levels of ballista ports were open on her starboard side with ten blazing bolt tips protruding. The *Jeonham* slipped past the *Korsan* at no more than twenty feet away. The top volley of ten fired simultaneously into its side setting the raider ablaze.

Immediately the Man-O-War banked hard to starboard in a maneuver not capable by a sail ship of that size. It maneuvered in a tight circle to the *Hurley* and released the bottom row of burning bolts into the disabled Rayth raider. By the time it had gone around to the adrift merchant ship both pirate vessels were engulfed in flames.

Commander Benteen chewed furiously on the end of his carbana as he listened to the screams of the trapped mariners below. Pulling the roll of tobacco out of his mouth he glanced over at Admiral Lasia who stood beside him on the quarterdeck dispassionately watching the pirate ships burn. "Well, that's two we won't have to fight later."

"Wow, she's a beauty!" Twitch gushed as he regarded the *Haraka* slowly descending in the cavernous room.

"She gets the job done," Mal said proudly.

"I guess so!" The Akina said as he ran his hands along the sides. "Who wouldn't want to fly this baby. Whatcha runnin'?"

"We're moving a shipment of gems back to Immor-Onn," Mal replied.

"Immor-Onn!" Twitch cackled as his eye fluttered. "That's halfway across the damn Annigan!"

"Yeah," the Spice Rat acknowledged. "I'm learning the hard way about Flavian Portals."

The Akina scratched behind his ear. "You know, I may be able to save you a trip. I've been known to move a few gems."

Mal smiled. "Sorry, we've already gotten paid. We gotta get those little fuckers back to their owner, whoever that is."

"Speaking of gems," Orich said stepping toward the side hatch. "I have a request."

"Yeah?" Twitch asked warily.

"Something I discovered in the gem shipment," he said disappearing into the airship.

Mal glanced at her pilot leaving then turned back to Twitch. "So now that you see what we're dealing with, how the fuck do we get outta' here?"

"There are a couple of ways," the Akina answered. "None are pleasant."

"Oh?"

They were interrupted as Orich came out of the ship carrying the mysterious box.

"Can you tell us anything about this?" the albino asked handing it to Twitch.

The Akina's eye fluttered wildly as he examined the chained rectangular cube. "Beats me. I've never seen anything like it. How about you Voda?"

Taking it in his pudgy blue hands the Yupik examined all sides before meeting Orich's gaze. "These chains were crafted using a hybrid of fire and water magic."

"Exactly what does that mean?" Orich probed.

"Well, fire and water are on opposite points of the elemental spectrum. Whoever fashioned these chains had to possess formidable skills and a production operation."

"Like what?" Mal piped up.

"A forge would be handy," Voda offered.

Zaad pointed at the chains. "Each of the three EEtah houses use forges to craft magic into metal using fire and water."

"Interesting, however these chains aren't metal," the Yupik countered.

"Maybe a lapidarist over in the Dark Waste?" Mal guessed.

Twitch scanned the chains again. "That's where you found it, right?"

Mal nodded. "Can you open it?"

Voda exhaled loudly and examined the box again. "I think so. Are you sure you want me to?"

The Spice Rat chuckled. "Are you kidding. Anyone who went to that much trouble to keep me out is protecting something that's definitely got me interested."

The Ice Clansman became grim as he stared at Mal. "And maybe it was designed to keep something in."

The room was small by comparison to the others in No-Zann. The only blemish marring its perfectly square angles was a small stream which had etched out a narrow trail across the floor. All about, various boxes and a small bed lined the scorched walls.

Mal, Shom and Orich stood beside Twitch as they concentrated on the Yupik, his knees straddling the narrow band of slowly flowing water. Resting in front of Voda, half-submerged in the shimmering liquid, was the mysterious box.

The former Ice Clan shaman stared intently at the delicate black chains which bound the smooth ukko wood surface. After a short period of contemplation, he opened a small thin box by his side. From her position Mal could see it contained a multitude of different colored crystal beads each in three different sizes. Beside the beads was a twine of Darian silk and a three-inch-long orange shard of trinilic crystal with a needle-sharp tip.

Picking up the strand of spider silk, he held it up in front of him. The Yupik then chose three of the different colored beads and threaded them on the silk so they dangled inches above the box. He studied the configuration before reaching over and picking up the shard. With surgical precision he guided the tip to his thumb which held the spider silk against his forefinger and gave a small prick.

As a single drop of blood formed, he started a low, barely audible hum. Setting the shard down he reached into the stream. Cupping his hand, he brought up a small amount of water which he delicately poured over his bleeding finger and down the string. The water turned pink as it mixed with the blood and cascaded over the beads.

Mal and Shom ogled every move of the Yupik shaman in anticipation as they witnessed the pink liquid trickle onto the box and the chains began to melt. With the second handful of water the remnants of the chains were reduced to a thin black film which was washed away by the stream.

The Spice Rat and prodigal backed away quickly when the box top proceeded to rattle. Orich and Voda gazed on in wonder when rays of light burst from the sides.

As more and more light beamed out of the box's rapidly lifting top the ground rumbled and shifted below their feet. The two friends searched about in a panic as the room shook and shifted violently. Twitch frantically joined them as they bolted for the door. To their right a large crack had opened in the wall and debris was falling from the ceiling.

"Orich!" Mal screamed. "Out!"

The order went unheeded as the albino continued to stare at the ever-expanding field of light in front of him.

The trio made it to the doorway when the room exploded in blinding brilliance throwing them into Alto and Zaad who were standing guard.

The blast was over in an instant. The moment it subsided, so did the quaking.

Five curious associates cautiously stared into the room. Orich and Voda both lay unconscious on the bedrock. The box was still in the stream. Its top had blown off and came to rest ten feet away.

Inside the box, emanating a softly pulsing glow, was a large pearl the size of a human fist.

Entering the room, all paused and gazed curiously at each other. Each face contained a serene smile as a wave of peace and contentment swept over them.

Twitch made his way over to Voda and kneeled. "He's dead," the Akina reported solemnly looking up from the lifeless Yupik's grin.

Alto kneeled over Orich. "He's alive."

The quartet standing by the stream didn't hear him. They stood staring, totally entranced as the pearl gently pulsed.

"What the fuck is it?" Mal gasped.

"Not a clue," Shom confessed. "However, even though it killed our magical companion over there, I really don't feel any fear or anger toward it. If anything, I feel kinda…"

"Peaceful and content," Twitch finished his sentence.

"Yes, exactly," the royal confirmed.

A sly leer crept across the Akina's face. "Sell it to me. Name your price!"

Orich saw Alto leaning over his prone body. His business was elsewhere. He had heard the summons of the tilting cosmic scale carried on the voice of a distant mawl.

Upward he rose through the rocks and crystal.

Upward, over the rooftops of Shun-Dra he floated.

Soaring over the foothills of the Kel-Raku Mountains he observed great herds of antelope-like beasts run the grasslands like an undulating cloud.

He came to a landing in a large open track of prairie before a thick forest of yellow and red conifer trees. The moons rays were beginning to illuminate the eastern sky as a cloaked figure emerged from the shadowy forest.

The Bailian said nothing as the figure silently approached. Pausing several yards from Orich it stood motionless.

"I heard your call," the albino said in a hushed tone.

Slowly, paw-like hands reached up and pulled back the hood. Kind, tired features studied the Bailian as the elder jaguar's face became serious. "That which was foretold to you has come to pass. The pearl god has been released. It has begun."

Within the borders of the High Holy City of Zor there exist over one hundred different temples. All are dedicated to the various major deities worshiped across Lumina represented in one central neutral location. None however, is more opulent and splendid than the temple of the Golden Avatar.

Located in the far western catacombs of the city, its entrance is a large cave in the cliff just off the beach. This huge, pearl-encrusted opening beckons all who would choose to worship the eleventh incarnation of the entity which brought life from the Shallow Sea so long ago.

These sentient pearls have always been known as an ever-present force for good. Their pervasive song permeates the very fabric of Lumina, causing boundless fertility in both the oceans and on land, especially throughout its epicenter, the Goyan Island Chain. This hauntingly beautiful and virtually undetectable melody also acts as a nurturing cradle of balance for all the other various gods, both dark and light to provide for their believers.

Though worshiped by many sentients throughout Lumina, its most devoted followers and true apostles are the Otick.

These humanoid crab people were the first sentient life forms raised by the first Pearl Avatar ten thousand grands ago. They were the ones who lovingly tended and valiantly protected the sacred oyster beds on the bottom of the Shallow Sea which spawned the pearl deities.

Each thousand grands a new pearl avatar would arise from one of these three beds, all singing their own distinct melody. Each of the unique songs was directly responsible for all life evolving in Lumina. With the recent arrival of the ten thousandth grand, all were surprised and delighted to discover that the new avatar which rose from the beds of House Awa was golden, larger and more powerful than its pearl-colored predecessors.

The Otick priestesses rightfully judged this as a sign, heralding a new golden age all across Lumina. As predicted, prosperity, fertility and innovation swept the sunlit world above and below the Shallow Sea.

As the Kan fog receded, two lone Otick surfaced and waded onto the sandy shore. To the human fishermen readying their boats for sea, the Otick were a common sight. As far as the anglers were concerned, the crab-peoples were virtually indistinguishable from each other and generally ignored.

The glyphs on the backs of their shells marked them as generals of House Awa. Rising to their full height of seven feet, they regally paraded up the sands toward the temple's entrance.

"Our first audience with the Golden Avatar," Wallack excitedly remarked. "This is a great honor."

"Blessed be the Golden One," Raydan replied.

At the cave's entrance both Otick bowed down on one knee and respectfully lowered their gaze. From the cave's interior a female Otick in blue robes approached.

"You may rise," she said extending her hand.

Both Otick generals came to their feet.

"The Golden One awoke during the Kan," she informed.

"We heard the summons," Wallack confirmed.

The priestess indicated they should follow. "Blessed be the Golden One."

The tunnel sloped gently downward. A soft orange glow was reflected by the pearl-coated walls and the air in the tunnel was electric. Following closely, both Otick warriors quivered in anticipation.

In the first anteroom the generals removed their ooDs, setting the protective shells against the wall. The priestess glimpsed the interior of the individual shells which were covered in runes chronicling their deeds. In the second preparation room the generals were showered for purity. Only then were the double doors opened allowing access to the First Golden Avatar. All bowed as they entered.

"Blessed be the Golden One," they chanted.

The holy chamber was built as a small theater in the round. In the center was a shallow pool no more than two feet deep. Nestled there in the water, a giant oyster shell lay open. In it, a large golden pearl softly pulsed.

Descending the stairs, past the empty seats, the two Otick bowed on one knee before entering the water.

When they settled into the shallow pool directly in front of the gently glowing orb, it immediately began to throb. Waves of golden light bathed the room causing the two man-crabs' eyes to change from black to gold. Rocking back and forth they gave out a high-pitched holy chorus in unison as the avatar's song permeated their consciousness.

The one that was lost so long ago to war, has been found
The Fifth is among us again, in the distant,
Mist- filled land to the east where you journeyed before
You must seek it out
Find it before the darkness does
Protect it
The humans will aid you
Fly with them
Take it to the shining city,
to the beautiful blue queen
You are the only one of your numbers that can accomplish
this quest
You must not fail
Now go, the time of darkness draws near

The Oticks' eyes returned to normal as the intensity of the light in the room dimmed. The song's volume also ebbed, leaving both of the sentient crustaceans struggling to catch their breaths. Wallack and Raydan took a moment to compose themselves as the last notes of gentle pulsating rhythm subsided. With a reverential bow they backed out of the pool and swiftly left the presence of their deity.

The two donned their ooDs in silence and traded excited glances.

"Another quest," Raydan finally said as he secured his shell.

Wallack adjusted his ooD. "This quest comes from the golden light, not the Pearl Avatar as before. The Fifth is among us again. This quest we cannot fail."

"I do not like to fly my brother," Raydan admitted in a concerned tone.

Wallack was still trembling slightly as they exited the cave and made their way across the sand into the bustling city of Zor. "The prophets teach: 'Place your faith in the Avatar and your spirit will soar.'"

"Blessed be the Golden One," Raydan said as they entered the city streets and traveled eastward toward Valdurian Air Station Three.

The young, male, Tiikeri mongrel rarely left the boundaries of Shun-Dra. It was the only place in the land where he was truly safe. Tiikeri mongrels were considered an abomination to the tiger peoples and for the sake of racial purity, always killed on sight.

Now, as he followed the attractive grey mongrel out of town, he knew the risks. However, she was attractive and had the scent. He had the fever and could barely contain his penis which continually poked lustfully from its sheath.

"Where are we going?" he breathlessly asked as she pulled him along a path off the main road out of town.

"Just over there," she playfully enticed, pointing twenty yards away to a lone stand of trees rising up from the mist.

"My room's a lot more comfortable," came a half-hearted protest.

Stopping, she spun and embraced him. Gazing lustfully into his young face she felt his rampant erection poking her stomach. "I make a lot of noise," she breathlessly stated. "Besides I don't want my master to find out."

"Well, I guess this is secluded enough for you to make all the noise you want," he amorously rationalized.

"Come on," she coaxed as she playfully tugged on his hand.

"I don't even know your name," he said as she pulled him along.

"No-Le," she replied, stopping at the entrance to the small grove of trees. Playfully peeking inside, she glanced back at the Tiikeri mongrel. "This is it," she cooed seductively.

Curiously, the young male entered the clump of twenty trees. In the center was a small clearing and a wide tree stump.

"That stump is perfect," she said slipping up behind him.

He chuckled lecherously. "Something tells me you've done this before," he said as he started to unbuckle his belt.

"A few times," replied Ma-Tah as he appeared from behind the tree directly in front of him.

The mongrel's mouth fell open and froze in horror. Before he contemplated running, he felt No-Le's knife at his back. His attention then darted to the left as Stryder stepped into view. The young mawl was now fighting panic as the full blooded Tiikeri calmly strode over to him. Quaking with dread, he stared into Ma-Tah's hate-filled expression.

"Mongrel scum," the Tiikeri sneered as he delivered a punch to the side of the head knocking him unconscious.

The urge to gag woke him. The sleeve of his robe had been torn off and shoved in his mouth. His other sleeve bound his hands behind him and he hung upside down from a low branch.

No-Le knelt dutifully facing away. Stryder stood to the side watching Ma-Tah take in his suspended victim.

"You should be thankful that Pa-Waga has a use for your miserable life," the Tiikeri growled before slicing open his throat.

Torrents of blood cascaded down past his eyes frozen open. Ma-Tah reached into the rush of vital fluids as it flowed from the top of the mongrel toward the ground. Softly chanting, he methodically constructed an intricate field of binary numerology on the tree stump's flat surface. Twice he stuck his hand into the diminishing fountain of crimson, writing line after line of the same two runes.

When finished, he bent over staring at his work with labored breath. Slowly, the various characters on the stump started to smoke. Through bated breath Ma-Tah reeled in shock and staggered back as the top of the stump burst into flames.

The Tiikeri royal stood silently contemplating the mysterious event he just witnessed when Stryder approached. "Still more parlor tricks?"

The quartermaster's tone changed when he saw the tiger's grim expression. "Something bothering you?"

"There's something here that shouldn't be."

"What are you talking about?"

Ma-Tah scrutinized the flames as they subsided and died out. "I'm not sure, but whatever it is, it's dangerous to our cause, and it's very close."

Orich woke with a start. Alto was kneeling over him with Mal and Shom standing directly behind. All were staring down at him with concern etched upon their faces.

As he gazed around, Alto gave a sympathetic smile. "Are you alright my friend?"

Orich indicated he was and started to sit up. Alto rose and offered his hand.

"Am I ever glad you're okay," Mal's voice was noticeably relieved. "What the fuck happened?"

Twitch sadly gazed over from the body of the dead Yupik mage. "I'll tell you what happened. The resistance lost a powerful ally."

Zaad stood completely absorbed, staring at the silently pulsing orb completely entranced. "Would ya look at this thing."

"I would advise against touching it," Orich warned.

"Oh, don't worry about that," the EEtah said. "Just standing next to it makes me feel funny."

"Speaking of *it*," Shom pointed to the pearl. "What in the name of the gods is it?"

"Precisely," Orich replied.

The prodigal furrowed his brow. "I'm sorry, but my grasp of esoteric riddles is failing me at the moment."

It's not a riddle," Orich said firmly. "We are in the presence of the Fifth Avatar."

Everyone's gaze fell on the gently pulsing orb as Zaad backed away.

"They arise from the Otick oyster fields in the Shallow Sea. Lumina's very calendar is based on their thousand grand reigns. This one went missing five thousand grands ago when Nocturn attempted to attack the Goyan Islands."

"What the fuck was it doing over in The Barrens?" Mal asked.

"It can't be destroyed," Orich explained. "All they could do was bind it and hide it."

"Did it speak to you?" Alto asked.

The albino shook his head no. "It doesn't speak. It sings."

"Sings?!"

Orich stretched his back. "It is singing right now, for those who can hear it. Each Avatar since the first has sung a song which corresponds to the various stages of the development of life on Lumina."

"Well okay. It looks like the buyer of these gems is going to be getting more than they bargained for," Mal said. "As far as I'm concerned our job hasn't changed. We've got to get those gems and the singing god over there to Immor-Onn."

Orich's mouth went taunt. "There's more."

Shom threw up his arms. "Of course, there's more! There's always more! Don't tell me. This is the dangerous part!?"

The Bailian's stare bore into the ranting prodigal. "Catastrophic."

"Well sure," Shom continued. "Things can't be only dangerous anymore; they've got to be..."

"Shommy, shut the fuck up!" Mal admonished. "What's going on Orich?"

The albino took a deep breath. "Since leaving Immor-Onn, three distinct entities, each calling themselves Harbingers of Balance sought me out. They tried to warn me about this, but I didn't understand their cryptic messages. The warnings have now come to pass with the release of the Avatar."

Alto stroked his goatee. "I'm afraid I don't understand."

"This Avatar is not supposed to be here." Orich warned. "The first Golden Avatar now reigns. It has greatly upset the balance of this world. The Black Mural is poised to destroy the entire Annigan as we know it and allow life to try again."

Alto was genuinely confused. "I was under the assumption that the Avatars were a force for good."

Orich's expression betrayed a grim foreshadowing. "Its presence upsets the balance, so much so that the Black Mural is now poised to destroy us."

"Are you telling me there is now too much good in the world?" The swordmaster skeptically asked.

"In this case yes. All of this rises above the simple concept of good and evil. One cannot exist without the other. Every prophet is a heretic to their adversary and every revolutionary is a freedom fighter. Balance is the only thing that keeps the Black Mural from destroying us."

"All right," Mal piped up. "You keep talking about a Black Mural. What the fuck is that?"

"It grows with each act of imbalance on the Annigan. From the smallest to the largest, all are recorded there. It lies in the deepest oceans of Nocturn. As each act is recorded on its surface it grows. Soon it will plunge into the very core of this world. This will cause cataclysmic natural disasters. Life as we know it will cease and be replaced."

"Well isn't that cheerful," Shom moaned. "Replaced by…?"

Orich walked over and retrieved the box top. "I don't exactly understand. But I can feel it." The albino gently placed the top back on the box, covering the pearl. "It feels very different from life as we conceive it."

Reverently picking up the box, Orich joined his friends.

"Nothing's changed," Mal said. "We've still got a job to do. That means we've got to find a way out of here."

Zaad stepped up behind Shom and patted him on the shoulder. "Perhaps we should let the funny man guard the singing god."

Shom winced at the force of the pat then spun in frustration. "Shom! My name is Shom dammit!"

The EEtah gave the royal an amused grin. "I know."

As they left the room Twitch looked over at Mal. "By the way, I'm taking back that offer to buy."

The debris field stretched hundreds of yards down the beach. Charred scraps of wood, rope and sail juxtaposed the gentle rolling surf on this rare, calm winter morning.

Fia's gaze slowly followed the stretch of devastation and fixated on a badly burnt, half eaten torso in the sand. A series of shallow waves gently rolled it into a partially buried section of mast.

"It's the *Hurley*," Fia said in a low grim tone.

Blenda stood silently beside her admiral in the cold sand, unable to look away from the scene of watery destruction. Several sisters, chattering nervously, rushed past them to comb through the wreckage.

The Hill Sister gave a deep, sad sigh. "To be so close…"

"Not necessarily," Fia said. "The current that brought this ruin to us runs almost the entire half of the northern coast of Amarenia."

"What do you think happened?"

"Perhaps they took on flammable plunder and there was a mishap. I don't know."

"Think the *Korsan* met the same fate?" Blenda asked as the pair started toward the wreckage.

"That's got me concerned," Fia replied as she inspected the littered beach "If they didn't meet the same fate they still may be in trouble. I'll order Captain Csaba to take the *Craven* and follow this current back out."

Both Rayth commanders stood over the remains of the mariner. Any features were now indistinguishable.

"Let's get her body ready for full immersion with honors. Unless any more bodies wash up, she will represent the crew in the ceremony."

"Yes admiral," Blenda said as she watched Fia worriedly search the horizon line.

Twitch and Mal led the way as they returned to Rapscallia.

"Ya see," the Akina began as he raised a finger for emphasis. "There's only three ways in or outta this place. One unfortunately, is in only."

"Yes, we witnessed an arrival," Shom's tone was cold and sarcastic.

Stopping abruptly, Twitch spun and once again pressed up to the prodigal, "Looky here sonny!"

Blinking in astonishment, a superior grin appeared as the royal stared at the man-fox. "Sonny? Really?"

"I seen plenty of your type before…"

Shom reeled back in indignation. "My type?!"

"Yeah, whiner!" Twitch said angrily. "They don't last long down here!"

Shom threw up his hands. "Splendid, when do we leave?!"

"Well you boys just circle jerked your way around that conversation!" Mal admonished. "Shom, knock it off!"

"Me?!"

An angry glare silenced the royal.

"Now," she said returning her attention to Twitch. "The other two ways?"

Throwing Shom a dirty glance the Akina continued. "One of those died with that mage back there. That only leaves one other way." The fox creature paused as a sinister grin pulled at the corners of his mouth and his eye began to flutter. "The bug tunnels are the only way out."

Everyone stared at each other in stunned silence.

"Surely you don't mean those fire bugs that almost got me?" Alto asked.

"Nah, those were Na-Kab. You'd never stand a chance getting through their fire hive. The bugs you can deal with are the Do-Tarr's northern hive."

The Spice Rat slowly nodded and exhaled loudly. "Do-Tarr…"

"They're not so bad," Twitch assured. "Their tunnel system stretches practically under the whole continent. It's how we get supplies and such. There's only a few things to keep in mind."

Mal gave a resigned sigh. "You've got my attention."

"The first thing to know, these bugs all share a hive mind, except the king. They work as one and the queen sees everything they do. You'll probably need to get her permission by the way. And ya gotta understand, the hive is everything to them. So, don't damage it, *period*. The Do-Tarr don't got a word or the concept of 'accident.' They're merciless."

Twitch saw the hesitation in their expressions. "On the plus side, they're fair, they're neutral and they always keep their word."

All attention went toward Mal. She studied her comrades, then gave a probing glance at the Akina for an alternative.

Twitch shrugged. "It's the only way out."

Out of a clear, cold Lumina sky the *Drakin* gently banked southward over the rocky, western Goyan coast.

Captain Demetrius de Vana slowly circled the High Holy City of Zor to affect a lasting first impression on his four passengers. The tiered community stretched from the beach up into the foothills of Mount Goya until the massive forum protruded from and dominated its western face.

The first Bailian diplomatic delegation had been staring in wonder as they left the monotonous view of open ocean and passed over the lush eastern agricultural islands. The numerous cities illuminated by the sun's constant radiance filled them with awe as they finally trekked across the Goyan continent.

"Almost as impressive as Immor-Onn," ambassador Ar-Sut begrudgingly admitted in an autocratic tone. "Wouldn't you agree?"

The three in her party followed her gaze. The young male and female concurred with sycophantic abandon. The older Bailian bodyguard with bald head and thick snow-white handlebar moustache quietly observed the city passing beneath them.

Demetrius grinned at the ambassador's arrogance as he performed a gentle bank to the left and descended toward the massive entrance to Valdurian Air Station Three. The huge rectangle swallowed the relatively small craft. Once inside the young seneschal and runner stared about, mouths agape. The older man merely leaned forward in his seat, leaning on his cane as he stared out the windows.

"Immor-Onn's Air Station East is much larger," ambassador Ar-Sut said in a haughty voice.

The air boss on deck waved him to a docking area and given his passengers' status he was not surprised to see an official contingent waiting for them.

"Seems like you've got a welcoming committee," Demetrius said over his shoulder.

"Well I would certainly hope so." The ambassador sounded on the verge of indignation.

The seasoned pilot wisely held his tongue. He would be glad to get rid of the snooty Bailian female.

"Welcome to the High Holy City of Zor, ambassador," the pilot said as the *Drakin* gently settled into its slot. Immediately getting up from his lone pilot chair, he dropped the side hatch and the Bailian delegation disembarked.

Straightaway the line of six officials dressed in yellow robes advanced on them with welcomes. Demetrius exited well after the initial introductions were over. Running his hands along the side of his beloved ship he began his manual inspection of the craft. A task he never omitted.

As he started around the nose of the craft, a young human female wearing the green jumpsuit of the Valdurian Air Service stepped from the crowd which was now leaving with the ambassador's party. She was extremely attractive with long brown hair pulled back in a traditional ponytail. She was also tall, at almost six feet with voluptuous curves. Her rank patch indicated she was a captain. The Logistics Division patch on her other sleeve might have indicated she was clerical were it not for the pistol crossbow on her hip.

"Demetrius de Vana?" Her tone was formal yet friendly.

"You got him!"

His effervescence caused a thin smile to appear on the officer. "I'm Captain Okawa. I'm here to escort you to Joc' Valdur."

The pilot's jovial mood transformed into a serious stare. "Really? I mean, you're sure?"

"Right this way sir," Okawa said as she gestured him on.

As Demetrius entered the spacious office, the Valdurian emissary to Zor stood and came out from behind his desk. Captain Okawa positioned herself in the doorway, hands behind her back.

The Valdurian representative broadly beamed as he extended his hand. Demetrius was genuinely surprised at his youthful appearance. The scraggly moustache and long thick black hair were striking.

"Demetrius!" He greeted warmly as they shook hands. "So good of you come on such short notice."

"Not at all sir," the pilot responded in a meek voice.

Joc' indicated two chairs facing his desk. "Sit, sit!"

Demetrius waited for the young ambassador to be seated before he chose a chair.

"So, how are you enjoying the *Drakin*?" Joc' began.

The airship captain's palms started to sweat and he could feel his stomach begin to knot up. Nervously licking his lips, he sat forward. "Is this about my charter? It is, isn't it? Look, I swear I didn't realize what was in that shipment to Odari. They said it was rice. How was I to know…"

Joc' calmly shook his head no and held up a few fingers for silence. At the door Captain Okawa was looking at the floor, unsuccessfully fighting an amused grin as Demetrius halted his flustered babble and stared down at his lap.

"It's not about your charter."

Immediately the pilot perked up, obviously relieved. "It isn't?"

Joc' once again shook his head no, then stopped. "Well, a little."

Demetrius' joy evaporated. "Oh?"

"I'm invoking the cooperation clause in your loose charter," the ambassador said.

Once again relief descended upon the pilot. "Sure," he replied sincerely without hesitation. "A deal's a deal."

Joc' reached into a side desk drawer. Pulling out a small bag he placed it on the desk in front of the overwhelmed airship captain. At the ambassador's prompt Demetrius warily opened the bag and peered in.

He jolted back up eyes wide in amazement. "These are veros pearls!"

Joc' grinned, "I know."

"This is a small fortune!"

"I know."

Demetrius quickly closed the bag and stared suspiciously the Valdurian official. "What's the job?"

"Passenger transport. Right up your alley," the ambassador assured.

"If you don't mind me asking sir, why me? Plenty of pilots do passenger transport."

Joc' hesitated and his tone became complimentary. "Because you're the only pilot that's flown where our clients need to go."

The pilot slumped. "Nocturn."

"That's right and they need to get there fast."

"How fast?"

"You leave immediately. We desperately need that little trick of yours." Joc' flattened out his palm and shot it upward at a steep angle as he gave the pilot an understanding nod.

An exasperated Demetrius sat up in his chair. "You're sending me to Nocturn alone? Can I assume this is a suicide mission?"

Joc' remained calm. "You won't be alone. Captain Okawa is going with you for protection."

Demetrius sputtered in shock at the woman in the green jump suit then back to Joc'. "Sir, no disrespect to the captain but when I was there before we had two Avions, a Sunal EEtah and a couple of crack Zerian Rangers and we barely made it back in one piece. Some of us didn't. Some came back changed. I mean…"

"Captain," Joc's tone was firm. "I don't want you to go exploring. You go there, you drop off your passengers and you come home."

Demetrius slumped in resignation. "Well, I mean, okay…"

Joc' nodded sympathetically. "One more thing."

Demetrius dropped his gaze again.

"You won't be flying the *Drakin*."

The pilot's gaze was the only thing that moved as he silently questioned the Valdurian ambassador.

"They won't fit," he explained.

Now Demetrius was uneasy. He would be piloting an unfamiliar ship through insane conditions. He took some solace in the assurance that his beloved *Drakin* would be cared for. His mind was spinning as he and Okawa walked from the Forum directly to the air station's flight deck. *Joc' said the provisions were already loaded, but how could any of them know how to prepare for Nocturn?*

As the duo stepped onto the central flight deck, Demetrius nervously peeked over at Captain Okawa who had remained silent the entire trek. "You don't really talk much, do you?"

The nonconfrontational, noncommittal smile was all the answer he needed. Sighing deeply, he pushed on.

Demetrius heaved a sigh of relief when he saw the ship was a resistance class cruiser. It was the first thing he had ever flown. This one's name was written on the side — *Catori*. Two Otick man-crabs stood beside the craft. He assumed they were his passengers and Joc' was right, they wouldn't have fit in the *Drakin*. He now also understood his method of payment.

Walking confidently over to the craft Demetrius addressed his passengers, trying desperately to sound confident. "Okay everyone. We've got a long rough ride ahead of us. The sooner we get going, the sooner I get to spend some of your hard-earned pearls."

The Otick slowly reacted to the voice. Wallack opened his mouth in astonishment and pointed at Demetrius with one of his claws, "You!" he squeaked in common.

The pilot had a hard time believing who he saw. "What are you two doing here?"

Raydan laughed, "It is the will of the Golden One that we meet again!"

Wallack raised his claws skyward. "It is as the prophets said: Comrades in the holy cause do not forget and all share the same destiny."

"I see you guys haven't changed," he said before becoming aware of Okawa staring at him. The Valdurian agent displayed a puzzled expression and raised eyebrow. "You know them?"

The Rod-Ema Trench stretches across the western ocean floor of Nocturn from the Land of Mists to the massive outcropping of etheria crystals at its origin, the Agar-Goyot. All along the walls of the trench, a black wall of obsidian covered with the runes documenting the sins of a planet plunge into the depths of the abyss.

Glittering water, thick with etheria sediment sparkled through the blackness of the Ocean Deep. The goyot pulsed with energy. Giant shafts of softly glowing, multi-colored magical gems rose majestically from the apex of the trench several hundred feet above the seabed. In the center, a towering purple crystal a hundred feet in diameter climbed upwards toward the frozen ice floes of the surface.

A few feet off the seabed, various smaller crystals that terraced up the goyot were carved into giant phallic pillars. Perched atop each, tentacled beings could be made out in the murky, sparkling void. Their long appendages lovingly caressed the shafts as their upper bodies placidly swayed in the currents. Occasionally, one would jet away, disappearing into the dark ocean, only to reappear shortly after. Periodically, large bubbles would form around one of the beings and they would float upward.

Now the mood was anything but calm. The Chenoans reeled at the tremor from the mural in the trench. They all felt the presence. The pearl god which they had captured and hidden so long ago was now free. Claw-like hands resembling crab legs undulated furiously as the ancient beings silently conversed. The deliberation ended with all of them raising their arms and emitting a high-pitched squeal which resounded outward.

Slowly, the seabed began to shift and move as thousands of fish humanoids emerged from their resting places under rocks and fissures. They gathered about the goyot looking upward at their masters in mindless anticipation. Now, a low series of pulsing tones swept among the crowd from the Chenoans. The intonation quickly inflamed them and they angrily rippled in mass. With a dramatic wave of the Chenoans' arms, the army of Gar-Kal fish creatures began to ascend toward the surface and the Land of Mists.

Shom shuddered as he worriedly scanned over Mal's shoulder and out the *Haraka's* windshield. "You know, between that incident in the fields of Amarenia, and now this, I fear I'm developing a serious aversion to insects."

Mal sat staring at the lone figure of Alto. The swordmaster walked directly in front of the airship as it cautiously navigated the tunnels of the Do-Tarr's northern hive.

On all sides of the airship the insect workers scampered about completely ignoring the slow-moving craft suspended in the exact center of the tunnel. They were just as Mal remembered them from the streets of Immor-Onn. Chest high to humans, with a mantis shaped skull, human torso and insect lower body. To her perspective, each one was identical to the next. She was still pissed at Alto too. The crazy ass swordsman volunteered to lead the ship from the ground. He argued that his presence out front along with Orich-Taa's piloting and navigational skills would keep the *Haraka* from colliding into the walls or any other disturbance to the hive. When she vehemently protested, he cited Twitch's ominous warning not to provoke the Do-Tarr in any way. Her throat tightened any time one of the industrious insects got near him as they dutifully slipped past the human on some unfathomable errand.

Pressing slowly forward, Shom swallowed hard as the number of the sentient bugs increased. They moved rapidly along the floors, walls and ceilings, scurrying around Alto and the ship. Many of the workers carried flat wide shovels and long-handled hammers.

All inside the *Haraka* tensely scanned the cabin's interior as they heard the sound of Do-Tarr climbing across the hull.

The tunnels now widened considerably. Mal clearly saw intensive mining activity going on to their right. The Spice Rat and prodigal gawked in horrific fascination as the bug people worked with rapid precision. Initially, two of the creatures would scurry along a section of wall. Every five feet the tip of their thorax would mark a spot. Once the section was stamped, a single Do-Tarr moved between the parallel points. Keeping his mouth inches above the rock wall he vomited out a thick yellowish-brown liquid which quickly smoldered. That worker was followed by another with the shovel scraping the melted rock from the wall. The liquified slag accumulated along the blade of the tool until it reached the end. There it was dropped to the ground and another would take away the boulder-sized scraping. Moving along the work area they perceived similar scenes taking place all around them.

Suddenly, to their left a loud crashing sound followed immediately by a rumble caused work to instantly stop. All of the Do-Tarr stared in the direction of the sound. The clatter roused Zaad from his seat as he joined Shom behind the captain's chair. Mal pointed to a large section of wall that had fallen and left a massive crack.

From the direction of the toppled wall a high-pitched squeal began to slowly rise. Building in volume and tempo, it spread through tunnels until it encompassed the entire hive. Shom covered his ears and reeled in disgust as all the Do-Tarr in the immediate area swarmed onto one of their own. All inside the ship winced at the sound of body parts snapping as they witnessed the offending worker being swiftly dismembered and devoured by its hive mates.

Don't disrupt the hive, no fucking shit! Mal recounted blinking in astonishment. "Bugs don't forgive," she uttered remembering the Akina's warning. She was also thankful to Twitch for the large vial of Tiikeri pheromones as well as a small bolt of brightly colored fabric as a gift. The pheromones would come in handy if they needed to disappear and make a hasty exit. Still, even that advantage would eventually wear off. It wouldn't help if they were lost in the Do-Tarr's catacombs. The cloth was an essential diplomatic tool, because according to the Akina, the Do-Tarr queen liked pretty things. The Spice Rat's anxious gaze was fixated back on Orich's stoic frame as he concentrated on keeping the ship on course. "You sure you know where we're at and where the exits are?"

"Captain, I recognize exactly where we are," the Bailian said confidently.

Satisfied, Mal turned her attention quickly back to her lover, who despite the deadly interruption, continued to guide them slowly onward.

As they passed the construction area, the tunnel resumed its prior shape and the number of workers dwindled. Approaching a large intersection, a group of twenty Do-Tarr blocked their path. Orich stopped the *Haraka* and hovered immediately behind the swordmaster. Mal's stomach knotted as she saw two approach Alto. All in the cabin were fixated on the human interacting with the ominous-looking giant bugs.

Mal sighed and relaxed when she saw him bow. She could hear his introduction in her mind. *Alto de Gom, at your service.*

All were relieved when he approached the ship. Taa cracked the side hatch. Everyone's attention restlessly centered on a smiling Alto as he popped through the opening. "It appears we have an audience with the queen."

What do gods utter,
when perchance they speak to one another?
Things mysterious and unknowable to mortal kind?
The old pearl god
and the new golden avatar,
across the distance,
each sensing the other
Pulses of gold
Pulses of white,
and a bond, in a new city
Bright, shining, radiating potential
A beacon of good,
and a bridge to the dark, distant Annigan
The newly crowned jewel of the east, Immor-Onn

All across Lumina, from the leaves of the trees to the wind chimes of Immor-Onn, the song of the Golden Avatar vibrated on the wind. The Fifth Avatar's new home was to be among the Bailian people.

It was more than the oppressive heat and humidity that was making Mal sweat like the condemned on execution day. Standing just outside the perfectly formed pentagon-shaped entrance to the queen's chamber she caught a whiff of the stench emanating from within and Shom's reaction to it.

"Knock off the disgusted looks," she ordered under her breath. "And for the love of the goddess, keep your mouth shut. Let Orich do the talking."

Shom was about to protest when a Do-Tarr appeared in the doorway. "The queen will see you shortly," it said. "You may enter but remain silent until the birthing is done."

The Do-Tarr clacked its mandibles and motioned for them to follow. "She'll be in a much better mood then."

Once inside the large pentagon shaped room, Zaad was the only one not overwhelmed by the acidic, ashen stench. The EEtah appreciatively assessed the brightly colored cloths draped from the ceiling then fingered the small bolt of fabric in his hand. Twitch had chosen their gift wisely. The nine-foot man-shark couldn't help but notice that the queen was immense in comparison to her brood, standing easily as tall as him. Anatomically, she resembled the rest of the Do-Tarr with the exception of six massive breasts with jet black nipples on her humanoid torso. The sacs heaved with each birth contraction.

Her thorax rested on a low riser and faced away from them to the far point of the room. Two Do-Tarr stood behind her attending to her birth canal by lapping at the thick yellow fluid which oozed from the dilated rear end of the queen.

Two attendants stood in front of her and one stood directly at her side holding her hand. "Push, push," the two chanted.

"Yes, my love, push," parroted the Do-Tarr holding her hand.

The queen who had been staring down and concentrating snapped a nasty look at the Do-Tarr king. "You should try this sometime!" She lashed out as her mandibles quivered in pain.

Wisely, the king remained silent.

Lowering her gaze, the queen grimaced again and cried out as a massive rush of fluid hit the floor with a wet plop.

"It has arrived!" one called out in joy as it lifted the still dripping white sac for all to see. The room erupted with the Do-Tarr clicking their approval. The queen lifted her mantis head up, visibly relieved.

Immediately, the one carrying the embryo sac walked over to a row of large, open jars and gently lowered it into one. Behind the queen, the other was making loud slurping sounds as it hungrily cleaned her.

The two that stood in front now moved over to the queen. One picked up a deep bowl and held it up in front of the new mother's chest. The other reached up and began massaging one of the breasts and tugging on the nipple. As it milked the bloated sac an oily, greenish-yellow fluid squirted into the bowl. Great care was used to ensure no fluid escaped. With each breast milked the queen's expression became more and more serene.

Out of the corner of her vision, Mal humorously noticed that despite the proximity to naked breasts, Shom didn't display his usual lecherous stare.

As the last bowl was filled, the attendant offered it to the king who took a deep drink. It was then passed around to all the Do-Tarr in the room who took small sips.

Finally, the queen's attention settled on Mal and the group.

"None carry the curse," the Do-Tarr that led them in announced.

The sovereign nodded, with what Mal assumed was a smile, as she indicated the bowl be passed to them.

Orich immediately stepped up, bowed slightly and accepted the vessel. Taking a sip, the Bailian paused. His mouth contorted slightly and he loudly inhaled. He then handed it to Shom who warily inspected the half-full bowl.

"This is the Do-Tarr queens' nectar. It is very valuable and has been known to accentuate skills and powers. Even though its effects are sometimes short lived, this is an honor."

Reluctantly the prodigal accepted it and took a sip. Surprisingly it had almost no flavor, merely a slight hint of pepper. He thoughtfully assessed the taste and passed it on as a wave of confidence and heightened awareness swept over him.

When all had taken a drink, the attendant took a full bowl and poured it into the row of jars. The other four bowls were emptied into a narrow chute in the wall.

Orich leaned in close to Mal, "Her nectar now nourishes the hive."

The Spice Rat appeared confused. "How can that amount nourish the whole hive. There's got to be thousands of them?"

"It trickles down the hive via the waste of the Do-Tarr in the level directly above."

"Are you telling me the dinner table to one is the privy to the others just above?"

"Yes captain, with each progressively lower tier in the hive the nectar is diluted until it reaches the bottom rung of their society. The bearers of burden."

Mal stood in stunned silence as Orich took the bolt of cloth from Zaad and stepped forward.

"Oh queen," he began. "Thank you for honoring us with an audience. We bring a small token of our appreciation."

"How very thoughtful," the king gushed as he accepted the gift. "Look dear, aren't the colors wonderful?!"

To Mal, the queen's once-over of her mate was disdainful as she silently extended her hands. A slightly dejected king handed her the bolt. She stroked it softly as she trilled. Then handing it back to her husband she addressed the group. "We've encountered your kind in the past and you were a friend to the Do-Tarr. You are without the curse and have drunk the essence. The hive welcomes you. What brings you to our home?"

Orich extended his arms indicating the group behind him. "Oh queen, we seek safe passage through your tunnels. Our destination is Shun-Dra."

"Why do you seek the unaligned city?" the queen calmly asked.

From Mal's right, Shom cleared his throat and took a purposeful stride forward. "Um, Your Majesty, if I may interject..."

Mal held her breath and crossed her fingers. *Oh, by the goddess!*

All attention was now focused on the Eldorian royal. "We seek supplies for the trip back to Immor-Onn. We are carrying a very special shipment personally authorized by Queen Shula."

"Shula!" the king sputtered. "You know Queen Shula?!"

Shom's tone was confident and pleasant. "The cargo we carry is bound for her."

The king could not contain his excitement. "Shula and I are the best of friends!"

The queen's annoyed gaze descended quickly on her husband.

"You must take me with you!" he added.

The queen stared at her mate in shock. "What?!"

"Oh, do not be angry my love," he pleaded as he peered upward at his huge mate. "There's a work detail there and I must go to check on them."

"The workers are fine," came the unconvinced response.

"Yes, yes I'm sure," the king said. "But in this case my personal appearance is called for. Yes, that's it, it's settled, I'm going to Immor-Onn!"

Mal skittishly shifted her feet. "Uh, Your Majesty, no disrespect but…um, your size and shape, there's not enough room in the *Haraka*."

The king laughed, his head bobbed and mandibles clicked furiously as waves of heated air rippled in front of him, briefly obscuring their view. When it faded, Mal gasped as the group now saw a young, handsome Bailian male with smooth features standing in front of them. "Is this appearance more functional?"

To the Otick race, fear is an unknown emotion. Millennia of devoted service to the Pearl Avatars and the martial ability granted them has bestowed a veneration and well-earned reputation in their reclusive numbers. This however does not exclude them from reverential awe in the case of stimulating new experiences, such as flight.

Wallack and Raydan stared wondrously out the windshield of the *Catori* as Demetrius guided her smoothly out of the entrance of Air Station Three and hit the accelerator.

"I'd hold onto something," the pilot warned.

The cloudless blue sky of Lumina filled the window as the sudden velocity knocked the two large crustaceans back onto their decorated shells.

Raydan reeled from the rush of sudden momentum. "Golden One be praised!"

Wallack was attempting to get to his feet. "Deetus, perhaps it was a good thing we did not get a chance to travel with you before."

"Sorry about that," Demetrius apologized glancing backwards at his prostrate passengers. "But I've got orders to get you to your destination fast."

"The prophets tell us that undue haste can lead to unholy results," the Otick general replied as he finally stood.

The pilot chuckled. "We'll worry about that once we're there."

"So, are you going to fill me in on how you know each other?" Okawa impatiently asked from the chair next to him.

Demetrius raised his eyebrows in surprise. "She speaks!"

The Valdurian captain's response was silent and unamused.

The pilot concentrated out the windshield, keeping the curious agent in his peripheral vision. "About three grands ago we ran into each other in the Land of Mists. I'd hooked up with a pretty impressive group of, oh well, let's just call them fortune hunters. Their pilot got killed and I was the only one qualified to fly. I really wasn't, but I was the closest they had. A bunch of Otick eggs had gone missing and we were searching for them. Wouldn't you know it? These two knuckleheads back there were over in Nocturn looking for the same thing."

"Our children were stolen by the tentacled ones in the darkness," Wallack added. "They sought to breed a race able to move about in the sunlight."

"The only difference between them and us, was they were on a mission," Demetrius said. "We were only trying to line our pockets. As things turned out, they got their eggs back and we ended up caught in a big ruckus in the Land of Mists. We helped overthrow the mutant Tiikeri king and restore the Cub Prince to the throne."

Okawa sat back, quiet once again in contemplation of the story she had been told.

"How soon before we arrive Deetus?" Raydan asked as he finally regained his feet.

The pilot's voice took on a menacing tone. "That all depends on Ash-Ta airspace."

The pale blue and yellow foliage parted with a loud rustling as a startled flock of black and red birds took to the air squawking noisily. In stark contrast to their emergence from the concealed Do-Tarr tunnel the *Haraka* silently rose and hovered. Only the top of the craft was visible above the mist-covered ground.

Mal warily surveyed the surrounding area for movement. "So, what was the queen talking about when she mentioned the curse?"

Orich steadied the wheel and joined his commander in her reconnoitering. "If anyone's ancestors ever harmed or harassed the Do-Tarr they receive a genetic marker which is carried by the offender's decedents."

"You're kidding!"

The Bailian's response was calmly sobering. "No captain. The Do-Tarr do not forgive or forget."

"How many generations does this go on for?" Mal asked.

"Forever," came the grim reply.

The Spice Rat exhaled loudly. "Good thing we all passed the test."

"We all would've paid the price in guilt by association," Orich said as he completed his survey of the fog shrouded landscape. The Bailian then closed his eyes in silent consultation with his brother in the hull of the craft. "There appears to be no hostile activity in the area."

Mal adjusted her sword belt and faced the group. "Alright folks. We're going into town. Alto, you and Shom are in charge of procuring some food stores." She glared directly at the prodigal. "For the love of the goddess get something we all can eat."

Shom's response was both innocent and outraged. "I'm certain I have no idea what you could be referring to!"

"No more fucking olives!" she sternly said.

"I've got plenty, thank you," his smug reply was met with an annoyed glare from the Spice Rat.

Scowling at the royal, she looked up at the EEtah. "Zaad, you're with me. Grab that spool of spider silk and let's see if we can convert it into something more useful. Orich-Taa take the *Haraka* to a safe altitude and be ready to come get us out of here, especially if the shit gets deep."

"Wow, does this fucking place stink!" Mal grimaced as they sloshed through the boulevards of Shun-Dra. From the moment they entered town the Spice Rat immediately noticed that the level of the pervasive mist had lowered to ankle level and was substantially thicker.

Even Zaad reeled at the predominate stench of cat spray. "I can hear the funny little man now."

Mal smiled at the thought of the pampered royal's visceral reaction as their boots squished in the invisible mud-covered streets beneath their feet. Mongrel mawls peeked out at them from open doors and windows from the small hovels on either side.

Keeping her gaze forward, she cautiously kept track of their audience through her decidedly enhanced peripheral vision. "Stay sharp marine."

The EEtah grimaced at the mawls surrounding them, causing the frightened inhabitance to immediately look away. "Yes captain." With that assurance Zaad felt a slight agitation in the mist around his ankles. Shifting his feet to disperse it proved fruitless, so he ignored it and continued behind his commander.

Slowly, the further into town they progressed the buildings became larger. To Mal's eye they still displayed an unkept appearance common to any remote location regardless of the race. The streets were also becoming more active as a parade of mostly mongrels passed, taking time to stare at the towering man-shark.

Coming to a large intersection they noticed the crowd becoming more diverse. Pure bred mawls, scruffy down and out Singa lions and Pomaku leopards moved along the misty streets. They stopped to let a procession of robed Yagur jaguars move across the crossroads and toward a bridge leading to an island in the river containing several large complexes. From the opposite direction in the crossroads, the Spice Rat saw merchants and customers alike making their way down the street to the distinct activity of a bustling marketplace.

"This could be promising," Mal said, motioning toward the commercial area.

The small square consisted of a dozen narrow intersecting streets lined with covered vendor stalls. The Spice Rat was disappointed to find that they mostly consisted of produce, meats, trinkets and implements of a low and functional nature. After crisscrossing the various roads filled with aggressive merchants, a dejected Mal huffed at Zaad. "Come on, let's get outta' here. These small-town jerk-offs wouldn't notice something valuable if it were jammed up their ass."

A snicker from behind caused both to spin. A middle-aged female Singa stood just outside an alley entrance with her hands on her hips and an amused stare. Mal had seen her loitering in the market. She stood out from even the other Singa inhabitants. Her fawn-colored fur contained a touch of gray along her ears and snout. Over her right eye was a simple patch and the left side of her head was shaved and adorned with an ornate blue tattoo. She carried no weapon and her multi-pocketed tunic was held closed with a seashell belt. "You're just now figuring that out?" she asked sarcastically.

Instinctively Zaad moved forward in a defensive position. Immediately the mist began to swirl at his feet. The Singa indicated down at the undulating clouds. "Easy does it, big fella. I get a feeling you're needed and I'd hate to see the mist get you too." She then winked at Mal. "I'm Zau and I'm pretty sure I've got an answer to your dilemma."

"Oh?"

The Singa motioned them toward an empty alley.

She confidently pointed to the item in Zaad's hands. "That spool of silk should fetch a good price if you know where to get rid of it."

"And you do?" Mal asked skeptically.

Zau grinned slyly, "Yep."

"What's the catch?"

"I come along with the deal."

The Spice Rat obstinately paused. "Thanks, but I've got enough friends."

Zau maintained her impish smirk. "Oh, I'm sure."

When she reached into the pocket of her tunic Zaad tensed. This caused the Singa to pause. "Will you relax. We're in Shun-Dra. I couldn't do something aggressive if I wanted to." With that admonishment she pulled a large walnut shell from her pocket.

Mal saw the curious object contained a delicate hinge on one side. Holding it up for all to see she opened it. Inside appeared to be a milky white eyeball. Lifting her patch, she removed the eye from its container and placed it inside the empty socket of flesh.

Turning away from the open end of the alley, her replacement eye began to glow. A radiating three-dimensional field of blue-green light projected in the air directly in front of her. Slowly the field of light started to take shape. Opaque landscapes were dotted with points of light. Some were stationary, some moved about, while others winked on and off.

Mal and Zaad watched the blue sparkles which now fully formed into a globe of the Annigan suspended in the air before them.

"Very pretty," Mal said sarcastically. "How does this make me want to take your deal, whatever that is?"

"Because," the Singa confidently beamed, "with this map, I can get you wherever you want to go."

Shom examined the three bales and sighed contentedly as he leaned over to Alto who stood next to him. "Well, I certainly hope this gives your girlfriend less to complain about."

The prodigal had procured a sizeable amount of meat and grain from a mongrel merchant with questionable motives when he caught sight of Stryder Aramos entering the market square. The lone human was accompanied by a large white humanoid tiger.

The intrigued royal placed his hands on his hips. "By the gods, this little endeavor gets more interesting by the luna."

Alto was finishing up securing the details of the delivery. "Say again?" he questioned his friend. Shom motioned toward the mismatched pair making their way into the crowded streets.

"Another human. That's odd," Alto said as Shom tracked the diverse duo across the far end of the market square.

"Not just any human," Shom added. "That's Stryder Aramos. I wonder what my dear brother-in-law is doing here?"

The swordmaster scanned the dirty fog-laden street bathed in the low twilight of the luna. "I doubt very seriously if he is here on holiday."

"Umm," Shom agreed.

Stryder and Ma-Tah had made it about halfway through the bazaar's stalls when the human spotted Shom. Their gazes locked and the quartermaster instinctively reached for his sword. His arm was blocked by the Tiikeri's furry hand. "Let's not destroy this alliance before it has a chance to get started."

Stryder paused as he trembled in frustration. Realizing the Tiikeri was right, he reluctantly nodded his acceptance and the mist swirling about his ankles calmed.

Alto caught the malevolent glower on Stryder and the twitch toward his weapon. "It would appear that one more of those wishing you harm have discovered your whereabouts."

"So it would seem," Shom agreed. "I think I'm going to capitalize on our location and perhaps secure a strategic advantage."

Alto gave is friend a bewildered smirk. Shom noted it and gave a mischievous wink. "Excuse me for a moment."

The last thing the lead quartermaster expected was to see a beaming Shom Eldor casually sauntering his way.

"What in the name of Pa-Waga does he want?" Ma-Tah said with an apprehensive sneer.

Stryder said nothing as a smirking Shom walked directly up to him. He stopped a few feet in front of the two with a contemptuous grin. "Why Stryder Aramos, I've not seen you since you and your stooges boarded that pleasure yacht I was on. When was that, five grands ago?"

The quartermaster remained silent. The corners of his mouth were pulled taut and his nostrils flared.

Shom continued with his contrived pleasantries. "So, what odious endeavor brings you to this dreary backwash of the Annigan?" The royal then swept a glimpse up to the Tiikeri. "Where are my manners," clicking his heels and bowing slightly, his voice dripped with sarcasm. "Allow me to introduce myself. I'm Shom Eldor, intercontinental man of pleasure and complete disgrace to my family name. And you are?"

Ma-Tah silently scowled, his whiskers twitching in irritation.

The prodigal reeled back in mock surprise at the silent treatment. "Well Stryder, I see you've found a traveling companion of like temperament."

Once again, silence. Shom cleared his throat as two very dangerous individuals angrily fixated on him.

"Well I really must be off. Apparently, there's some sort of bounty on my head. Quite a bit of money I understand," Shom paused and gave Stryder a provocatively knowing glance. "Surely that's not the reason you're here? I can't imagine *you* need the money." He gave a sly wink. "That is, unless House Aramos isn't quite a solvent as we've all been led to believe."

By now Stryder was trembling, his hands clenched into tight fists.

Shom was relentless. "Quite a shame really, I mean me being in such close proximity, and yet alas, local mores being what they are. Much like your bodyguard and aide unfortunately discovered."

Stryder swallowed hard at the taunt. Many a man had died for much less.

Seeing he was not getting the reaction he desired Shom sighed. "Well, as I said before, I must be going. I hope you and your equally silent friend have a pleasant day, luna, whatever they call it in these parts."

With that, the royal calmly walked away. Both indignantly glared at him strolling calmly back to Alto's side.

"Now, I want to help you kill the little shit," Ma-Tah growled.

This hardship was no more than they endured in their everyday life on the ice floes of the southern Frozen Sea. Ri'Da lovingly took in his wife and child as they and countless others trudged through the snow. He smiled, sure that this time their suffering would serve a purpose. This time the land of promise foretold so long ago awaited them. The land where the caribou would be plentiful and the Ash-Ta would not hunt them from the skies. A land where they could live in peace.

Pulling the hood of his parka tighter against the howling winds he marveled at the multitudes trailed behind him, then forward at the crowd preceding his tiny family. All the Yupik tribes now followed their new messiah; the one whose voice called out in their psyche, beckoning them to join him on this holy pilgrimage.

For it was told by the sages: *You shall be led by a stranger.* This mysterious tall, thin figure was indeed strange. He wore only a simple cloak and hood and no one had seen his appearance. His hidden body underneath was obviously impervious to the cold and he carried only a large black pearl in his hand.

He must be the messiah!

The pearl radiated energy. Gathering the different tribes with its pulses of blue light, it led the people steadily eastward, toward their destiny.

Without appearing to stare Stryder surreptitiously peered at Ma-Tah sitting calmly on his bed as he angrily paced the room.

The Tiikeri placed a stalk of Maudo Grass into his mouth. With a slow deliberate pull, he stripped the delicate blue flowering buds. Immediately he leaned back and gave a contented sigh as all hint of prior aggression evaporated.

"You know," he began as he waved the bare stalk in the air, "perhaps we are approaching this whole Shom Eldor situation all wrong."

The quartermaster stopped in mid-pace and angrily stared at his Tiikeri counterpart. "That pampered little fuckwad taunted and mocked me in public. You don't get to do that and live!"

Ma-Tah sighed, "I think this can be handled another way."

"You're stoned!" Spittle sprayed out of Stryder's mouth with each word.

Ma-Tah continued with his calm demeanor. "Perhaps, but hear me out."

"I'm listening!" Stryder said angrily.

The Tiikeri picked up another stalk of grass and waved it at the raging human. "Correct me if I'm wrong, but there've been several attempts on his life recently?"

Stryder impatiently watched him ingest the intoxicant. "Yeah, so?"

"It occurs to me if all previous attempts failed perhaps a new strategy is needed. One that does not involve killing him, but rather placing him in a position where he can be controlled."

The quartermaster searched the eyes of the intoxicated Tiikeri. Slowly a touch of curiosity began to permeate the waves of vengeful anger. "More parlor tricks?" he asked skeptically.

Ma-Tah rocked back on the bed and laughed. "Hardly. But removing certain family obstacles in House Eldor would allow his advancement. This could be doubly beneficial to our cause as well as your house's standing in Lumina."

Stryder stood defiantly. "You keep mentioning this 'cause' we share. I don't seem to remember any agreement between us."

The Tiikeri grinned slyly. "Oh, I think you're aware, and along with the Chenoans we can issue in a new era of cooperation and, might I add, profit unsurpassed in the history of the Annigan."

The human stood weighing the words. Anger eventually subsided, replaced by a diabolical curiosity. "Exactly what did you have in mind?"

The bottom bay doors of the *Haraka* were opened wide as the airship descended on Shom and Alto. Waving his arms, the swordmaster directed Orich as the Bailian pilot slowly lowered the craft until it engulfed the two and the bales between them.

When Shom's vision adjusted to the light inside the ship he noticed the female Singa seated at Taa's old seat beside the captain's chair.

"One cannot help but notice that there are more among us than when we left," the prodigal said cautiously.

Mal was standing mid-cabin in between the rows of seats taking note of Alto sliding the bales on board. "Shom, Alto, this is Zau. She'll be travelling with us for a bit."

The humanoid lioness nodded her greeting as she scrutinized the two recent arrivals. Shom cast a skeptical glance at the captain as Alto came up beside him brushing one hand on the other.

"Honestly Maluria," the prodigal said in a weary tone, "do we really need another complication to our current situation?"

Zau gave a sardonic chuckle at Shom. "So, I'm thinking, if the way you helped your friend there load the cargo is any sign, I'm gonna offer a lot more to this crew than you currently do."

There was an awkward pause before Zaad erupted in laughter. "The lady Singa has the funny little man figured out already!"

The prodigal shot an annoyed glance at the EEtah. "My name is Shom!" he corrected, slowly enunciating each word.

The nine-foot-tall man-shark was still chortling. "I know."

"Alright, everybody, knock it off!" Mal said sternly. "Zau, show 'em.'"

The Singa got up from her seat and stood beside Mal. Reaching up she raised her eye patch.

Alto innocently grinned as he stared in wonder. Mouth agape, Shom placed his hands on his hips in reluctant amazement. Her solid white eyeball began to glow blue. A beam slowly emerged halting about three feet in front of her. It undulated and formed into a three-dimensional globe. All across its surface were fixed blue dots. In between were smaller blue dots blinking at random.

"What in the Annigan are we looking at?" Alto wondered aloud.

"This is a map of the Flavian Portals on the plane we currently occupy. The corporeal reach," Zau said.

Pointing into the blue field, she indicated the stationary dots. "These are the permanent portals. They're big and potentially dangerous because they can take you anywhere. They've also got the most predators lurking around them."

"That's just the kind of news I want to hear," Shom quipped.

"Much like jungle watering holes, predators recognize where prey congregates. Every time you pass into a Flavian Portal you step through the Middle Realms before exiting at your destination. It's anyone's guess if something's waiting patiently for an easy meal to pass by."

"The few times I used them they made me ill," Alto added.

All went silent as they fixated on the blue globe pulsing in the air before them as Zau continued. "The slightly smaller dots are dedicated portals that connect one specific location to another."

Mal traced several which winked and faded across the glittering veneer. "What are the small flickering ones?"

"Those are Flavian Mages moving about. They don't need to find portals. They can open their own. It takes a lot of power to do that though. Most times it's etheria assisted."

Alto pointed to a medium-sized dot which came to life, lingered for a bit then reappeared elsewhere. "And this?"

Zau gave the swordmaster a knowing chuckle. "That's Konaleeta."

"The island of the lost?" Mal asked skeptically recalling her maritime lore.

The Singa peered over at her new captain. "The same."

Shom stared in disbelief. "It was my understanding the lost island was a myth."

Zau chuckled. "Hardly. This cursed island is caught in a permanent Flavian Loop. It can appear briefly anywhere in the Middle Realms." With a flick of her wrist she lowered the patch and the hologram wavered, then disappeared. "So basically, I can get you anywhere."

This caused Zaad to erupt in laughter again as he pointed at Shom. "The Singa lady may be right. The funny little man may be obsolete!"

"Lovely," Shom muttered under his breath.

Mal snickered at Shom's predicament. "Alright Orich, let's take her up while we figure things out. We're sitting ducks here on the ground."

The shadow of four airships raced across the agricultural fields of Durik-Dor in eastern Amarenia. The Valdurian Resistance Class cruisers had risen above the horizon line just before moonrise and made a course directly for the coast. Their destination: The occupied town of Durik.

Suspended out both sides of each craft, four archers were poised ready to strike.

In Durik harbor, the Rayth mariners were preparing the raiders *Orca*, *Borden*, and *Shakra* for an extended raid when they saw the Calden Man-O-War *Jeonham* rapidly approaching. Because the ukko wood vessel had no sails, the massive ship was upon them before any of the stunned Rayth could react. With a startled cry many prepared for what everyone on shore assessed as an inevitable ramming maneuver.

Displaying agility normally thought impossible for such a large ship, the *Jeonham* banked hard to starboard and released a volley of twenty flaming ballista bolts into the docked ships. In the time it took to weigh the situation sails and decks were aflame.

Mariner Yeva dodged a burning piece of sail and rigging as it crashed onto the deck of the *Orca*. Witnessing many of her sisters running about on fire she rushed for the side of the ship and vaulted over the railing. As she plummeted into the harbor, she noted at least three raiders ablaze before submerging into the frigid waters.

Surfacing, she gasped for air as the cold sucked the oxygen from her lungs. When she saw what was right in front of her, she froze in shock. A few feet away she found herself facing the snout of a large seahorse. The startled Rayth didn't get the chance to cry out again as a trident tip plunged into her gaping mouth exiting the back of her skull. It was yanked back out with a savage tug and cracking sound. As the sea around her bloomed red, the Nyanja and her mount slipped silently under the water.

Approaching the harbor from the south, Commander Benteen chewed furiously on the end of his carbona as he stood on the bow of the lead away boat. Behind him the entire contingency of fifty Calden Marines followed, their ukko hulls gliding swiftly above the choppy water.

Fia was in an early morning meeting with the newly appointed mayor of Durik when Blenda flung the door open and rushed in. "Admiral, we're under attack!"

The Rayth commanders sputtered in shock. Bolting past Blenda she rushed into the street. "Get the sisters rallied! We've got to get the fleet off the wharf!"

She reeled back in revulsion when amidst the smoke already arising from the docks, an explosion sent a massive fireball into the sky. "Belay that! Follow me!" She ordered as she sprinted toward the docks.

By the time Fia and Blenda made it to the Durik wharf the scene was complete pandemonium. Most of her fleet, as well as the docks themselves were consumed with flame and Rayth were running about in panic.

From her left, a roaring battle cry rang out as Calden marines stormed on shore a little south of the wharf proper. In the lead was a grizzled Benteen, carbona securely gripped in the corner of his mouth waving his sword furiously. Behind the charging men two EEtahs towered. Each brandished their yudon harpoons in the air and bellowed furiously.

"Get to the *Raptor*!" Fia screamed as she drew her cutlass.

By now the Calden support ships had placed themselves in a line across the mouth of the harbor completely blocking it. They peppered the wharf with arrows as the *Jeonham* circled back for another pass. Blenda looked on in shock at the flaming ballista tips as they peeked ominously out its port side.

The two Rayth commanders sprinted for the ship rallying mariners along the way. When they reached the *Raptor* through a hail of arrows, they had only managed to amass a small force of twelve.

Quickly removing the mooring lines, Fia ran to the bridge. Grabbing the wheel, she shouted out at her skeleton crew. At her command they struggled to raise the sails and get the largest and now only remaining ship of the Rayth fleet moving. Pulling away from the docks all witnessed a volley of fiery bolts rain down on the town of Durik setting most of the buildings ablaze.

"Admiral!" Blenda called up to her from the deck, as she pointed to the line of Calden warships blocking their path.

Fia scowled at the obstacle. "Full sails then everybody hit the deck!"

Admiral Lasia scrutinized the assault from the bridge of the *Jeonham*. All witnessed the *Raptor* plunge through the line of support ships as it weathered a hail of arrows. Her battering ram sprit crushed the bow of the end support ship sending the bowsprit and most of the front of the ship crashing into the water. It immediately began to sink.

"That's their flagship," her captain excitedly reported. "They're getting away!"

The seasoned admiral was calm and dispassionate. "Prepare for pursuit Captain Kort. Let's go get her."

Clack, clack, clack...

The noise came from all around them. It rose from the darkness above the howling wind of the Frozen Sea. Sounds that were meant to frighten, to confuse, out beyond the line of sight. Ri'Da's heart was pounding and he witnessed the panicked expressions on his Yupik companions as the tapping of weapons drew closer.

Clack, clack, clack...

Surrounded by the feared Reindeer Clans, the caravan had stalled shortly after descending the Southern Mesa and entering the Maura-Pia Flats. Unless a miracle intervened, all knew what awaited them — most of the men would be killed, their flesh eaten, their dense bones made into tools, weapons and jewelry. The women and children would be enslaved and eventually assimilated.

Terrified outbursts swept among the caravan of pilgrims. Eventually, everyone's gaze fell on the hooded figure Ni-Chek who stood at the front of the massive procession unphased by the psychological warfare now being waged.

It was then that Ri'Da and all the travelers heard the voice in their minds. The voice that had called them to follow, now called for a sacrifice.

The Yupik father's stomach knotted and his wife gripped their newborn tighter to her chest as the mysterious figure's cowl swept across the crowd. It stopped a short distance away deep within the throng of pilgrims. When Ri'Da heard the cry of the distant mother he knew the choice had been made.

The crowd of ice clansmen parted. Ri'Da could now see the distraught family. They were from a clan that had joined them shortly before ascending the mesa.

The mother cried and wailed. Tears streamed down the father's cheeks as he stared off in tormented resignation. Reaching for their newborn wrapped in warm furs his wife looked up at him pleading. Staring away sadly, unable to meet his wife's broken-hearted glower, he took his child and the mother fell to her knees sobbing hysterically.

With sorrow emanating from every step the father advanced toward Ni-Chek clutching his baby to his chest. By the time he reached the robed figure his eyes were frozen shut from his tears. Giving it one last kiss, he held the baby out in front of him. From under his cloak Ni-Chek lifted the black pearl into view. It softly pulsed as the mysterious figure reached out and touched it to the sorrowful offering.

Through the flurries of snow Ri'Da saw the pearl start to glow. The furs wrapping the infant went limp and empty as the orb consumed the baby. The father fell to his knees consumed with grief. The pearl emanated a bright blue/black light as it raised from Ni-Chek's hand. The sphere hovered a few feet above him as the light became brighter.

With the illumination, the travelers now saw the massive army surrounding them. All had some form of horns attached to their heads. Some wore reindeer skull helmets. They rattled their bone weapons, clacking them together and stamping their spears on the ground. Their enraged, blue oblong faces were streaked with red patterns.

The black pearl now began spinning as it emitted a solid beam of blue light from its equatorial axis. The horizontal sheet of radiance shot out in all directions passing through the mass of the threatening army then, into the distance and out of sight.

As the pulse of light penetrated the Reindeer Clan's bodies the clacking stopped and they slowly lowered their weapons. All hint of aggression left them, replaced by a serene expression.

Holding out his hand once again, the pearl descended into his palm and he slid it back under his cape.

Know that you have witnessed a triumph and deliverance, came the familiar voice echoing in their brains.

Ni-Chek then resumed his eastward trek. His people silently followed, joined by the newly converted disciples of the Reindeer Clan.

Blood was everywhere. The disemboweled goat hung upside down. Part of its life essence overflowed from a small bowl below it on the ground.

Stryder stared in macabre fascination as he and Ma-Tah watched No-Le arrange the entrails into patters along the side of a shallow berm.

Events had happened quickly since the Tiikeri's aide knocked on their door a short while ago. She had followed Shom back to an airship. *Ma-Tah's not the only one who wants answers*, the quartermaster mused to himself. For that No-Le needed a medium sized animal. *And here we are.*

The mongrel was standing back examining her work when Stryder leaned over to Ma-Tah. "I would propose that we are wasting time…"

He was silenced by the Tiikeri's upraised hand as he followed his aide's every move.

Starting on her left, she pointed to a grizzly configuration. "The disturbance you discovered is indeed on the airship. They are airborne and safe for now…and…there is a living presence in the ship itself."

With the news, Ma-Tah suddenly erupted in a sinister smile.

No-Le moved her outstretched finger to the next set. "The Chenoan's fish people approach in vast numbers from the east. The ice clans are on the move on the southern ice floes. They too travel eastward."

Once again Stryder leaned into his Tiikeri counterpart, his countenance much different this time. "That's what the bat creatures said," he whispered.

Ma-Tah silently nodded yes but held his hand up again as he followed his aide's finger.

"Something powerful approaches from the west…I, I can't be sure…"

"Dagnabbit!" Demetrius spat as he yanked the controls of the *Catori* to the right. The maneuver dislodged several small Ash-Ta with huge teeth-filled mouths as they attempted to hold onto the ukko hull.

He could make out Captain Okawa beside him, she was calm but alert. Behind him both Otick stared in wonder at the flying spectacle on the other side of the windshield.

"Chiro clan!" The captain announced as he adjusted the wheel once more. "The little so-and-sos are a real pain!"

Squinting in mild surprise Okawa stared at Demetrius with an amused grin. "Dagnabbit? So-and-sos?"

Keeping his attention straight forward, the pilot blushed. "My mom didn't like it when I cursed."

The grin became introspective as her gaze returned to the drama of swarming large-mouthed bats attempting to assault the ship.

As the number of Ash-Ta pelting the craft increased, Demetrius became more frustrated until he finally had enough. "Okay, that's it. We're gonna loose these little creeps and get us there faster."

"How?"

The airship pilot grinned. "We're going up. It's a little maneuver I invented that I call skirting the up winds. More dangerous, well, only slightly more than where we are now."

"May the Golden One bless this undertaking and guide your hand Deetus." Raydan said with claws raised.

"Here we go," Demetrius announced as he pulled the nose of the *Catori* upward toward the edge of the atmosphere. "Let me know when it gets hard to breathe."

Ma-Tah licked his lips as he concentrated on the entrail patterns. "There's very little we can do about this situation except help the Chenoans," he assessed.

Stryder studied the Tiikeri as he spun the suspended goat so that its side was directly in front of him. No-Le joined him and steadied the dead animal.

"When I signal, slowly lower the sacrifice to the ground," Ma-Tah ordered in a low ominous tone. Indicating she understood No-Le turned away respectfully.

Reaching into the blood-filled bowl the white tiger dipped a claw and began writing on the white fur of the dangling animal. After filling one side with multiple intricate binary fields, he spun the goat's body again, so the evisceration incision was within reach. Using both hands he reached in and pulled the carcass all the way open. Placing a hand on his aide's shoulder, she gradually lowered it to the ground.

Ma-Tah was bent over, panting in exhaustion when Stryder stepped over to him. With a look of amused distain, he examined the now mutilated goat corpse. "What was that all about?"

"I've just lowered and opened the airship," the man tiger gasped out his explanation.

The quartermaster's look was incredulous. "Wait, how?!"

Finally righting himself the Tiikeri's grinned, his demeanor pleasantly arrogant. "I serve a mighty god."

Everyone seemed to have an opinion as to what to do next.

"All I'm saying is that we are wasting time!" Shom said, his raised voice cutting across the debate. "We should be on our way to Immor-Onn right now!"

Mal was about to offer up a comment when Orich's concerned tone caught everyone's attention. "Uh, captain..."

The Spice Rat's mouth was agape as she leaned on the ship's console. "What the fuck!?"

A sea of green poured out of the Kel-Raku River and undulated wildly below them. The fields, all the way to the horizon line were rapidly filling with thousands of the Chenoan fish servants.

"Gar-Kal," Orich explained. "The Chenoans use them to do their bidding on land. They have simple minds and are immune to any influences save that of their creators. I believe they are after the Avatar."

Suddenly, the *Haraka* lurched and began to slowly descend.

Mal glanced about wildly. "Orich, what the fuck is going on?!"

The Bailian pilot frantically adjusted levers and controls to no avail. "Unknown captain, the controls are unresponsive and I've lost contact with my brother in the hull."

Everyone in the cabin traded fearful glances as the ground and the beasts slowly approached.

Shom huffed in frustration. "Did I not tell you we should've already been on our way!?"

A scowl from Mal silenced any further comment from the royal.

"Let's all be thankful for that ukko hull," she said.

A loud click resonated in the cabin as the sides and rear hatch started to open.

"Unless we are open to the elements." Alto added over the wind which was now howling through the ship.

"Orich!" Mal screamed over her shoulder.

"I'm trying captain!"

As the craft continued to descend all heard the scratching of claws on the bottom of the hull. When green, webbed talons grabbed hold of the bottom of the side hatch Alto drew his short sword and severed them at the wrists. They were immediately replaced by more as the fishy humanoids started to pull themselves up.

Pulling his knife Alto zeroed in on his stunned friends, "I would prepare for combat," he calmly advised.

Shom and Mal immediately drew their weapons as Orich grabbed the box containing the avatar and cowered in the captain's chair clutching it to his chest. Zau stood in front of the seated albino and flipped over one of the shells on her belt. It contained an intricate blue rune. Raising one hand in front of her she frantically rubbed the rune with her other thumb.

The Gar-Kal's fish heads were now plainly visible through the open hatches as they scrambled over each other trying to get in.

From the back of the *Haraka,* all heard Zaad cracking his knuckles in anticipation. "It's been awhile since I've had fish!"

There was no time to reel from the stench of decaying sea life. Webbed, clawed hands raked outward furiously as a tide of fish peoples overran the *Haraka*. They packed all around it, climbing over and pushing it at each point of access.

"Move those fuckers away from the hatches!" Mal screamed over the beasts incessant hissing. "Everyone stay clear of Zaad! This is gonna get ugly."

For Alto and Zaad, hampered by the cabin's close quarters, this order was good news.

Shom cringed. "You want us to go out there?!"

Slashing across three of the monsters, Mal kicked back a third. "Let's go!" Hopping to the ground, she was immediately confronted by a wall of frenzied Gar-Kal.

"Oh by the gods!" Shom groaned as he leapt to his friend's side.

Everyone noted Zaad's enthusiastic laughter coming from the stern as he punched one so hard the entire top of its body exploded showering the back of the craft with scales and fish head fragments. Grabbing the bottom half of the man-fish by its tail he began swinging it back and forth in front of him as he made his way out the rear ramp of the *Haraka*.

Once he reached the bottom of the ramp, he released the body, heaving it into a throng that were rushing him. The EEtah felt his bloodlust rising as he drew Bowbreaker and hacked at the wave of Gar-Kal assaulting him.

Alto leapt from the side door, slashing simultaneously with his short sword and knife. As the dismembered bodies dropped around him, he took advantage of the miniscule break. Before the next wave flooded in the swordmaster sheathed his knife and drew his long sword.

As the double-edged etheria blade cleared the sheath a lone, a lingering dog's howl rang out. Its doleful, familiar wail swept across the din of combat and caused the swordmaster to smile. Both blades then swept into a wave of attackers which descended upon him. To his left, an airship similar to the *Haraka* came into view.

"This is the place," Raydan proclaimed as he observed the conflict below. "The Golden One has truly blessed this journey."

Demetrius warily eyed the fight below as he backed off on the accelerator and began a steep bank, circling the area.

"The avatar is there!" Wallack emphatically said, pointing to the *Haraka*. "I can feel it."

Staring down at the conflict, Demetrius squinted in recognition. "Hey, I know that ship!"

"They defend the avatar!" Raydan said enthusiastically.

"The prophets say that those willing to sacrifice for the cause greater than themselves shall truly be called holy." Wallack added as his gaze remained fixed on the thousands of humanoid fish swarming over the area.

"Over there," Okawa pointed to an area close to the besieged airship.

"You sure?" Demetrius asked as he surveyed the tumultuous plot of ground. "Pretty dangerous."

Okawa kept her attention on the battle below. "You let me worry about that."

Both humans stared tensely at each other.

"Your orders are specific," the Valdurian captain said.

"Oh, alright," the pilot conceded as he banked the craft toward the embattled *Haraka* below.

Alto noticed the airship landing about twenty yards from him crushing a handful of Gar-Kal as his blades slashed across rows of advancing creatures. The long sword let out an almost continuous growl as it swept effortlessly through the slimy fish bodies.

Demetrius brought the *Catori* in fast and hard. He heard and felt the presence of bodies being crushed under the airship's weight as they landed. "Alright, this is it!"

The Otick were already standing by the hatch coiled and ready.

"It was the will of the Golden One that our paths crossed and his will be done. Perhaps we shall meet again soon," Wallack said with a clack of his claw.

"May the Golden One continue to bless you Deetus," Raydan added.

Demetrius pulled a lever to his right and the side hatch lowered. Immediately the cabin was filled with the clashing sounds of combat and a nose-stinging wave of dead fish.

"You two knuckleheads kick tail and get back safe."

With that final encouraging goodbye, the two Otick leapt into the fray.

When the side door opened, the swordmaster was relieved to see two Otick emerge from the craft. Alto had never seen the humanoid crabs fight before. He managed to catch glances through the fog of his own combat. The martial abilities he witnessed left him in reverential awe.

Their speed was blinding, even with the shells on their back. Their six limbs all worked in perfect unison. The top two claw hands served as all-encompassing weapons with the ability to club, slash and stab. The four smaller limbs below acted as efficient stabbing arms. All movements were blended in a highly coordinated multi-attack style unsurpassed by anything the swordmaster had ever witnessed. They made their way to the *Haraka* cutting down waves of fish monsters as if parting a cloud of nuisance insects.

When Alto felt a claw rake across the back of his shirt, he knew the ship had been breached. Spinning his short sword so the pummel was turned forward, he plunged the blade blindly behind him. There was no time to turn and assess the situation in the cabin as a fresh wave of aquatic vermin were upon him.

Mal and Shom's breaths were ragged and their limbs felt heavy. With weariness came mistakes. The duo had moved by the tide of combat a little too far from the open side hatch. Now the Gar-Kal had access to the ship's interior and they swarmed inside.

From off to her left Mal caught movement on the side of a nearby hill. The bushes swayed wildly as six Do-Tarr emerged from a hidden tunnel and rushed their way.

The distraction proved costly to the Spice Rat as three of the creatures toppled her to the ground. The fall knocked the wind out of her as she landed flat on her back with two of the pungent slippery beasts wriggling on top of her. She managed to move her head to the right as a set of jaws snapped into the soil, barely missing her. Surprisingly, there was no other attack as they rolled off her and blended into the throng as it now seemed to be moving away. Shom fought his way over to her side and kept the rushing Gar-Kal from accosting Mal until she regained her feet.

To their right both now witnessed the six Do-Tarr cut a swath in the tide of living green fish using large mining hammers. They swung in wide arcs, pulping fish flesh as they advanced.

Alto watched as the *Catori* quickly lifted from the battlefield and sped away. He also noticed the massive army of fish men were now making their way east. They rushed past attempting halfhearted harassing strikes as they left.

As the last beast scrambled away the swordmaster dropped his hands in exhaustion. As he leaned over to catch his breath, a sympathetic whimper came from his long sword.

Standing straight up, he lovingly ogled the etheria weapon and reveled as a single tear of joy made its way down his cheek. Closing his eyes, he touched the hilt to his lips. "You I shall call Defari."

His emotional moment over, he flicked both blades clean and sheathed them as the Otick approached.

"The Avatar!?" Wallack pleaded.

Alto spun and peered inside the open cabin of the *Haraka*.

Mal sheathed her weapon as the Do-Tarr made their way over to them. Shom put his weapon away and was aghast at his tattered clothing. "Another set of my finest dress, ruined!"

The Spice Rat ignored his rant as she stepped up to the insect people. White shimmering waves briefly obscured the lead Do-Tarr. When they passed, the same handsome Bailian from the hive led three armed humanoid bug warriors.

"Thanks for your help Your Majesty," the airship captain greeted.

The Do-Tarr regent was exuberant. "No need to thank me. That was truly exciting. I can see travelling with you will be a once in a lifetime adventure."

Mal wavered in stunned silence. *He really is coming along.*

With a cheerful grin the polymorphed bug king addressed his protection detail. "My brave hive mates, you served myself and your queen in exemplary fashion this luna. However, where I go, you cannot follow. You are dismissed and may return to the hive. Each of you is to receive a double ration of tier one nectar."

The Do-Tarr vibrated in excitement at the thought of their reward and hurried toward the tunnel they had arrived from.

All Alto could see inside the *Haraka's* cabin were Gar-Kal bodies littering the deck. Trading concerned glances with the Otick all three leaped through the opening.

The interior was eerily quiet. The Singa lioness lay unconscious beside the ship's wheel, right before the twin bridge chairs.

Orich lay in the fetal position on the floor between the captain's and navigator's chairs. Both shipmates were badly scratched but alive. The swordmaster's gaze locked onto the Bailians hands which were frozen in front of his crumpled frame. They held the shape of the box which was now missing.

"The fish people took the avatar!" He said to the Otick. "Maluria!" he screamed out the side door.

The timbre of Alto's voice ripped Mal's attention away from the Do-Tarr king.

"Excuse me Your Majesty," she said before bounding up into the cabin. The Spice Rat halted suddenly as she came face to face with Wallack and Raydan.

Reeling in surprise, she inspected the sentient crustaceans. "What the fuck are Otick doing in Nocturn?"

"The Golden One has tasked us to bring the Avatar to its new home," Wallack said in a terse reply.

"The fish people stole the avatar!" Raydan wailed.

Mal stared past the two Otick to Alto who was helping Orich into the navigator's chair. Pushing past the crabs, she knelt over Zau who slowly stirred. "Are you alright?" she asked softly.

Looking up at her captain, the Singa nodded weakly.

By the time Shom, Zaad and the Do-Tarr king entered the ship they had finally managed to get Orich and Zau seated. The Bailian unblinkingly stared in shock. The front of his tunic was shredded, and most of his upper body was covered in scratches.

The Singa was not as clawed up and she slumped against the back of the chair in utter exhaustion from maintaining the protection spell.

"I held them off for as long as I could," she panted. "There were too many of them."

Raydan was almost in a panic. "We must do something!"

"I'm not good for much of anything," Zau declared with a yawn. "In fact, if I don't lay down, I'm going to fall down." With that statement, her eyelids drooped then closed. Her chin dropped against her chest as she slumped forward, fast asleep.

All attention now focused on the wounded but conscious Bailian.

"They travel east, toward the ice city of Mos-Agar and the purple temple of Lila," Orich stated weakly as he attempted to stand.

Alto put his hand on the albino's shoulder. "You are still weak my friend," he said.

Orich gathered his strength and slowly got to his feet. "You don't understand Mora. The Otick's concern is justified. The purple temple is a giant Flavian Portal to the Labyrinth Plane of the Middle Realms."

The Bailian's knees buckled and Alto caught him. "Get me to the wheel," he pleaded. "I sense that the ship is now controllable and they already have a head start on us."

107

The moon at mid-luna cast a soft yellow glow on the ice floes of the eastern Frozen Sea. It reflected off the white snow-covered surface illuminating the desolate landscape as far as Ri'Da could see.

All around him, the vast throng of various Yupik clans, which would normally be battling each other, plodded over the bleak wasteland as a single organism.

When Ni-Chek led the preceding believers of the diaspora over a hill and out of sight he heard his fellow pilgrims rejoicing. Their cheers and laughter echoed across the hills and crevasses. The Yupik father's pulse raced as he traded excited glances with his wife and those near him.

When it was finally their turn to crest the snowy hill, they too let out a cry of exhilaration. Stretched out before them was a glimmering circular city made entirely of ice blocks. The opaque structures sparkled in the moonlight and were arranged in the shape of a giant wheel all emanating from a large purple dome at the hub.

Ri'Da's heart leapt as he spun to his equally enthralled wife. *Surely this beautiful city was the promised land!*

In the far distance to west he heard the faint rumblings of a large moving mass. Excitedly he hugged his wife. The herds of caribou, as promised. *Yes, yes this was the promised land and soon, a celebratory feast!*

The *Haraka* caught up to the Gar-Kal herd as it swept off the eastern coast of the Land of Mists and into the frigid, iceberg filled waters of the frozen sea. The ocean below them churned green as thousands of fish creatures skimmed across the surface. Fluttering in quick shallow dives, they rushed toward the ice floes beyond.

"The Avatar is among them; I can feel it!" Wallack said as he took in the scores of humanoid fish swiftly swimming eastward.

"Yeah, but where?" Mal groaned. "One of those fuckers has it, but I swear they all look the same."

"We must find it captain," Orich warned as he propped himself up on the ship's wheel. "If they make it to the Purple Temple it will be too late!"

"What in the name of the gods has this temple got to do with anything?" Shom irritatingly asked from his seat.

"They seek to hide it on the Labyrinth Plane of the Middle Realms," Orich said. "Nocturn is no longer a suitable place to hide it anymore."

The royal was clearly confused. "Why don't they destroy the thing and be done with it?"

"It cannot be destroyed," Raydan said. "It cannot be unmade. It is the Avatar. Just as it was long ago, hiding it is their only choice."

Orich lowered the craft to fifty feet above the undulating mass of racing fish monsters. "And that is exactly the kind of cataclysmic activity which can affect the Black Mural in an excessive way."

As they drew further away from the relative warmth of the land the ocean became an icy slush with large chunks of frozen water congregating closer together. The wave of Gar-Kal easily adapted, scrambling over the icebergs and dipping into the frigid muck.

"We can do nothing from up here!" Raydan complained.

"The prophets tell us that in order to be the change you must be willing to immerse yourself in the holy cause." Wallack said defiantly. "You must get us down there."

"We've got no time to stop!" Mal firmly said.

"There are doors in the bottom of the craft," Raydan argued. "Drop us into their midst. We will find it."

"Are you nuts?!" Mal said. "As fast as we're going!"

"The Golden One will protect us. It is his hand that guides us," Raydan said.

Mal lowered her eyes and briefly weighed the circumstances. "I've got nothing better. Go for it."

The two humanoid crabs stood over the twin bay doors. With a nod from Mal, Orich threw the lever and the two Otick disappeared in a rush of icy wind.

All crowded at the windshield to watch the duo land in a low crouch then scramble along the frozen surfaces, easily keeping up with the Gar-Kal.

"And now?" Alto asked.

Mal sighed. "Well, we know where they're going. I say we haul ass to this purple temple and maybe catch them as they get there."

No-Le quickly skinned the goat and offered up the ribs to Ma-Tah while she chewed on a hind quarter. Stryder silently noted the Tiikeri's white fur on his hands and around his mouth become stained red as the mawls tore into the raw flesh.

"Happens every time a numen is called forth," the tiger lord admitted between bites. "I either want to fuck something, or I become ravenous."

Stryder remained silent and Ma-Tah noticed he wasn't eating. "Join us," he said as he waved toward the partly dismembered body.

"That's quite alright," Stryder said. "I prefer my meat cooked."

Both the mawls faces shriveled in disgust.

The Tiikeri took another bite. "Yes, I encountered that barbaric ritual back in Immor-Onn. Why would you want to ruin perfectly good meat?"

"Isn't there something we should be doing?" the quartermaster impatiently asked.

Ma-Tah tossed a stripped set of ribs onto a pile of bones. "Yes, we are doing something. We're eating. Bringing that airship down took a lot out of me. I need to regain my strength."

"Yes," Stryder's voice was heavy with skepticism. "Exactly what did you do there, besides make a ritual of your mid-luna meal?"

The Tiikeri stopped eating and gave a wide knowing grin. "I delivered a gift to our Chenoan friends. The airship is on the ground where their fish men can get to it. Hopefully it will induce them to become allies." He then motioned toward No-Le. "Hand me a section of fur from the other side."

Kneeling in front of him she spread the tattered section of white fur on the ground in front of her seated lord.

"Speaking of which, I need to get them a message."

Stryder appraised the slaughtered animal. "You seem to be out of blood."

Maintaining his superior attitude, the Tiikeri raised his hand. "Fortunately, the message is short." With a claw from his other hand he made a small cut below the knuckle on his extended forefinger. As the tiger's fluids flowed across the sharpened digit, he quickly scribbled three small binary fields.

Sitting back, he applied pressure to the tiny wound as he examined the furry manuscript in front of him. By the time the bleeding stopped Stryder smelled burning hair and flesh.

Immediately below Ma-Tah's bloody numbers, other sets of X's and slashes began to appear on their own, burned into fields of intricate patterns which filled the rest of the pelt.

The Tiikeri scanned the smoldering numerals and sighed in satisfaction. "It worked. We've got another audience with the Chenoans. We must go."

Ri'Da broke his last strip of caribou jerky in half and handed a piece to his wife. *Soon there would be enough for all*, he thought as he returned her weary smile.

The masses had congregated outside the southwest arch into the city of Mos-Agar. Beyond the pale blue gateway, the city lights glowed and twinkled invitingly. There were eight such gates around the perimeter of the ice city. Each avenue led directly to the city center and the purple temple of Lila.

The Yupik father's small family huddled near the front of the giant caravan in the center. Visibility was difficult, but his fellow pilgrims shielded them from the brunt of the gusting icy winds as flurries of snow coursed over the now motionless assembly.

In the distance he caught sight of their mysterious savior Ni-Chek as he levitated above those in the front of the group. Everyone gasped as he rose and came to a halt in midair on the left side of the arch near the top.

His right hand was extended, palm up. Hovering above his outstretched palm the black pearl pulsed. Short bursts of blue lightning ran its surface and crackled outwards into the snowy blackness. The light cast eerie shadows across the hooded figure, as in the past, never revealing any details as to the being beneath the cowl.

Now in the back of their minds his voice rose yet again. Many times, along their arduous journey it soothed and cajoled; it encouraged and admonished. This time it congratulated and welcomed them to the promised land. But first, they would need to be purified. The temple of Lila was before them. Passing through the purple dome would wash away all prior transgressions and make them worthy of their new home.

Ri'Da quivered in anticipation as the Yupik tribes began a slow orderly march under the blue ice gateway parading past the levitated wizard and his pulsing black orb.

In the distance, drawing ever closer was the rumble of the herds of Ri'Da's beloved caribou, just in time for a feast.

The ice floes below the *Haraka* were a swiftly flowing torrent of bluish green as far as any could see.

"Damn, would ya look at all those fuckers!" Mal shuddered in amazement. "There must be thousands of them."

Orich surveyed the rushing mob of fish beings below as they swept over the ice. "If my calculations are correct, we are approaching the front of the Gar-Kal herd. An accurate assessment is difficult without my brother's aid. I've still not been able to contact him."

Mal consulted the rapidly spinning indicator on the console. "At this speed we should be able to get ahead of them. Then it's only a matter of spotting the Avatar or the Otick."

"I must say, my initial hunch was right." The Do-Tarr king gushed in excitement. "You all are the most exciting travelling companions!"

Everyone stood behind Mal peering out the windshield. All except the glamoured Do-Tarr was gripped in uneasy suspense. The bug king was actually grinning widely as his eyes darted about the frenzied scene on the ice floes.

Mal glanced at the king. "Uh, Your Majesty..."

Keeping his focus on the Gar-Kal flight he waved his hand; his tone was effervescent. "Please, we're traveling companions now; adventurers! You may call me Kyopp."

Mal rubbed her temples and sighed. It was Shom's cry of alarm which snatched her back to the present.

"What in the name of the gods is that?!"

Spinning rapidly, she and her companions witnessed the onrushing herd of Gar-Kal colliding with the outer crowd of Yupik pilgrims. The frantic fish people tore a giant swath in the ice clans' ranks. They pushed and climbed their way through the waiting diaspora clawing and biting with abandon. The startled Yupik cried out and attempted to get out of the way only to collide with their companions toppling whole segments of the panic-stricken multitude to the cold ground.

"Who the fuck are these people?!" Mal barked.

"Yupik, ice clans," Orich said as he moved the wheel slightly to the right. His voice trailed off as they rushed past the advancing fish and over a sea of parkas. All were standing, facing the small glimmering city they were rapidly approaching.

As the *Haraka* came upon the city's outer buildings the ice clans were standing shoulder to shoulder. Orich banked the craft upward over the pale blue archway.

"What the fuck is that?!" Mal's bellow preceded the collective gasp from behind her.

Ni-Chek levitated motionless. His dark robes, unaffected by the wind, contrasted against the arch of the city's gateway. The black pearl hovering above his outstretched hand crackled furiously lighting up the area. He ignored the airship as it swept upward to his right and banked to the left over the city.

Shom shook his head in wonder as he scanned the Yupik masses which surrounded Mos-Agar. The horde completely clogged the eight main roads which made up the city's design. "Is this some sort of preposterously large religious ceremony?" The royal noted that the crowd flowed into the city center and the purple domed temple, but none reemerged.

From behind, Orich gasped causing Mal to furrow her brow. "Captain!"

The Spice Rat stood transfixed at the chaos on the ground. "Here it comes," she stated flatly.

"Captain, I believe that entity levitating above the gate is luring those witless ice clans into the temple."

Mal's mouth grew taunt. "So?!"

The Bailian banked around the city for another pass. "Captain, they go in, they do not come out! That temple is a portal to the Labyrinth."

As the craft swept across the sky toward the southwest gate Orich's voice became almost frantic. "Thousands, perhaps tens of thousands of souls are about to be plunged into and trapped in another dimension, effectively killing them. The Fifth Avatar is also bound for a similar fate."

The albino pilot circled high so everyone could see the mob of Gar-Kal plowing into the Yupik ranks just outside the city. He circled until they advanced on Ni-Chek once more.

The tension-filled silence in the cabin was deafening as Orich continued. "Captain, if either the Yupik or the Avatar enter the temple it would be catastrophic. If both enter, there is little doubt that will be enough to set off the Black Mural."

Zaad slammed a meaty fist into an equally sizable palm. "Swing up beside that floating cloak and drop the back gate. I'll take care of the problem."

"The problem is much bigger than that," Orich said. "A decision must be made. Kill that thing and the Yupik may disperse. That means however, the Avatar must go into the temple to keep the balance."

"And we cannot control the Otick." Alto finished the Bailians though. "They are on a holy mission. If they are unable retrieve the Avatar, they will follow it into the portal."

Shom huffed. "Huh, sounds like, 'problem solved' to me."

Orich's glare at the royal was cold, as his voice dropped to a low calculating tone, "Is it?"

Shom gave a weary frustrated sigh. "Mystic riddles again Orich…"

Mal, had been listening intently to the exchange shuffling her gaze between her two friends. Suddenly, her eyes flashed with recognition. "Wait, I get it! The balance of good and evil, only one can go in or we're all fucked."

Orich nodded yes as all concentrated on the Spice Rat. "…and depending on who enters will influence the course of history."

"Exactly," Orich replied. "And we stand on the precipice."

Mal's throat tightened as she nervously combed her fingers through her hair. "Okay, park us over the western edge of the city. We all watch for the Otick. Orich, train the starboard ballista rack on our floating friend out there. If the Otick show up empty handed unload on the cloak."

"The black pearl may also be just as dangerous." Orich warned.

"Make it a full load on the entire area."

Everyone's attention in the cabin immediately flittered between the mass of Yupik flowing into the city and the floating cloaked figure. The black pearl was now spitting out larger bolts of blue lightning.

"Not good!" Mal said ominously. "Orich!"

Before the albino pilot was able to spin the wheel a cascade of lightning bolts erupted directly toward the *Haraka*.

A metallic taste filled Mal's mouth and a heartbeat later the windshield was filled with a blinding flash which brightly illuminated the cabin. Almost immediately the random surges of power started to coalesce onto a single field. Bolts of blue electrical power pulsed, engulfing the craft in a net of crackling energy. The *Haraka* was rocked violently sending everyone sprawling on the deck.

Zau gave a violent shudder and bolted up in her chair. "Hello, I felt that!"

Mal sat up and took stock of the situation and her companions alongside her on the deck. Orich had managed to hang onto the wheel, and the Spice Rat was relieved to see her new navigator finally awake. "Is everyone okay?

"I feel great!" Zau chirped

Zaad thumped his chest. Grumbling he got to his feet.

"How about you Your Majesty?"

Kyopp waved his hand as he climbed into a seat.

Alto tenderly touched Mal's cheek. "How are you?"

For the briefest of ellipses Mal fell into the moment, acknowledging that someone cared about her. As it passed, she cupped her hand over his. "I'll ask the questions around here," she halfheartedly jabbed. "I'm the one responsible for getting you assholes back in one piece."

Shom viewed the touching scene with indifference as he got to his feet. "Yes, I'm sure I can arrange a room for the both of you at our next port of call. That is provided we make our next port of call. Uh, Maluria…"

The prodigal's attention was fixed out the windshield. A net of crackling blue bolts of energy filled the windshield. A single strand of the electric discharge stretched back to the black pearl levitating above Ni-Chek's hand.

"The ukko hull protected us from the blast," Orich said as he tugged at the unresponsive wheel. "However, that does not prevent it from trapping us. Captain, we are being held immobile."

Mal frowned as she shook her head, searching her brain for a solution.

Zau's attention was focused on Ni-Chek. "You know something occurs to me? Whatever that thing is, it's expending a lot of energy on controlling that crowd and having to hold us in place isn't helping."

"So, what are you saying?" Mal asked as Zau studied the floating wizard intently.

"I think it's struggling," the Singa replied not breaking her stare.

"Splendid," Shom sarcastically moaned. "So, all we've got to do is wait it out!"

Zau snapped a nasty look at the royal. "Who is he again? I really don't think I like him!"

Mal put her hand on the navigator's shoulder to diffuse the situation. Her attention, as she struggled to see past the blue energy net, was torn between Ni-Chek and the colliding masses of sentients below. The Gar-Kal mob had successfully parted the crowd of Yupik pilgrims and was about to enter the city.

"Everybody stay sharp," she rallied. "Okay, if Zau's right...we've gotta do something to make it harder for that cowled asshat out there." No sooner had the words left her mouth when a devious smile flashed across the Spice Rat's face. "Orich, kill the engines."

"Captain?"

"If it wants to keep us prisoner, it's gonna have to do all the fucking work."

Nodding in approval the Bailian pulled a lever to his left, turning off the *Haraka's* twin etheria powerplants.

When the engine died the intensity of the electric net dimmed for an ellipse and Mal traded a knowing glance with Zau.

"Okay," Mal called out. "What else can we do to make this fucker more miserable?"

Orich reeled in protest. "Captain I must warn…"

"Relax, I don't want to kill it. All I want it to do is let us go!" Mal said with a touch of irritation.

Alto's cry of alarm as he pointed at the ground interrupted the contentious exchange. "There!"

All attention in the cabin focused on the stream of fish people sweeping violently through the Yupik throng.

In the center of the Gar-Kal mass, about a hundred yards from the city's gate were the two Otick. Wallack had the Avatar. His lower four legs gripped the box while his two claw hands slashed out in either direction. Beside him, Raydan was a blur of deadly motion as he utilized all of the multi-attacking Otick combat skills. As the fish creatures mobbed them, they were cut down and swept away by the crowd's momentum, only to be immediately replaced by more attackers.

"Those crusty fuckers pulled it off!" Mal beamed. "They got it!"

Shom stood beside his friend, arms crossed tightly against his chest. "It doesn't matter Maluria. They're being pushed into oblivion by a disgusting torrent of oversized bait."

Okawa had been keeping a close watch on Demetrius. They had only been flying a short while and the normally chatty pilot was unusually quiet. His gaze shifted back and forth as if he were sorting out a dilemma. She had seen the look many times while conducting interrogations.

Her conclusions proved correct when he suddenly banked the *Catori* to the left, turning the craft back to the battle.

Having some idea for the change of course she decided to ask anyway. "So, what's going on?"

"I'm going back to help my friends," Demetrius resolutely said.

"Those weren't your orders."

He peeked over and took in the Valdurian's stern demeanor. "You had orders, not me. I had an assignment of which I completed."

"You are not authorized to do that. This ship is property of the Valdurian government."

"I'm already doing it," he replied leveling the ship out in the direction they had just came from. "I've been given a loose charter from your house. It doesn't prohibit me from taking on my own endeavors."

"Demetrius, I'm serious. Turn this craft around!"

The pilot ignored her demand as he stared out the windshield. "Sorry. I had to leave them once before. I'm not going to do it again."

"I can't let you do this," she stated, drawing her pistol crossbow.

Demetrius turned when he heard the gears clicking as they pulled the bow back. He gave the weapon and its wielder an amused expression while assessing the projectile aimed right at his head. The shaft was surrounded by reed slats. "Isn't that one of those new expanding bolts? Golly, I'll be that would make a real mess in here."

"I'm serious!" she growled.

Sighing deeply, he gazed back forward. "Unless you know something radically different about this assignment and are prepared to fly this craft through an unknown and hostile airspace, I suggest you put that away. I've got a feeling we may need your aggression in a little bit."

The tense stand-off lasted a very long centi. Okawa finally acquiesced with a terse snap of her head as she uncocked the weapon. "Fine, but if we make it back, I'm going to have to report this."

Demetrius gave an ironic chuckle as he adjusted the wheel. "If, we make it back, I'll help you file it."

"So?"

"We follow their path," he said as he motioned to the tail end of the Gar-Kal herd rushing eastward over the ice. "These guys look familiar."

The moon finally set in the west and a cloak of darkness descended. On the horizon, both could make out continuous flashes of blue lightning. "I'm betting that's the party we need to crash."

Okawa stared out at the unnatural flashes they were approaching rapidly. Demetrius caught the concern etched on her face. "Relax, Nocturn only seems scarier. There's things over on our side of the world that'll kill you just as quick."

Not very reassuring, she reflected to herself as she cocked her weapon again.

The crew of the *Haraka* peered helplessly through the lightning bonds which held them as the massive tide of fish-like denizens from Nocturn steadily swept the Oticks and their beloved Avatar toward the city gate.

"We've got to do something!" Zau said.

"We're not in a position to do anything," Shom scoffed loudly. "Obviously that, whatever that happens to be, is stronger than you anticipated."

Mal's lips were drawn tight as she followed the mammoth procession toward Mos-Agar. "Maybe the ship can't get out, but something smaller can. Orich drop the side hatch," she ordered as she grabbed her pistol crossbow beside her seat.

"Captain!?"

"I'm going to distract it. We've got to do something, now drop the damn hatch!"

The Spice Rat positioned herself with weapon ready as the door was lowered. The intense electrical field, a few feet from her, caused her hair to stand wildly. She winced as she tried to aim across the crossed bolts of energy. The potency of the voltage all around caused the air in front of her to shimmer making a clean shot all but impossible. Shuddering in frustration she backed away from the opening and Orich closed the hatch.

Everyone was still staring at Mal, when Alto caught movement in the skies to the west." "It appears we have company."

Okawa was frozen in shock as the *Catori* sped toward the chaotic scene outside the city gates. "What in the name of the empire is that?!"

"I have no idea, but it seems like whatever that floating thing is, it has my friends' ship trapped."

"We can't fight against that!" she said incredulously pointing out the windshield.

"We don't need to fight it," Demetrius said defiantly as he hit the accelerator. "We're gonna handle this the good old-fashioned way."

Everyone in the *Haraka* was now fixated on the airship speeding toward Ni-Chek.

"I've absolutely no idea what's going on, but I'm certainly glad to see them," Shom said with a touch of optimism in his voice.

The *Catori*, increased speed as it rushed directly at the levitating robe and orb. "Hold on!" Demetrius warned as he wrenched the wheel to the right at the last moment. The nose of the speeding ship narrowly missed the hooded figure as the *Catori* violently banked away.

Mal and Orich held their breath as the rear fin clipped the front of the robe sending it spinning to the ground along with its contents; a long rod of grey and red crystals. The black pearl continued to levitate and crackle with energy but the lightning net which had bound them quickly dissipated into the night sky.

A cheer went up in the *Haraka's* cabin as Orich fired up the engines and Mal jumped back in her seat. "Alright! No time to lose! Orich get us down there. Alto, Zaad be ready to get out there and give those Otick some operating room!"

The swordmaster and EEtah positioned themselves by the side hatch as Orich lowered the airship directly in front of the unwillingly propelled crustaceans. As the door dropped Alto was the first out, drawing his long and short sword in mid-leap. Defari growled loudly as it was unsheathed. This gave enough room for Zaad to exit and draw Bowbreaker.

"Get in!" Alto screamed as he slashed at several Gar-Kal who approached. Zaad's roar reverberated across the ice as he swung his massive long sword in a broad, deadly arc severing fish bodies as it traveled along its deadly path.

The Otick quickly entered the ship with the fighting duo covering their exit. As another wave threatened to overtake them the *Catori* banked and came in low, mere feet over Zaad. It then rapidly lowered to a foot above the ice, plowing a large swath in the waves of approaching oceanic denizens.

Seeing their opportunity, Alto motioned at the EEtah and they followed the Otick into the *Haraka*.

"Get us outta here!" Mal yelled as the side hatch closed.

The craft quickly lifted off and moved away from the floating orb and Mos-Agar as the Gar-Kal and Yupik hordes continued to flood into the city.

In the center of the cabin both Otick fell to their knees with the Avatar's box between them. "The Golden One has blessed us and this holy endeavor," Raydan proclaimed through ragged breath.

"All thanks to the Golden One!" Wallack said.

"More like thanks to that airship out there," Shom retorted under his breath.

Mal shot him a dirty look then took note out the window as the *Catori* came along side. Smiling broadly, she gave Demetrius a thumbs up then indicated for him to follow.

The Yupik crowd surged, almost knocking Ri'Da and his family to the cold hard streets of Mos Agar.

Something was wrong.

The crowd had been picking up speed as it rushed along the wheel-shaped boulevards toward the purple temple. The living tsunami carried everyone and everything along with them.

The roar of the caribou herd, once a source of comfort and promise of plenty was close behind them, *Too close.* The Yupik father glanced around in a panic, then cried out in disappointment and frustration. The rumbling caribou herd was in actuality a raging wall of the Gar-Kal charging through and pushing his people into the awaiting purple edifice.

In front of them, the towering entrance to the temple loomed ever closer. Ri'Da saw the people immediately in front of him slipping between the heavy arches. There were no doors and the second the ice clansmen in front of him entered, they disappeared from view.

The tiny Yupik family were now at the complete mercy of the panicked crowd which propelled them forward.

Ri-Da saw the giant beetle descend from the sky and land in the road behind him as he felt the pull from the open doorway. There was no time to marvel at the fantastic beings that emerged from the beetle's shell as the ice clansman and his family were swept inside the temple of Lila and into the Labyrinth Plane of the Middle Realms.

It took a while for the excitement to finally wane and the adrenaline to fade from the system. Once depleted, a profound sense of exhaustion descended over the occupants of the *Haraka*.

Zau was by far the most energized of the group. She gladly took over the wheel as an exhausted Orich plopped into a seat.

"Captain," the albino began with a weary sigh as he settled back into the navigator's chair. "That electrical assault woke my brother."

"That's good news Orich," Mal's voice was weary but relieved.

Orich displayed no joy in his brother's awakening. "Captain, I sense my brother is now somehow, different…"

"How?"

"Unsure, at this time." The Bailian's expression changed with the subject, from reflective to curious. "Tell me captain, how did it feel to make decisions usually left to the gods?"

The Spice Rat paused and stared pensively at her pilot. "Those two made the decision for me," she said indicating the two Otick.

Sensing there was nothing more his captain could explain, Orich gave a sad nod and settled back closing his eyes.

Shom sat forward in his seat unable to contain his curiosity. "Can someone for the love of the gods tell me what that thing was back there?"

King Kyopp cleared his throat. "I might be able to help." He straightened up and beamed as he commanded everyone's attention once more. "It was a large etheria rod of howlite and amber. The grey howlite effects glamour and polymorphs. The amber gives the power of attraction. With that combination along with the power of that black pearl it was no wonder it coerced all those ice clans to their doom."

Shom tilted his head skeptically at the Do-Tarr regent. "How is it you know all this?"

The handsome Bailian peered downward as the corners of his mouth turned slightly up. Reaching inside the neck of his shirt he pulled out a grey oval pendant on a chain and dangled it for all to see. "It is how I maintain my appearance to you. My people also mine the raw etheria."

Alto was cleaning his long sword. As his hands ran the cloth over the length of the blade a soft contented panting sound was heard throughout the cabin. "Why would anyone wish the destruction of thousands of sentients?"

Orich opened his eyes. "Someone is attempting to get the Black Mural to surge."

The swordmaster stopped cleaning and stared at Orich with an alarmed expression. "Who would do such a thing, and more importantly why?! If what we've been told is true, everything on the Annigan would die."

"When you discover the answer to one of those questions, it will answer the other," Orich said wearily. "All we just accomplished, was putting the cork back in the bottle. The Mural still teeters precariously."

With that dire warning the albino closed his eyes once more.

Alto's sword began a soft whimper. Smiling at the blade, the distracted swordmaster went back to stroking it with the cloth and the contented panting resumed.

"I should bring up one curious thing though," Kyopp perked up, happy to be the center of attention again. "Unless something was remotely controlling that crystal, which I doubt. That crystal was acting on its own."

"Why do you doubt it?" Mal asked.

"Anything with enough psychic power to remotely control such an endeavor would use a much more efficient means to do so." The Do-Tarr gave an exuberant shudder. "Did I not tell you this would be a grand adventure!"

Mal sighed and scanned around the cabin. "One thing is for sure; we can't compromise our little enterprise on account of theirs." She motioned to the meditating crabs and their deity in the cargo area. "We've gotta make sure those two get wherever they need to go."

Out the window to the right she spied the *Catori* paralleling them amidst the surrounding snow flurries. From their lit cockpit she could make out Demetrius and a female seated next to him. Catching his attention, she motioned below for a spot to land.

A cheerfully grinning Demetrius gave her the thumbs up and began a shallow decent.

The floor was wet and slippery. Choking humidity permeated the massive room. Water dripped from the ceiling and oozed from the cracks in the marble walls.

Stepping lightly so as to make no noise, a nude, one-armed Kai, body glistening in sweat, cautiously slipped around a wide pillar. Pausing, she strained to hear anything.

Her caution was rewarded. Off to her left a slight splashing sound caught her attention. Gripping the stones of the pillar she shimmied up with the front of her body facing out. Toes and fingers found their way into the tiniest cracks and fissures as she pulled herself upward toward the expansive vaulted ceiling.

With her position now cloaked in the shadows, she spied two figures in skintight bodysuits warily making their way between the wide columns that ran in three long rows across the room.

From the omnipresent orange crystal glow, she saw the two males, both carrying barbed spears. Moving slowly in a crouch, they paused just below her concealed perch.

Not daring to move, she became acutely aware of the perspiration running down her from the matted swath of shoulder length hair. She tried tipping her body upward, but it was too late. Droplets of sweat dribbled off the end of her nose and plummeted downward.

The salty drops landed on the back of the neck of one of the spearmen. He immediately paused, as did his partner. Uncertainty briefly swept across the two. They peered upward in time to see the small-framed female plummeting directly at them.

Her heels connected with the two startled sentries' foreheads and they toppled to the ground with a splash and a thud. Their spears clattered noisily beside them.

From twenty feet away, she heard the rapid splash of running feet. Her location had definitely been compromised. Leaping back onto the pillar she vaulted to the next one and scrambled to the far side as the footfalls approached.

When the splashing stopped on the other side of the pillar the assassin knew she had precious little time. Gripping the column with one hand she vaulted outward with her feet and swung out from the colonnade in midair.

Two more spearmen were examining the bodies of their fallen comrades. The scraping sound from behind of Kai taking flight from the pilaster caused them to spin.

They were met by a small, one armed woman leaping at them. Reaching out she smashed one's skull back against the pillar while she locked her legs around the neck of the other. As the first one slumped against the column unconscious, she rotated her body sending the man between her legs flipping over. He landed with a wet thump. She kept her tight grip on his neck until she was sure he wasn't moving. Unlocking her legs, she crouched and meticulously scanned the area.

At the far end of the room, an archer popped out from behind cover and fired an arrow. Kai traced it arcing across the distance toward her. Ducking slightly, she reached out with her only hand, snatching it from the air. Tossing it up, she caught it so the tip faced away. In a quick, fluid motion she sent the projectile hurtling back at her attacker. By then the archer had slipped back behind the column and the arrow clattered harmlessly against the far wall.

Not waiting for another shot she launched her body up the pillar and out of sight.

The bowman had already nocked another arrow when he cautiously made his way forward. He spun several times when he though he heard something but each time there was nothing.

As he crept forward, he saw the others sprawled out twenty feet from him. Checking on both sides, he decided to advance when he heard a familiar crackle and felt the top of his head tingle.

He slowly gazed upward to see Kai hanging upside down on the side of the column. She held on by her toes and steadied herself using the stump of her missing arm. The other hand was pointed directly at the top of his skull. A glowing blue spike emanated from her outstretched fingers. The tip had gently touched the crown of his head and now was pointed directly between his eyes. He swallowed hard and lowered the bow.

The assassin smiled sweetly at the very surprised attacker. "Tag."

"Very good!" boomed a loud disembodied female voice.

Kai awoke with a start. She was in the familiar gardens inside the Free City of Tannimore. The floating city-ship's spired skyline loomed above surrounding the recessed garden of Orad. She was nude, levitating a few inches above a sweat-stained mat. Immediately obvious was that her legs folded up below her had gone to sleep and she could no longer feel them. Sweat was profusely dripping off her chin, nose and nipples.

"You healed well and recovered nicely," said a complimentary voice which seemed to come from everywhere as she lowered herself onto the mat.

"While you will be encumbered with one arm, you convinced us of your ability to compensate."

Kai lowered her gaze in reverence. "When may I begin in my new capacity?"

"You have one more task before you," the voice informed. "When completed you will receive the gift and can begin your life anew."

"Until Boran calls on me," Kai added.

The voice betrayed no emotion. "It was you who made the bargain. With great gifts come a great price."

"What is the task?"

"This task comes in two parts. And they are as great as the gifts and price."

The wind howled, blowing vast sheets of snow across the top of the mesa. Mal concentrated on two figures in heavy coats as they approached from the *Catori* which had landed beside the *Haraka* on their temporary eyrie. Gripping the front of their garments and keeping their cowls leaning down, they staggered against heavy gusts which assaulted them.

Some of the white flurries followed them through the side hatch before Orich closed it. Pulling back their hoods Demetrius and Okawa shared a self-conscious moment as everyone in the *Haraka* stared at them.

"Deetus!" Wallack joyously cried out.

"The Golden One is truly watching over us!" Raydan said as he stepped up to Demetrius and lovingly placed a claw on his shoulder.

Mal stood up from the captain's chair. "You really pulled our asses out of the fire back there. I owe you a big one."

Demetrius blushed. "Aww, I couldn't leave these two knuckleheads out in the cold."

The Spice Rat's attention immediately shifted to the uniformed Okawa. "Who's she?"

Demetrius jerked a thumb in Okawa's direction. "She's my protection."

Mal's unconvinced gaze swept over the Valdurian captain. "If you say so."

The two human females traded silent, steely glares before Mal turned her attention back to her friend. "So, where ya headed?"

"West," Demetrius confirmed. "Back to Zor. I've got to trade in this rattletrap for my ship."

Mal chuckled to herself at Okawa's reaction to Demetrius's description of the *Catori*. "Well I've got another favor to ask, seeing how you're going that way." She pointed to the Otick. "I need you to drop these two and their special cargo in Immor-Onn."

Demetrius appeared confused. "Isn't that where you're going?"

"Yeah, but it's gonna take us a little while to get there and I don't want their mission or cargo to interfere with my ship."

He gave a mischievous grin. "You could always skirt the upwinds."

"Nah, that's your thing," Mal said indifferently. "Hanging where the air is thin freaks me out."

The two captains enjoyed a short sympathetic laugh.

"Sure, I can take them," Demetrius agreed. "The Valdurians paid me a small fortune to cart these two across the Annigan. I may as well give them their money's worth."

The Spice Rat chuckled then motioned to the Otick. "Okay, looks like you got an express ride home."

Both humanoid crabs excitedly clicked their claws.

"It is the will of the Golden One we soar together again," Raydan proclaimed.

Wallack came up beside Raydan and put one arm around him and pointed his other claw at their reunited comrade. "The prophets tell of the journeyer who aided in a holy quest was forever blessed."

Demetrius blushed slightly. "Alright you two. Let's get you to your new home."

As Orich lowered the side hatch Mal yelled over the howling wind. "That's two I owe you!"

Zau was at the wheel again. Projected out in front of her was the three-dimensional Flavian Portal map. Mal stood beside her studying it.

The moon was gone and most were asleep. Orich sat cross-legged in a seat along the hull next to Alto staring out into space.

Unseen by any awake, Orich and Taa's astral bodies were seated on the ship's deck facing each other.

Orich leaned into his sibling. "I'm glad you are back unharmed my brother."

"I felt as if I was trapped under a thick wet blanket," Taa confided.

"You were here all the time; you didn't reach out?" Orich sympathetically questioned.

"My entire mind and consciousness were consumed with glyphs."

"Glyphs?"

Taa nodded yes. "Two of them. They kept repeating in endless combinations and patterns."

"It's a wonder it didn't drive you mad," Orich said.

This caused Taa to laugh. "Quite the contrary my brother. They parted the curtains of ignorance and showed me many things."

Taa's vaguely ominous tone was beginning to concern Orich. Even now, as close as they were to each other he sensed his brother's presence but still lacked the ability to share his thoughts. "What sort of things?"

Taa stared at the floor. When his gaze returned to his brother it was hardened and sullen. "Things you wouldn't understand." In an instant his demeanor softened a bit and became morose. "We will talk later."

With that good-bye, Taa dissolved into the deck below him.

They're making for the Banok Atoll admiral!" came the frantic navigator's report.

Admiral Lasia confidently stared off the railing. "Good. If we don't get them, the portal will."

The *Jeonham* had been perusing the *Raptor* for two full Lunas. The pirate ship always managed to stay outside of the Calden Man-O-War's forward ballista range and the crew was becoming frustrated.

"We should've caught them by now!" said the helmsman, a twenty-grand-old raw-boned young ensign.

Lasia calmly raised her spy glass and examined the escaping ship.

"She's got all her sheets in the wind and caught a favorable current," the seasoned Calden officer assessed. "She's also getting carried along by the portal, as are we. It won't be long now."

On the *Raptor*, Fia was personally at the wheel. The wind was gusting to well over gale force blowing everything around the deck. This normally would have been considered inclement weather to her and her skeleton crew. With a Calden war ship in hot pursuit, this wind was keeping them alive.

With a quick glance back over her shoulder she saw the sail-less ukko wood craft slicing through the heavy seas. The best and only plan she could formulate was losing the more advanced craft in the infamous waters extending well out from the Banok Atoll.

Above the thick clouds she noted the moon dipping toward the western horizon accentuating the dim sun in the northwestern sky. For a short period, the daylight would flare, as the two celestial orb's positions lined up. When the moon dipped below the sun's location, she would attempt a break away at the atoll. The plan had to work. It was all she could think of.

As Blenda came up the stairs and joined her on the quarterdeck both felt the ship's speed increase. "Admiral, we're going faster, and I don't think it's the wind!"

"I don't either," Fia agreed as she assessed the sails then glanced back at the *Jeonham*. "Its speed increase matches ours." She noted with a puzzled tone.

"Yeah, but this is strange," Fia fired back. "And the helm's getting sluggish."

The crew on the quarterdeck of the *Jeonham* felt the acceleration too and a wave of anxiety swept across the anxious crew.

"Relax. I've made the Banok Run," Lasia grinned and indicated toward the Raptor. "She hasn't. The strength of the pull says we should be coming up on the atoll any time now. Before moon-fall for sure."

"What then admiral?" the navigator asked surveying the horizon.

"That all depends on them. Either way, they're finished."

"Should I prepare a team of boarders admiral?" Came a voice from the stairway as Tuko the deck boss came up onto the landing.

Lasia looked over at the fat, bald officer. "There's no need. Prepare all ballista ports. Get the flame pots going. If the portal doesn't claim them, we're going to wipe that ship off the face of the waters."

The deck boss gave a sadistic sneer. "Aye-aye admiral." He replied before disappearing down the stairs.

Lasia exhaled loudly. "I almost feel sorry for them," she admitted. "Whoever is in command of that ship is a gifted mariner. It's such a waste."

"Land, admiral!" Blenda shouted.

Fia saw the small dot of land on the horizon as she absentmindedly chewed on her lower lip. Her plan now formulated she checked the western sky. "Okay, the moon will be setting by the time we get there. We're going to come around the eastern tip of the atoll. Then cut it hard to port which will bring us up the south side where we'll run its length. At that point we'll drop smoke and burning oil and make a run for the next steering current north."

As the *Raptor* moved closer to the speck of land, their speed increased again and Fia was struggling with the wheel. When the atoll was close enough for details on shore to be seen Blenda was needed to help control the stubborn wheel. Fia thought it strange when a small settlement on the far eastern island came into view.

Now as the Rayth rounded the eastern tip of the atoll the ship was yanked hard to port. It was caught in one of the swiftly moving currents of the turbulent southeastern ocean as it circled the seven-mile crescent of small islands. At first Fia inwardly celebrated, as this made their western swing easier. Her relief was short-lived as the *Raptor* nearly doubled in speed, knocking anyone to the deck that wasn't holding onto something.

Fia had never been on a ship traveling this fast. Her heart pounded and she fought to stay calm by focusing on straightening out the wheel. The ship continued to pull to port despite Fia and Blenda's futile efforts. It was hooking them into the shallow waters of the atoll and a potential grounding of the ship.

"Get over here!" Fia screamed as the navigator got to her feet.

Three sets of hands on the wheel proved as ineffective as two. The *Raptor* rounded the far islands and was swept into the atoll.

"By the goddess!" Blenda called out as she felt the ship straighten out. They were racing directly into what appeared to be a giant hole in the ocean.

The circular opening was almost as large as the interior of the atoll itself. Water rushed over the circumference in a giant crashing waterfall.

The sound of creaking and breaking wood, along with the startled human cries, were drowned out by the deafening crash of water as the Rayth flagship dropped over the edge and out of sight.

Admiral Lasia and the bridge crew witnessed the *Raptor* drop into the massive Flavian Portal. For most on the *Jeonham*, this was their first Banok Passage. Experiencing one of the Annigan's largest permanent portals this close was perilous.

"Hold tight!" she warned at the top of her voice as massive ripples of dimensional displacement swept outward. The waves of radiating energy would ultimately be felt hundreds of miles away.

The *Jeonham* rocked violently as the fluctuations passed them. The Calden admiral stared briefly at the area she had navigated so many times. It was not a place for the faint of heart. Brightstar were the only ones comfortable here.

"Give me hard to starboard helmsman," Lasia ordered. "Let's go home."

To Stryder Aramos, the docks of the northernmost Tiikeri port city of Tan-Du had the appearance and smell as bad as all the rest. Mongrels and orange Tiikeri clogged boardwalks in a constant hum of activity. Ice ships docked and cargo was loaded as well as unloaded. This was punctuated by the occasional line of chained slaves disembarking from the special slaver ships, bound for the market.

No-Le led both he and Ma-Tah to the northernmost dock which was situated farther apart than the others. Mongrel dock workers quickly got out of the white Tiikeri's way and bowed as he passed. Preparing the way, No-Le cleared fishermen and workers from the end of the dock itself. The three now stood alone at the edge of the dock as the cold winds from the ice floes beyond caused the mist around their feet to swirl and churn. Loose flaps of clothing whipped about in an attempt to go airborne.

"I keep waiting for this Tiikeri hospitality I'd been promised," Stryder grumbled as he held his jacket tighter.

"Soon," Ma-Tah placated as he kept his hands tucked in his sleeves.

The moon was rising over the distant ice floes in the east when No-Le pointed out onto the waters. "There!" she said as the moonlight reflected off a giant milky white orb surfacing in the bay. The light from the rising moon reflected the water streaming across it as it surfaced and made its way slowly toward the docks. Behind them Stryder heard the cries of shock and alarm from the simple dock workers.

The bubble stopped right at the edge of the platform. It was twenty feet in diameter and half submerged.

No-Le checked back with her master who nodded. With that approval she placed her hand on the bubble and pushed. The pliable shell swallowed the limb and the mongrel proceeded to step through, disappearing into the cloudy liquid beyond.

Stryder paused, seized with apprehension as he watched Ma-Tah calmly follow his aide, allowing himself to be swallowed into the orb.

"Come now," the Tiikeri said to the astonished human just before his head disappeared. "We mustn't keep our hosts waiting."

ACT TWO

Traveller Obscura

According to the early morning dispatch, the crime was horrific even by this neighborhood's reputation.

Zekoff de Corab, colonel of the Zorian city guards stepped out of the two-seat buggy and onto the streets of the Sedam Sestasra Plat in southern Zor. He glanced briefly at the rickety shacks stacked precariously upon each other lining the narrow streets. His nostrils flared at the smell of sewage and animals. The nickname Seven Sisters Slums fit aptly.

The dampness of the Kan fog had yet to burn off. Everything glistened with a dewy brightness in stark contrast to the bleakness of the location. Zekoff measured his gait on the slick cobblestones as he made his way to a nearby alley swarming with activity.

Just outside the alley, in the street, three city guards milled about investigating the scene around the corner, out of sight. A small crowd gathered on the other side of the avenue and people stared out their windows in bored acceptance of the neighborhood's constant violence.

A patrol sergeant greeted him.

"Sorry to call you out so early sir, but this is a big one."

The commander's mood was grim as he walked past his subordinate, not breaking his slow cautious stride. He smelled the blood the second he entered the alley. The metallic taste cloyed at the back of his mouth.

The sergeant followed closely.

"An apparent robbery, but unusually savage."

139

Zekoff froze as he stared at the body. Lying on his back in the narrow passage was Hoyt Eldor's mangled six-foot-three frame. His blue eyes stared lifelessly upward and his long salt-and-pepper hair was mangled in a pool of gore. Fear and rage were etched permanently on his stiff, lifeless face and both ears had been cut off. His arms were pulled to one side, adding to the mangled appearance of the body and several fingers were cut from each hand.

Standing by the corpse's head, blood surrounding the soles of his shoes was his spymaster, Captain Rafel. His thin, effeminate features were pulled tightly inward as he stared silently downward in shock and horror, twirling a strand of his long black hair with trembling fingers.

The commander of the city guard's heart sank. The romance between his spymaster and the Eldorian ambassador was one of the worst kept secrets in the Forum. Both took their jobs seriously and were concerned about the appearance of conflict of interest. Zekoff didn't care about political impropriety. He had never seen his spymaster happier or more productive.

Stepping past the body he put his hand on the captain's shoulder. "Rafel, I'm so sorry. Let's get you…"

Rafel focused on his commander, his eyes beginning to well with tears. "I'm not leaving him!" His attention immediately returned to the body.

Zekoff paused, caught between duty and compassion. His stomach tightened and his voice took on a fatherly tone. "Rafel."

No response.

"Captain!"

Rafel looked back up. Tears were now streaming down his cheeks, tumbling onto and staining the front of his winter tunic.

"Captain," Zekoff gently admonished. "You're contaminating the area."

The spymaster stared at the puddle of coagulating gore around his feet and began to sob uncontrollably.

Zekoff signaled to one of the city guards who came up on the other side of the grief-stricken officer.

"Get this man a drink," the colonel ordered. "Rafel," his voice lowered, "let these people do their job. You need to go with the corporal."

Numbly lowering his head in acceptance, the spymaster allowed the young guard to lead him away.

Sighing deeply the old colonel reached for his pipe, then realized he had left in a hurry and forgotten it. "Okay sergeant, what else have we got?"

"Like I said before sir, seems like a classic robbery."

Zekoff stroked his gray beard and studied the grizzly scene. "It would certainly indicate that. The extremities removed probably contained jewelry. His throat was cut, but not execution style. Looks like they were cutting off something hanging from his neck. Still…"

The sergeant gave a quizzical look. "Still, sir?"

"What was the Eldorian Ambassador doing in one of this city's most dangerous neighborhoods in the middle of the Kan?"

"Searching for something exotic," the sergeant lewdly offered.

Giving his subordinate an unconvinced glance, he concentrated on the avenue to which the body had apparently been dragged.

The seasoned old commander slowly ventured farther away from the corpse. He studied a wide trail leading through the extensive amount of debris littering the alley. The abnormal path led to the street beyond.

Zekoff halted as he surveyed the peculiar valley. With fixed gaze the commander contemplatively stroked his beard. "Perhaps…"

The massive dead tree trunk was leaning at a forty-five degree angle high over the forest floor. The view was good, even though the perch was precarious. The lone Pomaku leopard man surveyed the vegetation below. He had lost sight of a small herd of wild pigs and needed a better view.

The giant ironwood tree had fallen so long ago there was no record of it in any of the mawl's collective oral history. It had always been called Maoh Arroon — the leaning giant. Its angle would be relatively short lived though. It would soon enough plummet as those supporting it died and rotted. Across the millennia, Maoh Arroon was always the same.

The Pomaku gave a satisfied smile when he saw the bushes rustle twenty yards away. Checking his short spear and lanyard he prepared to jump in pursuit of his reacquired prey when he felt the bottoms of his feet tingle. He shifted position quickly as he felt the tree trunk shudder. Before he could jump, the ancient column of wood vibrated as a massive blue flash of energy burst from below.

The Pomaku hunter was flung to the ground. He landed flat on his back in a thick patch of moss, startled but alive.

The flash was immediately followed by what appeared to the startled mawl like a giant beetle. It catapulted from the ground, crashing upward past the surrounding trees. Terrified, the man-leopard scrambled backwards into a large clump of bushes.

When the blue flash cleared, Mal gasped in surprise. They were barreling upward toward the underside of the forest canopy. "What the fuck?"

"For the sake of the gods watch where you're going!" Shom chastised as branches crashed past the nose and windshield of the *Haraka*.

142

"Unavoidable," Orich said as he attempted to navigate away from the larger limbs.

"I thought you said you knew where we were going!" Shom snapped at Zau.

"I said I knew where a local portal was!" the Singa angrily clarified.

"Both of you shut the fuck up!" Mal loudly interceded as the airship broke through the treetops into a moonless sky full of stars. The Spice Rat exhaled loudly and sat back staring at the serene forest canopy below twinkling and glowing all the way to the horizon.

"That was exciting!" Kyopp beamed as he enthusiastically shook Shom's shoulder. "Wasn't that exciting?!"

The prodigal gave a loud, resigned sigh. "Yes, Your Majesty, very exciting."

Mal gave a solitary chuckle at Shom's predicament as she kept her vigil out the windshield. Zaad, who was seated across from the prodigal pointed and laughed. "The funny little man…"

Zaad's jest was cut short by the sound of Alto starting to heave. Mal shot a glance to Orich who opened one of the bottom bay doors.

"Over the side blade slinger!" she shouted against the howling wind.

While Alto relieved himself out the hatch, Shom formally addressed to the Do-Tarr king. "Your Majesty, I mean Kyopp, I do apologize for sometimes forgetting how you wish to be addressed. Please believe me that I always strive to accommodate your wishes."

Kyopp gestured his thanks. Shom turned to Zaad and continued. "Why in the name of the gods can you not afford me this small courtesy? My name, is Shom!"

The EEtah kept his grin as Alto walked between the two. "Feel better Mora?"

The swordmaster silently raised his hand as he took his seat. Focusing on Alto safely taking his seat, Zaad looked directly back at Shom. "I know."

An amused grin played at the corners of Mal's mouth to see her friend frustrated in such a manner. "So, where the fuck are we?"

In the navigator's seat beside her Zau examined the forest canopy below. "If only I knew."

Kyopp had wandered toward the bridge and was peering over their shoulders. "Oh, I know where we are."

Both spun to the Bailian who relished the attention. "You do?!"

"Sort of, I mean, I've never seen it from this vantage point, but that's the great northern forest down there. Our hives are below it."

Mal huffed as she spun back to the windshield. "Damn, we're still in the Land of Mists. We didn't get very far."

"So, what are you saying?" Zau muttered defensively.

"I'm saying we didn't get very far off those ice floes. Damn, stop being so touchy about everything!"

"Touchy? Me?"

"Ahm," Alto interrupted. "Perhaps there is a nearby alternative portal?"

Zau paused and shot Mal an irritated glance with her good eye while she lifted the patch on the other. The blue three-dimensional map projected outward between captain and navigator.

"That's the one we just came out of," the Singa declared as she pointed to one of the glowing dots. "Based on our current path, it appears there's a small two-way portal very close to us which leads directly to our destination."

"That's good news. How far away?" Mal asked.

"About six miles," Zau calculated.

Kyopp studied the terrain below. "There's a narrow gorge about that far away."

"Punch it Orich."

"Yes captain," the albino responded as he pushed the accelerator forward.

The trip took less than six centi and everyone heard the rushing river as they approached. The Spice Rat anxiously watched the thin blue ribbon far below, as it flowed through the steep, narrow tree-lined valley. The *Haraka* slowed and performed a graceful bank around the area.

"According to my calculations, it's right over there in that cliff wall," Zau announced pointing to a rectangular patch of rock amidst the carpet of thick trees leading to the river below.

"Sure doesn't look like much of a portal," Mal said skeptically.

"And the last one did?" Zau responded.

Shom was aghast. "Are you proposing we fly into that cliff wall?"

"Precisely!" Zau replied.

"The funny little man may have a point," Zaad spoke up. Mal noted a touch of concern in the normally fearless EEtah's voice.

"I mean, we're all familiar where your last calculations landed us!" Shom hammered at Zau.

The Singa navigator huffed defensively. "That was a quick way off the ice! Calculations had nothing to do with it, mister smart-aleck!"

"To ask us to fly into a wall is the ultimate request for trust." Alto said as he gave Mal a questioning look.

Mal quickly pondered the quandary. "Either way, the trip ends quicker. Let's go!"

Shom's eyes widened in disbelief. "Yes, but with one of those options we are not going to be present to spend any of the money we've earned."

Mal's voice to her navigator was low and calm. "You sure of this?"

Zau gave a single confident nod.

"Okay Orich, aim for those rocks," the Spice Rat ordered.

Shom threw up his hands and grunted in disgust. The Bailian pilot pulled the nose upward for height, then plunged into the tree lined crevasse, aiming directly at a barren patch of rock on the side.

Everyone in the *Haraka* was nervously focused at the side of the cliff as it rapidly filled the windshield. Mal's solemn demeanor broke into relieved amusement as the rocks just in front of them started to emit blue sparkles. "Okay, good news! We're probably not going to die. HOLD ON!"

The natural first reaction is to hold your breath for as long as you can. Then, the initial panic sets in as the lungs, starved for oxygen, seize up, causing the throat to involuntarily gulp for air, only to draw in liquid.

After several swallows, usually accompanied by frenzied thrashing, shock begins to set in and with it, the realization you are drowning and these frenzied undulations are your last living act. As your lungs fill you gently float away, physically and mortally.

Stryder Aramos knew all about drowning. It had almost happened to him once as a child at the hands of his older cousin Harper. It was also the favorite torture techniques of the Ironmark Maji the Torrent.

This however, was different. Once the quartermaster realized that he was actually breathing the liquid inside the bubble he relaxed. The sensation of warm fluid moving in and out of his nose and mouth felt somehow soothing. The womb-like environment calmed him and he became aware of the forms of Ma-Tah and No-Le barely out of reach in the murky, glittering fluid.

He also became aware of the sensation of movement. Shifting over to the side of the bubble he witnessed the slow descent into the dark, icy depths. All across his field of vision glowing bioluminescent fish darted about. A giant school of inch long fish, glittering like gems rapidly approached the sinking orb. They encircled it with their masses then rushed away. As they trailed off, a large black object rose from the darkness. It jetted through the school, devouring all it was able to in a single gulp. Stryder saw its long, slender body and huge jaws set against the glow of the remaining school as they made their escape into the inky blackness.

"Magnificent, isn't it?!" Ma-Tah marveled as he came up behind the human.

The sensation of actually talking in water was another strange first for Stryder. "Yes," was all he could initially manage. The fluid coursed into his lungs and once accustomed to the sensation of forming words without air, he actually found the experience enjoyable. "We're deep," he noted as he attempted a few words.

"And we're going a lot deeper," the Tiikeri said.

"How far?"

"On the bottom of this ocean is a massive trench. At its easternmost point is a giant outcropping of etheria crystals. That is our destination."

The quartermaster remained silent as he watched the various forms of glowing sea life pass around him. Each became slightly different the deeper they plunged into the ocean's depths. After two decis of constant descent the rim of the trench became visible.

In the midst of the deepest ocean rests the true abyss, Stryder reflected as their protective orb now traveled along the length of the Rod-Ema trench, moving steadily eastward. They trekked another two decis. All along the journey Stryder observed an army of fish humanoids crawling over both sides of the trench, tending to its black walls covered in mysterious runes.

147

Coming into view, he marveled at a large, multicolored glow which illuminated the distance. Slowly, the ball shifted slightly northward on the sea bottom and the base of the glow. All along the seabed, a multitude of creatures scurried along the sandy bottom as they drew near the giant etheria outcropping.

The entire area was well lit for hundreds of yards from the thick pillars of glowing etheria crystals rising from the end of the trench. The field of crystals was easily a hundred yards across. Stryder stared upward in amazement at the sheer size of the raw gems. One purple column in the center of the field, rose upward toward the surface and out of sight.

Perched atop each crystal pillar was a being that looked exactly like the Chenoan ambassador he had encountered in Shun-Dra. Their long tentacles undulated along the facets of the gems beneath them, stroking and sensuously caressing the phallic objects.

The orb slowed and hovered in front of the Chenoans. Ten feet below them, the ocean floor glittered with shards of multicolored magical gems.

"Exalted ones," Ma-Tah began. "We give thanks for this audience."

The voice that responded resonating within the confines of their chamber seemed to be comprised of hundreds of voices speaking as one. "You honor us with your presence."

Stryder noted the voices were the same as the ambassador, old and gentle.

"I'm certain ours can be a beneficial union for all our peoples," the Tiikeri praised.

"Indeed," the voices confirmed. "But first, a gift, as both a token of cooperation, as well as appreciation for guarding the life of one of our numbers."

To their left, a half dozen of the Gar-Kal minions had constructed two separate three-foot-high piles of white crystals on the seabed. Each of the individual gems was about a foot in length. Between two pale, blue etheria pillars,

Stryder saw a small strand appear connecting the twin columns. The linking tissue undulated and quickly grew into an orb much like the one they occupied only slightly smaller. Breaking loose, it floated over to the piles of gems. Lowering itself over them, it engulfed the stones. It then gently rose and attached itself to the visitor's bubble with a resounding plop.

Stryder became aware of Ma-Tah speaking. He was giving thanks and beginning the negotiations. His attention however, was fixated on the gems within close proximity. He felt his heart rate pick up as he greedily licked his lips. *This is a good start.*

The Endless Ocean stirred,
Ripples transformed to swirls,
One feeding off the other,
Growing and joining
The many becoming the one
A raging vortex of circling water formed,
Open to the multiverse,
And any who dared travel it

From deep within the massive whirlpool an expanding blue glow refracted across the spume of the churning ocean. In the midst of an enormous blue flash a towering explosion of water launched the *Raptor* from the depts of the sea into midair. The sound of groaning and cracking wood along with human screams preceded an enormous splash. The Rayth flagship crashed into the water. The impact sent giant plumes of displaced seawater skyward which quickly fell, showering the deck of the warship. It drenched a white knuckled Fia and Blenda as they held on for their lives.

Behind the ship, the whirlpool slowed, then closed, replaced by gentle ocean swells.

When Fia finally managed to unlock her hands from the ship's wheel, she realized she was trembling. The pirate queen didn't know how long they plummeted through the darkness. She grimaced, still hearing the strange menacing sounds that had surrounded them, as well as the screams of her sisters as they were thrown from the deck into the unknown.

The ship finally settled. The chaos of their arrival was replaced by the gentle lapping against the sides and the wind rustling in the sails. Both Rayth commanders stared at each other, speechless. Simultaneously they stared upward at the grey, featureless sky and the wind which seemed to blow from everywhere.

"Admiral, where are we?"

Fia peered upward quizzically. "No clue. I've never seen a sky like that, no sun, no clouds…"

"What do we do?"

The admiral shifted her gaze down at the empty decks, normally bustling with activity when under sail. "Check the ship for damage and see how many of us remain. I'll try and find a course to steer."

Exactly as he had done every morning since being assigned, Lord Julius, Avion ambassador to House Pyre and the Nine Golden Masters, rose with the moon. Still nude, he strolled out onto his balcony and surveyed the gentle snowflake spires as his adopted city of Immor-Onn came to life. The gently discordant notes of the city's windchimes echoed upward and a feeling of calm gratitude swept over him.

A stiff breeze fluttered at the outer feathers of his wings and he opened them to their full outstretched length. Extending his arms and gazing upward at the swiftly passing clouds, he launched himself skyward.

This was the routine he practiced every morning. Fly straight up to the place in the sky where the air became thin. Every luna, a little higher. It was a grand game. Climb until unconsciousness overcame, then plummet helplessly to the ground.

So far, it had been the will of the gods to awaken him in time to pull out of the fatal plunge. However, the gods were a fickle lot and could just as easily let his body be dashed to the ground like a fallen bird. Ultimately, this was the Avion royal's daily test to see if he soared in the gods' favor.

Climbing swiftly, he punched through the layer of clouds into the clear sky above. In the distance, he saw a falling object, little more than a dot racing toward him. It was at this point he also heard the faint singing. The Avion shook his head to clear it, thinking this must be a new symptom of oxygen starvation. However, he wasn't anywhere near the atmosphere's edge, and the song, was very familiar.

The *Catori* was making its descent from skirting the upwinds. Demetrius squinted as he caught sight of an object in the distance spiraling upward from Immor-Onn. "What in tarnation is that?"

As the object barreled closer, the pilot did a double take. It was an Avion ascending at a high rate of speed. Okawa beside him viewed the object suspiciously but said nothing. Demetrius's studied the naked winged man as he streaked past the *Catori* off to the left. His wings were arched and his long black hair flowed out straight behind him.

"Julius?!" Demetrius uttered in confusion.

151

"Julius?!" Wallack perked up.

"As in Lord Julius?!" Raydan's voice quivered.

Demetrius now settled back in his seat and Okawa searched his perplexed expression. "It sure looked like him," the airship pilot replied.

The two Otick shared excited glances.

"The Golden One has truly blessed our cause," Raydan chirped.

Wallack raised a claw in agreement. "As with meeting Deetus again, the songs of the prophets tell many tales of reunited comrades, who join together once again for a holy cause."

"Well, I wouldn't get your hopes up," Demetrius glanced over his shoulder at his two passengers. "Julius is ambassador here, but word has it he's crazy."

"Have you not checked on him?" Wallack incredulously asked.

Demetrius chuckled. "I'm an air jockey and he's royalty. We hardly run in the same circles."

"Still," Raydan challenged, "a former comrade in arms?"

"You remember how Julius was when we finally made it back from Nocturn?" Demetrius reminded.

Both Otick nodded yes.

"Well, he hasn't gotten any better. In fact, word from the palace says he's a real pest to the queen."

"I guess you don't talk to her either?" Wallack asked in a disappointed tone.

Okawa had been listening intently to the exchange. "So, wait a centi," the Valdurian security officer pointed a finger at Demetrius and the Otick. "You're telling me you know the Bailian queen?"

Raydan was genuinely perplexed at the question. "Of course. She was a pleasure slave of the tiger people's mutant king. We liberated her when Deetus and his friends helped the cub prince to his rightful place on the throne." The Otick general appeared sorrowful. "She is a truly gentle soul. I can only imagine the things she endured. The Tiikeri can be a cruel people."

Okawa stared at the crab men in amazement. Her gaze then moved to the pilot. She said nothing, but her bearing contained a hundred questions.

Catching her inquiring stare Demetrius' exhibited a modest but confident gleam. "Who do you think flew them out?"

Okawa now understood why Joc' Valdur had insisted on *this* pilot. "That must've been some operation?"

"Darn near killed us," Demetrius confirmed.

Both shared a mutually reverent moment. Out the windshield, off to their left, both missed Julius' body plummeting toward the ground. The unconscious Avion was on his back, his wings, hair and limbs fluttering furiously upward as he fell.

Once again, I have found favor with the gods, Julius marveled, as several hundred feet from the ground he rolled over, pulling himself out of freefall. Catching a gust of wind, he circled the city before returning to his residence high above the metropolis below.

Settling gently onto his balcony, he exhaled and stretched his wings then folded them against his back. It was always good to find himself in favor of the gods, but he couldn't help but get the feeling something was different.

Behind him the decorative glass door opened. Joining him on the wide wind-swept platform Dak, his faithful seneschal ceremoniously approached the Avion, robe in hand. The giant fifteen-foot man-shark greeted the much smaller winged humanoid with a smile. "Did we have a good morning flight sir?"

"Yes, yes, splendid," Julius energetically replied as he accepted the garment. "Let's get freshened up for the luna. Somethings going on and we're going to the palace to see the queen."

"Sir?"

As Julius and Dak stepped onto the main covered avenue leading to the palace the Avion stopped and studied the windchimes which hung above every street.

He concentrated on the clear street covering and the crystal chimes slightly below. Throwing his seneschal a frustrated glance, he motioned upward to them. "Do you hear that?"

"Sir?"

"The chimes, the chimes," his voice raised in pitch. "And you can feel it too, can't you feel it?!"

The EEtah stared upward, obviously confused. "Sir?"

A confounded Julius contemplated the citizens of Immor-Onn as they bustled past him, apparently blissfully unaware. The Avion ambassador enthusiastically fidgeted. *It was obvious, wasn't it?* The chimes which served to calm the populous no longer kept a discordant jingle. Now the melodies came together in complex chording and unification.

The queen must be made aware, if she didn't realize it already.

Most humans, especially those across Lumina, believe however erroneously, that their race is superior over the myriad of others which populate the Annigan. This is especially peculiar when one considers that humans are but a few of the sentients that can only breath above water.

Stryder Aramos now contemplated that dark irony on his hands and knees as he vomited the murky, sparkling liquid onto the docks of Ka-Beer. Ma-Tah had subtly relieved himself over the side of the boardwalk. He now stood staring down, obviously amused, over a gagging and sputtering human.

"The first time is always the hardest," he assured.

The quartermaster gasped a few more times before sitting back. "What was that stuff?" he panted.

"Pagos," the white tiger answered simply. "Living water. The oceans in Nocturn are teeming with etheria crystal sediment worn away from the deposits along and in the trench."

Stryder squinted up at him. Ma-Tah laughed and offered him a hand up. "Come, we've got quite a bit to do before your return to Lumina."

Taking a moment to steady himself Stryder disdainfully took in the mongrel dock workers then glanced back over to the small orb floating at the end of the wharf. "Shouldn't we take the gems with us?"

The Tiikeri gave an ominous grin. "Even if any of these simpletons dare try and steal from a guest of the king, they wouldn't know what to do with their spoils. They're aware of the penalty too. Come, now that you've been introduced to the Pagos, there's something else I need to show you."

"You know this really is quite inconvenient," Julius dramatically tossed his head in a grandiose display that sent his thick mane of black hair swaying in the wind. "I mean, she's always in the palace at this time of the luna. I don't really…"

Dak had stopped listening. His employer possessed the ability to blather on for decis if allowed. Most of his diatribes were ramblings. However, every now and then, a glimmer of the brilliance that once was, would surface. Touching his left shoulder, the EEtah guided the Avion ambassador into the main boulevard leading eventually to the city's twin harbors and in this case, Valdurian Air Station East.

They had been told at the palace the queen had gone to meet an unexpected dignitary who recently arrived. Lord Julius decided what he had to tell her couldn't wait and so, they followed. This type of impulsive behavior was hardly new to the seneschal. Lord Julius called on the queen almost daily. No matter how busy the sovereign, nor how incoherent Julius's ramblings, she patiently listened and appeased him. Dak loved queen Shula. He recognized something in her from the first time they met in Nocturn. The petite Bailian woman had a good heart and calm nature under duress.

"...and now we've got to walk all the way to this air station. By the by, have I ever been to this place?"

Julius going silent in expectation of an answer snapped the daydreaming EEtah back. "Uh, no sir, ya haven't visited there yet."

A thoughtful guise swept across the Avion's handsome features. "Ah well, I guess something will come of this. I'm not at all sure how I feel about..." Julius suddenly stopped. "Oh, how do you do!?" he cheerfully greeted a grimy old Bailian housekeeper. "So good to see you again!" The woman gave a weak, surprised quiver before they moved on.

Julius would've normally kept a much brisker pace and the EEtah with his short legs appreciated his lord's regal stroll. The distractions along the way however were absolutely maddening. They had barely gone another twenty feet when the Avion was enthusiastically shaking hands with a very stunned merchant.

After several more impromptu stops, Dak finally guided his boss up the wide ramp leading into the air station. The facilities' large twin doors were closed and two Outer Clan EEtah dressed in the uniforms of Valdurian Marines flanked either side. In earlier times, the Sunal EEtah would be tempted to mock the smaller EEtahs of the outer clans in their green jumpsuits. He reflected however, that he now wore an orange tunic and carried a messenger bag on his arm. Clearly, he had no room to tease anyone. Still, one thing he possessed that they did not, was strapped to his back — the yudon harpoon. It was issued upon your admission to the Sunal and was always with you. No outer clansman dared carry one. For any unqualified sentient caught with the EEtah symbol of rank, meant their death.

Passing into the air station, the seneschal became immediately grateful of the EEtah marine's discipline. Each stared forward at attention as Julius attempted to give them a martial pep-talk. Dak was also impressed with the sheer size of the newly built facilities. This one was easily the size of the one in Zor. In fact, the whole newly rebuilt city of Immor-Onn mimicked the High Holy City in its expansive, accepting architecture and urban planning.

To the left, the massive opening to the commercial flight deck and hangars was cordoned off. Two more EEtah marines stood guarding it. A few flight crews attempted to enter but were denied admittance. The two Valdurian guards nodded and silently stepped aside when Julius approached. In a way, Dak was glad his boss was a fixture around the city. The ambassador had been stopped once, early on in his assignment. The scene he caused, flying to the top of the rafters and screaming his protests to passing traffic was still talked about. The queen herself was the one who finally had to come and talk him down. Ironically it was that incident which initiated the mad Avion's infatuation with the Bailian queen.

The hangar was empty except for a medium sized airship. A crowd of a dozen sentients were congregated on its right side. There was something very familiar about the scene they were approaching: the ship, the crowd.

"By the mighty winds of Salar, I don't believe my eyes!" Julius shouted, as he extended his wings and leapt over to the ship. Dak followed behind in an excited sprint.

"Julius! Dak!" The Otick happily cried in unison as they excitedly fidgeted clicking their claws.

Okawa held back in stunned silence, taking in the surreal moment. She was used to dealing with spies, thieves and assassins, not demigods and royalty. *Obviously old friends*, she deduced as they greeted and hugged each other. The queen actually teared up as she welcomed the Otick and their most special delivery. The pompous Avion was especially entertaining as he babbled on to them about some song only he was able to hear.

Raydan stared at the box containing the Avatar that he carried, then back up at Julius with a stunned expression. "How is that possible, a non-Otick hearing the Avatar's song?"

"Absolutely no idea, but it's quite a catchy melody," the Avion ambassador exuberantly replied turning his attention to the queen. "It's affected the city's windchimes, have you noticed? No, let me sing it for you!"

"Julius…" the queen gently admonished with a slightly raised eyebrow.

The Avion ambassador frowned as he slumped in disappointment.

Wallack raised a claw. "The prophets tell us that in order to hear the Avatar's song, all that is necessary is the heart of a child."

The Valdurian security officer was so intent on watching the Oticks she barely noticed Queen Shula make her way over to her.

"This all must be quite overwhelming?" the sovereign sympathized with a warm smile.

Okawa appeared a bit surprised, as she studied the group. "You could say that, Your Majesty."

Demetrius joined the two. He bowed slightly to the queen when he approached, but she was staring longingly at the group. "You can trust any one of those sentients with your life," she stated, in a hauntingly distant voice that caused Okawa to pause. "I'm sorry," the sovereign said snapping out of her maudlin tone. "So, where to from here?"

"We're on our way back to Zor," Demetrius spoke up. "The captain here has to return to, whatever it is she does. I've got to swap out this tub for *my* ship, and then, I'm officially retired, courtesy of the Valdurian government."

Okawa discreetly signaled her agreement.

Demetrius huffed. "You'll have to excuse my secretive traveling companion Your Majesty. She's not much of a talker."

Okawa responded with a silent, sarcastic grin and roll of the eyes.

Unphased, an enthusiastic Demetrius spun back to the group. "Hey, who wants to buy an airship?!"

The prime minister heard the screaming from down the hall. Scowling in disbelief, he sighed as a stream of bellicose obscenities reverberated past the bedchamber door. The unlucky guard on station outside, stood at rigid attention.

Basbakan de Boger tensely tapped the papers in his hand against his other palm as he assessed the situation. The king had been drinking. The darkly ironic factor in all of this was the king never really stopped drinking. The intensity and volume of this bender however, indicated the drunken sovereign wasn't far from physical violence.

Starting toward the door, he studied the guard who passed him a relieved sigh. Basbakan took a moment to steady himself, then rapped loudly on his king's bedroom door. There was no reply and the incoherent yelling continued unabated.

"Stay sharp young man," Basbakan said as he opened the door.

Entering the room, the prime minister's bulbous nose flared with the stench of stale liquor and body odor. The king staggered about the middle of the opulent but unkept chamber, screaming in between taking healthy swigs from a bottle in his hand. Droplets of collected whiskey flew from his massive handlebar moustache with every bellow.

There was another smell too — blood. To his left the queen lay motionless on the white marble floor. A stream of crimson flowed from her temple to the far corner of the room where it began to pool.

Taking another drink, he pulled the bottle away quickly, spilling liquor the length of his heavily stained satin robes. Leaning forward the Eldorian king continued his tirade at his dead wife, as drink and spittle sprayed out in front of his enraged mouth.

Basbakan gasped in horror. He inhaled sharply as he quickly closed the door. "Oh sovereign!" he panted as the king stopped yelling and pivoted toward him. The royal's robust frame teetered as he tried to focus on his right-hand man. Then, once again, raised the bottle to his lips. When he lowered it, he was still angry, but now with the distraction, remorse quickly rose in the king. He blurted out an angry incoherent statement as he dramatically waved the bottle wildly.

"Sovereign!" Basbakan interrupted as he glanced over at the body. "We need to get you out of this room."

Eldorian King Warbel Eldor blinked as he attempted to comprehend. Shaking his head, no, he took another long drink then erupted into a sorrowful, unintelligible explanation.

Raising both hands in front of him the Eldorian Prime Minister interrupted again. "Sovereign, I'm going to send the guard away. You stay put. I'll be right back and we can get you out of here."

Warbel defeatedly lowered his head, then launched into a sorrowful ramble.

Opening the door barely enough for his pot-bellied frame to slip through, Basbakan slid into the hall and quickly closed it. As the latch clicked, Warbel spun back to his dead wife and began to sob.

He was about to raise the bottle when he heard the tapping. Swaying, he wheeled to the glass doors leading out to the balcony. Squinting, he focused on a small figure. It tapped once again, then backed up and lowered its cowl as it kneeled, hand out with palm open.

In the hazy fog of memory, he recognized the one-armed beggar girl from the streets around the palace. What in the name of the gods was she doing here?! He would have the insolent welp hung for trespassing.

He staggered to the glass doors and flung them open in drunken indignation. His full-throated admonishment was as unintelligible as the rest of his ramblings. The figure remained silently crouched — its only hand extended out in a pleading gesture past a simple tattered cloak.

Waving his hands so wildly it sloshed the pungent liquid out of the bottle, he continued his slurred rant at the trespassing beggar girl.

"So, you killed your wife tonight," came a deep and metered female voice from beneath the cowl.

The timbre and cadence penetrated the royal's intoxicated anger. He stopped his yelling and stared at the mysterious crouched figure.

"How does that make you feel?" the voice from beneath the cowl became hypnotic. "Guilt, sorrow…"

Warbel Eldor choked as a whimper escaped his lips. Peering back through the glass at his wife, his weeping gave way to wrenching sobs. The bottle tumbled from his hands shattering on the floor of the balcony.

The sloppy sovereign didn't see the beggar bound gracefully backwards out of her crouch. Her solitary arm gripped the bannister and she twirled upward. He felt her legs as they wrapped around his neck and locked. The king gagged and sputtered as she spun, pulling him off balance and launching him into the air and over the balcony. The sound of his own neck cracking was the last noise Warbel Eldor heard. His corpse plummeted out of sight, into the dense Kan fog, landing on the courtyard below with a dull thud.

Kai allowed her body to follow her victim's arc as it fell. She released it in time to attach herself to the wall below the balcony.

As screams echoed from the plaza below and out across the city of Rophan a one-armed figure scurried along the façade covering the castle walls, disappearing into the fog and shadows.

The destruction extended for miles. Prime, old growth conifer forest now lay broken and decaying. The old Yagur brushed away a tear which had fallen and inched its way down the orange fur on his snout, tickling his whiskers.

Inhaling deeply the musky aroma of the forest, the humanoid jaguar examined the trees on the perimeter of the devastation. His gaze settled on the blooms of golden mushrooms sprouting from the base of the trees around him.

The infection has begun here too, scraping away a layer of loam at his feet confirmed the shaman's assessment. Thin black tendrils connected the golden crowned parasites to their remote and growing host.

In the distance, a huge puff of what appeared to be smoke, accented by blue lightning, ascended quickly into the moonless sky and was carried away on the wind. He knew it wasn't smoke, but rather spores erupting from an immense growing mushroom field that would soon reach his location. At this rate it was inevitable, within a thousand grands the great northern forest of the Land of Mists would be overtaken by the massive fungi that was the Bel'-Vese Forest. Then, with no host to supply it with nutrients, it too would die, completing the circle.

A thin, delicate web of blue lightning raced across the windshield of the *Haraka* transforming the view from black, to a smoky white. Before any could cry out, the airship erupted from the cloud of spores, straight up into a starry sky.

Orich was prepared when he saw the lightning. Moving the wheel, he banked the ship in a gentle circle around the blighted area as Alto dry heaved in his seat.

"Nocturn!" Mal gasped, as she peered back in shock, first to Zau, then back to Orich. "Why the fuck are we still in Nocturn?!"

Shom stared impatiently at the back of the navigator's partially shaved head. "So much for your calculations!"

The female Singa sat forward staring into the distance, silently mouthing the numbers again. "No," she replied defensively, after brief contemplation. "My computations, I'm sure were correct."

"It would appear not!" the prodigal shot back.

"Alright you two!" Mal warned.

"Captain," Orich interrupted. "I believe Zau was correct in the course she set. No more than an instant before the lightning appeared in front of us, I felt an ever so slight flux in the ship."

163

Mal remained silent as she continued her inquisitive stare.

"Captain," the pilot continued. "I believe my brother had something to do with us being off course."

"Exactly what are you saying?" Shom's voice rose a register.

"For the most part my brother's essence lies sleeping in the hull," Orich explained. "We are separated while he sleeps but when he awakens, we partially connect automatically."

"Why does he keep fucking with us?" Mal asked.

The Bailian appeared doleful, "As I said before, my brother has changed."

"Oh lovely," Shom groaned. "So now we've got a ship that's trying to kill us!"

"No," Orich corrected. "If my brother wished us harm, he would simply divert us to the Middle Realms or fly us into a mountain."

"What's your brother's strategy?" Zaad asked from his seat.

Orich changed his scrutiny back to the windshield. "My initial guess would be he seeks to delay our return. However, I'm merely guessing."

"Kyopp," Mal called out. "Come see if you can spot where we are."

The Do-Tarr king sat up with an excited grin. "Yes captain!" He looked over at Shom next to him as he quickly got to his feet. "I just love saying that!" he beamed.

The blue-skinned humanoid bounded to the bridge and studied the terrain below. They were circling a massive field of large erupting mushroom buttons. To the east, was a strip of dead trees which led to a conifer forest which stretched to the horizon. To the west, beyond the erupting field was a jungle of towering mushrooms and fungi which also stretched out of sight.

Carefully, the glamoured bug king studied the terrain below. "Unless I'm mistaken, we are over the border of the

164

great northern forest and the gigantic mushrooms of the Bel'-Vese Forest."

Mal ogled the blossoming mushroom crowns below which regularly discharged thick clouds of spores. "How the fuck did we end up here?"

"Those spores must contain Flavian conducting properties," Zau offered.

Mal froze. A mischievous smirk played at her lips. "Impia!"

Zau's eyebrow's scrunched as she followed her captain's gaze. "Impia?"

Mal was almost beside herself as she rocked in her seat. "It's a mushroom from my home in Lumina. The spores are what Oldust is made from."

"Soshi?!" Shom blurted.

"You bet your ass!" the Spice Rat confirmed. "Except in the Spice Islands, they only grow a few inches tall. The little fuckers are also a real pain in the ass to collect because they tend to be found in really dangerous locations." Mal nodded around at the group for emphasis. "Now, here we are, circling over the biggest impia mushrooms this smuggler's ever seen, pumping out a shit ton of spores."

Shom, warily studied the all too familiar greedy demeanor in his friend. "Maluria…"

There was only the two of them left. Thankfully the *Raptor* only sustained minor damage in the passage to wherever this was. How long they had been there was anyone's guess. Without sun, moon or stars time was meaningless while up above, the blank grey sky gave no hint as to location.

Fia had seen signs of life — a pod of dolphins surfacing, agitated water where schools of fish were feeding and sails, always in the distance.

Now a current carried them along some unknown watery path. The two Rayth managed to adjust the sails to assist the watercourse in taking the *Raptor* to some distant or perhaps nonexistent location.

Fia was watching Blenda securing a rope on the main deck when the hairs on her arm stood straight up. The Hill Sister felt the tingling too. Both surveyed the area, searching for the source of the strange sensation.

A mile off the port bow the sea turbulently churned and swirled. As the diameter of the whirlpool increased, tendrils of blue lightning crackled upward into the featureless sky. The *Raptor* lurched as the wind increased and the ever-building swells flowed outward from the rotating vortex buffeting the ship.

The hole in the ocean was showing no signs of stopping its development, as larger waves were spun outward. Fia noted that they were being pushed away instead of being drawn in.

As a monster wave crashed into the port side of the ship Fia abandoned any idea of paralleling the disturbance. The vortex was growing faster than the *Raptor's* ability to outrun it. Fearing being either overtaken or overturned the Rayth commander spun the wheel to port, directly into the now stadium-sized aquatic cyclone. "Ease the sheets!" She screamed over at Blenda. Immediately, the burly Rayth rotated the two-handed crank and the sails began to slowly lower.

Wave after giant wave now crashed over the bow, spraying the decks and soaking the two mariners. With the sails partially lowered, the war ship made almost no progress toward the still growing turbulence and that was fine with

Fia. She had handled rough seas in the past but nothing like this.

Gripping the wheel, Fia felt the muscles in her arms and shoulders begin to seize in protest. She steadied herself for the giant white-tipped crest rushing their way with unforgiving abandon. It blasted over the bow in an explosion of water which almost cast Blenda overboard.

As the spray subsided, both Rayth stood mesmerized on the pitching sea sprayed decks. Rising from the whirlpool, the upper spires of a crystalline city came into view between the sheets of blue lightning. It continued to steadily rise as parapets, walls and finally a small patch of surrounding rocky ground rose above the angry sea. As the last of the island surfaced the wind and seas calmed.

Gentle ocean swells now lulled the Raptor toward the land mass and Blenda bolted up the stairs to Fia's side. The Hill Sister kept shifting her bewildered stare from the island to her commander.

"Admiral, what, what is it?"

There were four distinct levels to the towers of multicolored crystals. A lower circular tower slightly above the docks and two levels of buildings with no apparent windows or doors. There were no obvious signs of life.

Fia continued to stare at the floating city ignoring Blenda's troubled questions. Slowly, an air of recognition crept across her. "I thought it was just an old sea legend..."

"Admiral?"

"Konaleeta, the lost island," Fia proclaimed. "What's that Brightstar shanty?

Konaleeta straight ahead,
Give me hard to port instead,
That ghostly island
Will draw you in
And never will you
Be seen again."

"Admiral, we're going straight toward it!" Blenda's voice was strained.

Fia flexed her hands and stretched her shoulders before taking the wheel again. "I'm heading in that direction, it may be our only way out of here, wherever here is. One thing's for sure, it never stays anywhere for very long."

"Maluria, have you completely taken leave of your senses?"

"Not sure I take your meaning there Shommy."

"Don't give me that innocent look and don't call me that! You know very well what I'm talking about!"

Mal glanced away dismissively. "We'll only be on the ground a short while."

"Given our luck so far, those are famous last words," Shom protested. "This is an unnecessary risk!"

The Spice Rat shot a disappointed scowl at her friend. "Don't tell me you've gone soft on me? Are you aware how much potential money is laying on the ground down there?"

Zaad sat forward in his chair and leaned on Bowbreaker. "The funny little man may have a point captain."

"This isn't a debate," the airship commander proclaimed. "I'm getting as many of those damned spores as I can carry. Anyone that wants to help gets a full share."

This caused a thought-provoking murmur to pass around the cabin.

Kyopp perked up and excitedly shook Shom's shoulder. "I for one think it's a smashing idea!"

Shom sighed. "As long as we're going..." he said in a defeated voice.

"Don't worry Shommy," Mal consoled. "Since Taa is unavailable, you and Zau can stay with the ship."

Grumbling the prodigal sat back in his seat.

Shom's pouting always amused Mal. "Zaad, consolidate those gems back there and get us a bag. Orich find us a spot in the blighted area near those erupting 'shrooms."

"Yes, captain."

Nervously checking her uniform, captain Okawa veered to the right instead of her usual direction at the all too familiar intersection in the Zorian Forum. Her well-worn path to the left led to the office of her boss; Ambassador Joc' Valdur. The busy corridor she now traveled led to the main Forum and the various meeting rooms.

Briskly making her way through the bustling crowds of dignitaries, emissaries, and clerks she stopped in front of a wide door guarded by a Valdurian Marine. The seven-foot tall EEtah remained at attention as she smoothed her jumpsuit then knocked briskly. Without waiting for a reply, she entered.

The sweet, evergreen aroma of pipe tobacco was the first sensation to greet her as she closed the door. This immediately identified colonel Zekoff, who sat at the large table which dominated the room along with three other men. Her boss Joc' Valdur sat next to the commander of the city guards with an empty chair to his right. Across the table from them were two ambassadors of the other houses in the mutual defense pact. The scruffy Pierce Calden and the hulking Tate Whitmar sat silently. Both appeared grim.

Standing at the head of the table, obviously leading the discussion, was Zekoff's spymaster Rafel.

All eyes fell upon the tardy captain. She merely gave a slight nod of her head offering no apology or explanation

Joc' raised his hand and motioned to the chair beside him. "Okawa. Good, you're here." Everyone, this is my top security operative. Okawa, Captain Rafel was catching us up on recent events."

Taking her seat, everyone's attention returned to the Zorian spy chief. He stared down at the edge of the table he was leaning on. His long strands of black hair tumbled around him, obscuring his face.

When he started to speak, his voice was hollow and melancholy. "As you all probably are aware, three cycles ago..." Rafel's voice cracked and he paused briefly before composing himself. "Three cycles ago, Eldorian Ambassador Hoyt Eldor was killed in an apparent robbery."

All acknowledged the tragic event.

Rafel looked up. His eyes were sunken and swollen. "Last Kan, Warbel Eldor and Queen Imia also died in what appears to be a murder suicide."

The table burst into shocked, puzzled chatter.

"It appears, the king and queen were arguing. The king was quite drunk, He struck and killed her in a rage," Rafel continued over the waning jabber. "He then, in a fit of remorse, threw himself from his balcony into the royal courtyard, breaking his neck."

"Well don't that tear the tail off a yak!" Tate Whitmar said as he drummed his fingers restlessly on the table. "Who in the name of the gods is in charge over at House Eldor?"

"The prime minister is in temporary command while they sort things out," Rafel explained. "Reports are he's been running things anyway lately due to the sovereign's excessive drinking."

"That's a deadly coincidence," Pierce Calden said with a touch of suspicion in his tone. " So, the entire royal lineage of House Eldor met their demise in the course of three short cycles?"

"Not all," the spymaster corrected. "There's still the matter of Shom Eldor. He's still in the royal succession."

Joc' quickly covered his mouth as a snicker erupted.

Rafel regarded him curiously for the outburst. "Ambassador?"

"Sorry," Joc' said, quickly lowering his hand. "But if you knew Shom, that would probably be your reaction too. He's hardly the bureaucratic type. More like the drunken lecherous type. Right now, he's running with a crew on the *Haraka* operating under one of our loose charters."

"I ran into the *Haraka* recently over in Nocturn," Okawa offered. "He was there."

Tate leaned back in his chair stroking his chin quizzically. "What was going on in Nocturn?"

Okawa smiled slyly. "I'm sorry sir but I'm not at liberty to discuss that."

The Whitmar ambassador rocked forward laughing loudly. He smacked his fist on the table and pointed at the security operative. "By the gods, I like you little lady!"

Pierce Calden had yet to shed his skeptical demeanor. "I find it disturbingly convenient that the two top Eldorian leaders died so close to one another."

"That's certainly not unreasonable," Zekoff said as he fiddled with his pipe. "None of the baubles stolen off the ambassador have made their way into the city's pawn shops. This could be an indication of more nefarious intentions"

"Perpetrated by who?" Okawa found herself blurting out.

The old colonel chuckled as he lit his pipe. "The list is long and distinguished," he quipped. "Including some sitting at this very table, I'm sure."

The two ambassadors shifted about uncomfortably but remained silent.

Blowing a column of aromatic smoke in the general direction of the ceiling, Zekoff studied the people at the table. "The question is, who directly benefits from such actions?"

"Why House Aramos, of course," Rafel answered immediately. "And speaking of House Aramos and Nocturn — Stryder Aramos left unexpectedly for Immor-Onn last quinte. He was then observed leaving for Nocturn with a white tiger sentient. He returned to Zor two cycles ago and no one's seen him."

"Tiikeri," Okawa stated.

Rafel pushed his hair back. "I'm sorry?"

"The tiger people, they're called Tiikeri. From what I understand they're the controlling race over in the Land of Mists."

"You encountered them?" Rafel couldn't disguise the curiosity in his voice.

"Not directly..."

"You may speak freely captain," Joc' reassured. "We're all on the same side here."

Okawa cleared her throat. "My mission was to bring certain personnel to and then from the Land of Mists, to Immor-Onn. They had direct dealings with them."

Joc' sat forward, leaning his elbows on the table and noisily exhaled. "I'm afraid Ambassador Calden's wariness is rubbing off on me. It sounds like something is going on."

"An alliance with the Tiikeri?" Rafel posed.

"Maybe," Joc' replied. "One thing is for sure. With the Eldorian high command out of the way, life just got easier for anything House Aramos might want to attempt."

Tate doubtfully threw up his hands. "Then there's always the chance these were two coincidental deaths and we would be runnin' in circles trying ta' catch a whip tail."

"You may be right," the Valdurian ambassador conceded. "But in case things aren't so innocent, I think it would be wise to keep an eye on the situation."

All the participants mumbled in agreement.

Joc' peered around the table. "With the colonel and Captain Rafel's permission, I'd like to get Captain Okawa here to do some poking about and perhaps discover what's going on."

"A wise move," Zekoff complimented as he took another puff on his pipe.

"She would report directly to Captain Rafel or myself," Joc' clarified, "with authority to use whatever force deemed necessary by circumstances."

Once again, the table clattered in agreement.

The Valdurian royal addressed his security operative directly. "Captain, you'll be operating without official acknowledgment, permission, or protection from any of the houses present, so, no uniform. Do you understand?"

Okawa nodded grimly.

"You may need to get to Immor-Onn and other distant locals quickly as well. I'll need to assign you a pilot."

An illuminated grin slowly replaced the captain's dour disposition. "And I know just the pilot."

A few hundred yards from the steep, rocky shore the current carrying the pirate ship abruptly increased. The glittering battlements and towers of the lost city loomed rapidly closer over the bow and rigging. Completely raising the sails and attempting to bank proved fruitless as the *Raptor* was swept into Konaleeta's small harbor.

"We can't stop her in time!" Fia shouted from the bridge.

Blenda took in the rapidly approaching wharf. It contained a half a dozen empty slips protruding from a jetty. There was a large flat dockside area a few yards beyond. On either side of the receiving area were a wide staircase and ramp leading up to a large round building with battlements.

Up on the quarterdeck, Fia frantically searched for any possible way to stop the ship in time. They were practically on top of the harbor when she finally concluded that all options had been exhausted. Her heart sank as she screamed out to the Hill Sister. "Abandon ship!"

Blenda stared up at the bridge and her commander in disbelief.

"Jump!" Fia bellowed, as she climbed up on the railing.

Reluctantly, Blenda made her way over to the port side of the speeding vessel. When she saw her commander leap into the water the Rayth realized she wasn't kidding and followed her over the side.

Both heard the resounding crash of colliding structures and cracking wood while still submerged. The two surfaced in time to see their dreadnaught flagship smashing headlong into the extended stone jetty.

The Rayth treaded water in horrified silence as they saw the bow collapse in on itself, sending the foredeck and main mast toppling forward. By the time the ship ground to a halt, the *Raptor* lay impaled on a phallic outcropping of stone. The two individual docks on either side of the jetty had clipped the hull from halfway down the bow line, shearing the bottom of the ship to mid-keel.

When the last of the wood creaking subsided, a chilling silence descended. Blenda heard the wind whistling through the vacant streets. On the docks, metal latches on the rigging clattered against the pilings. In the distance, a whale's blowing drifted across the water. Both Rayth were breathing heavily. Still stunned by the crash, both began swimming toward the nearby harbor.

Chests heaving in exhaustion, they pulled themselves up on a nearby outcropping of boulders. All Fia was able to do was sit, panting and staring at her badly damaged ship.

"Goddess be damned!" Blenda cried out in frustration as she surveyed the wreckage.

Slowly, Fia's ragged breath returned to normal. Seeing her commander had no intention of getting up, Blenda sat on the hard stone beside her.

They remained silent for quite a while. Fia's stare never left the *Raptor*. Her expression hardened into a menacing scowl with each passing inspection. Blenda was becoming anxious and she fidgeted, hoping her commander might notice. Fia however refused to move.

Sensing she needed to do something she leaned over. "Admiral..."

"Don't call me that!" Fia snapped.

Blenda reeled in surprise as Fia slowly faced her.

"I'm not the admiral of anything," she stated in a defeated voice. "The Rayth are no more."

Blenda placed a comforting hand on her shoulder. "We can discuss our future at a later time. Right now, we should get off this wharf. The sound of that crash must have been heard all across this island. Who knows what it will attract?"

Fia resumed her morose vigil to the destroyed craft. "There's nobody on this fucking island but us," her voice was hollow and devoid of hope. "It's no more than a pile of rocks that bounces around the Annigan, picking up stragglers like us along the way, then casting them out into who knows where." She gave a sarcastic chuckle. "The stuff sea legends are made of."

Not thinking of anything to say, Blenda joined her former commander staring at their dreams of empire as it lay crushed on a solitary rock jetty.

Once again, they sat in silence until they heard the chanting. It came from deep within the city and moved parallel to them echoing dolefully through the empty, windswept streets.

Both Rayth's attention snapped toward the buildings as they followed the moaning chant which tracked from right to left in the distance.

Blenda slowly got to her feet. "Nobody?"

Mal peered out the windshield and double checked their location as the *Haraka* hovered a foot above the decaying forest floor. All throughout the surrounding blighted area, large patches of mushrooms of various sizes and colors bloomed. A half a mile to their left was the Great Northern Forest. It stood in direct contrast to the copious variety of fungi to their right, which led back to the Bel'-Vese Forest.

Satisfied the ship was secure, the Spice Rat briefed her crew. "Good job Orich, you're coming with us. I'm definitely going to need to be aware of what's going on out there. Shom, you and Zau stay with the ship. Take her up to a safe altitude and keep watch on us. Don't hesitate to pull our asses out of there if things get sticky. Got it?"

Both nodded weakly.

"Everybody else with me," she continued. "Zaad, you're in charge of the bag. Okay folks, let's work as a team and we can be on our way a whole lot richer."

Zau dropped the side hatch and the musky scent of rotting vegetation filled the cabin. Mal's nostrils flared as she hopped out onto the ground. Her feet sank several inches into the dead leaves and moss. As she stepped forward, the ground immediately rebounded to its original shape as if she had never been there.

When all disembarked, the *Haraka* ascended into the Nocturn skies leaving five sentients staring about, listening to the sounds of forest life surrounding them.

Orich stared briefly at the spongy soil below their feet. "It knows we are here," he said ominously.

Mal shot her pilot a concerned glance. "It? It what?"

"Captain, I'm detecting a vast interconnected network of fungi slightly below the ground. It is apparently spreading eastward as indicated by this growing blight."

The Bailian's explanation was interrupted by the sound of wood cracking behind them. Everyone spun in the direction of the rustling. Alto's hands hovered inches above his sword's hilts.

Five yards away, a small stand of fallen dead trees were being pushed upward and to the side as a red dome nudged through the eroding woodland.

Mal held her hand up for everyone to be still. "Orich, what've we got here?"

The albino stared intently as a red crown, atop a grey stalk a foot in diameter fully sprouted and continued to quickly grow. "A rapidly growing fungi bloom of some sort," Orich said as he inched closer. "I'm not receiving any hostile intentions. With your permission I'd like a closer look."

The buttoned stalk stopped growing when it reached four feet tall. Mal gave her pilot an anxious squint. "Just be careful. I don't need anything happening to you."

With an understanding nod, the Bailian moved toward the quickly growing object. He travelled only a few feet when the red dome flowered open. It was definitely a mushroom of some sort. The ribbed underside of the dome contained a light blue tint. The extended dome now revealed five small, lidless black eyes set into the upper stalk. The dark dots blinked curiously as they darted from side to side taking in the surroundings. From the center of the woody stalk five thin, foot-long appendages broke free at one end and slowly waved in the breeze.

Orich stopped and glanced back at the flabbergasted group for direction. "And now it sees us."

Noticing the group tense up, he gave a reassuring signal. "Captain, I'm still not detecting any ill intent, more like curiosity. I'd like to approach."

Mal paused as she weighed her pilot's request. "Alright, Alto…"

The swordmaster took a deep breath and joined the albino. As the two cautiously advanced, the creature's tendrils slowly waved in their direction. Orich noted Alto's sudden worried demeanor. "Sensory organs I believe."

Mal tautly stared at the two as they slowly progressed toward the mysterious fungi. A sudden shimmering to her right brought her attention to Kyopp who assumed his insectoid form. His fingers played with the end of his long-handled hammer. "Captain, the Bel'-Vese is unpredictable and completely self-serving," the Do-Tarr's normally jovial tone was now ominous. "I would suggest discretion."

"You heard him," Mal called out. "Watch your ass!"

Making his way in front of Alto, Orich crouched slightly, poring over the strange fungal entity. The arms slowly fluttered inches from his nose and each eye searched in a different direction. When one of the tendrils actually touched the Bailian's chin he shuddered slightly. Alto reached for his blades only to be stopped by Orich's outstretched hand.

The contact lasted only a few ellipses with three appendages gently brushing the albino's face. Alto stared intently at the interplay, on guard for the first hint of violence against his friend. He relaxed a bit when he saw a slight smile cross the Bailian.

When he straightened up, Orich looked back at the group. "It is as I suspected. This organism's primary function is a watcher."

The two rejoined the group. All were hanging on the pilot's words except Kyopp who scrutinized the surroundings with wary trepidation.

Orich gently caressed the locations on his face the tendrils had touched. "The mushroom forest beyond is not the entity, merely an extension. The controlling force lies in the vast network of fungi right below the surface."

"Is it dangerous?" Mal asked.

Orich's demeanor was matter-of-fact. "It's curious as to why we are here."

Mal chortled nervously. "What the fuck, as Shommy would say in this instance; I guess we *have* to tell the truth. Sell it."

The albino brought his attention back to the watcher. All of its eyes were trained on him. Silently, he indicated himself, then the group. He then pointed to the white, grapefruit sized pods lying about on the ground, then back to his companions.

Several ellipses passed before the ground rustled at various points close to them. Everyone formed a circle with Orich in the middle. Alto's thumb and forefinger flicked together above his etheria blades and Kyopp hefted his hammer.

Mal silently snapped her fingers just over the hilt of her sword, as throughout the immediate area larger brown domes began erupting from the dead and displaced vegetation. Immediately, the air was filled with the intense smell of damp earth.

The mushroom heads bloomed to a three-foot diameter the moment they cleared the terrain, revealing two very expressive eyes which darted wildly about.

"Everybody stay calm," Mal said in a low authoritative voice.

Directly below the eyes, all could see these living fungi had shoulders. Once enough of their arms were exposed, the stalks pulled themselves free and pushed their way out of the soil. Their torso was crude and woody with two legs. The stubby bottoms contained no feet, but rather thin tendrils, which connected them to the terrain they previously emerged from. They slowly flexed their arms and legs, easily pulling them from the soil. With a slow and plodding gate, they moved toward the apprehensive visitors.

Zaad set the sack beside him and absentmindedly played with Bowbreaker's hilt. "Perhaps the funny little man was right this time captain."

The moon had fallen over the Tiikeri port of Tan-Duu when Stryder and Ma-Tah returned to the opulent suite the dignitary had procured.

As No-Le closed the door behind them, the white tiger huffed in frustration. "You humans are a most stubborn lot! How is it you still cannot accept the things you have witnessed? You claim to be a man of numbers!"

Stryder nonchalantly unbuckled his sword belt. "I am a man of numbers, as is my whole family. It's only because you've failed to persuade me that this god of numbers you serve is responsible for anything." The quartermaster paused. "So, convince me."

Ma-Tah's face radiated with a satisfied glow at the challenge. He nodded at No-Le, who bowed and left.

"I don't need to convince you," he said confidently. "Pa-Waga will. The numbers will show you."

Walking over to a low desk below the room's only window, the man-tiger opened a drawer and took out a large sheet of paper. Holding it up to the light of a nearby crystal, he carefully examined it while his fingers tested its composition. "Well, it's not the quality I'm used to, but it will do."

Stryder curiously paid attention as the Tiikeri placed the sheet on a table beside a shallow bowl. "Do for what?"

Ma-Tah remained silent as Stryder stared in amused frustration. "How can it convince me if I already don't believe?"

The human's protest was interrupted by No-Le returning. In her arms was a small humanoid mawl. The two-foot-tall animal nuzzled the mongrel's neck affectionately, as its contented trill filled the room.

The quartermaster's gaze narrowed at the adorable bundle of fur in the mongrel's arms. To his dismay, No-Le walked up to him and extended her arms presenting the cheepa to him. The huge almond shaped eyes of the charming biped blinked innocently at a totally dispassionate human.

"I don't need a pet," Stryder said with a touch of irritation in his voice.

Ma-Tah motioned for him to accept the offering. "Belief is not important right now. Belief will come." The Tiikeri met the human's gaze and held it. "All that is needed now is a gesture of intent."

Stryder reached out and reluctantly took the cheepa which stared endearingly at him. No-Le immediately retrieved the bowl from the table.

The creature began to coo as it licked the quartermaster's hand. Ignoring the affectionate gesture, Stryder drew his dagger. He had witnessed the Tiikeri in such instances and assumed the actions needed.

When the tip of the blade pierced the cheepa's abdomen, Stryder's vision became slightly cloudy. He vaguely heard Ma-Tah chanting in the distance as he felt the fluids run the length of his wrist. Excitement began to stir in his loins, gravitating outward through his entire body. Chest heaving, Stryder watched as the angelic beast poured out its life blood into the bowl No-Le held up from her kneeling position in front of him. Its adoring eyes never left the quartermaster as it continued licking his hand and trilling until it slumped over limp in his firm grip.

Ma-Tah stopped chanting as No-Le stood reverently, holding the blood-filled bowl at arm's length. She crossed the room and placed the vessel on the table next to the sheet of paper. Without a word, the mongrel slave moved to a corner on the far side of the room where she discarded her tunic and knelt facing the wall.

Stryder's was flush with excitement as Ma-Tah extended a hand toward the desk. The Tiikeri was calm and confident. "Write."

Exuberance and apprehension played with the human as his gaze moved quickly from the Tiikeri to the table. "I, I don't know what to write."

Ma-Tah tried to remain calm but his expression bubbled with excitement. "Just write. There are only two characters. Pa-Waga will guide your hand."

Slowly moving over to the table, the quartermaster stared down apprehensively at the paper and bowl. After a brief contemplation he dipped his right forefinger into the bloody vessel. The Tiikeri held his breath as he witnessed Stryder make his first crimson glyph on the paper's surface.

The energy in the room continued to build as the human slowly etched the binary figures in a bloody line across the sheet. As he continued, his pace increased along with his breathing. Stryder's breath quickly became ragged as he now furiously scrawled, transferring the life essence of the cheepa onto the paper before him. As his crimson-stained finger reached the bottom of the page he stopped and stared at his work.

Panting furiously, the human finally peered over at the Tiikeri. Ma-Tah gave a knowing confirmation as Stryder, chest still heaving, leered diabolically.

"I, I...what happened?" the quartermaster said as he gulped for air. "I've never felt anything like that! The power, it was..."

"Intoxicating," Ma-Tah finished his thought.

Slowly the quartermaster gained his composure.

Both stared at Stryder's rampant erection through his pants. The Tiikeri chuckled. "Pa-Waga inevitably raises powerful passions."

Seemingly on cue No-Le rose and moved to the center of the room. Slipping down on all fours she arched her back and thrust her hind quarters lewdly into the air. Her tail twitched then flattened out against her back revealing her engorged lips.

Ma-Tah's voice became low and seductive. "No-Le will assist you as you share with her the majesty of Pa-Waga."

Without hesitation Stryder unbuckled his belt. Crossing the room over to the prostrate mawl he began to open the front of his pants. *A mighty god indeed.*

They traveled cautiously down the empty streets, Fia on one side and Blenda directly across. The road was apparently composed of pearl, making silent footfalls difficult. The two Rayth stared continually at the strange architecture as they progressed onward in the direction of the slowly moving chorus.

All the structures appeared to be made of solid crystals, each a different color. The shapes mimicked traditional stone buildings, but these contained no windows or doors. As the two crept between the monoliths they noticed the various-sized obelisks were extremely cold to the touch. Casting simultaneous glances along the street, each saw the other's confusion at the faux city.

As they drew closer to the chanting, the discordant tones caused each of the sisters to become jittery. Moving parallel, each unsuccessfully tried to get a glance at the source of the curiously haunting intonations.

Jerking her body in the sound's direction, Fia silently indicated she was going in for a closer inspection. Holding up her hand, she signaled for Blenda to stay in position.

A chill swept through the pirate queen as she flattened herself against one of the frigid walls and slowly crept forward. Arriving at an intersection identical to all the others, she cautiously peeked around the corner.

Moving in a straight line to her right, was a procession of six robed figures. Their bipedal bodies were almost translucent and gave off a slight bluish glow. Their heads were covered with domelike hats. Long scarfs circled their necks and crisscrossed their faces, covering their eyes.

Fia's gaze was fixed in amazement as the line approached a purple crystal edifice directly in front of them. Instead of veering away and staying on the street the mysterious monks marched directly at the solid wall. As the first one encountered the building's façade a glowing oval appeared in the same blue hue that emanated from the marchers. All paraded solemnly into the shimmering opening and their humanoid façade faded away, revealing a four-foot-tall oblong block of crystal which merged with the structure itself.

The column exited the other side in the same manner, first appearing as multi-colored blocks before assuming their prior form. Paying no attention to the voyeuristic humans, they entered another crystal edifice in the same manner.

Blenda anxiously stared at the back of Fia as she spied on the mysterious entities. Her hand flexed tensely on the hilt of her war hammer as she searched warily about. From behind, she suddenly heard more of the chanting. Spinning, she saw another line of monks exiting a structure only feet away. Keeping the line of advancing figures in sight, she bolted toward Fia. Sensing her approach, the senior Rayth placed a solitary finger over her lips.

The mariners were now surrounded as several more lines of chanting forms appeared. Both drew their weapons and stood silently with astonished expressions. Surrounding them, multiple lines of chanting acolytes moved in and out of the nearby structures. All morphed into a crystalline form with each passage.

Both the pirates felt a tingling from the wall they had been against, at the same time as the hair on their bodies stood up comically. The jolt that followed knocked Blenda to the ground. Her hammer clattering beside her was drowned out by the chanting only inches away. The Hill Sister Rayth looked up, gasping in shock as a portal had opened directly behind them.

The line of monks now exited the wall they had been leaning against. Their opaque forms were passing directly through Fia's body. The Rayth was frozen in shock with eyes bulbously opened wide and mouth agape in a silent scream. Her body jolted with each form that invaded her, but despite one trauma after another, she remained standing. When the last crystalline torso exited her body, Fia dropped to the ground unconscious.

Blenda scrambled over to her shipmate and friend. Fia was completely unresponsive as she stared blankly upward. Back across the street, her gaze followed the line of bodies as they disappeared into another building seemingly unaware of their effect on the comatose human.

The *Haraka* circled lazily over the blighted area between conflicting forests. Shom strained to see any details of the group below. "I say, could you hold this ship still for a few ellipses? A few is all I ask."

Zau scowled at the royal's irritated tone. "So, what? Now you're an expert on flying?"

"You really are quite disagreeable, aren't you?" the royal said as he spun in his chair to confront the Singa.

Zau's snout wrinkled as she stared past the spokes of the ship's wheel. "Looky here mister smarty pants!"

Shom huffed in frustration. "I am merely trying to get a look at my friends on the ground. It appears as if they've made some sort of contact!"

"I'm a navigator, not a pilot! Basic maneuvers are all I got. You think this is easy? You come back here and fly this thing!"

Shom scoffed in sarcastic amusement. "I've no intention of flying anything. That my dear, is your job. Now, I'm asking you to do your job and…"

The prodigal's voice trailed off as he observed Zau's mood go from irritation to concern.

"Uh oh," she said as her mouth dropped open.

"Uh oh? What do you mean 'uh oh?' I don't like 'uh oh' very much." The royal spun in his chair gaping back out the windshield. "What in the name of the gods is that?!"

Approaching rapidly from out of the darkness were twelve winged creatures. A quick gauge of their size put them at about seven feet tall. Their individual flight paths were erratic, rapidly banking and diving. As a group they were moving rapidly for the area on the ground occupied by his friends.

Zau stared intently at the advancing giant bats. "Ash-Ta."

"Ash what?"

"Ash-Ta, bat clans from the west." Zau's tone contained a hint of dread.

Shom gave an unnerved glance back at Zau. "Are they dangerous? Oh, what am I saying? Everything's dangerous over here!"

Zau ignored Shom's griping. "Less dangerous than some of them. By their size they appear to be the Acero clan. They're vegetarian."

Shom rapidly drummed his fingers on the dash as he watched the massive leathery wingspans draw closer. "Vegetarian. That doesn't sound so bad."

"Yeah, one problem though…"

Shom spun back again. The worried look asked the obvious question.

Zau banked the craft toward the group. "Kyopp's with them."

"So?"

"The Ash-Ta and Do-Tarr are natural enemies." She said as she started a decent. "The captain said come and get them if anything looked dangerous. I'd say this qualifies."

The air was thick with the smell of damp earth and wood. By Mal's count they were surrounded by twenty of the slowly ambling mushrooms. Now, all in the circle had drawn their weapons. Orich stood in the center, unarmed and studying the intriguing beings' halt barely out of sword range.

Mal's heart was pounding as she pointed her blade at the nearest fungal entity. "Everybody stay calm."

Slowly the walking mushroom took a step forward toward the Spice Rat with its hands raised. As Mal relaxed a bit, a crude woody arm pointed at the pods littering the ground, then back at her.

Orich leaned her way. "Captain, it seeks to confirm that you want some of the spores."

"It's why we're here," she said not taking her attention or weapon off the being.

The living mushroom silently moved its arms in a back and forth motion between the two.

Orich scrutinized the animated mushroom carefully as it communicated the fungal forest's demands. "It says the Bel'-Vese will gladly give up some of her children for a trade. Something of like value."

Mal's mouth opened in surprise, keeping her pilot in the corner of her gaze. "Trade?" She glanced back at the bulbous head which was staring at her with an expectant pose. "What the fuck do we have to trade?"

The mushrooms eyes took on an amused twinkle as it pointed toward Zaad.

The albino's tone dropped an octave. "The Bel'-Vese wants the EEtah."

Mal was genuinely taken aback. "Are you fucking kidding me?!"

Zaad waved Bowbreaker menacingly in front of him. "Me?"

The fungal diplomat and Orich traded a lingering glance.

"You wish some of its children," Orich said in a solemn voice. "It demands a suitable trade."

"What in the name of the gods do they want with me?!" Zaad bellowed.

"Apparently, there is something in your aquatic makeup that is good for the growth of some of the various fungi of the forest." The Bailian shifted in trepidation. "Fertilizer."

The EEtah's deafening roar of laughter reverberated off the forest in either direction. "Fertilizer huh? Well it's gonna cost ya more than a few pods!"

Raising Bowbreaker he brought it in a wide arc, heaving a path of destruction across the three mushrooms that were in front of him. The first virtually exploded from the force of impact. The others were cleaved violently in half, their legs falling as their tops were propelled onto the decaying area.

With a resounding howl from Defari, Alto's blades were already a blur beside him. Mal noticed more mushroom men erupting from the ground all around them. Raising her sword in the air to signal the *Haraka* she dropped it in front of her severing the cap of the fungi that had been communicating with them. "Okay, this is not what I had in mind!"

The fungal army kept advancing as new members were added to their ranks. Mal gave a quick glance skyward. "Come on you guys," she grumbled uneasily as she surgically sliced through another with its arms reaching out for her.

The sound of combat was suddenly overshadowed by loud screeches. All gazed upward to see large humanoid bats swooping and diving toward them.

Kyopp had finished a massive swing of his hammer. It pulped several attackers when he caught sight of the undulating wings almost on top of them. "Ash-Ta! They're probably upset because of me."

Shom frantically pointed out the windshield. "A signal. Did you see it?! She signaled us!"

Zau was alert but calm as she cautiously adjusted the wheel. "Look, I see it. Shut up, you're making me nervous."

By now the flock of bats were swirling about frantically over the group. Shom now also saw dozens of walking mushrooms closing in on his friends.

"Will you hurry up!" he said in a distraught tone.

"Any faster and I'm gonna crash this thing!"

Shom's mind desperately searched for an idea. "You can open the bottom bay doors and come in on top of them. I've seen Orich do it."

Zau shook her head incredulously. "I don't know how to do that!"

"Are you kidding me?!"

The Singa maneuvered the wheel to avoid colliding with the enraged Ash-Ta.

"Looky here mister helper, I told you, I'm a navigator not a pilot!"

Any further protest was silenced by a loud thump on the windshield. Crying out in surprise, a stunned Shom was met with a large snarling bat attempting to hold on. Its long blunt teeth clattered against the glass causing opaque swaths of slimy drool to paint the window.

"See? See! Now you've done it! You've distracted me and now this!" Zau said defiantly as she jerked the wheel to the right.

The Ash-Ta was thrown from the front of the ship as Shom was pitched to the deck.

It didn't take long for the prodigal to regain his footing.

"You did that on purpose!"

Zau gave a wink. "You bet! And our hitchhiking friend is gone too. Now I'm going to try and get this thing as close as I can to the captain."

Shom fretfully ran his hand through his hair. He scrutinized the sky, alive with human sized man-bats and assailing giant mushrooms on the ground.

"Have you ever even landed one of these?"

Zau gave a sarcastic grunt.

"Are you kidding? Up until a few cycles ago, I'd only heard about them."

Six mushroom bodies exploded as Bowbreaker cut a destructive swath across their ranks. Their broken, fibrous shafts littered the ground around the enraged EEtah. As a dozen more made their slow advance toward him, he heard a screech and ducked as a human sized man-bat swooped narrowly above him. Swinging his massive sword upward he missed. The Ash-Ta ignored Zaad and dove toward Kyopp.

A penetrating squeal resonated over the area as the Do-Tarr's hammer struck center mass on the bat before it landed. It doubled over and dropped like a rock on two mushroom men who were almost upon him.

As the *Haraka* neared the ground, Shom was incredulous. "You call this close?! We're at least thirty yards away!"

"You think you could do better mister critic you come on over here and give it a shot!" Zau said defensively, as she accidently bounced the bottom of the ship off the ground. With another try she gained control, holding it a few inches over the ground. "See what you made me do!" The Singa paused, assessing the rows of levers to her right. Choosing one, the front pincers clicked together. "Okay, how do you open the damn door?!"

With a frustrated sigh, the prodigal threw the lever by the side hatch. As the ramp lowered, the sound of arms clashing and Ash-Ta's screams filled the cabin.

Zaad moved over so he was standing behind Kyopp. "We gotta get to the ship!" The Do-Tarr nodded in agreement and the two slowly made their way to the airship fighting back to back.

Sprinting, Mal and Alto were behind Orich who was bounding over a field of large flat fungi carpeting the ground. Both swordmaster and captain kept their weapons up, but it appeared the assaulting Ash-Ta were only interested in the EEtah and Do-Tarr.

Mal had taken a swing at an Ash-Ta that had gotten too close when she heard a whooshing sound behind her. Back in the direction of the ship, she saw Orich enveloped in a cloud of spores as he toppled to the ground.

"Alto!" Mal screamed.

"Cover me," Alto said, as he sheathed his weapons and picked up the unconscious albino.

Shom met them at the ramp. The swordmaster handed the limp pilot over to the Prodigal. Mal then assessed the combat slowly advancing in their direction.

Zaad and Kyopp were halfway across the fungi field when another blast of spores enveloped the duo. Zaad teetered then dropped as Kyopp continued swinging away at the attacks from the air.

As Shom and Mal carried Orich into the ship Alto observed mushroom men beginning to spring from the ground beside them. A massive irregularly shaped fungi also erupted right beside the prone EEtah. The mushroom shot up with amazing speed to ten feet. From under the crown it then released a dense white net covering the immediate area, entrapping them both.

Kyopp was now pounding on the fungal webbing to no avail. The dense fibrous material bent and shook but remained intact. The Ash-Ta, now realizing their enemy was trapped, swooped lower to the ground. Five landed and were making their way over to the caged pair in short hops. The three mushroom men had almost completely emerged out of the ground when Alto charged.

The swordmaster drew both long and short the instant he reached the now fully formed mushroom minions. They had taken their first steps toward the cage when Alto's long sword swept through them with Defari's baying howl. The stalks toppled silently to the ground, cleanly severed in two. Running his short sword vertically down the cage he created an opening on the opposite side of the approaching man-bats.

"Can you get Zaad to the ship?!" Alto asked as he saw an Ash-Ta hop out of the cage then toward him.

Wordlessly the Do-Tarr king easily hefted the burly man-shark and took off running at an astounding speed. Alto had no time to marvel at Kyopp's abilities as two angrily chattering Ash-Ta leapt at him.

Dodging to the side, he simultaneously slashed out with a yowling Defari, severing the wing of the one closest to him. The other spun to find the swordmaster's blade pointed inches from its throat, a menacing growl emanating from the tip. The bat clansman froze, fearfully eyeing the snarling blade as his companion with the severed wing rolled on the ground wailing in agony. The remaining three were hopping over toward him while the ones still airborne swooped and screeched.

Alto solemnly took in the approaching Ash-Ta. "Cease this attack and retreat or this one meets the same fate!" He said in a commanding tone. The group paused, assuring the swordmaster they understood.

"You are friend of the Do-Tarr," the closest one screeched.

Alto remained grimly calm. "My travelling companions are none of your concern. Now I will tell you a second time, desist or perish!"

The Ash-Ta hissed and was about to jump closer when Alto plunged the tip of the snarling etheria blade through and out the back of the bat. Its spinal cord severed the Ash-Ta immediately dropped. As it screamed out in pain the swordmaster bolted for the ship.

He was certain he could outrun the ones on the ground. It was the ones in the air that proved more problematic. One landed in front of him right before the ramp and hissed as it prepared to lunge.

With no time to stop, Alto crossed his blades in front of his chest and did a diving roll directly at the Ash-Ta. As he came up, he slashed out with both swords in an X pattern, quartering the bat. The gruesome sections of flesh toppled to the sides of the ramp drenching it in gore. The swordmaster raced into the ship showered in the flying remains.

The nine remaining Ash-Ta furiously assaulted the *Haraka*, pounding fruitlessly on the hull.

Shom closed the hatch and leaned wearily against the barrier breathing heavily. "Alright, what do we do now?"

Mal skittishly scanned out the windshield as enraged mushrooms and bats violently attempted to breech the airship. "Zau, I'll take the wheel. See if you can find us a portal."

"I've already checked. There's nothing close," the Singa said with authority. "I can open one, but a portal large enough to move this ship would knock me out."

Mal sighed rejecting the idea. "No. My pilot's useless. I can't have both of you out of commission."

"Captain resume a westward course," Kyopp said as he morphed into his Bailian form. "They won't follow."

"How do you know that?!" Shom asked with a touch of optimism.

"First, they were only coming to feed. I just happened to be there. They're hungry and this clan doesn't eat flesh. Secondly, we're going to be crossing Ash-Ta clan borders. Believe me, if one clan is in another's air space uninvited, we'll be forgotten because they are going to want to fight each other."

Mal took over the wheel. "What the fuck. It's worth a try."

The *Haraka* lifted off and sped west as angry winged creatures swirled, circling the escaping craft. After a few miles, the frustrated attackers stopped and retreated back to the Bel'-Vese.

"Looks like you were right Your Majesty," Mal said, the sound of relief evident in her voice.

"My people only call a few races enemies and we understand them well," the king said smugly. "And please, call me Kyopp."

Mal smiled as she handed the helm back to Zau and wearily lowered herself into the captain's chair.

Shom was settling into his seat when he leered over at his friend. "So Maluria, I hope we've learned a valuable lesson here about greed?"

Forgetting her fatigue, the Spice Rat was on her feet confronting the royal. "You're fucking lecturing me on greed?!"

Shom appeared astonished. "Surely you must realize that you put all our lives in danger, and we came away with nothing."

Mal was about to react to Shom's admonishment when Alto slipped over to her.

"Perhaps not completely empty handed," he said grinning as he reached inside his robes and pulled out a spore pod the size of a grapefruit. "A little something I picked up along the way," he said with a grin as he awarded it to Mal.

The Spice Rat's mood changed instantly from combative to delighted. Her eyes lit up as she accepted the offer with a broad grin. "I knew I loved you for a reason," she said jubilantly before grabbing the swordmaster and passionately kissing him. As his lips slightly parted, Mal stopped suddenly, recognizing she had inadvertently admitted something long unsaid.

After a few ellipses of stunned silence, Shom noisily cleared his throat. "I'm sorry what did you say?"

The two broke slowly from the kiss. The airship captain's expression resembled a child caught stealing candy. "What?" she said innocently.

Kyopp, ignorant of the group dynamic, appeared confused. "What?"

"What?!" Mal's tone was insistent and a touch embarrassed.

"Oh, by the gods Maluria, we all heard it!"

"I don't know what you're talking about Shommy," Mal taunted coyly.

Shom shook his head and gave a frustrated sigh. Zau stared forward out the windshield as she silently guided the craft, sympathetically grinning for her new friend.

Brother Pameten had not come out of his office for two cycles now and the rest of the scribes were growing worried. The Cali Master and chief Marassa had cloistered himself away immediately upon his return from the main library at the University of Marassa in Zor. He had issued strict orders not to be disturbed to the extent of having his meals delivered. The book he brought back needed to be studied.

Now as the Kan lifted on cycle number three, brothers Nadseny and Murrisch trudged through the narrow, congested inner city streets of the Ndani Tract in central Rophan.

"It's not right," Murrisch said as the wheel from a passing cart splattered the hem of his robes. "Why can't our temple and library be located in a better tract?"

Nadseny grunted, pulling his robes tighter against the chilly wind. "Because the name of the god we serve isn't Toma."

"You would think with your family connections," Murrisch grumbled under his breath.

The pair rounded the corner filled with noisy vendors and heavy street traffic. They slowly approached the largest building in the impoverished neighborhood of the Eldorian capital city.

There as always, standing guard by the front doors, was the EEtah Tlata. The ten-foot-tall sentry had been with them for several grands and with the light duty, was getting a bit pudgy. His face was a mask of pure delight as he munched gleefully on a fish provided by the newest scribe, brother Adisi. The young man was regaling the guard with a recounting of some minor incident. The EEtah was clearly not listening as it greedily devoured its morning meal. The young scribe balanced a sizeable stack of papers in his hands atop which, perched precariously, was the Cali Master's breakfast.

Nadseny's and Murrisch's stomachs grumbled at the drifting aroma of spiced porridge. Both hungry scribes ironically valued the meal he carried more than the copious ramblings of Eldorian nobles they would inevitably need to copy. Unfortunately, their solitary meal was not until midcycle.

Seeing the senior scribes' approach, brother Adisi paused. "Good morning brothers!" he said in an overly cheerful chirp. "I hope you slept well."

"Well enough," Murrisch said fighting a wave of irritation at Adisi's enthusiasm.

All three nodded greetings to Tlata as they entered. The portly EEtah absentmindedly waved them into the modest double doors in between bites. Respectfully, the junior scribe followed his superiors through the entrance to the scriptorium.

"Brothers," Adisi pleaded as he stepped across the threshold. "Would one of you take this stack of papers. I've got to deliver brother Pameten's breakfast before it gets cold.

"Thank you brother Adisi," came a weary, yet confident voice from the far end of the room.

All three scribes stared in surprise down the twin rows of desks, inkwells and stools to Pamaten's now open door. The exhausted Marassa stood in front of it, arms folded. He weakly nodded at Adisi. "Please put it on my desk."

As the junior scribe rapidly obeyed the Marassa's order, the leader's gaze focused on Nadseny and Murrisch. "Find brother Falta. We meet within the deci."

Assembling the scribes was accomplished quickly. They met in Pameten's office with the door secured. Even though the chamber pot had been carried away, the room reeked from three cycles of being closed off.

Murmured suspicions of the meeting's nature swept amidst the various scribes as they arrived for work. Most could guess. The prime minister had called an emergency Marassian genealogy council. A new sovereign for House Eldor must be named.

Pameten stared out from behind his desk at the three Marassas under his charge. Directly in front of the Cali Master on the desk was a large open book. The very tome he procured in his emergency trip to Zor and to the main library, the Marassian Calisma.

"Brothers," he began. "We enter an unknown era. No doubt the goddess' wisdom will lead us with her flame of truth."

The statement caused a murmur to erupt among the monk scribes of the fire goddess Milo.

"This is because of the deaths of the sovereign and his brother, isn't it?" Nadseny said as he leaned forward excitedly in his chair.

Pameten studied the scribes intently staring at him. "As you are aware, this council was convened at the direction of the Prime Minister. Unfortunately, the list of successors to the throne is murky." The lead librarian indicated the open book in front of him. "Because of this political ambiguity I was authorized to borrow and consult the Zauvek Eldor."

All three monks leaned in for a closer inspection. This was unprecedented, for the grand tome of Eldorian lore, traditions and history never left the Calisma in the high holy city of Zor. Access there was only granted to high Eldorian scholars. As with every book or scroll loaned out from the Calisma to the individual Calis, the borrower guaranteed its return with their life.

"What guidance did it offer?" Nadseny innocently asked.

Pameten sighed loudly and sat back in his chair. "I've been sorting through this whole mess. Traditions go back thousands of grands."

Murrisch anxiously rubbed his hands together, "And?"

The Cali Master remained wary. "The inevitable decision everyone thought would be political chaos, is actually quite cut and dry."

Nadseny appeared perplexed. "Sir?"

Pameten blinked thoughtfully over his desk at three very different yet inquisitive scholars. "Put quite simply, the way I read it, the sovereign's decree of three grands ago that banished Shom Eldor, violated Eldorian grand tradition and is null and void."

Nadseny gasped, "That means…"

"Exactly, Shom Eldor, is the legal — by every recorded family tradition — rightful successor to the Eldorian throne," the Cali librarian grimly acknowledged.

A few ellipses of astonished silence were abruptly punctuated by Murrisch scoffing loudly, "Preposterous! Shom Eldor is a libertine and one degree removed from being called a traitor to the house!"

In a rare display of emotion, Pameten, shrugged and threw his hands up in resignation. "The book is open," he said. "You all know how long I've been going over it. I encourage all of you to read the relevant passages. I really don't think there's a choice."

Murrisch's eyes narrowed. "We shall see."

The Cali Master regarded the only brother who had not spoken. "Brother Falta, you are a well renowned law scribe. What do you make of all this?"

The middle-aged man with greying temples stared thoughtfully at the open book. "I can provide no opinion until I read the text. I think it safe to say my wife and child are going to see a lot less of me in the coming cycles."

Pameten gave a sympathetic chuckle. "Quorum committee rules apply here and, in this instance, couldn't carry more weight. You learned brothers must agree by majority. I am merely a guide and arbitrator and am ineligible to vote."

All signified their understanding.

The leader's mood suddenly brightened. "I do come with a bit of good news."

The solemn air was broken, and all bristled with anticipation. Pameten leaned forward on his desk. His enthusiastic expression was contagious. "I've secured permission to copy the Zauvek Eldor for our Cali!"

Exuberant accolades immediately bubbled about the room at the news.

"We only have one quinte to complete it," Pameten said, his tone blanketing the effervescence. "So, that means you three need to review it and make a ruling quickly. Then all current projects are to be put on hold. Copying this tome will receive top priority."

All nodded in agreement.

The group stood to leave and Falta touched the open page. "With your permission I'd like to get a look at it first."

He arrived near the end of the first act, wincing at the pungent smell of body fluids the instant he stepped inside the ornate doors.

So, this is the Prazer Teatro. Talk about your weird assignments.

There on the stage, a middle-aged woman with outrageously large breasts knelt provocatively. The skinny young man with badly pock-marked skin, wielding a penis of astounding proportions and rigidity, stood directly in front of her. His head was thrown back in the deliria of ecstasy.

The enthusiastic, near riotous crowd was howling and clapping as the ascetically challenged youth pumped furiously between the woman's well-oiled matronly mounds of flesh.

Peligro de Aris ran his hand across his bald head and chuckled. *Damn kid. How'd ya get this gig?*

Standing in the aisle next to stage left, he watched most of the preparations going on backstage.

She was there, casually tuning her lute.

Not half bad looking, he assessed. *No wonder she's a hit.*

In his five grands as an Aramos Black Talon, Peligro had experienced some extremely weird and dangerous incidents, but the axioms were right: *Your first visit to the Prazer Teatro will always stick with you.*

Centrally located between the merchant and inner-city tracts of Rophan, this pleasure theatre was wildly popular. He had been assigned to the Eldorian capital city for two grands now and for some reason had never visited.

Peligro was feeling a little reluctant as he felt the folio under his coat. This was hardly a typical assignment; it did however come directly from the top.

I never leaned on a musician before.

According to his briefing she was hardly an average musician. Her particular type of bard supposedly had special abilities. No matter, he had his orders.

The crowd exploding in appreciation brought his attention back to the stage. Hooting, screams and stomping lauding the young man who was ejaculating like a geyser, covering everything close in a shower of white liquid. The thunderous crowd slowly subsided and the two saturated performers bowed and retreated backstage. Some in the crowd got up and started for the exits.

The Aramos agent saw that the intermission team was about to take the stage. *Three outer clan EEtah and six naked humans. Looks like a party!*

She led the procession. The initial chord from her lute filled the theater as she leapt onto the stage. In the audience, the effect of the music was evident. The tide of those leaving quickly subsided and most retained their seats, groping in their pockets for the next act's payment.

Now Peligro realized why he had never visited. The three dancing EEtahs were ridiculous, but it was the six humans impaled on their bent, upraised arms which was truly shocking. The tune she played and sang was humorously bawdy dealing with anal sex and all on stage sang along.

A quick scan backstage revealed the next act. Mistress Shima, a human Kinjuto Dominator, had three Cul-Ta rat creatures securely bound to a cross.

Yeah, I don't want to know...

The intermission act danced off the stage and the humans dismounted from their impaling. Making his way around several horny, rowdy groups the Aramos agent slipped backstage.

Once out of the public eye the speed in which the actors shed their stage persona amazed Peligro. All participants scattered back to their everyday lives the instant the next act took to the stage.

The lute player lingered to retune her instrument. Golden locks tumbled forward, framing aged wood as she listened intently.

"You play well," Peligro said as he nonchalantly approached.

The young woman glanced warily at him but said nothing. The clean shaven, well-dressed man halted a few feet away. Looking back at her instrument she continued her tuning.

Peligro sighed,

Aww, come on ya stupid fucking quim. Don't make this hard on both of us! The Aramos agent cleared his throat loudly.

"If I can have a moment of your time Mz..."

Stopping again she glanced up with a bored, slightly irritated expression. "They call me Sabini, and it seems like you already do."

Peligro's annoyed smirk was transparent and the bard gave an overtly manufactured grin.

"I carry a very generous offer for your services," the Aramos operative said calmly in an attempt to keep the meeting professional.

The young lady hoarsely scoffed then returned her attention to her instrument. "I'm under contract with this place for the next grand."

"That will not be an issue," the Aramos agent said. Reaching over he touched her shoulder in an attempt to show sincerity.

The moment his hand made contact she plucked a single note.

The blast of pain erupted from behind Peligro's ears and stormed across his skull. The seasoned agent staggered as he gripped the sides of his head. His vision severely blurred as he valiantly attempted to stay on his feet.

Thankfully, the agony was brief. A sweating, tearful Peligro teetered as his vision cleared.

The freckle-faced young lady was plainly unintimidated as her green eyes stared directly at him. In her hands, the lute was ready to play again. "The same note four frets up and your head explodes."

Fucking Boustian! Now his orders made sense.

The Aramos agent placatingly held up his hands.

Okay soldier, now you know why you pulled this gig.

Forcing himself to stand upright Peligro smiled wearily, his expression admitting defeat. "Let's start again, please? My name is Peligro. I represent a wealthy patron who has written some innovative songs and is convinced you are the one to perform them."

Drip,
drip,
drip...

The droplets striking the floor shattered the silence of the near empty room.

Something is wrong. Stryder Aramos sat cross-legged on the cold stone facing the far corner. The two adjoining walls were filled to the ceiling with crimson binary fields of X's and I's.

In the opposite corner, the body of an eight-grand-old street urchin was suspended upside down, her life blood all but expended. By the door was the orb filled with the Chenoan gems.

Drip,
drip,
drip...

Stryder now regretted killing the young girl. Not for moral reasons, but rather her small frail body hadn't contained nearly enough blood for his use. This was new to him and he vowed to pick up the nuances eventually.

These numbers make no sense, he grumbled to himself.

Waves of frustration sent his gaze sweeping back and forth along the glyph-covered walls. Shouting in frustration, the quartermaster and newest acolyte to Pa-Waga searched his recent recollections.

They had returned to Immor-Onn five lunas ago under cover of the moon-less. Ma-Tah went back to his duties as finance minister. Stryder decided to remain anonymous while his cousin secured him a vedette boat home to Zor. The quartermaster set up temporary quarters in the ever-shrinking available regions of the city.

Once again inspecting the walls, he scowled at the nonsense he had written. Nothing came to mind which would cause this, this…aberration.

A winter gust swept through the streets of the Bailian empire's capital sending the windchimes above the thoroughfares clattering melodically. Stryder heard them just outside. Snorting, he chastised himself for being distracted by something so blatantly banal.

He was about to dismiss the thought entirely when he was hit with a flash of recollection.

Wait, something's different!

The windchimes, those jangling irritants that he attempted to dismiss as background noise, were, different…more melodic.

That's it! By the sacred numbers the reports are true.

The pearl god reawakened, the one that should not be, had somehow made it here, to Immor-Onn.

Stryder erupted in maniacal laughter as he realized that this was the warning given to Ma-Tah on the burning stump in the Land of Mists.

But was this possibly affecting his master's written revelations to him? How could it be that powerful?

Staring at the two walls full of meaningless strings of numbers, he felt his anger and frustration rising.

Surely this is a result of those damnable windchimes. He rationalized. *Yes, yes, that must be it! Concentration is impossible!*

His breath became more labored as he lamented over his failed masterpiece.

I serve a powerful god. I refuse to believe an ancient pearl and a fairy tale queen can prevail!

Outside the wind gusted. The chimes loudly collided causing Stryder to pause. He gasped in surprise as the glyphs on the wall started to melt. The individual numbers streamed down the stone surface becoming sheets of blood cascading to the floor. The crimson liquid flowed onto the ground, surrounding the seated quartermaster in a shallow sea of the sticky liquid. It stained his naked legs, and groin as it swirled around him.

Stryder's laughter became more maniacal as he pounded on the ground before him sending oval splashes of blood into the air. The scope of his adversary had been revealed.

"You reveal yourself," he screamed at the ceiling. "You may keep me from my master's words here in this place…"

Stryder's demeanor became childlike as he swirled his fingers in the pool of blood surrounding him.

Despite your trickery I have prevailed. I know who you are!

In a sudden outburst he pointed upwards into space. Spittle sprayed from his mouth as he screamed at the ceiling. "I prevail!"

"I know who you are!

"I know who you are!"

A profound sense of loneliness swept over Blenda as she stared at the gray featureless sky. Her only companion Fia, was still unconscious and the Hill Sister's gaze settled on her prone form. She had managed to carry her back to the *Raptor,* barely missing streams of parading monks which steadily increased.

The quarterdeck was damaged but habitable and there were food stores in aft compartments, but for how long would they hold out? The bow and one third of the ship were totally destroyed, smashed on the rock jetty. Realizing they were stranded in some far-flung location in the multiverse, amplified her feeling of isolation.

Fia had stirred a few times since they arrived. She mumbled some unintelligible words, then laughed hysterically before drifting back into unconsciousness.

The chanting was now coming from all over the crystal city. Blenda saw multiple lines of monks passing between and through buildings. She was relieved none came near the docks.

Fia's twitching brought the Hill Sister's attention back. Blenda kneeled over her in case she needed to be steadied. As usual the ramblings started when Fia rocked from side to side. Sweat poured off Blenda as she held her admiral's hands, listening for anything she might understand.

The babbling lasted longer this time but ended abruptly, replaced with a low hum. Finally, Fia awoke with a start and began to laugh. Blenda happily gasped as she gripped her hands tighter. "Are you alright?"

Fia abruptly stopped laughing when the question was asked and blankly glanced up at her first mate. "It's so simple," she said in a low hoarse voice.

Blenda's next intonation was more forceful. "Are you alright?!"

Fia weakly nodded yes, then returned Blenda's grip. "I saw…"

"Saw?! Saw what?"

The pirate queen's vision shifted wildly back and forth as if she were taking in an invisible performance.

"The new lords of the Annigan grow impatient."

Blenda was confused. "You mean like Morax and the Chenoans he told us about?"

Fia gave a weak laugh.

"The Chenoans are pawns and Morax, with his revolution, are fools of the pawns."

"Admiral, I don't understand."

Fia stared obstinately at Blenda. "I asked you not to call me that. My name is Fia. The Rayth are no more."

The Hill Sister swallowed hard at the confession issued from her commander's own lips.

Fia sadly shook her head. "The Black Mural teeters!" Coughing, she focused back on a rattled but attentive Blenda. "...and we've been playing along like fools!" She started coughing again and it converted into a choking laugh.

Blenda noticed Fia's eyes were wild and erratic.

"What've those things done to you?!"

Fia stopped laughing. "Lifted the blinders," she said in a hoarse whisper.

The Hill Sister was still contemplating her friends' latest statement, when the chanting abruptly stopped.

Blenda quickly spun and Fia gasped when she propped herself up on her elbows.

The entire dock area was filled with monks. They stood silently, staring at the *Raptor*.

Blenda scowled as she reached for her war hammer. "I've had it with their tricks!"

"It's almost time," Fia said in an optimistic tone. "It won't be long now."

"By the goddess I'm going to get some answers!" Blenda said standing.

"No!" Fia weakly pleaded.

Unable to stand, the former Rayth could only watch and cry out, as the Hill Sister shook her hammer and cursed at the crowd surrounding them.

The group of mysterious monks remained unresponsive as Blenda leapt from the jetty into their midst, shrieking obscenities.

Fia screamed as loud as her physical strength would allow, to no avail. The last memory of her loyal Rayth sister was a scene of docile monks surrounding Blenda and obscuring her from view.

"It's time!" Fia yelled, falling back onto the deck in exhaustion. Once again falling in and out of consciousness, she felt the tingling and shifting surges of power beneath her.

The last sensation Fia was aware of before completely succumbing to the darkness, was the sound of the *Raptor* being torn off the jetty. The lost island of Konaleeta sank beneath the waves in the same manner it had arrived. In an explosion of blue lightning it gated out of the Endless Ocean Plain of the Middle Realms.

The northern docks in the high holy city of Zor cater to a slightly more upscale crowd than their southern counterpart. This is especially reflective in their drinking establishments. One was less likely to find trouble in the dozen pubs and taverns, however, the wise visitor always observed caution. The largest bar of the northern docks, was not on the wharf proper, but rather a few streets in. The Nuna Pub was constantly busy, but the early Kan was always the most hectic.

As the Turine in the harbor rang seven bells, the thick Kan fog was already pervasive throughout the city. Captain Okawa stepped inside the pub's warm boisterous interior. As she unbuttoned her coat and scanned the crowded room, many broke from their conversations and revelry to stare. There was good reason for the men to leer and women sneer. The Valdurian captain appeared radically different than she did in her uniform. The simple yet form fitting blue dress clung to the voluptuous, statuesque woman. By far the most striking feature was her thick, silky brown hair that flowed past her shoulders and gently swayed as she made her way across the room.

Ignoring lecherous stares and comments, she followed the sound of a distinct male voice, which was unfortunately at the time, singing.

Slipping gracefully past a cluster of patrons, she peered down the massively long bar, billed as the longest in Zor. Midway, Demetrius, along with three disheveled sailors were belting out a bawdy tune at the top of their lungs. She chuckled slightly when she realized the airship pilot was not singing any of the dirty words.

Coming up on the drunken quartet, Demetrius perked up when he saw her.

Thankfully the song was ending.

"...*she's a Zorian lass*
And she lives by her wits
But it sure doesn't hurt
That she's got great tits!"

Okawa rolled her eyes at the juvenile song as all four men erupted in celebratory laughter, slapping each other on the shoulder and slamming mugs onto the bar.

Demetrius teetered a bit as he feasted his eyes on Okawa moving gracefully over to him. His three companions stared lecherously as the pilot warmly greeted her.

"Why Mz. Okawa, you're, you're *beautiful!*"

The seasoned agent found herself helplessly smiling at his innocent nature. "Hey Demetrius, got some time to talk?"

The airship pilot gave a drunken chortle. "I've got plenty of time to talk! Didn't you hear? I'm retired!"

With that announcement, the trio surrounding Demetrius erupted in cheers, back slapping and feet stomping. More drinks were promptly ordered.

Okawa grinned broadly at the rowdy celebration. "So, I see..."

Demetrius leaned toward the beautiful brunette and wobbled as he raised a finger. "And, and, you know how I know I'm retired?" The drunk pilot didn't wait for a reply. "Because, I've already been drinking for quite a while now..."

This revelation set the surrounding trio into another fit of revelry.

Okawa ignored the surroundings and stared at Demetrius. "Whadd'ya say? A word?"

Demetrius's shoulders fell as he slumped back against the bar. "I don't know..." he said in a low whine.

Sensing the decline in the festivities, the pilot's drinking companions leered menacingly at the interruption.

"Here now," the man with a lazy eye on the outside of the group protested. "Who are you to butt in on our fun?!"

"Yeah, we was getting on just fine without you!" spat the one to Demetrius' immediate left, with a long unkept beard.

The third companion behind her had thick greasy hair and a three-day stubble. "Maybe you best move on," he said ominously.

Demetrius shifted hesitantly as he saw the Valdurian captain's shoulders tense.

"That is unless you want to help us out," he said lecherously as he attempted to grab her shoulder from behind.

The scene exploded, as Okawa leaned back into the sailor, elbowing him hard in the sternum. He groaned, leaning slightly forward as the wind was driven from him. Using the same arm, she dropped it, made a fist and delivered a devastating blow to the groin. The man's eyes crossed as he doubled over in agony.

Both of the others reached out for the Valdurian. A quick, short side kick to the knee stopped the man with the lazy eye. He staggered backwards with a yelp then leaned on the bar to keep from falling.

Rage flashed across the face of the one directly in front of her. Saliva ran down his beard as he reached out to grab her. Okawa deftly grabbed his wrist and twisted. Demetrius winced at the snapping sound. The man went from enraged to engulfed in pain.

Without a word, she calmly pushed him into the one with the injured knee. The altercation was over in an instant and imperceptive to anyone more than five feet away. The trio limped away fading among the crowd, nursing their wounds.

"Something tells me you've done that more than once," Demetrius slurred as Okawa reached into her coat. Pulling out an envelope, she placed it on the bar in front of him.

He stared at it for a moment before catching her gaze. "You didn't have to do that. Those were Okay guys, just drunk."

"I know," she said in a calm, confident voice. "That's why they're not dead." Winking, she turned and disappeared into the crowd of boisterous patrons.

Peligro hated these kinds of assignments, but being a former sergeant in the Aramos Forsvara Guard, he knew how to follow orders.

Sipping the warm liquid from the plain cup, it was hard not to be fond of the attractive woman across the table. *This tea is the same kind mom used to make*, he reminisced.

Brother Falta paused nervously when he came home that evening and found the Aramos agent seated at the table with his wife Miadi. They were getting along well, laughing and chatting casually. The smell of freshly brewed tea scented the room, and both had cups in front of them.

On the far wall, his eight-grand-old son Nadany worked studiously on an assignment his tutor had left him.

All looked over as he closed the door. Peligro noted Falta's gaze shifting quickly about as he took in the scene.

"Hello father," Nadany said in a bored voice as he glanced up briefly from his studies.

Miadi was on her feet immediately, greeting him warmly. "Oh, hello dear. I'm so glad you made it home a little early."

Falta's voice was hesitant and low. "Yes, well, I reached a good breaking point…"

"Dear, this is Brother Peligro. He's here all the way from the Head Marassa in Zor!" Miadi said, unable to mask her excitement.

Peligro stood and enthusiastically presented his hand. "Brother, I apologize for this unannounced visit. I must say though, your wife's charm and hospitality are only exceeded by her beauty."

Miadi blushed at the compliment.

"And your son," Peligro continued. "Such a diligent young man. Both have made this task of mine bearable."

Falta took his hand apprehensively, as he searched his memory for the name. "Not at all, how can I help the main Marassa's office?"

Alright, let's do this and get it over with. Please go along. A shy, somewhat embarrassed bearing crossed Peligro's face. "I was hoping we could speak in private."

Miadi took the cue. "Nadany, come with me to the market."

"But mother..."

"Come," she cajoled. "I'll get you something special for supper."

With a peck on the cheek, wife and son were out the door.

Peligro motioned to the chairs. "May we?" he said with a friendly shrug.

"Of course," Falta's voice was hesitant as he took a seat.

"You are not a Marassa," the scribe said staring directly at the charming young man.

Peligro glanced at the floor as he chuckled. When he looked back up, he carried a harder, more confident demeanor.

"You're smart. I like that," he said sitting back in the chair.

"Am I in some sort of trouble?" the concerned scribe asked as he leaned forward on the table.

Peligro smiled broadly. "No, no, you haven't done anything, yet. In fact, so far, you've done everything right. You're a successful law scribe with a beautiful family."

"So why are you here?"

Keeping the pleased demeanor, the agent rapped lightly several times on the table. "Straight to the point, I like that too."

A number of tense ellipses passed under the umbrella of civility.

"Right now, you are researching parts of a very important book," Peligro said as he nonchalantly examined his pants leg.

"The Zauvek Eldor," Falta said nodding. "I was working on it today."

"And would you care to share your thoughts with me?"

The scribe vigorously shook his head no. "Not until my findings are released to the council."

Come on...don't be difficult, Peligro became pensive as he brushed a piece of lint off his lap and locked eyes with the suspicious scribe. "I see. You do realize you are the deciding vote in a very serious matter?"

Falta's demeanor slowly dowered as he started to put the pieces together.

Peligro was serious but nonthreatening. "I represent certain groups. Groups which seek to keep a respective order and balance to society."

Falta was growing more concerned by the sentence.

"Now, the chaos of not having a direct line of succession in a major human house is, well, counterproductive."

Falta swallowed hard as he stared at a slightly maniacal young man whose smile had reappeared.

"So exactly what are you saying?"

Peligro leaned forward on the table mirroring the scribe. "I would very much suggest your ballot promote a smoother transition of power."

"You mean Shom Eldor?" the scribe said focusing on the topic.

Peligro sat back beaming. "Like I said, smart!"

Falta lowered his head as he summoned the courage. "And if I told you there is solid legal precedent in the last thousand grands to challenge that?"

I knew it. Of all the scribes, I've got to get the one with some integrity. Peligro sighed as his disposition took on a sad nuance. "You know, I seem to always draw the most unpleasant of assignments. Now, out of necessity, I've embraced a philosophy that you don't have to be unpleasant, to do an unpleasant job."

The scholar stared blankly at the obvious folk logic. His superior notion quickly faded as he watched the well-manicured young man lean back on the table.

"I would hate for something *unpleasant* to happen to your family," he said not breaking his friendly demeanor.

The words hit Falta like punch in the stomach and radiated quickly through his entire body. His folded hands on the table were visibly trembling and he felt his bowels loosen.

Witnessing the scribe's petrified reaction, the agent adopted a more consolatory tone. "Not all at once," he defended. "I mean, you'd be able to recant...but the wife would probably be first, then if you still held out, the kid would of course be next. I got it! You could even choose which one goes first, how about that?" Peligro paused and sadly sighed. "Then, if you still wouldn't be reasonable, you'd force me to deal unpleasantly with you too."

Tears were welling up in Falta's eyes as Peligro took on a more resolute tone.

Aw geez, come on pal... "Look, you're good people. Please don't make me do this!"

Falta was quaking. "Why in the name of the gods would you do this. You, you seem to favor us?"

This, this is why I hate these jobs, he thought. "Orders," the Aramos agent said with a shrug. "So, what will it be?"

"There's one coming up on our left." Zau said squinting into the map projected out over the ship's wheel as she struggled to keep it steady. The gusts of wind swirling around the jagged peaks of the Spine of the World whistled constantly and shook the airship from side to side.

"This may be a chance worth taking," Kyopp said authoritatively. "We've entered the most dangerous airspace on the entire Annigan. Even with this ship, the Ash-Ta are not something you want to deal with especially in great numbers."

They followed the late luna moon, setting in the west. The weak illumination cast long shadows on the huge rocks jutting from the dark sea to their left.

Mal's attention was pulled away from the map when the light level changed outside. In the distance, the moon's silhouette was obscured by what appeared to be undulating clouds. "Did you ever see something and say to yourself; 'we could be really fucked here?'"

All crowded around Zau at the wheel to get a look.

"Speaking of which," Kyopp said pointing. "I believe we are observing two flights of Chiro clan. They're quite a way off. Each one of those clouds contains hundreds of Ash-Ta."

"Surely you don't think they would be able to get to us in here?" Shom asked in a panicky voice. "I mean the hull is that ukko stuff...am I right?"

Kyopp shrugged. "With numbers like that they might damage the craft. I can assure you on the Spine of the World there is *no* place to land for repairs."

Mal signified she understood and sighed deeply.

Zau had not taken her attention away from the map. "Coming up on it now Captain," she said calmly.

Mal guardedly approved and Zau pulled the ship suddenly to the left aiming the bow of the airship directly at one of the jagged peaks.

Everyone standing was thrown into a pile on top of one another, against the right-side hatch.

"Sorry.... sorry!" Zau said nervously.

"Just like the good old days," Shom sarcastically quipped as he sat up.

Any more comments or witticisms was cut short by *Haraka* plunging into the pillar of stone and disappearing in a giant blue flash.

Its emergence was equally as jarring. The craft was spit out of a crumbling tower of long abandoned ruins at a velocity none of the passengers had ever experienced.

Dangerously low, the airship barreled toward a partially constructed settlement. Astonished mongrel workers and their Tiikeri owners dove to the ground as the *Haraka* barreled forward a few feet over their rooftops.

In the cabin, there was an initial cry of alarm, but things were moving too rapidly for chatter.

Zau grasped the wheel tightly in a vain attempt to gain control of the ship. "Captain, I can't slow us down!"

"Better think of something!" Mal said as she watched them barreling straight at rocky, tree-laden foothills.

The Singa once again quickly consulted the map in front of her before it flickered off. "Hold on!" she said jerking the wheel to the right.

No one had the chance to get up from the last maneuver and were tossed about again.

"Sorry, sorry…" Zau repeated.

Peering out the window together Mal and Zau gasped in astonishment. They were now rushing directly for a small stand of trees surrounding a large pile of boulders.

"What the…" Mal cried out.

"This may be a little rough," the Singa said wincing.

When the first saplings snapped in front of the *Haraka's* bow, pilot and captain finally saw a faint blue glow emanating from the small cave.

"Here we go again!" Mal screamed.

The cave mouth flared open like a giant maw when the craft was within a few feet.

The speeding airship was bathed in sheets of bright light immediately before it was swallowed by the portal.

They were spit out again from the side of a cliff into a steep tree-covered valley, with countless shallow ravines and crags. The moon was considerably brighter. Mal noted the sun far off in the west between the mountain peaks in the distance. To their right, Mal saw a vast forest stretching to the horizon.

The sun and terrain's right. At least were in the Twilight Lands, was the Spice Rat's reassuring thought as she tightly gripped the edges of the front console.

"Between those peaks," Mal said frantically as she pointed.

As the rocky pillars slipped past on either side, everyone let out a shaky — and as it turned out — premature sigh.

Before any reactions were possible, all in the cabin were flung about as the *Haraka* suddenly decelerated. The jarring force vibrated the craft as it bounced wildly in an elastic fashion. The bobbing gradually slowed to a standstill.

Everyone slowly got to their feet, panting in confusion and relief.

"What the fuck!?" Mal said leaning against the hull.

Zau pulled herself up, assisted by the wheel. "Captain, as fast as we were going, I can't imagine anything that could have stopped us that rapidly and yet didn't tear the ship apart."

"Everyone okay?" Mal asked.

All gave an affirmative reply except Shom. The prodigal was staring out the windshield. "Uhhh…"

Stretched out across the valley was a massive, intricate field of spiderwebs extending in multiple layers between the peaks.

"Incredible!" Alto marveled.

"Can you even fucking believe this?!" Mal said, her voice a combination of awe and frustration.

"Captain, despite our current situation, I do have some good news," Zau said as she studied the sky.

"I could use some good news right about now," Mal replied staring out at the webbing.

"We're very close to our destination," the Singa said confidently. "I'd say Immor-Onn is no more than a luna away."

"Okay, I like that," Mal said as she indicated the strands which held them. "What the fuck is all this?"

Alto stepped up and indicated out the windshield. "A guess, but I believe we are trapped in the webs of the sentient spider race our guide told us about when we first arrived in Immor-Onn."

"Yes, as I recall the words 'very dangerous' was bandied about," Shom said flippantly.

"Obviously they can be dealt with," Alto said, searching for a positive angle. "I mean, they trade silk. We've got some."

"Why don't you cut us out?" Shom asked with a touch of urgency. "I mean those new blades of yours are pretty impressive."

Zaad was the one to speak up for the swordmaster. "It's not the string, it's the sticky." The EEtah pointed to his conical head. "Shom needs to think!"

"It's doubtful if the Cevots would be able to breech the hull," Kyopp said as he helped the still unconscious Orich back into his seat. "They will probably encase us and move us, either to a place where they can take their time getting to us, or maybe to their queen."

Shom was aghast. "You actually mean we should let them cocoon the ship, with us in it?!"

Alto gave the prodigal a sly smile then walked to the cargo area. Everyone focused on the swordmaster as he reached over and pulled at the end of Darian Silk on the spool.

In a flourish, he cast the end of silk into the air, spinning several feet of it from the roll into the air. As it slowly floated downward Alto rapidly drew his knife and positioned the blade beneath the falling strand.

"The problem is not the silk," he calmly said, as the strand drifted slowly onto the etheria blade. It was severed in two with no force necessary. "The problem is getting off this web. I would humbly suggest that the, Cevots you called them, are going to be much better at it than us."

"Is it possible for you do something in your original form?" Shom asked Kyopp as he now grasped at any idea.

The Do-Tarr king was stymied. "No, my race is suited for mining and tunneling through stone. I'd be as trapped as Alto's swords would."

Throwing his hands up, Shom whirled dramatically. "Fine!" he said in a defeated tone. He suddenly stopped and spun back toward the EEtah. His attitude changed completely to one of happy revelation. "You just called me Shom!"

Zaad motioned at the royal and chuckled.

"I know," he said, slapping a meaty hand on the prodigal's shoulders that made him wince.

The man-shark then looked over at Alto sheathing his knife and pointed at the silk. "Nice Mora," he praised before addressing the group. "I'm gonna go with his plan, mostly because you sentients don't know shit about blades."

Mal gave out something between a huff and a chuckle. "Yeah, you've mentioned that once or twice…okay, I guess we wait."

The stench of fear permeated every inch of the nearly empty room. He had stopped struggling a little while ago. Now, as he hung upside down naked, the young male prostitute whimpered and trembled uncontrollably.

"Please, no…," he choked amidst racking sobs.

A nude Stryder Aramos stopped assessing the ornate, shallow bowl in his hands. An amused, disdainful expression crept across his face as he slowly walked over to the bound young man. He certainly hoped this one had enough blood for his needs.

Still sobbing and sniffling, the young man followed the quartermaster with fear laden scrutiny as he placed the bowl below his head on the floor.

As he stood up Stryder gazed lovingly at the terrorized youth and gently stroked his cheek.

"Please? No? You should be thanking me," he said as he grabbed the man's naked buttock. "How long do you think you can rely on selling this. I'm about to give your pathetic life some meaning. My lord is going to elevate your existence."

The quartermaster's soothing tone and loving touch was confusing to the bound prostitute as he watched Stryder confidently survey the four blank walls. It was here, in his own mansion, on the outskirts of Zor, that he would create his masterpiece that was formerly denied him in Immor-Onn.

The young man panicked and wiggled furiously as Stryder raised his right forefinger. The nail had grown to over an inch long and was honed to a sharp tip. The quartermaster stared lovingly at it.

"My temple must be consecrated," he said steadying the boy and placing the nail against his throat. "Thank you for your sacrifice."

The brothers' astral bodies sat atop the *Haraka* as the moon dipped below the peaks of the Os'-Oni mountains. The entire ravine was alive with a million lights as the moon's waning illumination refracted off dew drops which clung to the intricate webbing connecting every peak in sight.

"I know it is you that hampers our return brother. Why?" Orich said in a gently confused tone.

Taa's disposition turned sly. "Timing my brother. Timing."

Orich blinked in confusion. "I don't understand."

"Why are you not among your friends?" Taa asked changing the subject.

Curiosity transformed to concern. "Don't you mean *our* friends?"

"Of course," came the disingenuous reply.

"The spores' influence caused me to reflect," Orich said in a slow deliberate voice. "Things are changing. Many things were revealed to me. I choose to remain unavailable while I meditate on what I've been shown."

"And have you been shown anything about me?" Taa asked.

"I feel an influence on you," the albino paused and stared outward. "And I now realize, eventually it will be our greatest asset."

Taa's coy demeanor instantly changed and he was noticeably intrigued. "Brother?"

Orich's explanation was interrupted by a slow strobing of the light across the ravine. Long, spindly limbs crept around the side of the western peaks. The hairy appendages undulated in the breeze, then stroked the webbing. Limbs gave way to bodies, as two giant spiders cautiously slipped from the rocks onto the webbing.

The albino mirror images looked back at each other, then began dissolving in a shimmer above the airship before disappearing. Within the cabin, Zaad's roar of alarm filtered outward through the hull.

With shoulders slumped and head hanging, Demetrius lumbered onto the flight deck of Valdurian Air Station Three. He had all day to sleep off the previous night's incident and resulting bender.

Now, as the grand Turine in the harbor rang seven times, the Kan fog rose in the streets, chasing away the bell's last echo.

Okawa stood by the *Drakin*, arms crossed, sporting an amused grin. A skin-tight grey body suit accentuated her curvaceous frame and brown hair. On her hip was a pistol crossbow and a matching grey shoulder bag was at her feet.

Slouching past her, staring forward, he reached out and slapped the paper from last night's envelope into her hands.

"Captain Demetrius, reporting as ordered," he said sarcastically, in a weary defeated voice.

The Valdurian agent rolled her eyes as the pouting airman climbed aboard his craft. "I hope you're not going to be like this the entire time?"

"I was supposed to be retired!" he said matter-of-factly, as Okawa came on board. "In a pub somewhere, with well-endowed wenches bringing me drinks!"

He glanced over as Okawa secured herself into her seat. "This is little more than blackmail by house Valdur," he said emphatically as he reached for the controls.

Okawa's grin changed from amused to sly. "I couldn't help but notice you didn't give back the five hundred secor air-note that was also in the envelope."

Caught, Demetrius scowled and switched on the etheria powerplant. "You do realize that flying in the Kan is inherently dangerous?"

"Yeah, that's why I requested you."

A startled Demetrius froze at the controls. "Darn it! You're the one responsible for this?!"

"No, Joc' Valdur is responsible for this. All I did was make a suggestion."

"In the name of the gods, *why*?!"

Okawa stared in disbelief with an entertained smirk. She had to admit though, his modesty was endearing. "Because you're one of the best pilots I've ever seen. You're one of the few who can skirt the upwinds and you've actually flown in Nocturn."

Demetrius glanced away, flattered but frustrated. "Fine!" he said as the airship started to rise. "Where to?"

"A private residence on the outskirts of Tuath Plat."

Demetrius threw her a quizzical side glance. "You need an airship to get you across town?"

Okawa grinned out the side window as the *Drakin* slipped out of the hangar and into the dense Kan fog. "It's not that simple. We're going to need to approach from the wilderness side of the plat."

The pilot quickly scanned the dashboard, his voice betrayed concern. "Slightly above the tree tops I would imagine?"

"Yes."

"In the fog?"

"Yes."

Demetrius spun the craft eastward. "I see…"

"You're not going to start pouting again, are you?" Okawa challenged.

Demetrius remained focused as he swept the airship over the barely visible rooftops of a retiring city. "No, but if I knew what the job was, I would've held out for more money."

The flight, as it happened was relatively simple. The Kan fog that far up in the foothills extended upward only twenty feet. The *Drakin* slipped mere feet above the treetops in brilliant Lumina sunshine.

On Okawa's direction, he lowered the craft into the thick mist. It circled the perimeter of an expansive estate, keeping below the upper foliage for cover. In the center of the clearing, a large three-story manor house rested behind a high wall. Three smaller structures were interspersed on the well-manicured landscaping.

"Residence huh," Demetrius said skeptically. "That's a gosh darn compound."

The Valdurian ignored the pilot's assessment. She took in the details of the area as he circled. "Okay, let me out there," she said pointing to a remote area of the grounds which bordered the tree line.

Silently the *Drakin* settled to the ground. Okawa grabbed her bag. "Get into the air and hang back. Wait for my signal to pick me up. It might come from anywhere in the compound, and I'll probably need you fast, so keep a lookout."

"Wait, signal? What kind of signal?"

The Valdurian operative smirked. "Oh, you'll know."

A confused Demetrius lifted off as he watched Okawa sprint across the grounds toward the compound.

Sabini had them in the palm of her hand, as usual. The blond, frolicsome bard was the toast of the streets in the Eldorian capital of Rophan. Her twinkling green eyes and infectious grin had been known to win over many a curmudgeon. This amazing ability almost always resulted in a handsome tip.

Her tunes would vary, depending on the audience. Most were funny, ironic ballads that sometimes bordered on bawdy. Today's songs were different. The words and cadence of her new material carried the timbre of a stirring march. Her beautiful voice was accompanied by the driving, unnaturally loud lute she strummed.

All in the crowd surrounding her bobbed their heads and tapped their feet along with the rhythm when the first chords were played. Then Sabini's soaring voice began:

> *There was a young man*
> *They called the boy king*
> *His bravery and courage*
> *Is that which I sing*
> *Shom, Shom, brave Shom!*
>
> *Oh, he was the youngest*
> *Eldorian by name*
> *He traveled the Annigan*
> *Seeking fortune and fame*
> *Shom, Shom, brave Shom!*
>
> *He sought not the crown*
> *But to fight for what's right*
> *With daring and muster*
> *And a heart that was light*
> *Shom, Shom, brave Shom!*
>
> *Shom always answered*
> *His country's true call*
> *The wayfaring sovereign*
> *Will deliver us all*
> *Shom, Shom, brave Shom!*

The majority of the crowd was singing along by the second chorus. Long after the song ended and the sound of coins falling into her hat faded. The lyrics; "Shom, Shom, brave Shom…" were heard radiating outward from the nearby street corners. It echoed across the city, transported by a substantial wave of enamored fans.

With an amused smirk Sabini inspected the interior of her open lute case. Accented against the dark lining she counted twelve pieces of silver; a good haul for a single song.

Slinging her lute over her shoulder, she moved to the next large intersection to sing the song once again.

Who the fuck is Shom? She pondered upon hearing the chorus drifting once again through the crowds in the streets.

"Everyone, freeze!" Mal said in a dire whisper.

Outside the windshield, six eyes peered inside the trapped airship, as one of the giant spiders studied their strange catch. They heard the second Cevot walking on the rear of the ship. Everyone traded fretful stares as they felt it testing the hull with a series of rapid taps.

The irony of having multiple eyes, is that spiders possess very poor vision. The one out front, sensing nothing, joined its companion in examining the rest of the craft.

Mal scanned the cabin to confirm they all heard the Cevot's low rumbling voices as they vibrated across webbing which surrounded them.

"What is it?" One of the spiders said in a low clicking voice.

"Something that fell from the peaks. Get rid of it!"

The one formerly at the windshield now sniffed at the side hatch. "No, I smell the faint essence of food."

"We can't get into it. This takes up too much space in the web for a waste of time."

"The queen should see it."

"No!"

"It may be valuable. Do you want to be the one to tell the queen we discarded something she might want?"

No one could make out the next few exchanges between the giant arachnids. They heard them slowly moving around the ship. When white strands of silk began to cover the windshield Mal sighed deeply guessing the spiders' next move.

Shom gasped, his utterance awash in fear, as the last portion of the sole window was blocked out plunging the cabin in darkness.

"This was your idea," one was heard saying. "You can carry it."

The other made an unintelligible reply as it picked up the cocooned ship. Inside the craft lurched on its side toppling all against the hull's interior.

The Cevot carrying them stopped. "I felt movement in there."

"Are you sure?"

"Yes, there should be some rocks in that cave over there we can use to break it open."

The two spiders, now determined to gain entrance, scurried along the web to a cave in a nearby cliff. Everyone struggled to hang onto something as they were jostled about the cabin.

"What in the name of the gods is going on?" Shom said in a panicked whisper when they felt the craft come to rest.

Mal had barely enough time to shush him, when they felt a heavy object bouncing off the outer hull. One of the spiders cried out in pain when a ricocheting boulder careened from the ukko wood exterior and struck them. As potentially comical as they envisioned the mishap, no one was in a spirit of levity.

The pounding continued for quite a while until frustration set in. One had made a comment about giving up, when a loud guttural clacking reverberated into the dark cabin.

All in the airship now realized the noise coming from the exterior of the *Haraka* was the clash of battle along with the cries of the combatants.

Sensing the attention shift away from them, Mal tapped an orange crystal filling the encased ship with light. With the return of vision came a collective, audible sigh.

Several times the airship was rocked as assaulted bodies in the throes of a struggle slammed against it, only to be repelled. Finally, the sounds of combat came to abrupt halt. Moments later they were replaced by muffled voices and multiple cracking sounds.

Mal stared at everyone's puzzled expressions. "Alright, open her up. Let's see what the fuck's happening out there."

Zaad pulled the lever, breaking the seal on the door. Alto drew his short sword and slipped it between the edge of the hatch. As promised, the etheria blade sliced through the silk cocoon with ease.

When the hatch dropped, the human and EEtah were greeted by eight humanoid rams, interrupted from their labors.

Alto remembered them from the group's arrival in Immor-Onn. These were the Fudomi. The humanoid ram creatures stood almost as tall as Zaad. Their feet were hooved and thick conical horns sprouted from the sides of their ovine shaped head.

Two of the Fudomi were busy chopping up the dead Cevot bodies with massive axes. The other four were occupied collecting spider eggs and webbing.

Both groups froze in position as they stared at each other in astonishment.

With a friendly smile the swordmaster sheathed his blade. "Well, hello!"

Okawa felt the cool dampness of the grass on the soles of her special boots. The Kan fog tingled on her cheeks as she raced across the open ground in a crouch. Reaching the compound wall undetected, she stayed low as she flattened out against it.

The Valdurian agent was reaching in her bag for a line of silk when she heard low clucking coming from directly around the corner to her right.

There was no time for the luxury of an assisted climb. Quickly scanning the area, she leapt straight up. Her fingers easily found the ledge of the eight-foot-high wall. In a fluid motion she pulled herself on top, lying prone on top of the wide barrier.

Okawa froze in position, as a large flightless bird with long legs and taloned feet stepped into view. It looked upward, clucked a few more times, snapping at the air with its serrated beak as it moved off into the fog.

Breathing a sigh of relief, she slid over the barrier into the grounds of the central estate. Crouched against the inner wall, Okawa reached over to the tubular holster on her left thigh, retrieving a nine-inch blowgun. From a side pocket on her pouch she pulled out a single dart. Putting the tip between her teeth she gently bit down and removed the wax covering on the tip. Spitting out the protective sleeve she loaded the projectile.

The main house was thirty feet in front of her. The entrances to the three-story ornate structure was dark, with the exception of a light in the servant's quarters on the first floor and glowing crystals above.

Pausing, she mentally reviewed her calculations from their arrival. The lone guard in the back should have been along by now. Deciding to take a chance, Okawa slipped up to the rear door. With a gentle nudge it slid silently open into a kitchen.

The room was kept warm in comparison to the damp fog outside by one of three ovens on the wall to her right. On the far side of the room, she detected movement and grunting.

Slipping up behind a row of large hanging pots, she finally witnessed the source of the noise.

She also now knew the location of the rear sentry who appeared to be a low ranking Forsvara Guard. He was seated on a long preparation table. His pants were lowered to his ankles and his sword belt was lying beside him.

Kneeling in front of the young man with her back to Okawa was a serving wench, her dress top pulled to her waist. Her head and upper body bobbed furiously in his lap.

The guard's head was thrown back in ecstasy as he grunted in satisfaction. Throat exposed, Okawa raised the blowgun and fired.

The dart, striking the side of his neck caused the sentry to involuntarily reach up to swat what he thought was an insect. In doing so, he drove the dart further into his neck. Almost instantaneously his eyes crossed, and he slumped back.

Oblivious to the attack, the servant girl only realized that the erection which filled her mouth had rapidly gone limp. Slowly, she stopped and peered up at the recipient of her affections, now fast asleep. Pulling the flaccid organ from her mouth, she nudged his thigh.

"Koyor?" she apprehensively stammered.

Seeing no response save that of his mouth dropping open, she smacked his thigh in frustration.

"Koyor!"

As the unconscious sentinel started to snore, the serving maid stood and angrily pulled the top of her dress back over her exposed breasts. Stomping her foot in humiliated indignation she slapped the unconscious guard across the face.

"Bastard!"

When there was still no response she stormed off, slamming the door on her way out.

Okawa chuckled and slipped over to the unconscious Aramos soldier. Taking the sword from the table and the embedded dart from his neck, she tossed them into the oven. From her bag she pulled out a small bottle of cheap pungent liquor and doused the front of his shirt.

Leaving the bottle uncorked she placed it in the guard's lap, then moved to the interior.

Through swinging doors, the Valdurian slipped into an opulent dining area. Beyond that, was a long receiving hall with large portraits adorning the walls and multiple doors on either side.

Thankfully, all doors were unlocked. A large public study was followed by an official-looking office, and a smaller private study. Seeing nothing out of the ordinary Okawa was about to move to the second story when she noticed a door on the rear wall of the private study. The exterior lock immediately caught her attention. It was a Reta seven, the most sophisticated key and tumbler lock available.

From inside her bag she removed a bifold pouch. Setting the bag beside her she opened the small folio. It was lined on both sides with picks of every size and variety. Choosing two she inserted them into the keyhole and deftly manipulated them.

She gave a satisfied grin as the last tumbler clicked and the lock slid open.

Standing to the side Okawa cautiously pushed the door open. The cool air that poured out was thick with an overwhelming rank, metallic smell.

Blood, she grimly assessed.

Carefully peeking around the corner, she saw stairs descending into darkness.

Retrieving a small orange gem, she tapped it against the doorjamb and it gave off a warm glow. Holding it aloft in her left hand, her right rested on the handle of her pistol crossbow as she took her first step onto the narrow riser.

The stairwell was short, and the stench of dried blood increased with each stair. They led to a twenty by twenty-foot square room. When she reached the bottom, she held the radiant gem up high and surveyed the dank quarters.

Okawa betrayed no emotion, but the ghastly scene caused even the seasoned agent to waver in uncertainty.

The room was all but bare. There was a crude harness in the ceiling to her right. On the floor, directly below the restraining system was an ornate shallow bowl. The entire area was covered in a large film of crusted blood. A trail of crimson swept from the stain to a single door in a nearby wall.

It was the walls and ceiling that left the Valdurian in horrific awe. All were covered in lines and patterns of crimson X's and I's. Each of the bloody glyphs were laid out in a complex configuration resembling lines of a poem. The groupings were of different sizes and lengths all connected by lines, which when examined closely, were made up of the same two runes of minuscule size.

Walking slowly by the walls of the room, she carefully studied the glyphs. Spotting an intriguing pattern, she reached out to touch it. As her finger drew near a spark arced to her fingertip. She snatched back her hand and made a mental note to keep a safe distance. Her examination was interrupted when she heard the front door slam.

Quickly extinguishing the light, Okawa went to the base of the stairs and scanned upward.

"Koyor?!" a male voice called out.

He's in the receiving hall, she noted as she slipped up the stairs.

Careful to relock the cellar, Okawa placed her ear to the door of Stryder's private study. She clearly heard the guard calling out to his comrade as he passed from the dining area to the kitchen.

"Damn ya Koyor!" she heard the front sentinel admonish at the top of his lungs as she advanced into the receiving hall.

"Ya just can't get enough of that wench can ya?! Ya smell like a damn whiskey bottle. Lord Stryder will have us both hung for this!"

Confident the second guard was well occupied Okawa bolted for the front door. She made it only about halfway there when it opened and a third guard entered. He froze in surprise when he saw the rapidly advancing woman.

He's seen me, Okawa reluctantly assessed. *I hate to do it...*

"Hey!" he screamed reaching for his sword.

He never made it.

The Valdurian agent launched herself toward the startled sentry and lashed out with a blinding solitary punch to the throat.

The blow crushed the man's larynx. Forgetting about the sword, his hands gripped his throat, gurgling furiously as he toppled to the ground.

Sprinting up the landing, Okawa bounded three stairs at a time. When she reached the second floor, she heard the kitchen doors fly open. Seeing his comrade lying dead, the now lone guard cried out and drew his weapon.

Not wasting any time, the Valdurian bolted up the final stairs to the third story which consisted of a wide hallway with four doors on either side. Dashing to the last door she slipped inside. The bedroom was moderate in size, with a bannister bed and dresser. There were two windows flanking the bed's headboard.

Opening the window facing east she pulled out a small sack. Yanking on the dangling cord that encircled the opening she tossed it out into the air. The pouch exploded in a yellow flash that trailed sparkling streamers on its way to the ground.

Sure hope he sees that, she said to herself as she inspected the room. Her attention focused on the dresser and the jewelry box sitting on top. Opening each of the drawers she took the clothing and miscellaneous items and tossed them about. Opening the box, she found it full of medium priced to fairly expensive jewelry of almost every variety. Reaching in, Okawa indiscriminately scooped up rings, necklaces and bracelets, dropping them into her bag.

She considered another flare when she heard the guard make the third floor and begin opening doors.

When she perceived that the guard was searching the room two doors down, the *Drakin* appeared out of the mist and swung its port side to the building. Scrambling out the window, she threw her bag on board then climbed in after it.

"Somebody call for a carriage?" Demetrius said jokingly.

The Valdurian agent's timbre was deadly serious. "Move!"

"Yes ma'am!" he said as he jerked the wheel to the right. The airship quickly disappeared into the fog.

The remaining guard opened the door. Seeing the dresser and jewelry box ransacked as well as the window open, he rushed in.

A quick scan of the room revealed no one. Bolting to the open window he looked out. There was no one to be seen in the thick Kan fog or quiet grounds below.

Fia awoke suddenly as a wave of cold water splashed across her. Gradually her surroundings came to her. The first thing she became aware of was she couldn't feel her arms. They were locked tightly together for who knows how long, holding her nude body tightly to a narrow piece of ship's deck which bobbed about in open water. From the position of the sun she guessed her location as somewhere in the northwestern ocean of Lumina. Thankfully the ocean swells were minimal, however from her vantage point she saw no signs of land.

Resting back on the planks, exhaustion took her once again and everything went black.

The next dousing of cold water to wake her was hardly a gentle ocean swell. She bolted up from a hard-stone base sputtering from the brace of icy liquid. Standing at her feet was a small man with blue skin. His head was tapered at the top and bottom. He set the bucket behind him and stared at her.

Standing beside the Yupik ice clansman was a tall human male in his early thirties. His long, angular features were accentuated by a high-collared jacket and tall pompadour hair style. Four other Yupik stood around her.

Seeing the human male, instinct kicked in for the Rayth. "Dag!" she spat as she attempted to get to her feet.

The stout blue humanoids on either side immediately grabbed her and lifted her onto a low red-stained stone table. To her surprise, the small statured Yupik were deceptively strong. The only thing moving on her nude frame, was the crystal pendant on her neck which had managed to stay with her through the present calamity.

Upon hearing the term, the human's eyebrow raised as his smooth, cruel features imparted an air of amused superiority.

"Splendid. You've decided to join us," he said in a disdainfully calm tone.

Fia's gaze darted about the windowless room. It contained cells of various sizes along the far wall, as well as half a dozen ominous looking torture devices in the center.

Seeing her stare, the man walked over to a torture cross. "You're in the city of Penaber," he said as he ran his hands sensuously across the worn wooden beam. "I am Calden Ambassador Tubig."

He casually wandered over to a stretching rack. "Now that we've established who I am, what say I guess who you are?"

Fia contemptuously sneered at the brash young man.

Hearing no reply Tubig spun back around at Fia with a gloating smile. "Yes?"

Keeping eye contact he slowly approached. "Let's see; you just used Rayth terminology, the wreckage you were found clinging to had Rayth markings on it…"

He paused. "Any of this sound familiar?"

Fia remained silent, her face contorted with rage.

"Several lunas ago one of our warships chased a Rayth ship, the *last* Rayth ship I might add, into the portal at the Bannok Atoll.

Tubig paused. "Anything?" he said with a superior smile.

Fia defiantly spat at him.

The Calden ambassador continued, unphased. "And now here you are, swept in on wreckage from the portal in the Innaca Deep."

He walked up beside her and gently brushed her cheek. She violently wrenched her head away.

"So, would you like to hear my guess?" he mockingly offered as he suddenly and intensely grabbed her chin, forcing her to look at him.

"I think you are the Rayth leader known as Fia!" he defiantly said as he brought his face close to hers.

She winced at the heavy garlic on his breath and tried to turn away only to find herself held fast. Letting her go he stood back up. The aura of desperate confusion on her face told him all he needed.

"I guess in the end it really doesn't matter," his tone was now condescendingly introspective. "As far as everyone is concerned, that is who you are. That's all that really matters, isn't it?"

A chilling deportment danced across the ruthless young man's face. "I imagine you're going to provide quite a show in the Calden halls of justice. A pity I won't be there to witness it."

Tubig laughed as he calmly sauntered to the foot of the table. "A boat will be along shortly for you."

He hesitated, as he gazed longingly at her struggle against the Yupik holding her motionless. "However, it now appears we've some time to kill."

The Calden ambassador opened his pants as the Yupik held her tighter and slid her crotch area to the table's edge.

"It occurs to me, that being out here on the frontier as it were, I haven't been with, or for that matter, even seen a human female in quite a while."

Fia cried out when she saw his rapidly growing penis.

This caused the young Calden ambassador to grin lecherously. "Oh, please feel free to make as much noise as you wish. No one will hear you, and I like it."

Not bothering with, nor needing the forest as cover, the *Drakin* slipped silently above the fog-covered rooftops of Zor.

"So, we're going back to the air station I take it?" Demetrius said as he stole glances of Okawa fishing around in her bag.

The Valdurian officer nodded yes without breaking her concentration inside the bag.

"What's that?" he said as she pulled out a handful of rings and bracelets.

Okawa hefted the loot in her hand. "Oh, jewelry," she said nonchalantly. "I had to make it look like a burglary."

"No, that," he said, indicating a specific ring. "I may not be a heraldry expert, but that looks like the royal Aramos crest."

"It probably is," she said returning to her sorting.

Demetrius' features tightened nervously. "Oh golly, oh gosh, we didn't break into Stryder Aramos' house, did we?!"

Okawa stopped and locked eyes with the pilot. "No, *we* did not! I may or may not have committed such an action. *You* were never there!" Her voice became hard and resolute, "Got it?!"

"Got it," Demetrius gulped nervously. "I'm pretty sure I wouldn't hold up well to torture. You start pulling at my fingernails and I'll probably tell everything I know. And if I don't know it, I'll make it up."

Okawa kept her intense stare. "I'll try and make sure it doesn't come to that." Placing the bag aside, her tone became more informative. "Alright, once we get back, I'm going to pull some people together quickly. There's a good chance that you're going to be needed, so stay close."

Demetrius shuddered in frustration. "You want to tell me what in tarnation is going on here?"

Okawa's stare morphed from intense to amused disbelief.

"Okay, okay!" Demetrius conceded throwing up his hands.

The queen always wept alone.

She resigned herself on the day of her coronation that her subjects would never see her angry, or in this case, sad. The common people of Immor-Onn had enough troubles trying to survive. She would not burden them with her distresses.

Now, as the tears would not stop, Queen Shula was consumed with racking waves of grief.

Her beloved pet cheepa, Manar was dead.

Shula's logical mind found it hard to grasp why she grieved so deeply for a pet that she only recently acquired. Lord Jo-Rakk, the Tiikeri ambassador, had promised her another. But she didn't want another.

Perhaps her sense of loss was due to the furry little companion's unconditional love. Or maybe the constant affection and willingness to please that it always displayed. All of those wonderful endearing qualities compounded the overwhelming sadness and guilt. She honestly believed the death was ultimately because of her own failings.

It had all happened so fast. Cheepas were naturally curious and always into everything. Until the everything proved deadly.

The table was draped in black. Lying in repose, the small humanoid feline was the picture of serenity.

Sniffing and clutching uncontrollably the Bailian queen leaned on the table for support. Several of her teardrops tumbled onto the creature's golden fur, causing it to glisten.

"You blame yourself," came a familiar voice from across the room.

Queen Shula gasped, startled that someone was eavesdropping, a witness to her grief.

"You shouldn't," said the cloaked figure as it stepped out from a darkened alcove.

Shula stood transfixed as the mysterious robed figure crossed the room toward her. Strangely, she felt no fear or malice. The individual stopped on the opposite side of the table bearing her dear Manar.

"It pains me to see you in such distress my queen," the cowled individual said staring at the dead cheepa.

Shula frantically parted the curtains of grief, searching her recollections. *That voice, I know it!*

Reaching out from beneath the robe, a human hand gently touched the cheepa's forehead. From the fingertips, thin strings of blue electrical current flowed gently outward, enveloping the tiny body.

As quickly as the energy was projected, it receded back into the fingers and Manar opened her eyes. Heartwarming recognition and a dimpled grin engulfed the revived pet as it gazed lovingly up at its master.

"Shula," she peeped extending her arms.

The queen's mouth dropped open as her disposition instantly transformed from grief to delight. Picking the cheepa up Shula cuddled it to her breast. Manar raised up and began licking the queen's neck.

The figure patiently stood watching in anonymity as the Bailian sovereign cuddled and cooed adoringly.

Now through tears of joy she stared back at the mysterious cowled figure and giggled despite her weeping. "How, how, can I thank you?"

The same lone hand reached up and pulled back the covering.

"No need my queen," Kai replied as she gazed fondly on her friend and monarch.

"You've come back to us my little savior!" she gasped as the cheepa continued to snuggle.

"It's always good to come home my queen," Kai replied with a loving smile.

Reaching over the table, Shula ran her fingers along the strands of hair framing her face which had gone gray.

"You've changed," the sovereign tenderly noted.

Kai gave the queen a sad smile. "In more ways than one."

Even the howl of the wind as it passed through the peaks of the Os-Ani Mountains couldn't drown out the constant drumming.

The trail winding up the mountainside was wide enough to accommodate everyone, with room to spare. Mal inspected the three Fudomi who led the parade, then uneasily checked behind. Peering past her friends to the three ram creatures following, the nimble, thickly muscled sentients carried the still cocooned *Haraka* with ease.

Their hosts were wary, but not hostile. There were a few initially tense moments when they insisted that weapons be surrendered. They quickly acquiesced when Alto handed his blade to the lead Fudomi. Upon leaving her master's side, Defari gave out a constant doleful howl that so unnerved the primitive people they abandoned the whole idea. At that point Kyopp's royal negotiating skills managed to broker a truce and a potential deal. Everything now hinged on what their leader had to say.

The volume of the drumming increased as they came along the side of the cliff into a deep narrow ravine between the peaks. Here the trail widened to a small plateau a hundred yards across. Dotting all sides of the peaks, rising high above and facing the plateau, were caves, each connected by a series of narrow trails carved out of the cliff. All led eventually to the clan's central square. In each one of the surrounding cave openings humanoid rams pounded in rhythm on tall single drums with a large bone mallet, welcoming the returning raiders.

From the corner of her vision Mal saw Shom reeling from the barnyard like stench which was impossible to escape.

The crowd that began to gather started cheering when the party entered the plateau. The lead Fudomi basked in the adoration, saluting the crowd. One reached into the large sack they carried and held aloft a Cevot egg. Upon seeing the delicacy displayed, another round of cheers and back slaps erupted from the throng.

Mal noted that the three carrying the airship placed it at the end of the plateau near the edge. Catching Alto and Zau's attention she directed it toward the ship with an ever-so-slight gesture.

Now that the victorious party was officially welcomed, everyone's attention settled on the strangers, especially Zaad who stood a foot taller than the largest of the clan. Mal was the first to admit that all the clan folks appeared very much alike. Were it not for some with small infants, distinguishing between male and female was all but impossible.

The drums abruptly stopped. The excited crowd went silent and parted as a Fudomi, larger than the others, dressed in leather-trimmed furs pushed through the pack. He glanced briefly at the strangers but stopped in front of the raider with the sack of eggs and stared quizzically.

"The raid was successful?" he said eyeing the sacks.

The young male was clearly proud and excited. "Yes, oh Doyen! We have eggs, and Cevot meat for our bellies along with silk to trade!"

The leader gave a satisfied bellow as he placed his hand on the younger Fudomi's shoulder. With that acknowledgement out of the way, his suspicious gaze fell on the five sentients clearly out of place.

The Doyen's attention immediately focused on Kyopp in his Bailian form. Nodding in approval he moved his way.

"One from the shining city to the west. Good, someone we can deal with," he said as the two approached each other.

The Fudomi chief then inspected the rest of the group. Mal leaned toward Kyopp.

"Play along," she said in an authoritative whisper.

In a regal flare befitting a king, Kyopp ostentatiously fluttered his arms. "Oh Doyen, we are ever grateful for your clansmen who spared us the Cevot's wrath. My friends and I are eager to get back to Immor-Onn. Your raider said you might aid us in exchange for the silk that encloses our ship."

The Doyen's tone became arrogant. "I am the only one that can make such promises!"

Mal lowered her head slightly to hide a grimace. *Here we go!*

"And what is that thing?" the Doyen said motioning at the *Haraka*, still covered in white silk.

"Best let me do the talking," Kyopp whispered back to the Spice Rat.

Mal signaled her agreement as the Do-Tarr king pointed at the airship. "This is our ship, oh Doyen."

The Fudomi leader' brow furrowed skeptically. "Why is it so far from the water?"

"Great Doyen, our ship sails on the wind."

With that revelation, the leader ignored Kyopp and became engaged in an animated conversation with those standing beside him.

"I don't think I like where this is going," Mal whispered loud enough for the group to hear. "We need to be ready to get the fuck outta here pronto. Zau can you fly that thing all wrapped up the way it is?"

The Singa surreptitiously surveyed the airship. "I'll need to cut the tail end out and at least some of the windshield so I can see. My knife won't do it."

Alto reached down and slid the etheria knife out from his sash. Surreptitiously, he passed it to the navigator lioness.

"Be careful," he said in a solemn whisper, "It is one of a kind."

Zau quickly tucked it up her sleeve as the Doyen's emergency council broke up and he addressed the group.

"This wind ship will be very valuable in getting our silks and goods to market in the shining city to the west. As of now it is a long journey over land, and the clans closest to the city have an unfair advantage."

The Doyen raised his fist and the crowd cheered. "No more!" he said, pointing to the *Haraka*. "This gives us an equal chance with the other clans!"

He spun toward Kyopp. "Sell it to us!"

Mal sputtered in indignation. "No fucking way!"

The Doyen's nostril's flared as he sneered at the Spice Rat. Kyopp placed a gentle hand on her shoulder.

"Unfortunately, the ship is not for sale. Perhaps there is another way we can help the Bree-Ah clan?"

The Fudomi leader remained firm. "No! The ship was found and retrieved in our territory. We call on the right of appropriation."

Mal's fists tightened. "Like fuck you do!"

The Doyen snorted loudly. "Then there is a challenge?!"

Mal marched forward pointing her finger ominously at the much larger Fudomi. "Fuck yes there's a challenge! That's my ship!"

The clan leader raised both fists in the air and gave out a braying cry. "Saa-Rot, Saa-Rot!"

The crowd immediately picked up on it and started the chant. In mass they started moving toward the opposite end of the plateau pushing the group along.

Mal consulted with the former marine commander. "Zaad, you've dealt with these folks," she said over the chanting. "What's this all about?"

The EEtah was unhelpful. "I only encountered them in town. They kept to themselves. I got no idea captain."

They were hustled over to a remote area with two circular rings etched in the granite floor, each thirty feet in diameter. The crowd stopped and the Doyen pointed at the circle closest to the cliff. "Ner-Rot." He stated soberly. His finger then drifted over to the other ring which was carved away from the cliff's edge. Three quarters of the stone circle was suspended over the side which plummeted thousands of feet. "Saa-Rot," he said with an evil leer. "We fight there."

Mal traded worried looks with her companions as she began to unbuckle her sword belt.

"Surely you're not going to attempt unarmed combat with that thing?" Shom said in disbelief.

Zaad put a hand out and stopped her. "You never struck me as suicidal captain." The EEtah grinned maliciously.

"These horn heads need to pick on someone more their size and temperament. I'll fight for the *Haraka*."

Alto affirmed his agreement. "If combat is inevitable, that is a much more sensible plan."

The Spice Rat sighed in a combination of acceptance and relief. Zaad gave Mal a confident smile as he removed Bowbreaker and handed it to Alto.

"Besides I've heard mountain goat is a delicacy," he said as he started for the ring.

The clan was now amassed on the cliff's edge chanting and shouting. The Doyen was already standing in the circle limbering his arms and stomping his hoofed feet to the delight of the cheering crowd.

Mal reached out and touched the EEtah's arm as he walked past. Her grimace was one of thanks and concern. "Zaad…"

The man-shark paused and gave an amused look at his commander. "Don't worry captain. He's a meaty one, they'll be plenty for us all."

The Fudomi leader was snorting furiously, spraying a mist of snot out before him as he worked himself up into a fighting frenzy. Zaad roughly pushed through the gathering crowd of Fudomi as he entered the ring. The Doyen stared at him with a rage-filled expression as he let out a loud bray and lowered his head, horns pointing forward.

Zaad arched his shoulders raised his head upward to the sky and let out a savage roar which reverberated across the canyon and caused the crowd to go quiet.

When the Fudomi prepared to charge the EEtah was already drooling profusely. "Alright meat, let's see what ya got!"

By the time Zekoff made it to the farmlands south of Zor, the agricultural compound was buzzing.

The colonel of the city guards could make out the barn through the thick, early Kan fog. Both its wide, double doors were open. A bright orange radiance streamed out becoming a diffused cloud of light surrounding the entrance. Dark silhouettes of Zorian guards searching for evidence danced in the murky glow.

The hulking form of patrol captain Gasata appeared from the mist and met the colonel as he passed between the gate. His presence radiated with intensity and Zekoff saw his mouth pulled taunt under his bushy handlebar moustache.

As usual, the patrol captain got straight to business. "The wife found him about two decis ago. We've got her in the house talking with one of my female guards. She's pretty shook up."

"Of course," the colonel said nodding sympathetically. Keeping a calm exterior, he fought the feeling of his stomach knotting. Recently losing his wife to violence, he now avoided dealing with grieving spouses. "The barn?"

"That's where she found him," Gasata said in a cold factual tone. "He was late for supper and she went to get him."

Both Zorian officers made their way in the visceral dampness toward the barn. As they passed the house, Zekoff peered in the window. Sitting at the table was a middle-aged woman with brown, slightly greying hair. Her face was buried in the palms of her hands.

The widower's throat tightened and his stomach gave a savage twist as he watched the grieving woman uncontrollably sobbing.

"Colonel?" Gasata said, pulling his leader's attention away from the heart-wrenching scene.

When Zekoff looked back at him, the captain gave an inaudible sigh of relief and continued. "This is the damnest thing I've ever witnessed in all my grands on the street."

The commander gave a loud huff as they stepped into the glowing fog of the barn's entrance. "Well, let's see what we've got."

As they moved into the crystal-lit interior, the colonel of the Zorian city guards halted abruptly. Mouth slightly agape, Zekoff stared in horrified reverence. "That now makes two of us," he said in a mortified hush as he scanned the room.

The barn itself was practically empty. Along two of the walls, tools and farming implements leaned haphazardly. Empty stables lined the third.

The farmer was suspended by his feet in the far corner, his throat sliced open. Directly below the corpse was a small red stain. Bloody footprints led from the body to the fourth wall.

The entire surface, from floor to ceiling was covered with intricate patterns painted in crimson. On the ground in front of the glyph-covered wall was a bloody pail.

Stroking his beard contemplatively and moving closer, the wily commander noticed the entire field of runes was composed of endless variations of only two characters, all penned in the farmers blood.

"Rafel?" Zekoff absentmindedly mumbled, unable to look away from the surreally macabre mural before him.

"He's on his way," Gasata said studying the empty pail stained red. "Look at all the splatters?"

"Frenzy," the colonel said in an authoritative tone.

Gasata inspected the rest of the barn and empty stalls. "The wife said that their two wagons and teams of horses are gone."

"This is hardly the work of horse thieves," Zekoff said reaching for his pipe. "And I have a sneaking suspicion this is not a lone incident."

With head lowered and massive horns pointed forward, the Fudomi Doyen charged. His fierce exhalations vaporized briefly below his flaring nostrils before being whisked off by the wind.

Zaad stood panting in excitement. His massive body was crouched, arms extended.

When the humanoid ram was fully committed to his charge, the EEtah leapt forward into the oncoming barrage, robbing it of its full impact.

The collision of the two behemoths thundered, reverberating between the surrounding canyon walls as the Fudomi's boney skull connected with Zaad's midsection. The force of the crash surprised the EEtah as both combatants were propelled in mid-air backwards into the crowd. Panicked clan folk scrambled to get out of the way as both fighters crashed to the ground.

Zaad bellowed, exposing his jaws and tightening his muscles to lessen the blow. Grabbing the base of both horns he savagely twisted the Fudomi to the side.

The crowd gasped in shock as Zaad's multiple rows of teeth snapped ferociously at the Doyen's exposed neck.

The ram creature's brute strength was enough to keep the EEtah's jaws from slamming shut. Zaad, sensing that a quick killing blow was not possible, gave a violent yank with his right arm tearing the horn from the Fudomi leader's head. The Doyen screamed in agony and Zaad took the opportunity to roll away.

Both slowly got to their feet, obviously stunned by the encounter and began to circle each other warily.

Zaad hefted the horn in his hand all the while studying his opponent. He saw blood running down the side of the Fudomi's head. With a contemptuous sneer, he cast the broken appendage to the ground. The crowd gasped at the disrespect and then murmured at the outsider's unintentional keeping with the Fudomi Rothas code of unarmed combat.

Seeing that all attention was on the deadly contest being played out before them, Zau reached to her seashell belt. Flipping over one of the shells she gently stroked the rune emblazoned on the reverse side initiating a spell to enhance the crowd attraction to the contest.

Now in close quarters, the Fudomi capitalized on the EEtah's main weakness, its stubby legs. Nimbly dancing forward, the sure-footed Doyen swept his arm upward delivering a powerful uppercut punch. Its huge fist connected with such force that the eight-foot-tall man-shark was driven upwards then onto his back with a resounding thud.

The crowd exploded in approval, then leaned forward, enraptured by the contest. Alto and Shom shared appreciative glances when their Fudomi guard's attention gravitated away from them. Mal gave an impressed glance toward Zau at the spell she was slowly working. The Singa smiled triumphantly then backed slowly up, slinking over to the tail of the *Haraka*.

Gasping to recover his breath, Zaad quickly rolled to his left as the Doyen dove at him. His thickly muscled forearms crashed to the ground where the EEtah once lay. With the Fudomi's back now exposed, Zaad delivered a punishing blow, barely missing his spine. The force knocked the wind out of the prone humanoid ram.

Mal nervously glanced back and forth as Zau slipped calmly up to the airship. With every passing moment the crowd's attention became more and more focused on the conflict. Catching both Alto and Shom's attention, Mal gestured back to the ship and Zau's surreptitious approach. Both swordmaster and royal indicated their acknowledgement.

The Fudomi's scream of pain was silenced by the wind being driven from his lungs. The crowd gasped as Zaad got back to his feet. The EEtah was panting furiously as he eyed the Doyen slowly struggle to pull himself to his knees. Not

251

waiting for him to stand, Zaad charged the kneeling the clan leader as the crowd hissed its disapproval.

The kneeling Fudomi was far from defeated. Dropping back to the ground the Doyen rolled in the direction of the attacking man-shark. With his target too low to grab and moving too fast to change strategies, Zaad tripped over the prone Fudomi leader crashing to the ground precariously close to the outer edge of the Saa-Rot circle.

By this time, their captives were all but forgotten. The entire Bree-Ah clan was now mobbed around the arena cheering and jeering the combat taking place precariously close to the cliff's edge.

Mal was torn as to where her concentration belonged. Zaad was fighting for his and their lives. Zau was already at work, using Alto's etheria knife to cut away the silk webbing that clogged the tail of her airship. The crystal blade sliced through the bindings with ease and the Singa quickly made her way to the windshield.

Both combatants were now on their feet and once again circled, appraising each other with cautious respect. Immediately beside them was the edge of the precipice. Surrounding them was the howling wind and cheering crowd.

As the Doyen circled Zaad he was able to take in his enthusiastically applauding clan. His rousing moment was short-lived as he witnessed the *Haraka* slowly lifting off. Crying out, he attempted to point and sound the alarm, but the crowd was too immersed in the conflict to notice the escaping ship behind them.

This was the distraction Zaad was waiting for. The EEtah lashed out with a savage punch to the side of his head delivered at full force.

The Fudomi screamed in agony as the wound from the broken horn was assaulted again. The force of the blow spun the Doyen backwards and he toppled over the side of the ring and into the void.

The crowd collectively gasped in horror then went silent. All were transfixed on Zaad, who stood triumphantly on the cliff's edge. From the corner of his vision the EEtah marine commander spotted the *Haraka* as it crept silently along the back side of the cliff behind the crowd. Once away, it slipped over the cliff's edge and disappeared.

From over the side of the Saa-Rot arena Zaad heard the sound of rocks falling. From this height he barely made out features from the bottom of the canyon far below. The sound of cracking stone just over the edge, was caused by the Fudomi Doyen. The ram grimaced as he fought to maintain his grasp on the crumbling cliff wall. His hooved feet flailed wildly in the wind as he struggled to find a foothold.

Zaad despondently observed the suddenly silent clan folk. The entire community was awash in shock and disbelief. All tribal unity was shattered with their leader's defeat. In this disheartened state, they would be easy targets for rival clans.

Sighing in resignation the EEtah knelt on the cliff's edge and extended his hand.

The Doyen glared up at the man-shark and scowled. "Never!"

"Don't be a fool," Zaad screamed over the howling wind. "Take my hand!"

"No! I will climb back! I will kill you!"

Zaad was actually taken aback by the Doyen's bravado.

"You are in no position to kill anyone," the EEtah said with a firm dismissive sneer. "And I would rather not leave these people leaderless when it is not necessary!"

The Fudomi's facial resolved faltered for an instant. Zaad continued to cajole as he kept his hand extended.

"Do you not care for your clan?!"

Slowly the Fudomi released a hand from the boulder and reached upward until it firmly grasped Zaad's. As the EEtah began to mercifully pull his adversary to safety the Doyen gave a powerful yank.

"I will kill you!" he screamed as he savagely wrenched Zaad over the edge of the cliff.

The once subdued gathering erupted in celebration when their leader gradually climbed back over the rim of the arena.

Their festive mood was immediately dampened as the *Haraka* ascended above the ring and crowd. The clan folk gasped when they saw Zaad on top of the hull, clinging to the silk covering of the ship.

Shom was beside himself when he heard the loud thump of the EEtah landing on top of the craft.

"I say, for a newcomer that was exceptional," the prodigal said as he gloated in satisfaction. "You may yet prove useful."

Zau glared angrily at Shom. "I may what?!"

"Knock it off!" Mal commanded. "He's still out there on the hull."

Kyopp's mood brightened and he exuberantly sat up.

"This is where I believe I can help," he said as a wave of opaque air streamed in front of him. When it cleared, the Do-Tarr king was in his insectoid form. "Kindly open the side door."

Shom silently consulted Mal for confirmation. She consented and the prodigal pulled the lever. As the hatch dropped, a blast of cold wind whipped through the cabin. The Do-Tarr's eyes twinkled at Shom.

"Isn't this exciting?" he beamed. Without waiting for a response, the insect man scurried out the hatch and along the outer hull.

All clearly heard the clicking of the Do-Tarr's feet above the rushing wind as he made his way over to the clinging EEtah. He soon reentered the cabin, carrying the man-shark with ease.

As the door closed, the roar of the wind subsided and an exhausted Zaad collapsed into his seat.

"Thanks," he weakly said, as he pointed to Kyopp. "I owe you one."

The air in front of the Do-Tarr shimmered once again and he resumed his Bailian form. His blue features were lit up in elation. "We are the ones that owe you my friend! That was an amazing contest!" The Bailian enthusiastically ogled Shom. "Wasn't that amazing?!"

"Yes, Your Majesty," the royal weakly agreed.

Mal sat back in her seat and gave a sigh of relief. "Alright Zau, get us the fuck outta here."

"Yes captain."

"You know where we're going, right?"

"Yes captain."

"No portals, right?"

Zau smiled as she banked the *Haraka* westward. "Yes captain."

Horse hooves clattered against the flat, well-worn cobblestone reverberating down the near empty streets of the Tuath plat of northern Zor. The high holy city was deep in the Kan.

The blurry silhouette of a wagon with a single cloaked driver, pulling an empty wagon and team moved deliberately out of the thick fog.

They were there, as ordered, waiting. Six men skulked in the shadows, all taken from the lower denizens of the southern docks. Out of work sailors and soldiers of fortune with strong backs and weak minds were easy to find. The only other requirement; none were to know each other. Nothing to be traced back to the quartermasters.

The wagons stopped. The metered echo of the hooves faded into the mist. The hooded figure silently turned to meet six large, unkempt men staring at him. Securing the reins of the horse team all caught a glimpse of the figure's right forefinger. The nail was over an inch long and sharply pointed.

All felt a twinge of apprehension as the cowled figure leapt gracefully from the buckboard and strode purposefully over to them.

Dur de Leeds broke into a cold sweat as the much smaller figure approached. The veteran of countless brutal conflicts couldn't explain his rising sense of dread. He gasped when he saw the human's features under the hood. Badly bloodshot eyes twinkled as the clean-shaven human beamed maniacally. Dur had seen madness before but he grimaced when he noticed the freshly carved characters. The man's entire head and neck were covered in the same two tiny scabbed-over glyphs. Reaching below the cloak he produced six blue sodalite gems.

Dur swallowed hesitantly as he accepted a large perfectly faceted crystal. The instant the gem touched the palm of his calloused hand the soldier of fortune was overcome with confidence in the man who just hired him.

"Payment in advance," the scarred man said in a deep whisper that resonated loudly in Dur's mind.

The mercenary made no attempt to stop the mysterious figure as he reached up to his head with his long, sharpened nail. He found himself flushing with pride as an X was carved into his forehead. He felt the blood trickle down, but he didn't care. A massive feeling of belonging swept over him and he found himself smiling at the man beneath the cowl.

The sentiment was cast back with a welcoming pat on the arm. He then moved to the next man where he repeated the same ritual.

When all six had been paid and inscribed, three with X's and three with I's, everyone silently climbed into the empty wagon.

The sound of the hooves once again echoed as they quickly made their way out of the city, to the northeast, into the mountains.

Through a pain-racked haze Fia sat on the table's edge and squinted at the naked young man across the room. Casually, he took a long drink from a silver flask then held it up, silently inquiring if she wanted any.

"No?" he shrugged, genuinely perplexed. "Pity. This brandy is shipped in from home. It's much more preferable than the swill they drink around here."

The Rayth wobbled then doubled over as a sharp spasm swept up her body. Her entire vaginal area and lower abdomen felt like it was on fire.

She refused to speak or cry out during the brutal assaults as she struggled in vain against her mortal restraints. The ice clansmen that held her securely viewed the horrifically savage rape with cold, expressionless stares. All the while the ambassador had been awash in sadistic glee as he mercilessly thrust himself into her.

As the agonizing wave passed, Fia sat back up. She watched Tubig calmly set the flask beside his neatly folded shirt. When he began walking her way the Yupik on either side of her grabbed her arms and legs.

Stepping directly in front of her he smiled condescendingly at her anguished features etched with rage and hatred.

"Our time together unfortunately will be coming to an end," he said in a low husky voice. "You leave on a ship at

257

moonrise. Then, all that will be left of our amorous encounter will be but a fond memory."

Wrenching her gaze away she refused to meet his smug mocking stare. Reaching over he gently put a finger under her chin and tilted her back up to evaluate her. The aristocratic Calden had to admit, even with her battered body she was beautiful, in a barbaric fashion.

"This would go so much easier for you if you just relax and enjoyed it," he said with a lecherous sneer. "However…"

Summoning her strength, Fia pulled herself forward and spat directly into the ambassador's face.

The young man kept his sardonic grin as a large glob of blood drenched spittle ran down his chin. Casually, not breaking his gaze he captured the visceral pink dollop on his fingertip and slowly carried it to his mouth. He sensuously savored the wad of body fluids and his erection began to rise again.

"I do love your spirit," he serenely continued as the specter of sadistic lust filled his eyes.

Reaching out he dispassionately examined the dried blood which covered her vulva and inner thighs.

"We seem to have exhausted this avenue," he said in a mockingly resigned tone.

"No matter," he declared resolutely.

Nodding to the Yupik, they lifted the Rayth and flipped her over onto her stomach. She squirmed in protest to no avail. The stout ice clansmen held her securely.

"Here on the frontier, we learn to improvise," he said roughly parted the cheeks of her buttocks.

An exhausted Zaad was slumped over in his seat. A long trail of drool escaped his open jaws as he reclined in a sound, silent slumber. Next to him Orich sat upright in a meditative, unconscious state.

Below the *Haraka* the thick foliage of the Os-Tor forest lay shrouded in pre-moonrise darkness.

"How soon till Immor-Onn?" Mal asked Zau. The Singa was struggling slightly with the wheel as the winds outside increased the closer they got to the coast.

"I'm thinking a little after moonrise. That is if the weather holds."

Shom took the final swig off his flask then held the empty vessel up for his inspection.

"Well Maluria, once again we've escaped complete ruin by the skin of our teeth."

"Yeah, no thanks to you," the Spice Rat said in an acrimoniously nonchalant tone.

The prodigal reeled in feigned shock. "I'm not sure I take your meaning?"

"This whole thing was your doing!" she said accusingly. "You took the fucking job!"

"The lady has a point," Alto added.

Shom shot the swordmaster an irritated glance then stared back at Mal.

"Are we not all significantly wealthier than before this little adventure?"

"All I got outta this was a spool of silk," Zau countered as she kept her vigil out the windshield.

"Excuse me!" Shom huffed. "But I do believe that roll of spider silk is extremely valuable!"

"Yeah, I'll make sure I cash that in as soon as we land." Zau said in a dry sarcastic mutter.

Kyopp chuckled at the banter, genuinely amused.

"This has been a grand adventure!" he said excitedly vibrating in his seat. "I absolutely adore you all!"

The Do-Tarr king's mood changed from enthusiastic to scheming. "But we also have something very valuable that you are not considering."

Mal, Shom and Alto traded confused looks and even Zau cast an inquiring glance.

Seeing all attention on him, Kyopp snickered. "All those portals we recently bounced through…"

"My stomach remembers them well," Alto said sardonically.

Kyopp became giddy, gesticulating wildly. "Okay, okay, okay…do you remember the cats?!"

Zau froze at the wheel and she lit up with recognition. "Ah hah!" she said then spun to the group.

Kyopp, overjoyed for someone to share the moment, pointed excitedly at the Singa.

"Gar-Yesh Point!" Zau said in enthusiastic revelation.

The Do-Tarr was no longer able to restrain his enthusiasm. "Yes!" he bellowed as he bounded from his seat.

The pair's elation faded quickly, as three confused humans peered back at them.

"Okay, ya fucking got me," Mal said with a confused shrug.

Kyopp leaned forward to make his point. His demeanor turned serious. "Gar-Yesh Point is on the eastern tip of *this* continent. What are the Tiikeri doing building in the Twilight Lands?"

The continued blank stares caused the king to sigh in frustration.

"Why should we care?" Shom said dismissively.

Zau cast a contemptuous glower at the royal. "Because you should care! The Tiikeri are only interested in one thing: Empire. *Theirs*! They don't care who they destroy or enslave to spread their control. They genuinely believe they are superior to all races."

"Well, isn't that cheerful," Shom said with a touch of arrogance.

Alto stroked his goatee. "I can imagine that certain strategists in the Bailian Empire might find this information useful."

"Exactly!" Kyopp said, enthusiasm rising in his voice. "All I'm saying is, why give the information away for free?"

The question caused Mal to erupt in a genuine laugh. "Why Your Majesty, you've a distinct mercenary side to you."

Kyopp gave a knowing smile. "In my race, the king needs to acquire that skill early on."

Three stunned men stared back at Okawa as she finished her briefing.

Rafel's brow furrowed as his mind raced. "You say these, 'blood runes' were actually charged with some sort of energy?"

Okawa soberly scanned those at the table. "Yes, they actually shocked me when I tried to touch them."

Demetrius cleared his throat and shifted awkwardly in his seat. All attention fell on him.

"Uh, I'm aware that I'm the new guy at the table, but am I the only one here that thinks this is creepy as all get out?" The pilot stared inquisitively around at the group. "I mean bodies drained of blood, then used to write on a wall..."

The Zorian spymaster leaned forward on his elbows. "A short while ago we encountered much the same scene on a farm south of town. Horses and wagons were stolen."

All paused as the disturbing coincidences were considered.

"You don't steal two wagons unless you intend to transport something," Zekoff said as he blew a thick column of aromatic smoke in front of him.

The cloud dispersed as he waved the match out. The commander of the Zorian guards was solemn.

"I'm not sure what Si Aramos is up to, but we've got to find those wagons, quickly."

Technically, the Eldorian capital of Rophan was still in a state of mourning. The deaths of both the sovereign and his wife had taken all by surprise. Black mud crosses still decorated the entrances of most buildings. The people, however, were anxious to get on with their lives.

The restless crowd had been growing steadily since the lifting of the Kan, just as it had done every day for the past three cycles. Eldorian Prime Minister Basbakan stared at the anxious mob and sneered.

"The sovereign was buried only a short while ago and now this!" he said in utter disbelief. "You're certain our informants are correct?"

"Yes rector," said a clean-cut young man in his late twenties as he joined him at the window. "They are waiting for a glimpse of their new sovereign."

"When I find out who leaked that Marassa royal lineage report I'll have them executed in the city square," Basbakan spat not relinquishing his view of the vista below.

"It's not just that," the assistant hesitantly said.

The balding, potbellied official finally looked away from the window. "Oh?"

"It seems there've been Boustian bards on the streets ever since the funeral. They've been singing ballads extolling the valor, wisdom and benevolence of Shom Eldor."

"And no one tried to stop them?!"

The assistant gave a defeated shrug. "Several of the city guard tried early on."

The prime minister's questioning expression prompted him to continue.

"A few plucked strings caused them to piss themselves in front of everyone. The Boustian disappeared into the crowd which was then laughing at them. The guards are spooked. Won't go near them now."

Basbakan sighed and returned his gaze to the throng which was still growing and now spilled out of the square.

"Shom Eldor is completely unfit to lead this house."

"Thanks to the Boustians, the people love him," the assistant said in a baffled tone. "There will be riots, perhaps worse if he's not crowned."

Basbakan huffed in frustration. "Half of those sheep out there never even heard of the little pervert before. He hasn't been seen in the city for at least three grands."

"Apparently, the people don't care."

The subordinate's flippant tone resulted in a stern glance from the prime minister.

"Sorry rector," he said meekly, averting his eyes.

Sighing in resignation, Basbakan leaned on the windowsill. Adding to his depressed mood the crowd could now be heard chanting Shom's name.

"Well we've got to do something. Maybe we don't need to stop him. If we can keep his liquor cabinet full and bedchamber occupied, perhaps he can be controlled."

The assistant nodded.

"Do we even know where he is?" the Eldorian noble asked as he fiddled with the sleeve of his yellow silk robe.

"Rector, the last word we received, he was flying around with a group of mercenaries. He was spotted over in Immor-Onn a quinte ago."

Basbakan stroked his double chin. "Flying huh?"

"Yes rector."

"Get word to the Valdurians through the back channels. Let's find out where he is and get him home."

"Yes rector," the assistant said before giving a short bow and leaving.

Now alone with his thoughts, the prime minister nervously paused and listened, as the chanting below grew louder.

The cell was cold and damp. Sitting naked on the floor in the furthest corner from the door, Fia clutched her knees to her chest as she shivered violently. Watching the steam escape her mouth she was thankful that the cold stone beneath her soothed her swollen and abused nether regions.

Never in the darkest of nightmares did she ever imagine her ending would be like this. The Rayth had always envisioned being killed in combat, on the deck of a ship, sword in hand and wind in her hair.

Even in the depths of despair Fia felt no self-pity for her situation. Her thoughts battled back and forth between searing anger and hatred for her captors, all the while ironically realizing they never were the true enemy. The events in Konaleeta had shown her that.

She now knew there were those waiting, slightly beyond the veil of perception, straddling the doorway between here and the Middle Realms. Soon the darkness would come to all of Lumina, as it did so long ago. Then, as before, they would try to usurp dominion over the Annigan. New and different beings, waiting for the balance to tip and the Black Mural to afford them their time. A reign they felt was stolen from them by pearl avatars. There had already been a few attempts recently. She didn't know where, or how, but she felt it. They were probing as they waited at the threshold.

The moon would be rising soon. Glancing about the cage suspiciously, she saw no one. Holding out her hands, she coughed and gagged until a small white disc with blue striations spat into her palms. The Chenakan necklace had broken during one of the ambassador's drunken assaults. She recovered it from the floor on the way to her cell by fainting. Her Yupik guards were strong, but not very smart or observant.

Manipulating the disc in her hands Fia inspected the intricate script in a mysterious language. As her thumb rubbed over the miniscule engravings, she remembered what the Chenakan had said about contacting him.

The instant Morax entered her thoughts the runes tingled against the pad of her thumb.

Her swollen cheek ached when a confident, slightly sardonic thought pulled at the corners of her mouth. As much as she hated the dags and their cock loving whores, this was bigger than any dared imagine.

The eclipse was coming and with the darkness, the Black Mural very well might fall, plunging all of the Annigan into chaos and destruction.

The Kan was lifting in the high holy city of Zor. As the fog slipped back into the Shallow Sea the streets slowly came to life. Street vendors from throughout the city and beyond were the first to arrive in the mercantile district of the Shemol Plat.

As usual, the small stout woman with long grey hair known as Meeka was already there. Every few cycles the spry widow woke early, navigating the murky streets from her home and loom in the small Kauppias enclave of the Tuath Plat to the north. She was wrapped warmly against the winter chill in a vibrant red and blue tunic of her own making. Spread out on the side of the street, were some of the most colorful, high-quality fabrics in the entire area: hers. Folding a swath of her best green muslin she amiably greeted the other sellers who also couldn't afford a shop as they arrived and staked out their coveted place.

Directly above, the shadow of Valdurian Air Station Three jutted from the hillside. The massive horizontal obelisk provided protection from the harsh constant Lumina sunlight. The station also provided customers, who arrived constantly. Within a short time of the fog lifting, the spots along the side of the well-travelled thoroughfare filled quickly.

A middle-aged man with a scraggly beard and long hair who smelled like a stable took the spot directly to her right. He carried a large sack across his shoulders which he placed before him and opened.

Meeka had seen him every sale day, but this was the first time he settled close to her. She winced at the pungent animal smell which was given off from a large blanket he retrieved and spread out.

As if the smell wasn't enough, the elderly weaver twitched in shock as the scruffy rancher pulled a large, dried horse penis from his well-worn bag. He held it up and examined it, then lovingly placed it on the blanket.

Meeka sat transfixed as the man reached in several more times. With each retrieval, another type of phallus was added to the collection before him.

He gave a mischievous chuckle when he saw Meeka's aghast expression.

"For virility!" he proclaimed clenching a fist to show power and sincerity. "Pickled, then dried!"

The weaver sat and stared in prurient wonder as the man pointed with pride to his priapic wares which came in various shapes and sizes.

"Horse, for stamina, bull, for power and deer for agility."

"Surely you don't believe that?" Meeka said blinking innocently.

The rancher laughed and brushed back his unkept hair. "What I believe is unimportant. What my buyers believe is all that matters!"

With salacious curiosity Meeka couldn't pull her eyes away from the display next to her. "There's so many different kinds."

Beaming, the man swept his hand theatrically over his merchandise. "I've got the largest selection in all of Zor! Even bigger than Orkat the alchemist. I actually had a whale cock once…"

Meeka had stopped listening. From up the street a commotion was approaching. A loud female voice rose above the clatter of the avenues. As a small caravan of wagons finally passed, she saw the nature of the furor. Even the enthusiastic rancher halted his babbling to stare along with the morning crowds.

Three foreigners, Bailian women, marched single file as the passing throng of the street parted. All were strikingly beautiful. Their braided snow-white hair hung like thick coiled ropes against their pale blue skin. They wore sheer robes and appeared to be unphased by the winter cold. All had three small gems embedded in a vertical line up the center of their foreheads. The last one in line silently held a large vellum sheet above her. The front of the document was filled with an intricate circular chart.

"Behold the wonder of Sofen as revealed through her true oracle Bu' Lan!" the first in line cried out repeatedly to either side of the street as they passed.

The trio stopped at an intersection a short distance away. The crier repeated her line one more time before the female in the middle stepped forward.

"Hear me people of Zor!" she announced in a lyrically haunting voice that filled the streets. Still addressing the crowds, she pointed back to the chart the other Bailian held aloft. "The Tanem Charts proclaim that the time is near!"

Reaching her arms skyward, her tone went from dire to rapturous. "Soon our beloved moon Sofen will black out your sun. All will rest in darkness and you will be able to behold her in all her full spectacle and glory!"

Meeka gasped in aversion at the words. Quickly she traced a spiral devotion to the sun god Suraja in front of her. *Such blasphemy!*

The Sofen priestess continued as she pointed to the passers-by. "But by the time you finally gaze upon Sofen's holy face it will be too late. Repent now! Come into her luminescent bosom. She welcomes you."

"That's what happens when ya let in those foreigners from the Twilight Lands," the rancher said disdainfully, "with their strange ways and nonsense religions."

Meeka was stunned. "What's this 'moon' she's spouting on about? And blocking out the sun? That's got to be the craziest thing I've ever heard of! Everyone knows Suraja is too powerful a god to allow that!"

"Preposterous I tell you!" the rancher concurred.

"All glory to Suraja," Meeka found herself saying from rote memory.

"His radiance blesses us all," they both said, finishing the benediction together.

The Bailians had attracted a small crowd of curious listeners. Most of the morning rush of street life noisily passed the exuberant proselytizers.

Meeka tried to ignore the blasphemers, but the Sofen priestess Bu' Lan's words cut through the waves of clatter which rumbled monotonously on the streets of the Annigan's largest city.

Even after the detestable apostates moved on to another corner, the dire warning resonated across her psyche, filling her with apprehension and doubt. The old weaver vaguely remembered stories her grandmother had told her about the darkness from so long ago, and the horrors that came with it.

Some exorcisms are easier than others.
Some demons can be dealt with…
Especially if the proposal presented, is in their best interest.

The brothers' astral bodies sat facing each other, with legs crossed atop the *Haraka* as it sped westward.

"I know who you are," Orich said in a calm resolute tone.

Both albinos stared deeply into each other's eyes until the sides of Taa's crinkled as a sly grin played at his lips. "Do you?"

"Yes."

Taa, adopted an innocent posture. "I thought I was your brother."

Orich remained solemn. "My brother is in there, somewhere."

Taa remained smug. "Oh?"

"I was able to track the trail of the spell across the Middle Realms. It led back to the Tiikeri, the one who now seduces in your name."

Taa's superior demeanor fell for the briefest of instances upon hearing his brother's discovery. He rebounded quickly.

"Well, aren't we the clever one," the demon said sarcastically.

Orich remained confident. "It was the mushrooms that afforded me my insight. So, considering, your delaying tactic in the mushroom forest has both betrayed and exposed you."

The demon remained silent as Taa's gaze narrowed angrily.

Sensing he was getting to the entity within, Orich continued, "You used the magical hull of this ship to attach yourself and suppress my brother. You somehow knew he resided there. I imagine you were delaying us to allow the Tiikeri and the human to get there ahead of us." Orich gave a shallow shrug. "Why, I'm not sure."

Taa leaned forward and the demon chuckled. "Not as smart as you thought, huh. Remember my pale friend, you are a new traveler and all may not be as it seems."

"I know your name," Orich calmly declared.

The smirk rapidly disappeared from Taa and the demon sneered.

"That means nothing!" he spat as the *Haraka* suddenly rocked below them.

Orich remained unphased. "You and I both know that is a lie."

Taa gave an evil smile and the craft pitched violently from side to side. "Well then, I might just plunge this craft to the ground, kill everyone and be done with it."

"I don't believe you are going to do that," Orich calmly stated.

"Oh?" the demon taunted as the airship once again pitched stormily back and forth.

"No," Orich said, unintimidated by the forceful, implied threat. "Because, I would try and stop you. You would inevitably prevail, but I believe your interests are now elsewhere. I don't think you want to expend that much energy on a part of your plan long since passed. You've already won in delaying us. Why do you linger? Ego?"

Taa sat back. Orich saw amusement dance in the demon's eyes. "Well, ego is my stock in trade."

Orich remained silent as he stared down the denizen from the Middle Realms.

"A game then?!" the demon proposed with Taa giving a wink and a nod.

"Game?" Orich said warily.

"Yes, something to make this more interesting." Taa paused as the demon's grin grew wider. "You say you know my name. I'm not sure I believe you. Prove it!" Taa pointed at his brother. "Tell me who I am. If you are correct, I will leave. If not…"

The *Haraka's* nose suddenly dipped and the craft began to swiftly drop to the forest below.

"If you are wrong," the demon cackled, "everyone on this ship dies."

The treetops of the Os' Tor forest were growing rapidly closer. Orich clearly heard Mal inside the ship swearing at the top of her lungs as she fought the wheel.

"You are Pa-Waga," he said confidently. "Tiikeri god of greed, gluttony and selfishness. Pa-Waga, the lover of power. You manifest yourself in this world by the power of numbers and their manipulation."

The ship suddenly stopped falling and righted itself. The demon's grin changed to one of begrudging regard. "You play a good game Orich-Taa," it said in a reserved voice. "You are correct. My full attention is needed elsewhere. I was leaving anyway. I do want to thank you for making my departure more amusing."

Taa leaned forward and groaned. Orich immediately felt the connection between his brother renewed. When his twin looked back up, he appeared weary but lucid.

"I was so cold brother," he said in a heavy voice. "Numbers kept swirling around my vision keeping me in a state of paralyzed confusion. I, I couldn't think straight. A few times the numbers cleared and I saw you and the others, but my voice was not the one that spoke."

Orich sympathetically put a hand on his brother's shoulder.

Taa peered about, suddenly aware of his surroundings. "We're almost to Immor-Onn!"

Orich lovingly reached out and touched his sibling. "Yes brother. Come, join with me. We travel home, to our destiny."

The lurching of the craft combined with Mal's tirade had awoken everyone. From his seat, Alto's concerned expression subsided once he realized everything was now under control.

"Honestly Maluria," Shom admonished as he straightened himself. "We're trying to get some sleep here. One would think you would've chosen a smoother route."

"Do you always complain?" Zau asked the royal as she rose and moved toward the rear of the ship.

"I like to think of it as a complimentary service to my fellow travelers," Shom said reaching for his flask. Hefting it, he remembered it was empty. "How else are you going to know the areas you need to improve," he said nonchalantly as he put the empty vessel away.

"Yeah, you're a regular saint," Zau wryly said as she knelt in the cargo area. Reaching in the side pockets of her tunic the pulled out several large folded pieces of vellum and laid them out on the deck in front of her. Ignoring everyone the Singa began studying the parchments.

Zaad and Alto, seeing there was no danger attempted to sleep, while Orich continued a low unintelligible mumble.

Examining the Bailian and finding nothing more unusual, Mal's attention was brought back to the helm.

"So, I imagine you're excited to see your friend Queen Shula?" Mal asked Kyopp who was standing beside her sharing the starry view out the windshield.

"Yes, yes, Shula and I have a very special bond," the Do-Tarr king said with a reminiscent stare. "However, once my little visit is over, I must resume my duties at home."

"Let's hope your queen doesn't find out about your *special bond*," Shom said lecherously.

"Oh, I don't need to worry about that," Kyopp replied not bothering to address the royal directly. "Unlike the rest of my race, I am not connected to the hive and my queen's ever-present gaze. What she doesn't know won't harm me." The Do-Tarr gave a smug, almost bashful grin. "Besides, variety is the spice of life. I mean, it can get pretty monotonous. My queen's libido is absolutely unquenchable. Her obsession is keeping the hive's population up."

Shom gave a chuckle of disbelief. "So, you're telling me your main job as king is, fucking?"

Kyopp gave an amused chuckle. "That about sums it up. After all, I am the only one able to produce offspring."

"In the whole hive?" Shom sputtered.

Kyopp gave a resigned nod.

"Well," Mal chimed in. "You're a pretty handy asset to our little group, and you seem to like excitement. You can always hang with us."

The bug king turned sorrowful. "Thank you, captain. That's very flattering, but there's only one of my kind born per generation. I will continue to serve my queen until my time is up."

"What's that mean?" Mal innocently asked.

Kyopp lowered his head soberly. "Once my successor is born, I will be devoured by my queen and my essence will be passed on for future generations."

Mal gave the navigator a questioning grimace. "Devoured as in eaten?"

"It has been that way since the beginning," the Do-Tarr said in a morosely resolved tone.

"Unfortunately, your time is already up Your Majesty," came a familiar voice from behind.

All turned to see Orich-Taa awake and glaring directly at them. The albino ignored the astonished stares of his companions and concentrated on Kyopp's concerned features.

"The future king has already been born," the Bailian said in his usual dispassionate tone. "The birth we witnessed while meeting your queen was your replacement. I felt his essence the moment the nectar was poured over his embryo. It contained the royal jelly."

Despite the albino's dire warning, everyone in the cabin, except Kyopp was overjoyed to see the *Haraka's* pilot reanimated.

"Orich!" Mal called out with a relieved grin. "It's about fucking time you made it back!"

The Bailian smiled weakly and nodded at the back handed compliment. "Thank you, captain. My brother and I are together again, this time for good. We are Orich-Taa and our time together with you, is short."

Mal was about to question the cryptic statement when Shom leered at Kyopp. "Well old boy, I imagine flitting across the Annigan with Maluria searching for suitable escapades, sounds much better than going home to be killed and devoured by a ravenous mate?"

As Demetrius closed the side hatch of the *Drakin* he took a quick look at the commercial hangar of Air Station Three. The massive room was all but deserted as the few remaining flight crews secured their airships for the coming fog.

"I'm telling you, it's dangerous to go flying during the Kan," he said watching Okawa settle into her seat.

"Can't be helped," she said matter-of-factly. "He's got practically a whole cycle's head start on us and we're not sure where he's going."

"So, your best plan is to go searching around in a blinding fog?" Demetrius asked climbing into the pilot's chair.

Okawa picked up her bag from beside her and grinned.

"Funny you should mention that," she said reaching into her shoulder bag.

The Valdurian captain pulled out two small, thin ukko wood boxes.

"Here you go," she said handing one to Demetrius.

The air jockey warily accepted the small oblong box, all the while keeping Okawa in his suspicious gaze.

Rolling her eyes, she huffed in frustration. "Oh for…will you just take the damn thing?!"

"Let's say, I'll relax once you start being a little more forthcoming with information," he said accepting the wooden object.

"Look, I've been authorized to speak freely to you, so relax. We're on the same side."

He held her gaze in a brief moment of acceptance before opening the box.

Demetrius' mood changed from suspicious to curious as he lifted a pair of spectacles from their protective case and held them up for inspection.

A pale blue circular lens was held firmly in place by a delicate metal frame. Attached on either side of the frame, right beside the glass, was a miniature arm and lever holding a pale orange lens. Pushing down on the arm Demetrius lowered the orange lens over the blue one, then flipped it back up.

"This should make your life easier," Okawa said with a smirk when she noticed Demetrius' perplexed stare.

Pulling out her own pair she pointed to the blue glass. "This glass has been blended with an etheria crystal that helps reveal things."

She then flipped the orange lens over the blue one. "This glass has been blended with an etheria gem for fire magic. When the two are combined it illuminates the heat given off by anything living."

"That's amazing!" Demetrius marveled as he put the spectacles on.

"It's important not to use the orange lens in direct sunlight. It'll fry your eyeballs right to a crisp. So only for use in the Kan or the dark. Got it?"

"Got it!" Demetrius enthusiastically confirmed as he faced the Valdurian captain.

The pilot expected to see the usual attractive brunette, hair pulled back into a ponytail, skintight smoky grey bodysuit filled with her voluptuous frame. The instant he saw her, Demetrius gasped and quickly spun away blushing.

Okawa's brow furrowed. "What?!"

"I can see through your ghost suit," he said in an embarrassed voice, keeping his eyes averted.

"Hmmm," she sighed putting on her pair. "Well, they are supposed to help reveal things," Okawa admitted.

"So, this makes flying easier, right?" she asked, addressing Demetrius directly.

"I guess."

"Oh, by the way, that thing on your thigh, I'd get that looked at."

"Yeah, thanks," Demetrius said as he continued to stare straight forward.

Pulling a lever to his right the *Drakin* lifted off.

As the airship silently made its way out of the main hangar, both equally silent occupants stared awkwardly forward.

"So...um," Okawa stuttered as she nervously peered out the side window. "Did you, um, like what you saw?"

Demetrius froze for an instant to make sure he heard her correctly.

"Yes indeed," he excitedly blushed, still keeping his attention forward.

Okawa gave a small, satisfied grin as they swept out of the immense rectangular air station entrance.

The craft climbed into the cold cloudy skies of Lumina. The Grand Turine in the harbor rang eight bells. Demetrius saw the fog rolling into town down below. Already the docks were all but consumed and the Shallow Sea beyond was invisible below the thick blanket of mist.

"We've still got a few decis before things start to get soupy in the mountains," the pilot assessed. "That is where we're going, right?"

Okawa looked back out the windshield, relieved to be getting back to business. "Follow the northeast road out of town. Let's hope he didn't go into the countryside."

"I don't think so," Demetrius said with a shake of his head. "It gets pretty rocky, pretty fast on that route. Another thing we've got going for us is that with the Kan setting in, farm traffic will be at a minimum."

The airship followed the wide road from thirty feet up as it snaked into the Goyan Mountains. Okawa was pleased that the pilot's description was accurate. They only saw a few wagons making haste for the safety of Zor and the sides of the road were too treacherous for a wagon to navigate.

When the Kan fog finally caught up to them, the ground leveled and the road forked off into three directions.

277

Demetrius sighed in frustration, as he halted the ship in mid-air. "Okay, decision time."

Okawa lowered her orange lenses, then studied the trail below.

"There," she said pointing at the three diverging roads.

"I don't see anything," Demetrius said concentrating out his side window.

The Valdurian shot him an irritated glance as she motioned for him to use his orange lens.

"Oh yeah," he said blushing.

Now he saw what the security agent was referring to. With the combination of magical glass, Demetrius clearly made out the indentations of recent cartwheels and footprints of both animal and human.

The road to the right, led up eventually to the volcano on Mount Goya. Not surprisingly there were no tracks there. The middle path was the main passage and cut directly across the mountain range. It was littered with impressions of constant traffic.

"It appears he went to the left," Demetrius said examining the trail of two wagons as they faintly glowed.

"He's headed for the Valley of Chains," Okawa said in an ominously contemplative voice. "I've got a bad feeling about this."

The Calden warship *Demiurge* hovered inches above the choppy water of Penaber harbor. Captain Maluk de Tinith stood on the quarterdeck and watched the moon rise in the east through a field of undulating masts as the sail ships were tossed about.

The veteran naval officer reminisced about his early days under sail but didn't miss them. The Calden fleet had recently been completely upgraded to ukko wood and he couldn't be happier.

The *Demiurge* had been called away from the end of its regular patrol in the northwest Ocean Deep. They had recently completed an Innaca run with several Brightstar trainees. For a few, it was their first dangerously close loop around the portal in the Innaca Deep. The warship was on its way back to the port town of Sammoz in the Zerk Atoll, when they received orders rerouting them here.

The layover would be short. There wouldn't even be enough time for his crew to go ashore. This was to be merely a quick prisoner pickup and transfer. Normally, this kind of mundane transport would be beneath this ship's capabilities and the captain's dignity.

Not this time and not this prisoner.

Maluk reveled in his good fortune. The *Demiurge* was the pride of the western fleet. Now, he and his beloved ship would be recorded in the annals of history as the ones that brought the pirate queen Fia back in chains. He pondered a dramatic entrance. Perhaps lashing her to the bowsprit. The thought of the cheering crowds made the handsome captain with short brown hair smile with satisfaction.

Perhaps a promotion, yes!

His musings of glory were interrupted as his first mate trotted up the stairs.

"We've added the extra restraints in the brig captain," she said as the wind blew a strand of red hair across her scarred forehead. "We'll chain her directly to the inner hull. She won't be getting away."

Maluk nodded and peered back to the harbor already bustling with activity. "And the marines?"

"Ready to take custody from the locals," she said, joining him at the railing.

"It shouldn't be long now," he said scanning the morning crowd.

"That's alright sir," she said with a curl of the lip. "I've been waiting a long time to get my hands on that quim. I'm gonna savor the moment."

"Laci?" Maluk said, as he peered quizzically up at the much taller woman.

"Oh, sorry sir," Laci said staring down at her feet. "My brother was a deck hand on a transport ship out of Leem, over in the eastern agricultural islands. Five grands ago the Rayth took the ship. My brother, Disparu, was never heard from again," her voice trailed off and Maluk sympathetically related.

Laci continued, scowling with every word. "I'm tempted to pay her a little visit in the brig and have a go at her myself."

Maluk leaned on the railing. "If everyone on this ship who had an axe to grind with the Rayth, 'had a go at her,' she wouldn't make it back alive."

Both laughed, but knew bringing her back, not merely alive, but able to stand trial, was paramount to this assignment.

Maluk suddenly stood up straight. "Ah, here they come."

"Looks like the locals beat me to my fun," Laci said with obvious disappointment, as the crowd parted and Fia came into view.

The former pirate queen was escorted by four Yupik guards and a tall lanky human with hair piled up in a pompous style. She was hunched over. Her hair was wild and tangled, obscuring her features. She limped badly. The Calden naval captain was aghast at the crimson splatters all across her chest and that her crotch and thighs were coated with dried blood.

As they approached the *Demiurge*, on cue a detachment of six Calden Maritime legion marched out onto the gangplank two abreast. They reached the dock and stood at attention as their sergeant stepped forward.

Twenty feet from the ship, Fia collapsed to her knees, convulsing with dry heaves. The thin young man leading them stopped and spun with an annoyed scowl. Maluk saw him motion to the Yupik, who roughly grabbed and wrenched her to her feet.

The Calden captain became enraged. She was in bad shape, perhaps too bad! If this prevented his grand entrance into Nader harbor.

"Too far!" he sputtered in indignation causing Laci to stare at her commander. "They've gone too far!" He roared as he raced down the stairs, his first mate trailing right behind.

Ambassador Tubig gave the marine sergeant a condescending smile and bowed.

"Sergeant," he greeted then moved aside. With a grandiose flourish he pointed back at the barely coherent Fia. "I present unto your care, the pirate queen Fia." Pivoting away his tone became flippant. "She's your problem now."

Any further posturing by the Calden ambassador was cut short by bellowing expletives emerging from the ship.

One does not rise to the rank of captain on your very own Calden warship by being timid. Despite his diminutive size, Captain Maluk's chiseled features and permanent late day facial shadow radiated intensity. Now, the enraged officer stormed the gangplank, plowing through the dual rows of marines.

The sergeant was attempting to hand Fia off to his men when the captain stomped up to them.

Grabbing Fia's hair, he pulled her head up to inspect Tubig's grim handiwork. Her blood-stained mouth was open slightly and a pink drool ran out the sides. The battered Rayth acknowledged nothing as she stared blankly outward.

Maluk released her hair and let her head drop. "Get her on board and have the Medikua check her out," he ordered.

The sergeant saluted and the marines led Fia up the gangplank.

Steely blue eyes then bore into the Calden ambassador.

"What is the meaning of this?!" Maluk spat, as he charged up to the mockingly indignant young man.

Tubig remained where he was, as an amused grin pulled at his mouth. "I'm sorry, you are?"

"Right now, I'm the one who's about to put a boot up your ass!"

Tubig retained his smug demeanor. "A naval officer threatening an ambassador. Well, I think you can pretty much kiss your career goodbye."

Maluk glowered upward at the much taller Tubig. "Yeah, I'm sure top dog of this frontier shithole has a lot of sway back home!"

The ambassador's mouth dropped open in indignation. Before any rebuttal could be delivered, the entire dock and ship rocked violently.

Tubig was thrown to the ground and Maluk was spun about but remained standing as a giant translucent bubble rose between the ship and dock.

Pandemonium swept the wharf and deck of the ship. The marines escorting Fia teetered on the rapidly undulating plank of wood. Tubig sat up in time to see Fia bolt to life.

Flipping her manacled hands back over her, she snared the Calden marine directly behind her. As his comrades struggled to help on the swaying gangplank, Fia gave the chain a twist completely snaring the legionnaire's neck. Keeping the flailing marine on her back between her and the rest of the men Fia desperately searched the area for an escape route.

Both captain and ambassador gasped in stunned, helpless disbelief as Fia suddenly leapt from the gangplank onto the bubble as she was about to be overtaken. The powerless marine was desperately grabbing at the chain tightly encircling his neck, as he was pulled along behind the escaping pirate queen.

A collective gasp went up as both were immediately swallowed by the malleable sphere.

The large, murky bubble undulated violently. The groaning and cracking of wood filled the air as dock and warship continued to shake. Then the top of the dome pressed inward. It bowed forcefully outward as the marine and chains were spit upward twenty feet into the air.

The body along with the chain still wrapped around his neck landed on the docks a few feet from the ambassador with a loud clatter and resounding thud. Tubig screamed in horror as he crawled back in a panic from the dead legionnaire. The unfortunate man appeared to be partially eaten. Large chunks of his body were torn away. His face was bloated and blue from the chain which had been strangling him.

As quickly as it began, the rocking stopped as the globe silently descended below the waves. Maluk bolted over to the edge of the badly damaged dock and searched the churning water to no avail. The bubble was gone.

Behind him, Tubig continued his panicked screams. "You allowed this! Your people let her escape! This is all your fault! I'll broil your ass for this! You're finished!"

Once the excitement of having Orich-Taa back dwindled, Shom and Zaad decided to go back to sleep. Alto and Mal opted to stay up. Their destination, as well as the moonrise were close. The Spice Rat especially wanted to continue questioning the Bailian, whose answers so far were too enigmatic to suit her. The albino immediately insisted on resuming his duty at the wheel.

With the moon's first rays peeking over the eastern horizon behind them, they got their first good look at the scenery below. The Os' Tor Forest was visibly thinning and agricultural fields appeared on the horizon.

"We should be seeing the spires of Immor-Onn anytime now," Orich-Taa said in a distant voice.

Mal took the cue and ended her friendly interrogation, choosing to concentrate on the scenery unfolding below as the *Haraka* swept westward toward the coast.

A wave of excitement swept over Mal when she saw the summit of the city's architecture peeking over the skyline.

"Our little adventure draws to a close my love," Alto said softly as he put his arm around her. "What's next?"

Mal grinned in anticipation. "Let's get this shipment delivered before we start talking about what's next."

"Pragmatic to the end," Alto said kissing her on the top of her head.

"We should be getting ready," she said as she indicated the sleeping duo of Shom and Zaad.

The Spice Rat chuckled at the ironically comical scene. The thin, blonde young man was draped across the massive chest of the snoring man-shark in the seat beside him. A thin ribbon of drool had escaped the royal's partially open mouth causing a small wet spot on the EEtah's jumpsuit.

"Those two sure have become cozy," Mal said with a touch of bewilderment in her voice.

Alto recalled appreciatively. "I believe the defining moment came was when we were trapped on the spider web. Zaad called him by his given name."

A confused Mal tilted her head and blinked, "So?"

"It meant a lot to him," Alto gently explained.

Mal shrugged in acceptance. "Hey, whatever keeps the crew happy, I'm for it!" The Spice Rat paused and gazed over at Zau who was still kneeling on the cargo deck. "And her? She's been at it since Orich-Taa got back."

Alto watched her move the six vellum charts on the floor.

"She's an Arron-Nin," he said with a touch of wonder in his voice. "Among other things."

Mal's gaze now bounced back and forth between Alto and Zau. "A what?"

The swordmaster's confident expression drew a quizzical glance from the airship captain.

"The patterns on those sheets are called Tanem charts and represent the stars of the night sky, the ones we cannot see in Lumina. I've seen those charts before," Alto explained. "In the Dark Waste Desert. They were much bigger though. Carved into a giant field of obsidian at the farthest oasis called Lor-Danta. There, the Arron-Nin astrologers study them."

"Are they any good?" Mal skeptically asked.

"In the Dark Waste one of those charts transported me back to you."

"Take heed in that which the charts tell you," Orich-Taa's voice resounded through the cabin. "Their wisdom is ancient." The deep utterance seemed to come from everywhere and caused Shom and Zaad to stir.

Zau stopped and sat back. She sighed in exhaustion, but her eyes darted quickly back and forth as if reading some rapidly passing scroll.

"It's coming..." The Singa then pointed at the configuration of the six rectangular charts spread out in front of her. "Soon!"

"What's coming?!" Mal anxiously asked.

"The darkness."

"The what?"

Zau enthusiastically pointed at the inner corner of a chart that partially overlaid another one. "It will last for ten cycles."

"Zau, what the fuck are you talking about?"

The lioness spread open her arms indicating the total pattern before her. "The eclipse!"

Mal quickly shot a confused glance at Alto. "The what?"

"The question is legitimate," said Shom as he rubbed the sleep from his eyes and yawned. "The last one happened about five thousand grands ago. Pre-human, she wouldn't be aware of it. Not many are."

Mal was becoming rapidly frustrated. "Okay, will someone, for the love of the goddess tell me what the fuck is going on here?!"

Alto and Shom smiled and shared knowing glances. A weary royal waved on his friend before lowering his head and yawning widely.

"The ancient texts are murky," Alto began. "They talk about a long period of darkness in which fish monsters from Nocturn surprise attacked the continent of Goya. No one is sure why. The Avions, Otick and EEtahs, led by the Piceans drove them back. Actually, it was the eventual reinstatement of the sun that truly defeated the forces of darkness."

Mal stood silently staring in astonishment at her lover. "How the fuck do you know that?"

The swordmaster gave an innocent grin. "To achieve the rank of Mora in Rohina-Takki I had to become familiar with history, literature, poetry and the like." Motioning to the charts he shrugged. "History, albeit from a distinctly Eldorian perspective, however…"

"Okay, okay, okay, I believe you!" Mal then pointed over at Shom. I'm just curious, how the fuck did *you* know it?!"

Shom was slumped over, forearms resting on his thighs. Slowly, he glanced over at his friend. "It must have been one of those damnable classes I actually attended…sober."

Finally convinced, Mal concentrated on Zau.

"How long 'til it hits?" she asked in a calm, calculating voice.

Zau examined the charts and pointed to one of them. "Five to eight cycles, ten tops."

"Okay," Mal said confidently. "That gives us just enough time to get rid of our cargo and get back to Zor to sound the alarm."

Shom squinted in disbelief. "Are you joking Maluria? That leaves us absolutely no time to spread any kind of alarm!"

Mal acknowledged the size of the task. "I recognize the Goyan Islands are a big place, but if we can use the Grand Turine in Zor's emergency bells v. That will cause the alarm to cascade from one to another across all the chains in the Goyan Islands."

Alto nodded his approval. "Bold yet attainable. The various regions won't be able to discern the nature of the danger, but at least they can be on guard."

Orich-Taa stood silently behind the ship's wheel to Mal's right staring ahead, unblinking.

"Alright," she addressed the albino. "You've been pretty quiet. Do you have anything of substance to add to this discussion?"

She saw the albino mouth the words as he remained facing forward. As before the deep voice seemed to come from everywhere.

"Kata-Ra Eclipse," he said to a wide-eyed Mal.

The Bailian' standpoint was ominous. "Change perhaps, the balance now teeters and may very well tip."

Mal gave a deep resolved sigh. "Alright, we've gotta job to do. Let's dump these gems and do it."

"There is one other thing captain," the Bailian's voice reverberated through the cabin.

"I'm counting seven humans and four horses," Okawa reported as Demetrius did a wide circle of the camp. "It also looks like these folks are settled in for at least a few cycles."

"Well, it appears you were right. This was their destination," Demetrius said nonchalantly as he skimmed the *Drakin* frighteningly close to the treetops. "By the way, these glasses work great!"

"I'll make sure I pass that along to the Landagar Group," Okawa said not breaking her stare out the window.

Looking perplexed, the Valdurian's tone became quizzical. "What in the name of the empire are they doing in the middle of nowhere?"

"Valley of Chains," Demetrius repeated aloud as he nimbly banked over a protruding treetop. "Old, right?"

Okawa gave a short gasp of surprise at the abrupt maneuver, but instantly recovered with a renewed clinical assessment of the ground below.

"Four thousand grands worth of old."

Demetrius stroked his chin in wonder. "Why would anyone want to string giant chains between mountain peaks?"

"Ask the monks in the area," she said, her mind on other things. "Right now, I've got to try and figure out what these people are up to."

"Just say where," the pilot said keeping watch on the forest canopy below. "There's not a whole lot of room to work with down there. The clearing isn't that large and those surrounding trees stretch right up to the edge of the cliff."

Okawa was serious as she surveyed the ground. "I've got to get to those wagons. They went to a lot of trouble to steal them. I'm betting whatever is in them will answer some of our questions."

Demetrius pointed to a spot on the steep trail a few yards before the clearing. "I can drop you there. You can come up on them from behind."

The Valdurian stared at the area as she considered his suggestion. Without comment the pilot circled the area one more time then swept down the rocky trail behind the wagons.

Settling quickly to the ground, Okawa opened the hatch. She quickly peeked back at Demetrius. "Remember…"

"Yeah, yeah, I know," Demetrius interrupted. "Stay close and wait for the signal."

Okawa smiled in satisfaction. "Good boy."

The pilot returned the grin and she disappeared into the fog.

As Okawa slipped up on the camp, she clearly overheard the sounds of the men eating their evening meal. The overall tone of the conversation was odd. The rowdy banter usually accompanying encamped men was replaced with restrained and somber tones, led by a single voice.

The dynamic piqued her interest and Okawa came up beside the camp behind a thick row of bushes.

She counted six men sitting around a small fire. All were eating. They faced a man sitting cross-legged on a stump. From her vantage point she noticed his cowl was pulled back and his entire head was badly scarred. He gesticulated as he spoke and she immediately noticed the long, sharp nail on his right forefinger.

She couldn't make out anything they were saying, but he was doing most of the talking. Occasionally one of the men would comment or pose a question.

Stryder Aramos, the agent noted silently to herself. *What are you up to?*

Deciding to take advantage of the lead quartermaster holding court, Okawa silently moved to the rear of the wagons. One was empty and open, she scowled upon finding nothing.

The second wagon was covered. Undoing the ties in the back, she peered in to see a large milky white translucent ball. Touching the surface, she found it soft and malleable.

Exerting a little pressure her hand slipped easily through the skin. It gently enveloped her wrist allowing none of the interior's smooth liquid to escape. Once inside, Okawa felt around, discovering it filled with small objects.

She pulled her arm out and curiously examined the shimmering liquid that coated her skin.

Collecting herself she tested the exterior once again. Pushing her hand into the orb she gripped one of the objects and pulled. It came out easily into her hand with a soft plop as the ball rebounded to its original shape.

The object was about a foot long and incredibly hard. It was covered in a white, dry paste which left a powdery film on her hand. Now the Valdurian agent was genuinely curious. Sliding out her knife, she scraped away a portion of the pasty layer. Below the coating was a raw orange gem, which started to glow and give off an incredible amount of heat.

The temperature immediately became unbearable and she dropped the radiant object to the ground. The bright orange light streaked outward, illuminating the nearby woods and spooking the horses which were tied up a short distance away. They whinnied and pulled at their restraints. She now heard the men hectically breaking camp and heading her way.

Three raced to the back of the wagon. Okawa recoiled at the looks of mindless rage. Their foreheads were carved with fresh wounds making their appearance even more menacing.

All three stopped immediately when they saw the gem glowing in front of her. They hissed manically at her over the heated waves of orange light but refused to pass.

The gem was casting progressively more light and heat as it melted away it's thin white covering.

To her right she caught sight of the other three running her way. Stryder Aramos followed at a brisk yet unalarmed pace, his black cowl fluttering out behind him.

"Alive!" He ordered in a deep malevolent voice which echoed off the surrounding trees. "I want her alive and someone tend to those horses!"

As the lead acolyte lunged for her, Okawa rotated her body slipping ever so slightly to the side. Using the man's outstretched hands and momentum, she tossed him onto the glowing gem. The man screamed as his clothing caught fire. He rolled on the ground flailing in a panic as the other henchmen froze in shock.

Okawa took advantage of the pause. Leaping into the air she delivered a savage flying kick to the one directly behind him. He grunted in pain and staggered back into the third as Okawa bolted for the trees.

Stryder scowled in frustration as the intruder sprinted away. Reaching under his cowl he pulled out a small reflective coin, blank on both sides. With a superior smirk, he flipped the coin into the air.

Okawa's breath was heavy and metered, her long ponytail stretched out behind her as she dashed toward cover. As the trees and trail grew closer, a slight wave of vertigo swept over her. She stopped and tried to clear her mind as waves of uncertainty clouded her vision. In front of her appeared six seemingly identical trails. She swayed slightly as she contemplated the conflicting choices.

"Well, what have we here?" Stryder pompously emoted, as he strode up behind her.

In a daze, Okawa slowly turned toward the voice. Stryder Aramos leisurely approached flipping the shiny coin in his hand.

"My, you're a pretty one," he said pompously as he caught the coin and held it up.

Moving his gaze between Okawa and the coin, Stryder's demeanor changed to mockingly academic. "Too many choices?

The quartermaster jeeringly finessed the coin in his fingers. "Simple really. Only two possible outcomes, but, infinite possibilities."

With her facing away from the illusion the dizziness began to fade. Now looking directly at Stryder she suppressed an expression of revulsion at the tiny runes carved into the man.

Behind Stryder's gloating frame she saw the gem was sparking uncontrollably. The ground surrounding it was burnt black. The growing etheria pyrotechnics were now showering the back of the wagon.

Okawa's senses were now almost clear, and she fought to put on a confident exterior. "In your situation right now, I should be the last of your concern."

"Really?" Stryder smirked.

"My lord!" one of the henchmen cried out in alarm.

The instant Stryder's attention was diverted, Okawa leashed out with a punishing front kick to the quartermaster's back. The force of the blow sent the cloaked man plummeting forward onto the ground. The coin flew from his hands and landed several feet away.

Not wasting any time, the Valdurian agent spun and sprinted for the tree line.

"Get her!" he sputtered as he tried to regain his feet. "You two, move that wagon, NOW!"

Okawa was twenty feet from the trees when she caught the sound of the pursuing henchmen. Her contemplation of what to do once she entered the forest was cut short by the startled cries of the men behind her.

The two shocked acolytes dove out of the way as the *Drakin* swept in quickly and hovered a foot above the ground between Okawa and her chasers. The side hatch dropped open and she saw a smiling Demetrius' peering over at her from the controls.

Without a word she leapt through the doorway and Demetrius raced the airship skyward.

Panting hard, Okawa ignored the grinning pilot.

"You know, we gotta stop meeting like this," he said good naturedly. "I'm beginning to notice a pattern in our relationship."

Throwing him an unamused glance, she settled back into her seat. "What took you so long."

Unphased, Demetrius banked the *Drakin* southward toward Zor.

"It looked like you were handling things," he complimented. "Anything important in the wagons?"

Okawa gave a shallow shrug. "Some sort of fiery gems."

"And that means?" Demetrius said with a perplexed expression.

The Valdurian locked eyes with her pilot. "I'm not sure, but that bad feeling, just got worse."

Stryder watched the airship disappear into the fog. His lower lip trembled in rage.

He had gotten a good look at her though. That was all he needed. His men successfully moved the wagon and the gem was burning itself out.

The possessed quartermaster needed more insight into the nature of the intruders. Pointing at two of his henchmen he glowered menacingly.

"Bring me one of those horses."

Fia hadn't slept or stopped talking for the entire trip below Lumina's ocean. She paced the deck wildly waving her hands. Her unkept hair swayed back and forth furiously and she never blinked. Morax listened in astonishment as she rambled on, barely finishing one thought before starting immediately on the next. There was no doubt the human female had changed drastically since he first saw her. It was obvious she felt guilt for the wholesale slaughter of her people. The revelations in Konaleeta pushed her grasp on reality and then her brutal rape and torture at the hand of the Calden had taken their toll.

Now she teetered on the very edge of sanity. Yet, in her madness, the Chenakan detected hints of a very bleak truth. If she was to be believed, the Chenoans, his people's enslavers, and sworn nemesis were but pawns themselves. The triumvirate between them, the Tiikeri and humans were but a ruse. The real threat was much greater and more terrifying than any cared to imagine.

According to Fia, the beings who waited at the dimensional threshold considered all life on the Annigan nothing but a nuisance to be done away with. A lesser lifeform, nothing more than the ants upon the ground. This new life form was uncaring, unfeeling and devoid of any emotions.

The Black Mural was but a means to an end. It had been thwarted twice recently, but that was no matter. Their time was at hand. They would rise and take what was rightfully theirs since the beginning of the world, before being usurped by the fleshy ones and their pearl overlords.

In a way Morax didn't want to believe her. The concept of an evil triumvirate was easier to grasp and seemed much more combatable. Her next statement however pushed even his sensibilities to the breaking point:

The Chenoans are gone.

Locals would say that the fog of this cycle's Kan was as thick as they had ever experienced. It provided perfect cover as the bubble surrounding Morax's ship surfaced in Narian Bay, south of the high holy city of Zor.

The unlikely duo stood on the deck as the translucent covering dissolved and the ship made its way toward the rocky shore. In the harbor the Grand Turine rang ten bells. Each chime hung dolefully in the air over a sleeping city.

"I owe you my life," the former Rayth said softly, as a wave of lucidity came upon her. "I should've listened to you when we first met. You were right. The only way to fight this is from the underground."

The Chenakan nodded sadly. "I am truly sorry for your people. I only hope your conclusions are wrong."

The craft landed on the shore with the grinding of pebbles beneath the hull and a soft thump.

Fia shuddered as the madness began to grip her again. "I'm not wrong."

The former pirate leapt onto the shore.

"Go to the trench, see for yourself," she said pointing up at Morax. "We don't have long."

As the Kan fog receded, Stryder sat atop the only remaining horse and surveyed the campsite which now resembled a battlefield.

The charred remains of the two wagons still smoldered. Grey smoke trailed lazily up into the cloudy Lumina sky only to be swept away by the cold winter wind.

Blood seemed to cover everything as six mutilated human corpses as well as three horses littered the ground.

A sadistic smile played at his lips thinking about the men as they viciously set upon each other. He felt his passion start to rise as the men marked with X's attacked the ones marked differently. When the last one standing begged for permission to kill himself, the quartermaster was breathing heavily in excitement and a rampant erection pushed at the front of his pants.

Of course, permission was granted. He had served Pa-Waga well, why deny this servant the chance to meet his lord. The last acolyte appreciatively thanked him with wide tear-filled eyes. When the groveling man slowly dragged the blade across his throat torrents of blood cascaded from the wound saturating the front of his coat. Quivering in satisfaction, Stryder ejaculated.

So much had been accomplished, yet there was still one more thing that needed tending. Their work had to be completed quickly because of the intruder, but that ultimately didn't matter.

Stretched between two nearby saplings was the skin of the first horse killed. Its dapple coat was filled with multiple patterns of the sacred numbers.

Her identity had been revealed in the figures. She and her accomplice would be dealt with. For that, he would need assistance of his ironmark and he knew the perfect one for the task.

Yes, his lord's time was at hand and he would not be denied.

Spurring his mount from the grizzly scene he started back along the mountain trail to Zor.

Shom let out a loud relieved sigh as the *Haraka* crossed over the farmlands and was enveloped in the snowflake spires of Immor-Onn. The moonlight played off the crystal domes and peaks, casting shards of multicolored light everywhere.

"Okay, spill it," Mal apprehensively said to Orich-Taa. "One more thing?"

The Bailian regarded his captain fondly. "We will be remaining here in Immor-Onn."

The simple statement caused the Spice Rat to pause and stare past him in contemplation.

"Well," she sighed. "I can't say I didn't see it coming or blame you. You've been through a lot and this is your home after all."

The albino gave a rare smile of thanks. "We can serve the queen and the people. They will need a Harbinger of Balance. The Annigan still teeters on the precipice and my brother and I are in a unique position to help. We are Orich-Taa."

"You did good," Mal praised.

Orich-Taa sighed contentedly as he guided the airship out over the ocean, banking it to the opening of Air Station East.

"And it was an honor serving under you captain."

"I suppose that means you're going to be getting back to your duties as marine commander, eh Zaad?" she said in a resolved tone.

The EEtah's laughter filled the cabin. "Not a chance!" he bellowed. "I haven't had this much fun since back in the day when we went tear-assing around the Shallow Sea causing trouble." The EEtah lowered his gaze and became serious. "I'm gonna give up my commission and stick with you."

Mal chuckled with delight. "Don't do that. I'm pretty sure I can get your 'temporary duty' extended indefinitely. No sense in risking losing any kind of military pension."

"Sweet!" the man-shark gushed as he stroked the handle of Bowbreaker.

"I've been thinking," Kyopp spoke up. "I'd like to tag along too. You were right. There's nothing for me back in the hive except death. If I'm going to die I would much rather it be on an adventure."

"You do bring a unique set of skills to the table," Mal admitted.

Shom noisily cleared his throat. "What about me?"

"What about you Shommy?"

"Well I…"

"Come on," Mal cut him off. "You're like a bad copper. You always keep showing up in my life. You're not going anywhere."

The prodigal shook his head whimsically and all attention fell on Alto who sat quietly. After a moment of awkward silence, all acquiesced to the swordmaster's austerity.

Alright," Mal said in a firm yet optimistic tone. "Let's finish this run. No one can say we didn't earn it this time. Take us in Orich-Taa."

"Yes captain."

ACT THREE

The Aramos Gambit

The horrifically chilling screams rising from dock six in the port city of Tunia mixed with the shrill cry of the gulls overhead as they circled and dove. Sixteen crew of the cargo ship *Zatecen* knelt shivering on the damp wood planks in front of the crates of contraband they were caught loading. Their hands were bound behind them and they uncontrollably trembled in terror. If they lived through this, all would be branded and have to endure many cycles of punishment slavery.

Guarding them, was a towering EEtah of Morrak Sunal, as well as a half dozen city militia. Most of the guards and crew, as well as the growing crowd of spectators looked away in shock and revulsion from the brutal spectacle on display before them.

Captain Dreisio's wrists were lashed to the railing of the docks and he stared out into the harbor. The grizzled old captain's pants had been shredded off him. His thin, boney legs were spread wide and blood ran down them in streams. The crimson rivers pooled on the deck at his feet until it mingled with the seawater and was washed away.

Directly behind him, an eight-foot-tall naked sentient with leathery, scarred, blue grey skin and a stubby row of fins running the length of his spine pumped away savagely. The brute grabbed hold of his victims' shoulders. With greater leverage he rocked the old captain back and forth on his massive penis with brutal rhythm. The much smaller human shrieked in agony as the creature bellowed with sadistic pleasure.

299

Standing a short distance away, a female Picean stood watching. Her slender, smooth, pale green features betrayed no emotion. Nor did she feel any pity for the man being brutally and humiliatingly raped. Smugglers knew very well the price of their crime. She raised her bald head and enjoyed the last remaining traces of the cool Kan fog as it receded into the Shallow Sea. Her gill flaps on the side of her head fluttered over her ears allowing the delicate membranes to translate the hushed, fearful languages in the crowd.

Her black, lidless eyes focused on one of the gulls as it broke from the circling flock and quickly descended, landing on the deck beside her. Squawking loudly, it circled, occasionally flapping its wings.

Pulling her attention away from the violent spectacle, she knelt beside the bird and removed the note attached to its leg. She glanced at the brief message then back over to her superior who howled and thrusted violently as he orgasmed.

The old man lurched forward over the rail against his restraints as the blast pulverized the interior of his torso. His agonized cries ceased as a torrent of blood and unrecognizable, gelatinized gore erupted from his mouth. His eyeballs popped from their sockets and flopped on his hollow cheeks as his now invertebrate trunk slumped over the rail like a deflated balloon.

With a satisfied grunt, the massive humanoid slid his immense member from the ravaged, bleeding corpse. Tendrils of red slime dripped from the semi erect cock and his entire lower torso was stained crimson.

The prisoners whimpered and reeled as he smiled, revealing short, sharp serrated teeth. Strolling over to the first mate his hairless, scarred features lit up in delight as the crotch of her pants suddenly stained and urine was leaking out beneath her.

"Sir," the Picean interrupted.

"Not now!" he impatiently snapped, as he leered at the young woman trembling in fear. His erection was rising again to full mast and he liked her mouth.

The Picean was persistent. "Sir, it's from Lord Stryder."

He stopped. His throbbing bloody organ mere inches from the terrified woman. "Eh…"

Glaring lustfully at her he sneered, then walked over and took the note. His erection slowly receded as Orrk the Undressed, Ironmark for the Goyodan Chain, read the short message.

"Get them chained and on a ship for Nier immediately," Orrk said to the EEtah, then callously laughed. "The slavers at House Whitmar are going to be busy today."

"Andha, get my ship ready to sail," the ironmark ordered the Picean. "We leave for Zor within the deci."

Air Station East, at one time seeming so cavernous and imposing, now felt like the embrace of an old friend as the Bailian pilot slipped the *Haraka* effortlessly through its massive opening.

The orange tunicked air boss flagged them into the commercial hangar, but that was hardly necessary. Orich-Taa was home.

Mal grinned in satisfaction when she saw Quadar standing to the left of their slip. Accompanying him was a detachment of six Valdurian marines, five Bailians and an EEtah. All wore the traditional green jumpsuits.

The enthusiastic young maintenance chief's red hair fluttered in the wind and his hands were on his hips. The

Spice Rat was relieved to see him smiling as Orich-Taa gently settled the airship into its slot.

When the side hatch dropped, Mal led the procession down the ramp. The exuberant young Valdurian kept his welcoming disposition, but his eyes gave away a pressing question.

"Boy am I ever glad to see you!" Quadar said as he opened his arms welcomingly.

Mal noted the probing look and grinned.

"They're in the back," she said in a confident, nonchalant tone jerking a thumb over her shoulder.

Immediate relief swept over the young man and his apprehensive smile broadened into a satisfied grin.

"YES!" he shouted, as he squinted and clenched his fists in celebration.

"Drop the back gate Orich-Taa," Mal yelled.

At the same time, Quadar directed the marines to the rear hatch as it slowly opened.

"Yes, well I do hope the queen enjoys her gems," Shom said adjusting his cuffs, as he strolled regally past the Valdurian maintenance chief. "We endured quite a bit to get them here."

A slightly defensive tone bubbled behind the redhead's jubilant mood. "I never said anything about the queen."

Shom stopped and eyed the young man with an amused smirk. "My good man, you have your skills, as do I."

"You really saved my butt on this one Mal," Quadar said, quickly changing the subject. "Anything I can do to help…"

"As a matter of fact," Mal interrupted. "This baby's got to be ready by moonrise next cycle. We've got to get to Zor in a hurry."

The maintenance chief scanned the airship. "Well, it appears she's taken some bumps, but is none the worse for wear. I'll get my people right on it."

Quadar watched the marines muscle the two large bags of gems onto the flight deck.

"That's all of them sir," the EEtah sergeant noted.

"Okay, that's my cue," he said, glad to be pulled away from the conversation. "I gotta get these to their rightful owner."

"Do give my regards to the queen," Shom said flippantly.

The redhead glanced back over his shoulder but said nothing as he escorted the marines out of the hangar.

Mal stared skeptically at the royal. "How the fuck are you so certain the Bailian queen was behind this?"

The Eldorian prodigal turned uncharacteristically insightful. "I believe it all started when I drank the Do-Tarr queen's nectar. My powers of deduction seem to have been enhanced, almost to the point of distraction."

The Spice Rat's face scrunched questioningly. "Wow?"

The royal's attention now flitted back and forth from Mal to Alto.

"Yes, you two also need to discuss things," he prophetically proclaimed. Reaching into his pocket Shom retrieved a pale blue gem the size of his thumb. "I do believe I promised you I would pay for your room at the next port of call, should ever we reach it."

He handed the gem to Mal. "We obviously made it. So, you two go and, well…" he fluttered his hands then started to walk away. "I've got my own matters to attend to."

"And you can give Attina my regards," Mal said slyly just before Shom got out of earshot.

The airship captain threw a lecherously apprehensive grin at Alto as Kyopp stepped out onto the deck.

"Your Majesty?" Mal inquired.

The Do-Tarr king gave a sarcastic chuckle. "Well, I've got a work team to check on. My dear bride will at least see that I'm doing what I said I would."

"Yeah, while she plots your death," Mal scoffed.

"Oh, there'll be no plotting," Kyopp said as he started toward the entrance. "She'll bite my head off then devour me." The Do-Tarr king took on a pragmatic tone. "At least it would be quick."

As he walked away, they saw the rippling air waves obscure Kyopp when he transformed to his insect state.

"I believe he made the wise decision in staying with you." Alto said casually to Mal.

"Speaking of which," Zaad's voice boomed behind them. "The sooner I give Commander Sandal the bad news that I'm not staying, the better."

"We fucking leave at moonrise!" Mal loudly admonished her crew as they headed out for their layover.

Sensing something was amiss, the Spice Rat peered inside the cabin of her ship. "Where's Orich-Taa?"

Alto joined her inspection. "He did say he was staying in Immor-Onn."

"Yeah but I didn't see him leave the hangar. The fucker could've at least said good-bye."

Alto reached out and gently touched Mal's shoulder. "It appears we have some time my love, what is your pleasure?"

Mal sighed and glanced back at her ship. "A drink, a meal, a bath and a bed. Not necessarily in that order."

Alto tilted his head quizzically. "I trust I'm included in these plans?"

Mal chuckled lecherously as she grabbed the lapels of his robe and led him to the exit. "Oh, yeah!"

"I tell ya, they should make the bastards from construction come down here and clean this up!" Bakos said as he steadied the horse next to him. "They're the ones that caused it!"

Rayor huffed at his coworker's complaining. Raising the glowing crystal, he continued sloshing through the ankle-deep water of the Zorian sewers. "It don't matter who caused it. If that clogged vent causes any of this shit water to back up into the Shallow Sea, it'll cause a ruckus no one will soon forget. Especially if it gets into the Otick oyster beds."

Bakos grunted his acceptance as he checked on the single horse pulling the empty wagon beside him. The animal, a fine sturdy draft horse, was doing well even under the current less than sanitary conditions.

"Turds!" Rayor called out as he dodged a large pile of feces floating by. The warning reverberated off the high ceiling and empty stone walls.

The alert came too late and the smelly, floating excrement collided with the front of Bakos' shins. The pudgy sewer worker launched into a torrent of obscenities as he danced about in the murky water. The horse beside him whinnied and bucked slightly causing the wagon to rock.

Glancing back, Rayor started to laugh as he kept up his soggy pace.

"Oh, you think that's funny?!"

"I warned you," Rayor said in between peals of laughter. "The wife's gonna make you sleep outside for sure."

Grumbling, Bakos swished his legs in the filthy water trying to dislodge the sticky refuse which now coated his ankles.

Rayor paused and consulted a vellum map, then stared out into the long tunnel ahead of them. "Looks like there's a junction room about a hundred yards up ahead," he said checking back on his work mate. "It's a good thing the boss found this old map. I don't think anyone's been down here in a long time."

Bakos peered apprehensively at the roughhewn stones which comprised the old sewers and noted the difference from the more precisely cut walls of the upper culverts he normally worked. "I been crawlin' around this city's sewers most of my life and I didn't even know this section existed."

"Yeah, well the sooner we get this done, the sooner we can get behind a tankard of the good stuff," Rayor said starting off again.

"I hear that," Bakos agreed giving a tug on the horse's reins.

As they sloshed their way noisily down the tunnel, both noticed the ground beneath them gradually sloping upward and the water level quickly receding.

"How's this happening?" Rayor quizzically said as with every step the floor beneath them became little more than slick, damp stone.

"Don't tell me we're fucking lost!"

Rayor continued to consult the map. "No, there's a large junction over there, like the map says. We'll be able to get our bearing."

The solitary glowing gem in the sewer worker's hand spread out, illuminating the large room as they entered. The ceiling towered twenty feet above them and each of the four walls contained several openings identical to the one they arrived through.

Peering into the darkness they gasped in disbelief. The light revealed the walls completely covered in complex binary patterns of X's and I's.

"What in the name of the gods?" Rayor gasped as he brought the glowing stone closer to the nearest set of runes. As the orange karabite gem drew closer to the mysterious crimson patterns, they began to emit small blue sparks and the crystal's light dimmed. Recoiling back the orange light returned to its original luminescence.

"Damn!" Rayor gasped. "I ain't never seen nothin' like this."

Bakos was staring upward toward the top of the walls, mouth agape. "Looks like whoever did this was starting on the ceiling," he said in morose wonder as he pointed to the far corner.

"I think this is blood," Rayor said as he examined the runes closely while keeping the karabite at arm's length.

"It's sorcery!" Bakos said, his voice raising numerous registers. "Fuck the blockage, we need to…"

The horse suddenly started to whinny and fidget pulling against the line in Bakos' hand. Both sewer workers gandered cautiously outwards as far as the light would reach. As the horse became more agitated, the men's curious scrutiny became an unnerved examination of their surroundings.

Both drew their daggers when they heard clicking coming from every entrance. As the clacking got louder the horse panicked, rearing up and braying loudly. It knocked a startled Bakos to the ground and bolted into the far tunnel.

As the portly worker got to his feet, the sound of the horse screaming in pain echoed out from the darkness of the passageway.

The clacking was growing louder and the terrified duo stood back to back. Their trembling hands held their utility knives in front of them at the ready.

"I'm gonna be sick," Bakos declared with a groan before doubling over and vomiting. Rayor winced at the smell of the bile, just as he caught the whiff of wet fur.

In the distance of the sewer passages, Rayor detected movement at the fringes of the light. With chattering teeth, he fought to keep the gem and blade in his hands steady.

The advancing commotion was now at a shrill level as the access tunnels filled with Cul-Ta rat creatures. Each was armed with various bladed weapons, some of comical proportions. The three-foot-tall denizens of the sewers no longer carried the smarmy demeanor they were famous for. These humanoid rats appeared hard and cruel. Their eyes burned with hatred.

"What do you want?!" Rayor cried out. "We don't have any money!"

A larger man-rat swaggered forward through the mob and laughed mockingly. "Just like a human," it said with near flawless diction. "You think money is the answer to everything!"

The huge junction room now slowly came to life with the Cul-Ta's arrival. They poured in from every opening, quickly filling the room. A ten-foot circle formed around the embattled sewer workers.

The young leader moved closer to the frightened humans. His grey and brown fur was badly matted over a thickly muscular frame which dwarfed his followers.

"You hunted us," he spat in a low, ominous voice as he pointed his dagger like sword at the two humans. "Put a bounty on our heads!"

Bakos and Rayor gazed about in disbelief, their bodies frozen in shock. Rayor was briefly distracted from his chattering teeth by the sudden pungent odor of urine. It was his.

The leader leaned forward menacingly. Spittle was forming at the sides of his mouth. "You killed and skinned my parents right in front of me!"

"It wasn't us! It wasn't us!" Bakos screamed in a shrill voice. "All we do is clean the sewers!"

The Cul-Ta stared uncaringly at the terrified sewer worker. "The only good Zorian is a dead Zorian." His malevolent gaze then slowly sized up the portly city worker. "You're a big one," he assessed with a sneer. "Our children will feed well."

The tension was briefly broken by the sound of a commotion growing closer from the tunnel.

"Well," a deep voice thundered from the darkness. "I guess I should count myself fortunate I'm not Zorian."

From the depths, a horse head approached, bobbing a few feet off the ground. Two of the rat torsos were sticking out the bottom of the severed neck. They pranced about, contemptuously imitating the animal as they moved its mouth from the inside, squawking away in their language. This caused the room to erupt in juvenile, sadistic laughter.

Behind the head, a small group dragged the horse's limp torso. They were followed by two who pushed a large cask filled with the animal's blood.

"I see you've met my new friends," the voice resounded once again. The menacing greeting was followed by a cloaked human who floated into the room, inches off the floor. The Cul-Ta mumbled excitedly and parted as the figure approached the men.

"I'm afraid they don't hold you city dwellers in very high regard," he said with a frown.

Both men winced in revulsion at the man's maniacal features and badly scarred face that sneered in contempt from beneath the cowl.

"And you've dropped by uninvited," he continued. "My temple isn't even finished yet." He stopped and gracefully extended an arm at the nearest rune-filled wall. The workers stared apprehensively at the man's freakishly long, dagger-like fingernail.

"But not to worry," he cajoled as blue sparks emanated from two rows of numbers on the nearby wall. "With your assistance, it should be completed in plenty of time prior to my lord's return."

Moving his outstretched hand, he pointed at the glowing gem in Rayor's hand and it began to dim.

"It's the least you can do," he said as the room went dark and the echo of his voice was replaced with the sounds of screams and tearing flesh.

Okawa sat forward in her chair and leaned on Zekoff's desk. "Stryder Aramos is back in Zor. I can feel it!"

The old colonel tapped out his pipe and looked up at Rafel. "Anything?"

"We've had no sightings," the spymaster said confidently.

The colonel reached for his tobacco pouch. "By the gods he's in charge of the Quartermasters' Guild! He can't just disappear."

"He's obviously changed," Rafel said with a shrug. "It appears he's practicing some sort of strange blood magic no one has seen before."

"Strange and dangerous," the Valdurian agent added with a twist of her head that sent her long brown hair swaying. "We must find him quickly. Something big is about to happen."

"Provided your assumptions are correct, that would be prudent," Rafel said calmly.

"Provided my what..." Okawa said quizzically as her attention shifted from the commander of the city guards to his spymaster.

"Captain, I mean no disrespect," Rafel said extending his arms. "But I make my theories and recommendations based on hard intelligence, not hunches."

Okawa was about to protest when Rafel cut her off.

"Once again, I don't disagree with your assessment. Stryder Aramos came back from Nocturn a changed man. I need more to go on before any action can be taken."

"I don't think we have the time," Okawa said, as she held the spymaster's gaze.

"Alright, alright," Zekoff said authoritatively as he packed the bowl of his pipe. "Put some people on the quartermasters' headquarters. Low key, comings and goings, the usual."

Rafel nodded.

The colonel lit his pipe and regarded Okawa through the cloud of smoke. "Let's find out about the residue we took from your hands when you got back. The results should be ready over at the university. Hopefully we'll gain some insight into those crystals. While you're there, see if there are any details you can find out about the Valley of Chains."

As Zekoff waved out his match he pointed the pipe stem at Demetrius standing quietly by the door. "And you?"

The pilot jumped at the unexpected attention. "Me?"

Casting the match aside he blew away the cloud of smoke. "You've been to the dark side of the world quite a few times I understand?"

"Uh, yes sir."

Zekoff opened his arms gesturing widely. His pipe gave off a weaving tendril of smoke. "What do you make of all this?"

"Me sir?" Demetrius bumbled. "I mean, I'm just a pilot."

The colonel chuckled. "Young man, if I only relied on the input from *experts*, I would've probably been dead a long time ago." The beard parted in a grin. "Speak up…"

Demetrius' nervous response was immediate.

"I never encountered anything like that when I was in Nocturn. But I will tell you, I'd listen to her," he said pointing to the seated Okawa.

The Valdurian paused in surprise. She knew better than to smile, but her eyes danced with appreciation.

"Oh, really," Rafel's tone was laced with subtle condescension. "And what brings you to that conclusion?"

The veteran pilot scoffed loudly. "Are you kidding? This is most I've ever heard her say at one time, ever!"

The Grand Turine in the Zorian harbor rang nine bells as Amarenian ambassador Alosus left the forum. It had been a long exhausting day. By now the Kan fog already engulfed the city and spread into the mountains. The dampness accentuated the winter conditions causing the ambassador to shiver. She pulled her wrap tighter as she stepped out into the near empty streets.

"I'm too tired for the baths," she said to Sareeta, her seneschal and bodyguard.

The Hill Sister acknowledged the disclosure with a scowl. The normally energetic woman's shoulders slumped and her gait was slow.

"Who would've thought negotiations for air stations would be so contentious?" Alosus said with a weary shrug.

"I thought everyone was on board?" Sareeta said as they began their short walk to the diplomatic compound.

"They are," Alosus said with a scoff.

The six-foot-tall Hill Sister loudly exhaled, *Politics. Unbelievable!* She thought. "We'll get back and I'll get you something to eat and then rub your shoulders."

"That sounds wonderful," the diplomat said as her voice trailed off in exhaustion.

Once Sareeta had the ambassador safely secured in her apartment, she set out for the kitchens, hoping they were still open. If not, she would have to locate a late Kan street vendor.

As she moved through the apartment's common area, Alosus removed most of her clothing on the way to her room. Opening the door, she shivered as a chill raked across her half naked body.

The esteemed sister immediately spotted the reason. The windows were wide open. Sighing deeply at the housekeeper's sloppiness, she treaded quickly toward the source of her discomfort. As she stretched forward to pull the twin windows shut, a female voice resonated from a dark corner in the rear of the room.

"Don't."

Alosus froze, blinking rapidly as she assessed her situation.

"It was getting stuffy in here," the voice continued.

The Amarenian ambassador's heart was racing and she found herself starting to perspire, despite the chill.

Alosus slowly turned keeping her hands out. "My bodyguard is outside…"

"Your bodyguard left on an errand," Fia interrupted the lie as she rose from the chair. "I'm not here to harm you. Quite the opposite. I'm here to warn you."

The ambassador warily lowered her hands.

"Do you know who I am?" Fia asked as she moved closer.

Alosus weakly nodded yes. "The reports say you were killed in the Bannock Atoll."

"And yet here I am."

"Why?" Alosus asked, obviously unnerved by Fia's wild and intense stare.

"I told you," the former Rayth calmly stated. "I come with a warning."

"Warning," Alosus repeated. "What kind of warning. About what?"

Fia's breathing increased as she waved her hand skyward. "The darkness, the eclipse, it's almost at hand!"

The ambassador stared at the former Rayth in confusion. "Darkness? What's an eclipse? What are you talking about?"

"The moon blocks out the sun. Darkness! The last time it happened humans didn't even walk the Annigan."

Fia's wild erratic motions and facial expressions rendered the stunned ambassador unwilling to question or comment on her passionate diatribe.

The Rayth held the ambassador's gaze. "Talk to the Otick! Talk to the Piceans! Time is short!"

Alosus' blank expression caused Fia to become even more animated. "Don't you see?! With the darkness comes things from the dark side of the world! It's an ancient battle.

And us," Fia waved her arms indicating everything. "All of us are nothing more than insects in the way."

The Rayth paused to catch her breath but Alosus remained silent.

"The Golden Avatar is the key," Fia proclaimed with labored breath. "Get to the Golden Avatar! Get to the Otick!"

From beyond the closed bedroom door both heard the outer doors open and close loudly. Both women's attention snapped toward the noise as Sareeta's voice called out from the next room.

"By the goddess, the kitchens were still open..."

When Alosus looked back, Fia was gone.

Sareeta was feeling happy and relieved she didn't need to go searching across a fog-shrouded city for her mistress' evening meal.

As she set the covered dish on the table the bedroom door flew open. Alosus, wide-eyed and frightened rushed into the room.

Sareeta's hand instinctively found the hilt of her short sword. "Esteemed, is there something wrong?!"

The ambassador said nothing as she retrieved a pen and sheet of paper. She quickly scrawled a short message.

Blowing on the ink, then folding the paper, she handed it to her concerned seneschal. "Get this to the quartermaster's headquarters immediately."

The door clicked closed as Sareeta quickly exited. Alosus dropped into the nearest chair and stared outward, going over in her mind the events which had just transpired. The Amarenian was both confused and concerned.

What in the name of the goddess does the Golden Avatar have to do with anything?

A coming darkness?

And her features, her mannerisms. She must be mad!

Mal had never experienced the feeling of being alone in a crowd, until now.

The Baths of Immor-Onn were busy as usual; naked Bailians of all ages, shapes and sizes relaxed in the warm water. Most of the patrons congregated into small groups chatting quietly, ignoring the humans. Some leaned back on the wide tiered steps, enjoying a relaxing soak. Now, they all faded off into a haze as the Spice Rat stared past Alto's chiseled frame in front of her.

As she shifted stressfully, the first sensation she became aware of since hearing the news was the feel of smooth stone below her buttocks and thighs.

The thought of Alto returning to Makatooa to open his school caused a profound feeling of loss to sweep over the hardened Spice Rat. The swordmaster's decision, delivered with tender, heartfelt regret was hardly a surprise. Nonetheless, the finality of his spoken words left her disheartened.

Alto gave a sad, resolved sigh. The act of actually verbalizing an — until now — nebulous plan, left him feeling drained and apprehensive. He glanced forlornly away from her penetrating stare. Ironically, his gaze fixated on a lone drop of water hanging precariously on the nipple of Mal's gently upturned breast.

Her breathing is labored, he silently noted.

"When?" Mal asked, her voice cracking. Alto watched as the drop of water tumbled from her fleshy peak plunging into and merging with the surrounding pool.

"We'll assess things after our current engagement," he said with a shy, encouraging smile.

Mal gulped and her gaze rapidly drifted to the ripples in the liquid at her waist.

Alto reached under the water and took one of her hands. Lifting it to his lips, his eyes met hers and held them in a captivating stare. "I would never leave you in danger," he whispered, slowly pressing his lips into the palm of her hand.

The kiss was soft and tender, causing Mal to sigh and stroke the side of his head. "It's just, you know, you're kinda handy to have around," she said softly.

The rare touch of vulnerability from a normally hard-edged Mal caused the swordmaster to pause, sharing the feeling of loss that only change can bring.

Mal suddenly sat up and composed herself. She playfully slapped the side of his face as she withdrew her hand.

"Asshole," she cooed.

Alto rubbed his cheek as Mal gazed at her surroundings.

"Okay, we've done the meal and the bath. We've still got the drink..."

"And the bed?" Alto interrupted.

Mal gave a wanton leer blanketed in a romantic glow. "We don't seem to have much time..."

"We never did," he interjected again in a touching whisper.

Mal cocked her head defiantly. "Then I'm thinking...we're burning daylight!"

The Spice Rat paused. "But first a drink."

"I love a practical woman," Alto said as they both stood to leave.

Glimpsing at the ominous runes covering the walls, the wary Cul-Ta apprehensively approached. Fearfully lowering his gaze, the young male held several folded papers in his outstretched hands.

"The papers you requested from above," it said with a quiver in its raspy voice. "They were where you said they would be."

Stryder stared at the ceiling, oblivious to his surroundings. The darkness was coming and with it, his lord's reawakening. His temple must be ready.

The quartermaster and apostle of Pa-Waga was seated in an elaborate makeshift chair fashioned on top of the slaughtered sewer laborers' work cart. Two of the Cul-Ta clansmen stood beside him reverently averting their gaze. Both stood ready to move the wagon and cleric across the already decorated junction room when directed. The messenger couldn't help but notice the blood-matted fur on their foreheads surrounding a solitary rune.

Stryder's left hand rested in a large barrel of blood beside him in the cart. With his claw-like right forefinger he traced the sanctified numbers in the air. As each line of binary marks was transferred, appearing high above on the ceiling, the level of blood in the barrel steadily lowered.

He shook his needle-sharp finger in dismay. The body fluids from the sewer workers and their horse turned out to be not quite enough.

Stryder gave a disappointed sigh. He loathed the distraction, but news secreted from loyal quartermasters was ultimately necessary, for now.

"Cantor?" it said timidly, holding out the papers.

"Don't call him that!" the leader snapped. As he walked past, he grabbed the handful of papers from his clansmen's extended hands. Ta-Chi angrily motioned to the nearest exit and the intimidated messenger quickly scurried away.

The Cul-Ta leader stood defiantly as he stared at the preoccupied human. An uncomfortable moment of silent, intense staring caused Stryder to stop his work and huff in frustration.

"What can I do for you Ta-Chi?"

"You promised vengeance! You promised a new age for my people! All you do is paint walls and place your mark on *my* people!"

Stryder slowly focused on the agitated Cul-Ta leader with a coldly ominous stare.

"And what exactly would you want me to do?"

"Guide us!" Ta-Chi pounded his chest with his free hand. "We need to show the cursed ones above our strength!"

Stryder grumbled in aggravation. Climbing from the chair he slowly approached the irritated Cul-Ta leader.

He gave a weary sigh. "I realize that through the miracle of cross breeding you've survived and progressed as quickly as you have."

Ta-Chi paused uneasily. The naked man's tone and cadence was low and disturbing. A few of the small rune scars on his neck appeared to be slightly glowing. The Cul-Ta's anger subsided, replaced by a rising wave of apprehension.

A wicked smile crept across the human's face as his nefarious gaze rested on Ta-Chi. "The impetuousness you now display is exactly how your prior generation died."

The Cul-Ta leader stood frozen as Stryder glowered malevolently. His mouth became dry as the first waves of panic began to rise in his chest and he found himself unable to move.

"Unfortunately, blind rage still dwells within you. This is a very dangerous factor which must be mitigated." He swept his hand around indicating the sacred numbers on the walls. "The numbers do not lie."

Still keeping his intense stare, the human reached back and snapped his fingers. Ta-Chi didn't see Stryder's two Cul-Ta attendants hefting the near empty bucket off the cart. He trembled as he felt Stryder's blood-stained hand touch the top of his head.

"Your leadership has now become a liability," he said, maintaining a soft menacing tone. "And liabilities don't add up very well."

In a swift fluid motion, the quartermaster grabbed the fur on the top of Ta-Chi's head and sliced his throat with his barbed forefinger. The two Cul-Ta henchmen quickly placed the bucket in front of their former leader as his life blood poured out of the giant gash.

The beguiled victim was frozen in shock as Stryder bent him over the container. Motioning for the two to hold him steady, he retrieved the papers from the dying leader's hand.

Three appeared to be usual dispatches from the main office but one was penned in an unusual hand and signed by the Amarenian ambassador. The fine paper became stained with red as he opened it and he quickly peered at the short contents.

Very interesting. Fia is in Zor, he mused.

Stryder scowled, crumpled the paper and tossed it to the floor. The report irritated him. In his current evolved state, news of this once principal adversary should be viewed as meaningless. However, something played at the recesses of his former consciousness. The thought of her subjugated form amused him. Orrk would be here soon. He would let him deal with her.

His vengeful thoughts were interrupted by the sound of the drained Ta-Chi's body toppling to the ground. Casually examining the crimson contents of the bucket, he grinned in satisfaction.

Should be just enough.

Zau spotted Shom first as he staggered into the commercial hangar. He was late of course. The elderly Singa's whiskers twitched and she raised an eyebrow as she observed the prodigal's unsteady gate.

Clearing her throat loudly to catch Mal's attention, she nodded at Shom.

The Spice Rat had been pacing outside the *Haraka's* open side hatch. She snapped her attention on the approaching royal.

"I fucking said moonrise!" her admonishment swept past Shom and was carried away on swift winter winds. "Where the fuck have you been?"

Shom stopped directly in front of the irritated airship captain.

"Hello Maluria," he greeted in an overly friendly tone.

Mal winced. "Damn! You smell like a fucking distillery."

With a look of distain, the airship captain started toward the hatch. "Never mind. I really don't care. Come on, we've gotta get going!"

"Uh, Maluria…"

The Spice Rat froze. Slowly she brought her attention, along with a wary look at her smiling friend. "What?"

"I've got some news," he said teetering slightly as he reached inside his coat.

A curious Zau and Kyopp stepped up beside Mal. Zaad filled the hatchway and Alto, who was seated on the ramp, took in the still intoxicated prodigal. Pulling out two pieces of paper he held them aloft dramatically. "These two dispatches arrived during the Moonless." He scanned the first leaf then returned his attention to the group. "It appears both my father, mother and uncle recently died, quite violently.

A shocked confused wave swept over the crew.

"What happened?" Alto asked with a genuine curiosity in his voice.

"My uncle was killed during a robbery in Zor. My father apparently killed my mother in a drunken rage then committed suicide."

"I would say I'm sorry," the swordmaster said standing up. "But they did try to have you killed on a number of occasions, did they not?"

"Well, not my mother," the parodical said with a touch of remorse. "She was a sweet, if not naive soul."

"So, where the fuck does that leave you?" Mal said, her irritation rising at their delayed departure.

"Funny you should ask," Shom said as he palmed the second sheet of paper. "Here's the interesting part. My presence is requested at a special heraldry council back in Rophan."

Mal huffed loudly, "Yeah, like that's going to happen!"

"Well, actually…"

The Spice Rat stared in disbelief. "Are you shitting me?!"

Shom shifted hesitantly. "It would appear that, well, according to this dispatch, I'm the new sovereign of House Eldor."

For the briefest of moments, the howling winds were all that could be heard as everyone stared in stunned silence.

Zaad's boisterous, uninhibited laughter was the first thing that broke the group's windswept reserve. The man-shark doubled over in the doorway pointing at the royal.

"The funny little man is now king! Who says the gods have no sense of humor?!"

Alto snickered as he crossed over to the royal extending his right hand. "You cannot escape the irony of this. From hunted to leader. Congratulations my friend."

"This is amazing!" Kyopp said effervescently as he patted the royal on the shoulder. "Your Majesty!"

Shom grinned at the enthusiastic Do-Tarr. "Why thank you, Your Majesty."

"Shommy, did ya ever think this might be a trap?" Mal suspiciously suggested as Alto and Shom shook hands.

"The thought did cross my mind," Shom said. "But with my father gone, most of that danger went with him. Besides my curiosity has been excited."

"So once again, we circle jerk back to my original question," Mal said placing her hands on her hips.

Shom gave a slightly sorrowful smile. "Well, I'm going to grab my belongings in the *Haraka*. Then, I've chartered an airship which leaves for Rophan in a few decis."

The news registered resoundingly in the Spice Rat, *First Alto, now Shom*. Time for remorse, however, was a luxury she did not possess.

Mal pointed an accusatory finger at her friend.

"You're backing out now, right as we're about jump into the shit?!" she said in a stunned staccato voice.

"Maluria," Shom's tone was defiant. "Did it ever occur to you that I will be much more effective helping you from a position of power. Say that of maybe, oh I don't know, sovereign?!"

Mal gave a frustrated sigh. "Whatever. You've obviously made up your mind. We gotta go."

The royal stood motionless for a moment as the weight of the moment descended on him. Giving a small, resigned shrug he made his way past Zaad into the ship.

"I will miss you Shom," Zaad said as the prodigal picked up his small travel bag.

The royal paused and gazed up at the EEtah. "You too, you destructive force of nature you."

The man-shark reached out and silently put his immense hand gently on Shom's shoulder.

"Make sure you put that sword to good use," Shom said glancing over at Bowbreaker.

Zaad's sentimental, reassuring reply was cut short by Mal leading the group into the ship and hopping into her seat. "Alright, if you're through with the tearful goodbyes, we are burning daylight!"

322

"Not even a goodbye Maluria?" Shom said as he started out onto the ramp.

The Spice Rat displayed an irritated smirk but remained silent.

Shom huffed, "Well, you never were really very good at them I suppose."

Shuffling out onto the hangar he watched with a touch of sadness as the ramp closed. The *Haraka* lifted off, disappearing out of the opening of Air Station East, as well as his life.

A winter squall passed over the high holy city of Zor slightly before the Grand Turine rang fifteen bells. A cold rain had fallen, soaking the city as it raced southward.

In the harbor, the waves were still sizable and the smaller sail ships were having a difficult time approaching the docks.

A lone Captain Rafel stood silently by an empty slip along dock number six. The wind blew his long dark hair wildly across his thin, pale golden skin. Remaining motionless, hands at his sides, he eyed the quartermaster's interceptor ship breaking through a four-foot wave crest on its way in.

The forty-foot Nolton Boat pitched and rolled inches above the turbulent surface of the water. The spymaster marveled at the sleek modified hull, designed to outrun anything that sailed. The light grey over blue hull was the perfect camouflage out on the waters of the Shallow Sea.

As the Brightstar captain deftly maneuvered the vessel into its mooring spot, Rafel curiously noticed that the ship wasn't flying the quartermaster's colors and the forward ballista wasn't loaded.

Delicately sweeping back hair out of his eyes he saw the gangplank lower and a female Picean disembark. The Zorian spymaster nodded a subtle greeting as she approached but kept his attention on the docked ship.

His wait was short. The hulking naked humanoid, apparently unfazed by the cold weather, lumbered off the ship and surveyed the unfamiliar wharf. Rafel took in his scarred, eight-foot blue-grey frame.

Orrk the Undressed also known as Orrk the Impaler, the captain silently noted. *Aptly named.*

He had never met the infamous ironmark and knew about him only by reputation. The reports were obviously true. He was the rare offspring of an EEtah and human female. This fatal union, forbidden by most societies and religions contained practical reasoning behind it. The female in such unions, much like Orrk's mother, never survived childbirth.

Rafel's gaze immediately swept down and ogled at the ironmark's massive penis as it swayed in front of him. He felt his heartbeat pick up and the front of his pants stirred. Even flaccid it was as large as some horses.

The spymaster had to admit, it was impressive. He remembered fantasizing when he first heard about it. He had never experienced anything remotely that large and his prurient curiosity played at the back of his mind. To be dominated by the much larger half man, half beast, bound and ravaged. He sighed as reality set in, realizing it would be the last fuck of his life.

Pulling his appreciative gaze away from Orrk's remarkable organ he strolled up to the ironmark.

"Orrk?"

The imposing, half human enforcer snarled at the thin effeminate man in black and scowled. "Yeah, who the fuck are you?"

"Captain Rafel, Zorian Guards."

Orrk gave a disdainful grunt. "So, what do you want?"

Rafel kept his demeanor pleasant as his gaze lackadaisically swept over the ship then back up at the ironmark.

"You're a bit out of your jurisdiction, aren't you?" the spymaster said nonchalantly.

Orrk snarled, revealing a mouth full of stubby sharp teeth. "I'd say that's none of your fucking business! I don't answer to you."

Rafel demurely smiled and let his gaze deliberately trail again to the ironmark's penis. He lingered, then stared back up to the grimacing half EEtah.

"Everything that happens in this city is my business," he said in a cheerfully husky voice.

Orrk noted the captain's attention on his groin and gave a domineering grin.

"I'm here on *personal* business," he said in an ominously seductive growl.

Keeping his amused expression, Rafel left no doubt he was blatantly unconvinced by the ironmark's story.

"I trust you will check in with us if your, *business* becomes more official in nature?"

"Sure," Orrk sneered. "I'll do just that."

"Your cooperation is appreciated," Rafel said in a slightly mocking tone as he stepped aside.

The spymaster's gaze followed the Picean and half-EEtah as they casually strode off the wharf and disappeared into the myriad crowd of sentient beings which coursed through the Zorian streets. His people were in place, their every movement was to be scrutinized.

Once again adjusting his badly windswept hair, Rafel returned to the city streets at a leisurely pace. *A rare half-EEtah. That should be fairly easy to keep track of*, he said to himself as he made his way toward the Forum.

Morax knew the trip was dangerous, but he had to know. Was Fia correct? Were the Chenoans really gone? Either outcome was disturbing in its own right.

They quickly made their way back to Nocturn on the reciprocal, traveling westward out of the Shallow Sea, the same route they used to deliver Fia to Zor. The Chenakan craft sped quickly over the steep banks of the Goyan Rise into the Ocean Deep.

"Give me two degrees to the south," Morax ordered the driver. The young helmsman complied, realizing this avoided the Parvat Seamount. The fiercely territorial Mer-Clans claimed those jagged peaks which stretched westward along the ocean floor. Time was of the essence and there was no sense in delaying their journey over trespassing a sensitive, ever-shifting Mer borders.

The increased presence of Calden warships around the northern coast of the Narrow Lands and Penaber where they had rescued Fia also required extra caution. The Chenakan submarine then finally navigated the Struja currents which insulated the etheria-laced oceans beneath the ice floes of Nocturn.

There was something both comforting and foreboding as the Chenakans passed through the glittery darkness of the crystal-laced home waters of Nocturn. The craft slowed as they guardedly approached the Agar Goyot in the distance. The towering purple crystal at its center beckoned to them as it stretched upward to the surface and the ice city of Mos-Agar.

Studying the swirling sediment near the seabed Morax seemed to grow more anxious with each passing moment.

"Something's wrong," he said to his helmsman whose hand rested on a blue-green crystal knob atop a clear lever. "There's movement below. Take us to the bottom."

The young Chenakan slowly pushed the handle forward and the ship began its decent.

As the cigar-shaped craft slowly rounded a small mountainous outcropping, both peered into the darkness below.

"All stop," Morax ordered as he assessed the surroundings. "We don't need to attract any attention. Let's keep this cliff behind us. Resume the descent"

Morax's tendrils became more agitated the farther the craft made its way to the seabed.

"And hold," he said raising his hand for emphasis. "How did…"

"It's, it's moving Morax!" the young pilot said as he stared out the window at the seabed below.

"Gar-Kal," the Chenakan leader said as he focused on the wide ribbon of fish-headed legions which marched across the bottom of the Frozen Sea and out of sight. "They're headed east, toward Lumina."

By now his three other crewmen joined them at the window. All ogled the humanoid fish army moving steadily eastward.

"There must be thousands of them," one said as he followed the masses below.

"What's going on Morax?"

The Chenakan commander gave a grim sigh. "If some are to be believed, they amass, waiting for the coming darkness."

"Shouldn't we warn someone?" the helmsman said, his voice filled with concern.

"Yes," Morax said breaking out of his stare. "But first, there is one thing we need investigate. Make for the goyot."

"Yes Morax."

327

The Chenakan craft cautiously approached the massive field of multicolored glowing crystals. Morax noted a distinct lack of activity both in the surrounding seabed and the Rod-Ema trench beyond.

"It's awfully quiet over there," Morex said in a curious mumble.

"Wait," the helmsman said pointing at the goyot. "There's movement ahead?"

Ahead, small radiant clouds seemed to swirl around each of the tops of all the individual etheria pillars.

"Let's find out," Morax said apprehensively. "Slow and careful helmsman, be ready to make a quick exit."

As the craft approached the outer columns of the goyot they noticed that the radiant clouds were not swirling but undulating with the current. They congregated on the swaying bodies of the Chenoans as they sat atop their crystal pilasters.

"They're not moving!" the helmsman noted.

"Why aren't they attacking us?"

The many questions weighing on the Chenakan's were answered as they drew closer and entered the field of etheria pillars.

The radiant clouds were actually schools of tiny luminescent fish. The small, darting undulation was ravenously feeding on the dead Chenoans.

The rebel Chenakans stared in shock as the submarine slowly passed into the etheria field. Atop every crystal pillar, half eaten Chenoans fluttered peacefully in the glittering current staring vacantly outward.

"She was right!" Morax said in a forbidding tone. "She was right!"

"Morax, what's going on?!"

The Chenakan commander looked over at his small confused crew.

"We've been played for fools," he said with a snarl. "All of us, for all this time…"

"Sir?"

"Make for Lumina helmsman, best possible speed!"

As the sleek submarine did a graceful bank out of the etheria field, the ship was rocked, tossing the crew about the cabin. Out the window, they now saw the purple pillar in the center of the etheria field glowing ominously. The ship lurched once again and all felt it begin to be pulled in the direction of the etheria tower.

The Chenakan commander stared helplessly as the purple tower loomed ever closer. "Give me full speed!"

The helmsman pushed the clear lever all the way forward. The ship's etheria power plant hummed and strained to no avail. The submarine continued to be dragged through the ocean toward the opening portal.

The helmsman grew panicked as the ship groaned. "Morax, if we keep this up, the ship's going to be torn apart!"

"We don't have a choice!" Morax said grimly as he desperately searched for another option.

A loud cracking sound came from the boat's right side. All gasped in horror as the main stabilizing fin snapped at the base and sailed past the windshield. The craft now spun wildly as it was dragged ever closer to the pulsing portal.

Morax stood mouth agape, staring helplessly as the massive, glowing purple tower now filled the window. The top hatch was beginning to buckle with a cracking sound. Thankfully, before the vessel was crushed, the Chenakan submarine was sucked into the undulating purple vortex, disappearing.

The room was oppressively warm in stark contrast to the winter chill outside.

Okawa stood in the back by the door of the Center for Alchemic Studies at the University of Marassa. Class was still in session. At the head of the room Marassa Hauts scribbled furiously on a chalkboard which covered, most of the wall. After each formula was written, she would address the class and give a detailed explanation

The middle-aged woman was dressed in the floor-length red robes of a senior Marassa. Her hair was bound into an efficient bun and her demeanor was passionately serious.

Okawa squinted at the unusual characters scrawled for all to see. She understood none of the alchemical equations, but clearly the twelve students occupying three long tables in the center of the room did.

All of the alchemists in training occupied their own station. In front of each was a beaker containing a cloudy boiling liquid suspended over a glowing gem.

At Hauts' direction each of the young students began slowly pouring an orange powder into the boiling liquid. As the two substances made contact a gentle cascade of sparks escaped upward from the open beakers. The room was immediately filled with impressed gasps and excited murmurs.

A flash and small explosion to her right caused the Valdurian agent to crouch at the ready. The brief scream of surprise was quickly silenced as one of the male students toppled to the floor. Beside him his fellow academics cried out in shock and jumped back away from the commotion.

Okawa relaxed a bit when she saw the Marassa nonchalantly glance in the direction of the disturbance.

Every damn grand, Hauts sighed in frustration. *There's always got to be one...*

The alchemist put down the chalk and calmly walked over to the convulsing student.

The beaker had exploded. Broken glass littered the area and the liquid dripped from the table's edge where it pooled beside the unfortunate pupil. The young man's face was burnt completely away. The now unrecognizable features were cauterized and smoldering. The front of his tunic was also gone, reveling burnt, blackened flesh.

Marassa Hauts stared at the dying young man, tapping her foot impatiently. When the pupil gurgled then went still, she addressed the remaining students frozen in shock.

Placing her hands defiantly on her hips the mercurial instructor admonished a harsh lesson. "It appears Si Werner has, through his carelessness, taught you a more effective example of what NOT to do, than anything I could possibly lecture you on."

The class was mumbling nervously as the Marassa returned to the board.

"This should impress upon all your minds the volatility and dangerous nature of the materials we are dealing with."

The teacher's eyes swept across her class still numb from the incident.

"We will take a short recess," she said sternly. "Now clean up that mess and get that body out of my classroom!"

All the young students stood silently gawking at each other, unsure of how to deal with the unpleasant situation.

"You are eating into your study time people," she warned. "I suggest you hurry."

On cue, the entire class led by a few of the senior students scurried about, tending to the lethal mess.

Catching Okawa's attention, the Marassa nodded to a door beside the chalkboard.

"That was some lesson," Okawa said as she closed the door behind her.

The instructor stopped in front of her desk then spun to gaze disdainfully at the Valdurian. Her matronly features were cold and dispassionate.

"I despise small talk, whoever you are," she said staring impatiently. "Almost as much as I despise being pulled away from my work on some mysterious municipal errand."

Okawa remained calm at the blunt greeting.

"Marassa, I can appreciate that you are busy. However, I feel this meeting would proceed quite a bit smoother and might I add quicker, if you didn't address me as if I were one of your students."

The two traded resolute stares until Hauts sighed and turned away.

"Very well," she conceded. "I analyzed the residue from your hands and under your fingernails. It appears to be finely granulated moonstone with traces of trinilic.

Having a seat, Haut rested her forearms on her desk. "I conferred with some of my colleagues over in the Etheria Studies department. That specific combination of the two powders was designed to melt when exposed to a certain type of light."

The Valdurian agent quizzically rubbed the back of her neck. "Exactly what kind of light might that be?"

The Marassa soured, obviously considering the question stupid. "Given the principal ingredient, I would say moonlight."

Okawa's mind was racing as she attempted to place this piece of information into the puzzle. "I see. Any ideas?"

The Marassa shrugged. "The chemical combination was interesting. I can't however imagine, here in Lumina, what a compound that interacts with moonlight would be used for."

The Valdurian paused, lost in thought until Hauts broke her concentration.

"Well now, if your questions have been answered, I've got a class to teach."

"Thank you for your time," Okawa said moving toward the door.

The cranky teacher ignored the appreciative statement and silently followed her out.

The Valdurian agent's next stop was the campus' main cali. There had to be something in those library books about the Valley of Chains.

Sister Pazach of the Sofen Sisterhood, keeper of the Tanem and herald of Bu'Lan, the anointed prophetess of Sofen peered around in dismay at the rising Kan fog. The crowds on the streets of Zor were gradually growing thinner which was usual for the end of the day.

"I miss seeing the goddess' beloved face in the sky," she said dolefully. "There is no comfort in this continual light."

The other priestess standing directly beside her grumbled in agreement as several merchants with empty carts clattered past on their way home.

"The people here reject the goddess' message. They refuse to repent."

"The constant light makes my eyes ache," Pazach added.

"Take heart sisters," high priestess Bu'Lan comforted as she studied the diminishing audience from the street corner. "All we can do is profess the word. They must possess the ears to hear us."

"Sister, what good is the word of truth if it falls on deaf ears?" Pazach said in frustration.

The high priestess gave a sympathetic smile. "We are the vanguard of a new age. The chart you carry does not lie. Soon all will see our beloved mistress in the sky, bathed in radiant glory."

The senior cleric's rally was interrupted by cynical laughter. All but the senior cleric gasped as Fia stepped out of the fog-draped alley behind them.

"Your goddess will be swept away like all the others," she said ominously.

The junior priestesses gasped as Fia proceeded over to them. Her hair was wild and unkept. The clothing she wore was tattered and by her smell they knew it had been quite a while since she bathed. The most disturbing aspect of the mysterious, blasphemous woman was her eyes. They were wide and bloodshot. Never blinking they darted back and forth wildly.

Bu'Lan was unfazed by the intruder's rebuke. Smiling, she beckoned Fia closer.

"Come," she said welcomingly. "See for yourself, the sacred chart proclaims the truth…"

"I know what the chart says," Fia interrupted confidently. "The chart is correct."

This unexpected agreement caused the sisters to pause.

"It is your interpretation that is dangerously wrong," the Rayth said pointing to the vellum sheet in sister Pazach's hands. "The new masters of this world are waiting, waiting for the darkness, waiting for their time to take their rightful place in the Annigan. The place they were cheated of long ago by the pearl avatars and the life they created, namely, us!"

Fia paused briefly, staring eerily at all three of the Sofen sisters. "We are the abomination to them; the beings that should not exist. Trust me, they do not possess emotions or feelings as we understand them."

Foam was beginning to form at the corners of the agitated stranger's mouth, causing both junior clerics to take an apprehensive step backwards.

Fia stopped directly in front of Bu'Lan and continued her dire warning.

"You want to save your goddess and yourselves?! Get on the next ship, or better yet, one of those new airships. Get to the farthest point in the Annigan you can. Pray that in the coming darkness the balance is not tipped. For if it is, if the Black Mural falls, there will be no place left for any of us."

High Priestess Bu'Lan adopted a condescending sentiment. "Our goddess looks down on us. She comforts and protects. Ours is to prepare a way so when she appears, all will be bathed in her beauty."

Fia chuckled sardonically as she disdainfully appraised Bu'Lan.

"Save yourselves, if you can," Fia's voice was now little more than a horse menacing whisper. "Gods die when they've no more followers."

From a short distance away, deep guttural laughter resounded through the fog. The sisters gasped as a moderately intoxicated Orrk, flanked by his Picean aide lumbered down the near empty streets.

"Ladies," he acknowledged as he passed.

All silently stared as the duo disappeared into the mist then back to where Fia had been standing.

She was gone.

It's unlike Rafel to be late, Zekoff thought as he shuffled the day's last pieces of paper off his desk.

He heaved a sigh of relief when he heard the gentle knock on the door. It opened immediately and Rafel's head popped in.

"I know, I know," the spymaster placated his boss' questioning gaze. "But uhh…"

The door opened completely, revealing Captain Okawa standing right behind him. "You're going to want to hear this."

The colonel stood and presented his hand. "Captain, you have news?"

Shaking it, both Okawa and Rafel took a seat in front of Zekoff's desk as the commander reached for his pipe.

"Uh, yes sir," she began. "I got back from the university a short while ago."

"And?" Zekoff said lighting the pipe.

"The substance on my hands was a powdered moonstone compound."

"You say it came from when you handled that burning gem," the Zorian commander said double checking his recollection.

"Yes sir," Okawa said. "The Marassa maintains it was designed to melt under the light of the moon."

The colonel paused as he watched a column of smoke slowly wind its way upward. "What does that mean?"

The Valdurian agent sat forward. "Well, the gems are obviously volatile and the coating keeps them in check. I'm not sure why anyone would choose that compound. It resembles more of a trigger than a protective coating."

"Still, not much of a moon here on Goya," Zekoff said as he examined the bowl of his pipe. "What in the name of the gods was Stryder Aramos doing with them in the Valley of Chains?"

Rafel sighed in frustration. "We are obviously missing a piece or two of the puzzle. Speaking of the Valley of Chains?"

"There wasn't much to find out sir," Okawa said pensively. "There's a monastery there. The Azorith Monks constructed the chains somewhere around four thousand grands ago. They still maintain them to this day. Supposedly, the lineage of monks has remained unbroken."

"That certainly sounds like something to check out," Zekoff said gesturing with his pipe hand.

"Yes sir."

"Speaking of Stryder Aramos," Zekoff's attention was back on his spymaster.

Rafel cleared his throat, "Still no sightings."

The colonel slumped at the news.

"However," Rafel continued, "We may have caught a break."

"Go on."

"This morning Orrk the Undressed, Ironmark for the Goyodan Chain arrived on an out-of-service quartermaster's interceptor."

Zekoff scowled, "A bit out of his element, no?"

"My thoughts too," Rafel coyly agreed. "I confronted him and he claims his visit is personal."

"Not sure I'm connecting the dots," Zekoff confessed.

The Zorian spymaster sat back twirling his moustache with a sly grin. "Orrk is Stryder's favorite enforcer; extremely brutal and intimidating."

"And you think…?"

"Yes sir, he's going to lead us to Si Aramos."

The colonel of the Zorian Guards sat forward and nodded in satisfaction as he tapped out his pipe.

"A break indeed," he concurred before facing Okawa. "The monks can wait. Find me Stryder Aramos."

"Yes sir!" Okawa said briskly.

"You got eyes on him?" Zekoff asked.

Rafel shifted restlessly. "I just got a spotters report before running into the captain here. He's headed on foot to the Seven Sisters.

The Valdurian agent gasped as she bolted up in her chair catching both Zorian guards by surprise.

"I know where he's going!"

Running his hands lovingly across the hull of the *Drakin*, Demetrius sighed heavily as he finished his pre-flight inspection of the airship.

"I can't get my head around why people want to keep flying during the Kan," he muttered as he examined the front landing skid. "I keep telling them that flying in the Kan is dangerous. Do they listen to me? No, they schedule a joy ride for the Bailian ambassador. I mean, why should they listen to me? I'm just the pilot."

"Ah, there you are!" came a high-pitch female voice from across the hangar. "Yoohoo!"

Taking a deep breath to compose himself, Demetrius pivoted toward the voice. The Bailian ambassador and her entourage were making their way toward him.

They were exactly as he remembered when he brought them here. The ambassador was an elitist, matriarchal type. She was accompanied by a young Bailian male and female aide. Trailing slightly behind was the quiet, older Bailian with a large handlebar moustache and cane.

Making this whole situation worse was, as Joc' Valdur informed him: He had been specifically requested by the ambassador.

Putting on his best diplomatic airs Demetrius stepped up to greet his passengers.

"Your eminence, it's good to see you again."

"Of course, of course," she said nonchalantly as she brushed past him.

The two aides followed closely behind, completely ignoring the pilot.

Demetrius found some solace in that the older Bailian bringing up the rear gave a courteous acknowledgement of his existence.

He had only walked a few feet past Demetrius when he stopped. Staring solemnly downward, the old man's eyes narrowed. Turning back to the pilot, he leaned on the bright green bulbous head of his cane as his nose and moustache twitched.

He lingered briefly as the rest of the staff made their way to the *Drakin*.

"Come on," Demetrius said as he passed him. "Can't keep the ambassador waiting."

The old Bailian continued to stare pensively at the main bay doors of the hangar.

"Is there some sort of alarm system on this floor?"

The seriousness in his voice caused Demetrius to pause.

"Sure. Remember this is primarily a military base," the airship pilot said with a touch of confusion. "There's at least one in every hangar. Ever since they were ambushed in the Unification War the Valdurians have been a bit paranoid. You know…"

Cha-Rod stood up straight and hefted his cane like a club, all the while not taking his attention off the entrances.

"Sound it now!"

"Captain, I gotta admit, I miss the funny little man," Zaad said as he settled back into his seat.

"Yeah, the pompous, whiny fuck does grow on you," Mal said from beside the ship's wheel.

The man-shark gave a sad chuckle as he closed his eyes. The Spice Rat's attention fell on a sleeping Alto on the other side of the cabin. His chest peacefully rose and fell. In between his legs, a sheathed Defari rested, tip down leaning in his lap.

"He's never far from that blade," Zau said from the wheel as she caught Mal's forlorn expression.

"Yeah," Mal scoffed. "His new solitary companion."

"You never can tell what's going to happen," the lioness said sympathetically.

Mal's mouth tightened as she stared vacantly back out the windshield.

Outside, the sun was becoming brighter as they approached the heart of Lumina. The *Haraka* rocked gently as it passed through rapidly moving winter clouds.

"It's just, everything's changing so quickly," the Spice Rat confessed. "People that I've been in some serious shit with are going away. These are the closest thing to family I've had since mine was killed."

Zau's whiskers fluttered as she sighed. "Change, huh? It's never easy. Especially in certain instances where, say, love is involved."

Mal gave a melancholy smile. "Yeah, I really put my fucking foot in my mouth, didn't I?"

"It's not like we all couldn't see it," the Singa said slightly adjusting the wheel. "I mean, I recently joined up and it was obvious."

"Yeah, I guess it was," Mal said with a dejected grin.

"You mean is," Zau corrected. "It's not like your feelings towards each other have changed. Besides, you're forgetting one thing."

"And that would be?"

"If this enterprise we're attempting is anything like the ones in the past, there's a chance we may not even survive long enough to worry about who's leaving who."

Mal sighed loudly as she stared out the window. "There is that."

"Personally, I would take things as they come. You've got each other right now. The future, contrary to popular thought," Zau snapped her fingers, "is an illusion."

She pointed a furry finger at Mal and clicked her jaws loudly. "Fretting about something that hasn't happened is only a distraction."

Mal nodded in agreement.

"You're right," Mal said patting the Singa on the shoulder. "I gotta keep focused or we all might end up seriously fucked."

Zau gave a compassionate grin. "Why don't you get some rest captain. I'll wake you in a bit and you can take her in. I've never landed in an air station."

"Good idea," the Spice Rat said. "As soon as we get to Zor we've got to get you to an optics shop. The sun in this part of the Annigan is going to be way too bright for you, even during the Kan."

"Thanks captain, it's already a bit uncomfortable."

Mal made her way, not to her captain's chair, but to a seat beside Alto. She gave her lover a lingering, melancholy glance, then rested her head on his shoulder and quickly dropped off to sleep.

The Cul-Ta's nose and whiskers twitched furiously as he took in the air station's flight deck. "That's the craft. Only one human," it said, obviously confused. "What about the blue people?"

"Kill them all," Orrk sneered. "The human is mine."

"I would do it quickly young man!" Cha-Rod said in a calm, emphatic voice as he deftly removed his tri-tailed cloak and twirled it in his free hand.

The warning was no sooner issued when a volley of six arrows, followed by Orrk and a dozen man-rats rushing into the room.

The old Bailian swept his cape in front of him capturing two of the arrows from midair, sending them clattering harmlessly to the ground.

Two of the missiles missed their mark entirely, bouncing off the ship and surrounding crates.

The other two plunged into the Bailian ambassador. One struck the back of her neck with such force the tip was now protruding from her throat. The other was embedded deeply in her upper back. Her aides watched in horror as the envoy plunged silently forward with a stunned expression, blood gushing from the wound and her open mouth.

Demetrius dodged two of the arrows as he bolted for a nearby pillar. Reaching for the red emergency lever, he nervously noted the rat creatures almost upon them. Half had bows and their second volley was nocked and ready to fire. The others were armed with human short swords which appeared massive in their tiny hands.

Seeing their leader fall, the two aides broke and ran. A number of arrows struck them in the back propelling them forward, dead on the cold stone floor.

Yanking hard on the lever, the station was filled with the sound of loudly ringing bells above. The alarm now sounded, Demetrius drew his short sword and took cover behind the wide rectangular pillar.

The storm of vermin was upon Cha-Rod. Two sword-wielding Cul-Ta attacked with vicious swings. The elderly Bailian's ukko wood cane swept away the attacks. Bringing the short wooden staff around in an arc the cudgel swept the attackers' legs from under them, crushing the bones with a loud crack. The ukko wood's repellent properties sent the crippled rats flying.

Shifting his body sideways, he swept the cape in a circle, capturing two more arrows. As he swirled the garment downward, the three tails entangled another advancing attacker's legs.

Yanking hard on the end the cape snatched the surprised Cul-Ta off his feet. It landed in front of its fellow assailants but was yanked away before any could react.

Grabbing the cape by the collar, the Bailian started spinning in place. The helpless Cul-Ta was now squealing in terror, twirling through the air at the end of the extended cape as a living weapon. After colliding with four fellow aggressors sending them staggering, the attack ended when the rat-man at the end of the cape collided with Orrk's large frame as he charged.

The half EEtah bellowed with rage as the helplessly spinning Cul-Ta collided with him, bouncing against his chest. He thundered forward delivering a punishing blow to the older Bailian sending him sprawling to the ground.

The ironmark continued past the prone Bailian to the pillar Demetrius was behind.

Rolling onto his back, Cha-Rod barely had time to regain his senses as several Cul-Ta attempted to pile on him.

Holding his cane in the middle the Bailian raised it in the air. As his arm fully extended the round green head of the cane erupted in a bright flash. The four assaulting rats were propelled backwards by a powerful invisible thrust. The top continued to glow as Cha-Rod got to his feet.

Demetrius was darting around the pillar, keeping it between himself and the enraged ironmark. Each time the half EEtah's bulky form grabbed at his quarry, the human would deliver a stinging poke with the short sword then duck back to the other side of the pillar, just out of reach. Orrk roared over the cacophony of the alarm bells as he lunged time and again at the agile airship pilot. The anticipation of the kill had the infuriated behemoth frothing at the mouth, his erection throbbing out before him.

Three remaining Cul-Ta now circled Cha-Rod probing for an opening. A few yards away another aimed an arrow directly at him. The Bailian was positioning his cape arm to defend from the missile when a crossbow bolt impaled the rat bowman from behind. The bow and arrow toppled from his hand as he dropped.

"You there, HOLD!" a commanding voice shouted from the entrance.

The three remaining attackers glanced up in a panic as half a dozen Valdurian marines with crossbows charged into the hangar. Screeching in surprise the rats darted for the far exit. Their route ended, as powerfully propelled missiles plunged into their bodies, dropping them in their tracks.

Demetrius, adrenaline still pumping, crouched warily along the wide column as the marines approached. The attacks had ceased but the piercing alarm reverberated through the hangar. Peering cautiously from the pilaster there was no sign of the irate ironmark. He lowered his weapon and leaned against the pillar panting as a marine sergeant approached.

Two marines were checking on the Bailian, while one aimed his weapon at the two Cul-Ta with broken legs who were attempting to crawl away. They cowered and cried out in pain.

The Valdurian sergeant lowered his crossbow and assessed the situation. Casually, he reached up and pushed the alarm lever back to its original position. The bells went silent, replaced by the persistent ringing in both combatants' ears.

Staring at the dead ambassador and her party the marines stared back at Demetrius who was now breathing heavily as he sheathed his sword.

"What in the name of the empire just happened? The sergeant demanded as he shouldered his weapon.

The problem with never sleeping also proved to be the greatest benefit; ample time to observe.

Fia spied the hideous brute from the shadows of the alley. In her former life as a Rayth she had a handful of near misses with him in the past. Many of her sisters were not so lucky and perished from his repulsive form of torture. However, this time he was not the object of her interest. He would lead her to the source of the disturbance she felt deep in her chest; to the instigator which was unwittingly hastening them to their doom.

Orrk, she recalled with a sneer. Lapdog of the head quartermaster. *If he's here, Stryder Aramos can't be far.*

She saw him enter the air station by way of a side service door. He hadn't been inside very long before alarm bells began to chime.

Her decision to stay put paid off. Shortly after the alarm, he reemerged and hastily turned south, slipping away along a side street.

During his trek across the city Fia almost lost him twice. The blue gray pallor of Orrk's skin blended well with the thick Kan fog.

She grew more wary as the buildings became more dilapidated. He was heading for the slums and she had no wish to fall into the hands of any predators which always lurked in such areas.

As he entered the Seven Sisters Slums the hybrid EEtah became more cautious. He now continually glanced around with each corner and shadowy alley traversed.

Fia flattened out against a wall when he stopped completely, waiting for a lone human prostitute to pass. When it appeared no one was close, Orrk slipped over the side of a sewer entrance and disappeared.

Fia's curiosity overcame her. Not waiting for the trail to grow cold she rushed over to the pungent rectangular hole in the ground. In the depths she detected nothing but fog and the sound of Orrk's fading footsteps.

The time to move was now.

Looking and seeing no one, she followed the ironmark into the tunnels below.

On the roof of a two-story building across the street, Okawa watched the two enter the Zorian sewers.

The Valdurian agent nodded in satisfaction.

She was right. Stryder Aramos was somewhere in the massive Zorian sewer complex and obviously there were other interested parties now involved.

The Kan would be lifting soon. There was no time to waste, the situation was quickly escalating. She crept from the roof and started out northward toward Judgment Square and Colonel Zekoff, confident her quarry was close.

The hangar was now swarming with Zorian Guards. Captain Rafel, appearing as if he had recently been woken, stepped through the entrance and took in the chaotic scene.

The spymaster glanced dispassionately at the impaled bodies of the ambassador and her party. He paused briefly where guards stood, crossbows trained, over the two wounded Cul-Ta. The frightened rat creatures' shattered bones protruded grotesquely from their upper legs and their hands were bound behind them. They whimpered and stared fearfully up at their captors.

"Get them to a cell," the spymaster ordered. "Alive!" he qualified as they muscled the crippled Cul-Ta to their shoulders.

As the captors were taken away, Rafel sidestepped a large pool of blood on his way to Demetrius and Cha-Rod who stood talking to a patrol sergeant.

"This might be a definite set-back in Bailian relations," he said with a weary sigh.

"Yeah, and apparently we didn't get all of those little rat fuckers either," the sergeant gruffly added.

"Never mind the rats," Demetrius said ardently. "What about the big, slimy, maniac with the huge, you know, thing?" The pilot waved his hand by his groin for emphasis.

Rafel threw a questioning glance at the sergeant.

The scruffy older man with short gray hair shook his head. "All we saw was the rats sir."

"He was behind that pillar trying to get at me," Demetrius explained.

"Curious," Rafel said absentmindedly playing with his moustache.

Demetrius couldn't contain his confusion. "Why in the name of the gods would Cul-Ta want to kill the Bailian ambassador?"

The Zorian spymaster glanced back at the bodies. "I don't think they were the targets."

Cha-Rods bushy eyebrow's furrowed. "No?"

"I think you were the target," Rafel said to a stunned Demetrius.

"Me?!"

"I'm betting the Cul-Ta were a diversion and maybe extra muscle. If Orrk was after you that makes the connection to Stryder Aramos."

"Orrk?" Cha-Rod said still confused.

"He's Si Aramos' favorite ironmark and enforcer," Rafel briefly explained before getting back to Demetrius. "You recently had a run-in with the chief quartermaster did you not?"

"Yeah," Demetrius said. "Over in the Valley of Chains."

Rafel ran his hand through his long hair. "It would seem Stryder Aramos is trying to remove any witnesses to whatever his rural escapade was."

Demetrius nervously shifted back and forth. He had been in quite a few dangerous situations in his life. However, he had never been the direct target of assassination.

"What do we do?"

"We need to let Okawa in on this," Rafel quickly replied. "She's been tasked with finding Si Aramos. This is a definite break for her."

"Yeah, I meant more about that thing trying to kill me," Demetrius qualified.

"Hopefully one will take care of the other," Rafel said in a vain attempt at optimism.

The Bailian cleared his throat. "Captain, my ambassador has been killed. I must of course report this. Nevertheless, I would also ask your permission to assist in bringing those ultimately responsible to justice?"

Rafel weighed the request. "We would probably appreciate the help, but that will be Colonel Zekoff's call."

"And it looks like you get that call sooner rather than later," Demetrius said motioning to the entrance.

Zekoff and Okawa swept into the hangar side by side at a brisk pace as the receding Kan fog swirled around their ankles. The colonel's hands were clasped behind him and his mouth was pulled taunt under his beard. Okawa was in the middle of making a point, her hands gesticulating sharply.

Rafel exhaled loudly. *This is where it gets interesting.*

Fia reeled from the stench of human waste which was growing stronger the farther she descended into the Zorian sewers. The Kan fog was slowly receding as she followed the sound of Orrk's splashing footfalls an earshot ahead in the darkness.

She halted and crouched in the refuse-strewn water when she saw the tunnel in front of her light up. Orrk grumbled at the sudden illumination but proceeded.

When Fia reached the lit section of sewer she noticed that the light extended along the expanse following the ironmark's route.

Taking a moment, the Rayth stared at the rune-filled walls and ceilings. The light was emanating from a specific multi-row set of binary numbers directly overhead. She scowled at the crude attempt to explain and command the elemental forces of the multiverse.

Moving on, Fia followed the lit tunnel as it descended. By the time she had made it to the crudely hewn older sewers, the Kan fog and water were gone, replaced by damp stone.

She now strode calmly, making no attempt to conceal herself. With the copious amount of number groupings on the walls the former Rayth was sure she was being watched.

Pausing briefly at the wide entrance to the cavernous junction room she nodded in appreciation at the massive amounts of interconnected binary fields.

Stryder Aramos stood regally at the far end of the room. Orrk towered beside him and all about were Cul-Ta and various humans. Each one had the numerologist's sacred numbers carved into their foreheads. All were staring at her.

"Do come in," Stryder said in a deep booming voice that echoed off the high ceilings. "We've been expecting you."

Fia entered slowly, eyeing the calligraphy adoring the walls and ceiling.

"Welcome to the temple of Pa-Waga," Stryder's voice dripped with pride. "Do you come to offer yourself to his service?"

"Perhaps," Fia said as she advanced toward the quartermaster. "But not in the way you might expect."

Stryder huffed. "It matters not. My lord's time is at hand."

Fia snickered. "Oh, there are those whose time is at hand, but your *lord* is not included."

Sticking his hand out from beneath his cloak Stryder casually gestured to a set of runes on a nearby wall. They immediately glowed blue and Fia felt herself grabbed and held immobile by an unseen force.

Stryder and Orrk crossed the room together. The ironmark lumbered beside the smaller, frailer quartermaster who floated inches above the floor.

In her past life Fia would have been repulsed by the sight she now faced. Stryder's cowl was back revealing a changed man. He was now clean shaven and bald. His eyes were bulbous and bloodshot. His once cruelly handsome features were now drawn and malevolently twisted.

The tiny, intricate binary carvings all across him that mimicked the walls, were the most disturbing.

He halted inches in front of her as Orrk came up from behind.

As they stared into each other's eyes both realized they were peering into the abyss. Madness always knows its own.

"I do believe that was heresy," Stryder said with a calm sneer. "I should sacrifice you to appease my god."

Fia continued her intense stare. "But you won't."

Stryder gave a domineering smirk. "Give me one good reason not to hand you over to my eager friend behind you."

Fia returned the confident grin. "Because I've already been touched by the etheria and you're curious. Otherwise I'd be dead already."

Both knew she was right.

A wave of his hands doused the runes holding her, and he nodded to Orrk. The giant seized her by the outside of her upper arms and lifted her off her feet.

"I am curious come to think of it," Stryder said inquisitively as he led them to a side tunnel.

Kneeling by the wall, the quartermaster pointed to a spot on the ground. The abrasive sound of Stryder's fingernail etching lines of numbers into the stone caused Fia to wince.

He signaled to Orrk and the obedient ironmark held her so that her feet dangled inches above the newly made symbols.

Placing his dagger-like nail above the top of her right boot Stryder pushed straight down, puncturing the leather.

The captured Rayth winced in pain. He retrieved it immediately and a small flow of blood seeped out at the tip.

As the crimson drops struck the runes, they began to glow blue. With a gesture from his master Orrk lowered the bleeding foot on top of the symbols.

"So you don't wander," Stryder said in a mockingly concerned tone. "The sewers aren't safe."

Fia tried to move. She managed to pivot on the foot, but it was otherwise held firm.

"Perhaps you can quench my curiosity at a later time," he said as he casually walked away.

The mood throughout the Bailian capital of Immor-Onn was nothing short of jubilant.

Commerce and trade were thriving. The available regions of the city were shrinking rapidly as displaced citizens came back to their beloved city. Diplomats and envoys from across the Annigan petitioned for a presence in the rapidly evolving city. The Do-Tarr had already begun construction on the temple of the avatar.

…and the queen had her gems.

"I just knew Quadar would come through!" Shula said as she held a beautifully cut red gem up and inspected it.

"From what I understand, getting them here was quite the ordeal," Kai said as she glanced around the queen's private chambers.

"I am well pleased!" The Bailian sovereign said jubilantly as she picked up a small green gem from the pile in front of her.

Kai smiled as she walked past the monarch's small circular desk. "I'm so glad my queen."

Glancing at a small stack of papers beside the gems the spymaster froze, gasping in horrific recognition. On the top sheet were four lines of X's and I's.

Staring at the binary field, recent gruesome memories flooded the human's consciousness.

She had been there on the scene several cycles ago when the marines found the body in the available regions. Little nine-grand-old Sa'Sha's body had been strung up like a side of meat in a butcher shop. Her throat had been slit and body drained of blood. The entire floor was stained red. On the walls, the same type of eerie glyphs were still faintly visible.

Because the young girl was an orphan of the streets, the incident was considered a singular event and brushed aside. Kai mourned with the rest of her street family, but death was a sad reality of their mostly bleak existence.

The writing she now stared at was the first indicator that it was not a solitary event. This displayed a depth and scope that agitated the deadly young woman. It gave rise to feelings of danger and vengeance in her.

"My queen," she said when finally able to speak. "May I ask what this is?"

Shula gave a brief glance at the stack of papers to her left then resumed examining her gems. "Oh, that's some boring proposal from the Tiikeri Finance Minister. I'm going to take it up with the next council meeting."

Kai felt her chest tightening in anger. *Tiikeri, Nocturn, no wonder no one had seen anything like it.*

Keeping her composure, she watched the content ruler playing with her new baubles. There was no sense in mentioning anything to her until she acquired more information.

There were questions that needed answering and the priestess of Orad didn't care how she got them.

"If I may be excused Your Majesty, there are matters which need attending."

The dream had awakened him. It was a call; a summons.

Junior General Onse, of Otick House Awa, climbed from the hole in the sand, which was the entrance to his austere home. The sun glistened off the damp shore of Zod Island as the Kan fog receded into the Shallow Sea.

Stretched out before him in the shore, thousands of other holes which constituted the Otick city of Hidet dotted the beach. Over each entrance was the occupants' ooD. The protective shell acted as a marker, identifying the resident. The outside of the shell showed their rank and house affiliation. The inside, now visible, was a chronicle of the owner's deeds.

The community was coming to life. Male soldiers were emerging in mass and donning their shells. They too heard the call. Surfacing from the waters were the female oyster bed tenders, plodding onto shore from their Kan shift.

Blessed be the Golden One, he recited to himself as he pulled his ooD from the sand and slid it over his back in one fluid motion.

As he made his way to the waterline, he was joined by three of his subordinate officers.

"Blessed be the Golden One," they said in unison as they saluted.

Onse repeated the greeting then stared out to sea.

"Something is coming," he stated grimly.

"We too heard the warning," one said as he excitedly clicked his claw. "Is there a threat so great as to arouse the entire Shelled Triad?"

The senior Otick started pensively out to sea. "I know not, but the house would not be rallied and we would not have been summoned by the Golden One if it were not dire."

All three clicked their claws in agreement.

"Double the guards on the beds," Onse said to the lower ranking of the trio.

He saluted and scampered into the breaking surf.

"We travel to Zor," he said to the other two. "The Golden One has called a war council of all the houses."

The three crab warriors entered the water. Their trip along the bottom of the Shallow Sea, up the Telassian Chain to the high holy city of Zor, thankfully would be a short one. Leaders from the other two houses had much farther to travel and the Golden Avatar would not be denied.

"Seems like we've got some commotion down there," Zau said as she maneuvered the *Haraka* into the main hangar of Air Station Three.

"Hey, that's Demetrius' ship!" Mal said as she spotted three Bailian bodies being carried away from the *Drakin*. "What the fuck happened here?"

Inside the commercial hangar, a Zorian city guard stood beside the air boss who directed the *Haraka* to a slip on the other side of the flight deck.

"More excitement!" Kyopp said enthusiastically as he squirmed in his seat. "I knew coming along with you was the right decision!"

Zaad gave a sardonic chuckle from the seat directly across. "Yeah, you're in the shit with us now. So, you really broke with the queen and your people?"

"The moment we left Immor-Onn she lost all track of me," Kyopp said definitively. "I've been to Zor quite a few times, but never without a tether to the hive. This is my first true taste of freedom."

The EEtah leaned forward in his seat. "Do you think she'll come looking for you?"

"There's always a chance," the Do-Tarr king conceded. "She can be very spiteful."

"Hey, you're getting the hang of this," Mal said to Zau as she gently settled the air ship into its mooring.

The Singa gave a sheepish grin as she shut off the etheria powerplants allowing the *Haraka* to float a few inches above the landing pad.

"All right everyone, we're here," Mal announced. "Remember, we got shit to do. Luckily a few of the people I need to talk to are in one place."

As everyone got to their feet Zau reached over and opened the side hatch.

With a wave of his hand a shimmering curtain of light appeared in front of Kyopp. It quickly faded, revealing a human male with the same facial features as his Bailian persona.

"That's some trick," Zaad said with an appreciative nod.

"I'll blend in easier," the Do-Tarr explained.

"Okay everyone, stay close," Mal said noting the change and she started for the opening. "This shouldn't take long...I hope."

Immediately, Alto tucked his swords in his sash and started after her.

She stopped midway on the ramp and glanced back.

"You're coming?" she said, her voice betraying both surprise and relief.

The swordmaster appeared confused.

"Why would I not?" he said in a gentle voice.

Mal's mouth tightened into a resigned smile. "Sure, come on."

They walked silently across the hangar making sure to stay out of the way of incoming ships being diverted around the incident area. A Zorian guard stopped them at the scene's perimeter.

"I really need to talk to Colonel Zekoff now," Mal said as she marched up to an intimidating distance from the young sentry.

The colonel's voice silenced the guard's objection. "It's alright, let them through."

Zekoff and Rafel curiously watched the duo as they approached.

"Maluria, it's good to see you young lady," the colonel warmly greeted. "What brings you to my city? Nothing illegal I hope."

Alto gave a subtle snicker at the "young lady" phrase triggering a quick scowl from Mal.

"Not this time colonel," Mal said stepping up to the group. "But I do come with a warning."

"Oh?"

"There's a potential shit storm coming to the Goyan Islands," the Spice Rat gravely said. "And we need to get the word out."

Rafel's moustache twitched. "Exactly what are you referring too?"

"An eclipse, darkness," Mal began, "and the things from Nocturn that thrive in it."

The group stood silently listening as Mal updated them on their discoveries and plan. When she finished all stood staring in silent disbelief.

"I've never heard anything about this. Did you call it an eclipse?" Rafel said skeptically.

Mal gave a questioning glance at Alto.

"The last one predates humans," Alto said grimly. "There's not much written about it."

Zekoff craned his neck in surprise. "I can't order the emergency signal on the turine to be rung on a potential threat. Besides, I would need to confer with the lead quartermaster to do it at all."

"And given Si Aramos' disappearance, that would be difficult," Rafel added.

"I saw Stryder Aramos over in Nocturn," Alto said. "He was in the company of a white Tiikeri."

"I don't like it," Zekoff said. "You may be right Maluria, there's something going on."

Mal huffed loudly. "Yeah, well when the eclipse hits everybody here is gonna have to learn to read by moonlight. If there's anybody left."

Okawa, who had been silently taking in the conversation suddenly gasped.

"You've something to add captain?" the colonel said hopefully.

The Valdurian agent paused briefly as she organized her thoughts. "The moon. Moonlight!"

"What of it?" Rafel said quizzically.

"Those gems Stryder Aramos had were covered in powdered moonstone. It dissolves under moonlight!"

"Without that covering, those babies put on quite a light show," Demetrius chimed in.

"Where are they now?" the colonel asked with growing concern in his voice.

"Unknown," Okawa said. "The last we saw them they were over in the Valley of Chains."

Zekoff stroked his beard. "Anything of note in the Valley of Chains?"

"Some reclusive monastic order," Rafel replied. "It's thought they utilize the chains for some obscure religious ceremony."

The colonel sighed. "We really need to find Stryder Aramos now."

"And time is not our friend in this instance," the Spice Rat ominously added.

"I'm pretty sure I know where he is," Okawa said addressing the group. "He's somewhere in the sewers. The Cul-Ta are on his side. It's not going to be easy."

Zekoff sighed. "Alright I'll start putting a team together."

"Colonel, with your permission I would like to be part of that team," Cha-Rod spoke up.

The Zorian commander assessed the small blue man with the determined gaze. "Well, it's your neck, but sure, we'd be glad to have you."

"Rafel, have a conversation with those two wounded Cul-Ta about a more specific location of Si Aramos."

"And I would like to be involved in that conversation," Okawa volunteered.

The spymaster smiled sinisterly. "Your reputation precedes you Captain Okawa. I would love to watch you work."

The brunette leered back at the spymaster. "I would say the same captain."

Zekoff directed a commanding stare directly at Demetrius. "I need you to get to the Temple of the Golden Avatar."

Demetrius recoiled. "Me?!"

"Yes you. Go and talk with the Otick priests about this eclipse. If it predates humans, they may give us some insight."

"So exactly who am I working for here?" Demetrius' tone bordered on indignant. "I thought it was House Valdur, and,

I would like to point out to both parties playing tug of war for my services, I am supposed to be retired!"

Okawa lowered her head and grinned.

Zekoff stared calmly at the frustrated young man. "Consider it a promotion."

The small school of snabb tuna propelled themselves through the Ocean Deep waters of Lumina at an astounding velocity. Their blue-green bodies and bright yellow fins iridescently glittered in the murky depths as they darted in erratic patterns as a single organism.

Swimming alongside, easily keeping up, a trim, muscled merman with long blonde hair steered them southward. The herder kept a watchful eye on the lead fish for any errant course change, all the while keeping a safe distance so as not to spook the school.

As they approached the Parvat Seamount deep below, the mer gave out a high-pitched alarm, warning the harvesters ahead of their approach. The sound echoed off the mountainous peaks of their home which ran along the Annigan's western equator from the Narrow Lands to the Goyan Rise.

He became concerned when there was no reply from the reapers of the Kombain Clan. All of the three high mer clans took their duties seriously and this was a serious breach of protocol.

As the peaks of the seamount appeared below, he called out again. Still hearing no reply, he decided on an alternative maneuver. They were moving too fast for errors. Perhaps containing them in shallower water might work. With a flick of his tail he guided the school eastward where the uninhabited summits graduated upward into the Goyan Rise and Shallow Sea.

Sensing the change, the wily fish attempted a tricky yet expected maneuver by darting into a narrow canyon. The experienced herder merely rerouted himself over to the canyon's egress point and waited. The school however didn't exit where he expected them to be. At their velocity there should have been no time for him to pause.

From below, a scraping sound resonated out of the ravine followed by the fish's distinctive grunting sound of pain. The confused mer felt a touch of panic rising within him. To lose a school was a great dishonor within his Cho'pon Clan not to mention depriving the community of much needed sustenance.

As he slipped down into the trench, his nostrils flared from the smell of blood. The tuna were nowhere to be seen. Scales and small various chewed fish parts floated about.

He reeled in shock. *What could have possibly decimated the school, so quickly?*

His answer came almost immediately. Beneath and around him the floor and walls of the gully seemed to be moving. Before he had the chance to give off a warning cry Gar-Kal were detaching themselves from the rocky partitions leaping at him. From below, the hideous fish creatures swam upwards toward him with webbed, clawed hands extended menacingly.

He spun quickly in an attempt to exit the way he came in, but it was too late. Searing pain coursed through him as multiple sets of talons raked across his back. He felt multiple bodies land on him from above driving him downward into a writhing mass of outstretched hands and snapping jaws.

Thankfully, the mer passed out before the first bite was taken out of him as he was pulled into the concealed, thrashing horde from Nocturn.

When the hapless fish tender was finally devoured the throng quieted, waiting for the coming darkness.

Religious temples of any kind always made Demetrius uncomfortable. They were always too formal, with too many rules. That, along with the chance of angering a powerful entity by breaking any of the myriad of regulations; the pilot decided it was best to avoid them.

Thankfully, growing up his mother had never forced him to participate. She was a scribe to the mayor in their hometown of Vana. A logical, well-read woman, Alyanna de Vana viewed all religions as hokum, designed to placate and loot a gullible populous.

Now, the recently conscripted airship pilot stood on the beach, in the hot sun. In front of him, the pearl-encrusted entrance to the temple of the Golden Avatar loomed.

Sighing deeply and summoning his reserve, Demetrius proceeded over to the doorway. As he was about to cross the entryway a high squeaky voice rang out in broken common.

"Halt, do not cross the threshold!"

Demetrius froze.

A female Otick dressed in a flowing blue robe stepped from the cave's dim interior. Admittedly, the pilot had only a few dealings with the humanoid crabs of the Goyan Islands outside of Wallack and Raydan. He knew they were a devoutly pious lot and extremely intimidating. Even the females stood a full six feet high and their hard exteriors weren't softened by any clothing they might choose to wear. To his human eye they were all difficult to tell apart. The only reason he knew this was a female was because she wore no protective shell on her back.

"Who seeks to enter the temple of the Golden One?" she challenged.

"Um, uh, my name is Demetrius," the intimidated pilot said nervously.

"Why do you wish an audience with the Golden One?" she asked impatiently.

The pilot fidgeted. "Well, um, actually I didn't. All I need is to talk to a cleric."

The accolade, sensing no sinister intent softened and studied him quizzically. "The attendants to the Golden One are busy. Come back later."

She started to leave but Demetrius' stammer caused her to pause.

"Well, actually," he began hesitantly, "it's kinda important."

"You wish to enter the temple of the Golden One?" she said in a haughty tone.

Demetrius gave an embarrassed shrug. "Well, yeah, kinda."

The Otick gave a resolved sigh as she pointed at the ground in front of her. "Kneel."

"What?"

"Kneel."

Always with the rules, he inwardly lamented.

"I gotta kneel?" Demetrius protested. "That sand is hot!"

The Otick was unmoved.

"And produce an offering," she said extending her claw hand palm up.

"And I gotta pay?!" Demetrius said, his voice climbing a register.

The humanoid crab stood in resolute silence.

The airship pilot sighed in frustration. "Look, the colonel of the city guards sent me. I need to ask if you know something about an eclipse. He says we don't have much time."

Her hand slowly lowered as she listened to the human's plea and her attitude changed to solemn recognition.

Suddenly, from behind her, the interior erupted in a bright flash. Beams of golden light illuminated the cave and backlit the sentry as they streamed outward and were diffused in the Lumina sun.

The sound of commotion behind them caused the female to move aside.

Demetrius followed suit as eight Otick warriors emerged from the light of the inner temple. They marched past the two ignoring them, as they made their way across the beach and into the waters of the Shallow Sea.

Adjusting her blue robes, the sentinel's demeanor shifted to reluctant acceptance as she studied the overwhelmed human.

"Wait here. The attendants are now free."

As they streamed out of the Ikusmen Optics Shop onto the busy Zorian street, Mal stopped and assessed her travelling companions.

"You know," she said putting her hands on her hips. "They look pretty good on you."

Cha-Rod, Kyopp and Zau, now adorned with round dark spectacles smirked at the compliment.

Zau touched the frame appreciatively. "I gotta say, my eyes don't hurt now."

The other two from the darker regions of the Annigan nodded in agreement.

"I can even project my map through the lens," the Singa added. "That guy's a genius!"

Mal huffed, "At those prices he better be."

The group's laugh was interrupted by the Grand Turine in the harbor ringing five bells. The Kan would be starting soon.

"Okay, this ate up most of our day," Mal said rallying the group. "Let's get over to the Demon's Gate Inn and hope Alto got us a spot to lay our heads."

As they started northward, they caught sight of Demetrius heading their way navigating the thinning but still crowded street.

"Hey," he said coming up to the group. "I've got news from the Otick."

"Did you inform Zekoff and the Zorian group?" Mal asked.

Demetrius shook his head. "I've spent the last two decis trying to locate them. No luck."

Mal grimaced. "So, what's up?"

The exuberant pilot exhaled loudly, "It's big!"

With a concerned sigh Mal directed the group to a nearby alley, away from any potential eavesdropper.

"Alright, spill it," the Spice Rat ordered.

Demetrius was practically vibrating with eagerness at finally being able to share his news.

"Well, the colonel was right. The Otick had complete records."

Mal rolled her hands expectantly. "And?"

"This eclipse thing happens every five thousand grands. The last time, Goya was invaded by those fish things. The battle set up a chain of events that led to the rise of us humans."

The pace of Demetrius' story was steadily increasing with his excitement.

"So, as it turned out certain groups of Avions, Otick and EEtah betrayed their own people and…" he glanced over at Zaad. "Didn't you know about this?"

The EEtah's response was immediate. "Way before my time, besides I'm outer clan."

"Anyway…" the pilot continued undaunted.

"Demetrius," Mal interrupted. "You got a short version of this?"

Catching himself, Demetrius sighed. "The Otick are ramping up. They expect something. They've got extra protection on their oyster beds and all three houses are martialing for a fight."

Assessing the news, Mal unconsciously ran her fingers along the side of her face.

"They even asked me for help moving them around," Demetrius chuckled at the irony. "I guess I work for them now too."

The pilot's next statement was cut short by a cacophony of chattering as a mob of armed Cul-Ta streamed into the ally from the far end.

"Fuck!" Mal barked drawing her sword.

Zau quickly backed to a doorway as Cha-Rod hefted his cane.

Rippled air appeared before Kyopp as he assumed his insect form and drew his hammer. He winced as his glasses, not designed for the narrower bug skull, toppled to the ground.

The alley was too narrow to draw Bowbreaker but Zaad smiled as he saw Orrk enter amidst a barrage of chattering rodents.

"Your ass is mine!" The EEtah declared pointing to the ironmark.

A motion of Orrk's hand sent a wave of rat creatures swarming over to the EEtah. He bellowed furiously as he punched the first so hard it exploded. The next managed to get a stab in with its small blade. This angered the man-shark and he grabbed the tiny assaulting arm wrenching it from its socket. Pulling the screaming Cul-Ta up he grabbed it by the tail. With a wide swing he started clubbing the other attackers.

The sound of stone crashing, followed by the spray of red mist followed Kyopp's hammer as he swung it from side to side, pulping rodent bodies and striking the alley walls.

Mal and Cha-Rod were taking care of several assailants each as Orrk charged straight for Demetrius. The pilot had drawn his short sword and was standing in front of the unarmed Singa.

From the doorway, Zau flipped over the same seashell from her belt she used on the *Haraka* in the Land of Mists. As she rubbed the rune on the shell's back, she closed her eyes and began to softly chant.

Demetrius swallowed hard and readied his weapon as the much larger Orrk charged him. The half EEtah screamed in frustration when he attempted to strike the human, only to be repelled by an invisible force.

Cha-Rod and Mal fought side by side. The Spice Rat was beginning to tire from the constant assaults by the more numerous enemy. So far, she had not been struck, but her sword arm was getting weary. The Bojo Vat master, by comparison, was the picture of grace. He deftly blocked the furious Cul-Ta's attacks with the shaft of his ukko wood cane, only to swing it and strike with the ornate head. As he dispatched an assailant to his right, he spun to see a roaring Orrk as he attempted to penetrate Zau's protective field.

Oscillating the cane in a wide arc he struck Orrk from behind on the side of his knee. The ironmark screamed in pain and lashed out, knocking the older Bailian unconscious and into Mal, sending both to the alley floor.

The Spice Rat readied herself as an enraged Orrk rushed at her. His massive erect penis jutted obscenely in front of him, the tip weeping in excitement. She attempted to scramble back and get to her feet but the ironmark was upon her. She cried out as he grabbed her and lifted her up in front of him.

"I know you…" he growled just as emergency whistles of the Zorian Guards went off all around them, one cascading into and being joined by another.

Orrk spun toward the alley entrance. There were still plenty of Cul-Ta keeping Zaad and Kyopp busy. He scowled in frustration at not being able to get his intended target and they were about to be joined by the city guards.

Leering evilly at the struggling Mal he head-butted the Spice Rat who went limp in his arms.

"Keep fighting!" he screamed to the remaining Cul-Ta as he made his way down the alley with the unconscious Mal still in his grip. "Kill them!"

Alto felt fortunate to have procured the same room that he and Mal had stayed in previously at the Demon's Gate Inn. The others would share a large common room next door.

His companions should be getting back soon from their search for eye protection. For now though, the bed was soft and his eyelids heavy.

Removing the blades from his sash, Defari gave out a whimper of protest at leaving his side.

Alto sighed as he propped the long sword by his head. "Easy girl, just a little nap."

The swordmaster drifted off quickly to the soothing sound of Defari's gentle panting.

It was the same dream he had ever since leaving Immor-Onn:

Maluria,

Marriage,
Children,
Peace,
All with an underlying, unrequited sadness.

The tender feeling of Mal's lips on his was shattered, as the door to his room burst open.

Alto sprang up instantaneously, hurling his knife at the sound while drawing Defari at the same time.

The Do-Tarr nimbly snatched the blade from midair as it flew towards him. The etheria long blade in the swordmaster's hands growled and snarled furiously as it pointed at Kyopp in his insect form.

"Mora!" he said, voice strained.

Alto heaved a sigh and lowered Defari.

"You need to come with me my friend," he said tossing the knife back to its owner.

Alto caught and sheathed it, not breaking contact with the humanoid mantis.

"It's dire," he said ominously.

The Swordmaster was now on his feet slipping the blades into their proper position.

"What happened?"

"We were attacked," he said in a penetrating voice. "They were after Demetrius."

Kyopp nodded at Alto's intense questioning stare. "He's fine."

Alto's shoulders relaxed slightly.

"Mora, they took the captain."

For the briefest flash, all movement in the room froze. The swordmaster grew calmly grim.

"Where?"

"By the optics shop in the Shimol Plat."

Alto started for the open door. As he passed Kyopp a mandible hand gently touched his shoulder.

"Humans are too slow," he said. "The rooftops will be faster. Let me carry you."

Mal awoke suddenly with a shiver. She was seated against a cold stone wall with her knees bent in front of her.

Immediately the Spice Rat was flooded with waves of pain from opposite ends of her body.

Her forehead where Orrk had butted her contained a large lump which throbbed almost to the point of obscuring her vision.

Focusing on her left foot she peered at a puncture on the top of her boot. All around the sole a small pool of blood had collected and her sock felt soaked.

She apprehensively peered about taking in her surroundings. The reeling stench of raw sewage permeated the air and the walls were covered with seemingly endless patterns of the same two glyphs. The most disturbing element of her current situation sat directly across the tunnel from her.

Fia's blank stare at the Spice Rat was relentless and unblinking.

Shaking from side to side, a rush of rage and vengeance swept away any discomfort Mal felt as she scowled at the pirate queen.

"Fucking quim, you're dead!"

Fia betrayed no emotion. "We're all dead."

"Yeah, maybe," Mal spat. "But I'm gonna make sure you lead the way!"

Fia ignored the taunt. She sat calmly, staring, as Mal attempted to stand.

Realizing she was unbound yet unable to move Mal stared quizzically at her left foot which seemed to be pinned to the sewer tunnel floor.

"Sorcery from Nocturn," Fia said calmly indicating her own appendage rooted firmly to the ground.

After a few more vain attempts Mal slumped back against the wall all the while keeping Fia in her contemptuous gaze.

"I'm sorry," Fia said as she continued her unnerving stare. "Who are you?"

Mal's aghast reaction at the question only fueled her own rage. "Are you fucking kidding me?! You fucking hijacked my ship and killed my crew back in Makatooa!"

The former pirate queen paused, searching her memory.

"Yes, I believe I do remember," she said with a thoughtful glance at the ceiling. "That was another life ago."

Mal's expression contorted in fury at being trivialized. "Yeah, I'm glad you've moved on. It's still pretty fresh for me!"

Fia gave an ironic chuckle.

"You think this is funny?!" Mal challenged.

Fia's blank stare transformed to one of grim resolve.

"None of this matters. If our *host* is successful, there is a good chance everything is going to die."

"How fortuitous," came a confident male voice interrupting Mal's shocked reaction. "That is precisely what I've come to chat with you about."

Stryder Aramos' black robed figure swept into the tunnel entrance. The pale, imposing Orrk followed immediately behind his master.

Mal gasped at his bald features completely scarred with the same two runes which adorned the walls.

Halting between the two rivals he studied them both.

"I never would have imagined," he said in a menacingly contemplative tone. "The two of you. I've finally got the two of you."

His attention fell on the smuggler. "Mal, the consummate Spice Rat. You have eluded me time after time."

"And the equally infamous Rayth queen," he said leering at Fia.

Stryder stared down remorsefully and sighed. "So ironic, now that you both are in my hands. It doesn't matter. My lord is about to issue in a new age and the past shall be forgotten."

Fia's mocking laugh echoed through the tunnel. "Your lord will perish right along with your worthless ass."

Stryder's scarred features became almost whimsical. "Yes, which brings us back to that curious conversation."

The young Zorian Guard swallowed hard as an angry Zaad, fresh off a blood frenzy, towered menacingly over him.

The six other members of Patrol Division were examining the Cul-Ta bodies littered throughout the alley in various states of slaughter. Two guards were interviewing Zau, Cha-Rod and Demetrius.

"They've got our captain," the man-shark said, his voice trembling with rage. "The questions can wait!"

The corporal was about to protest when Kyopp, with Alto riding on his back, skimmed across the adjacent rooftop and down the wall with astounding speed. The guards stopped and stared, mouths agape, as the humanoid mantis came to an abrupt halt in front of his companions.

Alto released his tight grip and slid off the Do-Tarr's back. As he swept over to the group, Zau noticed his features were taut and grim. The twinkle was gone from his eyes, replaced by an unnerving stare. As he glowered at his companions, all but Cha-Rod were struck speechless by the waves of controlled fury radiating from the swordmaster.

"Where?" Alto said in a low growl.

The old Bailian pointed to where the alley made a sharp turn. "He took her that way."

"He?"

"The big *campasino* that attacked us before."

Alto's attention snapped over to Zau. "Can you find them?"

The question broke the Singa from her trance. The lioness unsteadily nodded yes.

"You will excuse me corporal!" Zaad gruffly said as he joined his friends.

Reaching to her seashell belt, Zau swiveled two over, revealing the runes beneath. As she rubbed the glyph, she motioned in the direction where Mal had been abducted.

All followed her gaze. Alto grimly scowled when the glow of individual footprints appeared. They traversed the backstreet and out of sight.

The swordmaster was about to start out, when the Singa held up her hand. "I can get ya closer."

From behind her new glasses, the three-dimensional map projected outward. This particular emanation was scaled to city level and the glowing footprints were traced out on the map in a trail through the streets. They ended deep below the city.

"They're in the sewers," Zaad said.

"And all the way across the city," Cha-Rod said pointing to the location.

Zaad looked around apprehensively. "We don't have much time. Once the fog hits we won't be able to see anything down there."

Demetrius, who had been standing back silently, leaned forward. "What about a portal?"

All stared at Zau.

The Singa shifted anxiously. "Sure, but, if I get you there, I'm not going to be able to get you out."

"Why not?" Demetrius innocently asked.

Zau sighed. "Navigating Flavian Portals is one thing. It takes a lot of energy to open one, besides…"

"Get me there," Alto interrupted. His tone left no room for debate.

"You aren't going alone Mora." Zaad defiantly stated.

"Who could deny the chance to rescue a captured comrade?" Kyopp said retrieving the hammer from its sheath on his back and hefting it. "Besides, I know tunnels."

"Two have now fallen on my watch. Two failures for me," Cha-Rod admitted. "I would ask for a chance at some redemption."

Alto stared grimly at his companions then back at Zau. "Get us there!"

"You two," the patrol sergeant said pointing to the two interviewing officers. "Go with them, remember those pelts are still worth a silver piece each."

The older of the guards grinned evilly while the other younger guard with long brown hair swallowed hard.

Facing the doorway which had been her refuge during the attack, the Singa closed her eyes in concentration. Moving her hand to the second overturned seashell, she rubbed the glyph with the lightest of touches.

Slowly, blue sparkles began to erupt from the door jamb. They quickly spread until the entire entrance was bathed in a wavering blue light.

The swordmaster, unconcerned if any were going to follow, advanced toward the portal.

"Umm, do you want me to do something?" Demetrius hesitantly asked.

Alto quickly glanced at the anxious pilot.

"I don't care," he said in a cold, flat tone before proceeding into the blue radiance and disappearing.

Stryder had grown weary of Fia's tireless ranting. He didn't believe any of her preposterous story of sentient crystals bent on domination. He served a true and mighty god. The pirate blasphemer actually claimed these hidden ones waiting at the threshold, considered themselves the true masters of the Annigan, cheated out of their destiny by the pearl avatar in the very beginning.

Seeing his attention waning Fia opted for one final taunt. "Your time in this world is numbered."

"Fear has a number, death has a number," Stryder said in a low maniacal tone. "Everything has a number."

"Your numbers aren't going to mean shit in a few cycles," Fia said contemptuously.

Mal sat quietly, seething and in pain as she listened to the two people she most wanted to kill argue over the world's future.

"If either one of your fucked-up stories is right, why are you bothering with all of this?!" the Spice Rat said with a sneer.

The quartermaster paused, giving Mal an amused grin. "I just wanted to savor this moment, as brief as it may be."

From over Mal's head, two short lines of numbers on the wall started to glow.

"It would appear that guests are among us," Stryder said nonchalantly as he motioned Orrk into the main room.

Retrieving an orange wand from his robe, the quartermaster followed.

With Alto leading the way, the group stepped out of a glowing blue field which appeared in the sewer tunnel wall.

The two guards, Cha-Rod and Alto immediately reeled from the stench. The swordmaster doubled over and vomited.

"Come now," Cha-Rod said as his nostrils continued to flair. "It's not that bad."

"It's not the smell," Kyopp explained. "Mora doesn't react well to portals."

"What smell?" Zaad asked as he sniffed the air.

Alto stood up, gave his companions a resigned glance, then silently directed everyone's attention to the large junction room to their left. They made their way cautiously, inquisitively eying the rune-covered walls.

As they approached the glow of the huge room, Defari began to quietly growl from inside its sheath. Placing his hand on the hilt, the entombed dog's superior smell and hearing channeled through the swordmaster. From the room, he detected the pungent aroma of damp fur and traces of high-pitched chattering.

They abruptly halted in the doorway.

The large room was bathed in orange light which cast deep shadows on its many occupants. The glow made the rune-filled walls and ceilings appear menacing. Filling the far end of the cavern, spilling into the tunnels, were a sea of Cul-Ta. Standing in the rear, against the walls, a dozen human men scowled threateningly. All the humans and rat people had either an X or an I carved into their foreheads. On some, the blood stain from the recent wound was still visible.

In the very back of the foreboding mob, Stryder Aramos levitated so that his upper body rose above the sea of vermin equal in height to Orrk, who stood beside him.

"Ah, more worshipers," Stryder said opening his arms in welcome. "Come, receive your mark and join us. Our lord's time is at hand."

The swordmaster's penetrating stare bore into the quartermaster.

"Surrender Maluria!" his demand resonated off the walls.

"Alto!" Mal screamed upon hearing his voice.

The swordmaster's attention briefly settled upon the tunnel Mal's voice had come from, then back to Stryder."

The quartermaster took on a condescending smile. "Oh, but she only recently arrived."

"It was not a request," Alto growled drawing both his swords.

As soon as it was unsheathed, Defari let out a long baying howl which caused the Cul-Ta to pause uneasily.

Stryder continued his demeaning smirk at Alto.

"Kill them," he casually ordered.

The six rescuers fanned out into a wedge with the EEtah in the lead, aiming toward the tunnel which held their captain. The two city guards drew their weapons and stood back to back.

Zaad drew Bowbreaker and pointed at Orrk, "You're mine!"

The Cul-Ta nervously advanced toward the group, still intimidated by the howling sword.

Kyopp took advantage of the delay and scrambled up and along the nearest wall. With a wide swing of his hammer the humanoid mantis pulped the heads of the nearest two humans. When the red mist and brain matter showered their companions the Cul-Ta charged.

As Zaad raised his weapon, Cha-Rod twirled his cane and wisely moved out of the range of the EEtah's blade.

Hanging back Stryder pointed his orange wand at Alto. The tip glowed as a thin fiery tendril shot out at the swordmaster.

Alto had finished slashing at an attacker and his short sword was directly in front of him. When the fire struck the green malachite pummel it was immediately absorbed. The power then radiated up the honey brown axinite core of the blade causing it to glow slightly.

Zaad raised Bowbreaker and charged the oncoming mob, Alto fell in behind the EEtah to defend his flanks. Severed Cul-Ta bodies flew as the man-shark's massive sword cut a swath in the chattering throng.

Defending the charging EEtah from both sides, Alto swung his blades in deadly unison. Defari barked and snarled with every swing. The short sword in his left hand surprisingly severed three of the rats as the stored-up power from the averted flame strike was released. The shock wave sent destructive ripples of force deep into the sea of vermin, crushing bodies in its wake.

To the left, Cha-Rod was holding off two large humans. They swung their swords in a savage attempt to overpower the smaller Bailian. Both cried out in frustration as the Bojo-Vat master easily parried their clumsy attacks with his cane and gracefully danced to the side of them.

Suddenly realizing they had been outflanked, one spun with a wild swing of his blade. The Bailian was well inside the panicked attack. Grabbing the human's sword hand, he barred the elbow with the cane and violently thrust upward. The arm broke with a sickeningly loud snap. Screaming in pain the assailant dropped his weapon.

Cha-Rod kept his hold and spun him directly into the attacking sword of his companion. The impaled man gasped in shock as the blade punctured his chest.

As the second human attempted to retrieve his blade, the Bailian let go of his human shield. With a simple, yet forceful push on the cane's base he drove the head of the staff into the attacker's throat, crushing his windpipe. The astonished assailant gripped his neck, gurgling as he dropped.

Sensing movement behind him, Cha-Rod swung the cane in a graceful arc, catching several Cul-Ta attempting to attack from the rear.

Attracted by the despised uniform, the two Zorain Guards were surrounded by dozens of the waist-high rat creatures. Numerous fell to their disciplined attacks but the moment their blades became lodged in their target's bodies the others swarmed over them. The two dropped, screaming in pain as more and more Cul-Ta piled on the hated guards. Dozens of tiny claws and jaws shredded flesh, tearing it away and gleefully devouring it.

Kyopp continued to dart along the walls marginally above the reach of the combatants, striking at will.

Stryder, seeing the bug king assaulting with impunity, aimed his trinilic rod and fired another stream of flame. The magical assault missed as the nimble Do-Tarr scampered upward on the high wall. Stryder cried out in exasperation as the flame scorched numerous sets of sacred numbers.

Swinging Bowbreaker and bellowing with Alto directly behind, Zaad continued to cut a path through the attacking horde making his way toward Orrk.

Despite Alto's defense, the moment the giant sword cut a path in the Cul-Ta, more took their place jumping and clawing at the man shark. Batting them away, their claw and teeth marks dotting his body.

The ironmark saw the expression on the EEtah and knew what was coming.

"Lord Stryder," he said noting Zaad grow ever closer to a blood frenzy and them. "We need to get out of here!"

"Nonsense," the quartermaster said as he aimed his wand at Cha-Rod. "This is my temple."

Another streamer of fire lashed out, this time at the older Bailian. With his Ukko wood cane already swirling around him in combat, the ribbon of flame deflected to his left striking multiple attacking Cul-Ta and setting them on fire.

The rat men panicked as they were consumed in flames and attempted to run. In the congestion of battle they only succeeded in bumping into their comrades, setting them ablaze.

The burning Cul-Ta proved an excellent barrier. With one less flank to worry about the Bojo-Vat master now veered slightly, clubbing a path in the direction that Mal's voice had come from.

Stryder shook his head in disgust at the confiscated Chenakan weapon. "Worthless!" he said in frustration as he tossed it to the floor.

Throughout the room the humans were now all dead and even though the Cul-Ta still possessed vastly superior numbers, they were proving to be virtually ineffective.

"Sir, a temple can be built anywhere," Orrk said in a frantic attempt to convince his master.

Two more waves of rat men fell to the etheria blades when Alto detected Zaad's ferocity increase. When the first splattering's of drool flew back and struck him, the swordmaster wisely backed away from the beginning frenzy.

He now concentrated on fighting his way over to the tunnel that Mal had called out from. To his left, he saw the Bailian slugging his way toward the same destination. He felt the stinging of the scratches and bites on his back and arms but ignored the pain, concentrating on his objective.

Stryder took in the situation and huffed in annoyance.

"Very well," he said, touching three of the carved runes on his cheek. "Let's give them something to ponder while we depart."

As Stryder concentrated, the three scars glowed under his fingertips.

Kyopp watched from his vantage point on the wall, as sets of numbers blinked once in a line across the ceiling. They illuminated a path over to the tunnel they had originally entered from.

The Do-Tarr paused in shocked curiosity as a rumble and powerful wave of stench blasted out of the opening. It was quickly followed by a tendrilled monstrosity as large as an elephant.

The behemoth slid into the room on eight tentacled arms. Its entire shifting body was made of sewer debris held together by a sickening field of yellowish-brown fecal matter.

In what Kyopp assumed was the front of the monstrosity was a horse head. Its eyes darted wildly about. The heads of the sewer workers as well as Cul-Ta crania also jutted out from the stinking torso. The humans peered into space with blank expressions, while the rat heads snarled and snapped.

When the abomination reached the fighting, it raised its two front tentacles and indiscriminately grabbed two Cul-Ta. Savagely smashing the bodies together, it threw the mangled corpses to the ground.

Rearing back, an ear-splitting, otherworldly shriek erupted from the horse's mouth as the stinking monstrosity waded into the fray, killing anything it could get its tendrils on.

The screech of the rampaging beast unnerved the rats and they rapidly retreated down the various tunnels they had arrived through. Zaad managed to kill two of his attackers as they attempted to flee.

The frenzied man-shark quickly spun, chest still heaving. Drool ran from his open jaws and his body was covered with dozens of bite and claw marks. In mid frenzy, the EEtah hefted Bowbreaker aloft. The enraged marine bellowed in defiance, unintimidated by the much larger advancing leviathan.

With the Cul-Ta rapidly escaping, Alto and Cha-Rod easily made it to the tunnel. Mal was there, sitting along the wall to the right. Directly across from her Fia sat in the same bent-leg position. The former pirate queen was staring off into space, jabbering incoherently.

"About fucking time you got here!" Mal said in disgust. "If I had to listen to this bitch babble any longer, I would have fucking killed myself."

Alto smiled at the bravado as he knelt beside her. "Sorry my love, I was unavoidably detained."

Seeing she was unbound the swordmaster took her by the arm and attempted to aid her in standing.

"That fucker did something to my foot," she said in a vain attempt to move it. "Some kind of fucking magic!"

"Come on you freak!" Zaad taunted the monster as it made its way toward him.

Kyopp placed himself on the ceiling over the advancing creature. Several swings of his hammer broke away part of the rune-filled stone, sending it plummeting onto the sewer golem.

The creature shrieked again, as tons of rock buried its body. Slowly, the tentacles emerged and began to dislodge itself from the large pile of rubble. When the horse head emerged, the snout was grotesquely smashed and large shards of rock protruded from the fecal body. With an uncanny strength it pulled itself from its tomb and shambled forward.

Kyopp, with grim determination now knocked away larger sections of the ceiling sending them raining down on the advancing monster. It screamed again as rock pummeled its body. The Do-Tarr stopped when the raw rock above started to crack on its own.

Parts of the ceiling were now starting to crumble without any provocation on the part of Kyopp. Large clefts now started to run the ceiling as huge fragments fell.

"Come and get me you coward!" Zaad screamed above the sound of crashing stones as the creature pulled massive chunks of rock off of its back.

Deep fissures were now opening up in the ancient sewer walls and all felt the ground rumbling.

Assessing the weakened structural integrity of the area, the Do-Tarr's natural mining faculties told him it wouldn't be long until the entire area collapsed. Below, the creature was advancing on the enraged EEtah so caught up in his blood frenzy, he was unmindful to the precarious circumstances.

Scrambling at full speed across the ceiling and down the wall, the humanoid mantis raced over to the oblivious man-shark. Not bothering to stop, the Do-Tarr snatched Zaad from his feet and swept him away just before the creature's massive tentacles came crashing where he once stood. The force of the blow rocked the cavern and another shower of debris buried the behemoth.

Kyopp raced toward the tunnel with Zaad wiggling and screaming as he continued to wave Bowbreaker.

In the channel, Alto tensely squinted at the shuddering walls. Dust and small rocks were beginning to fall all around them. "We've got to get the both of you out of here."

"Fuck her!" Mal spat. "If you save that quim, I swear I'm fucking going to kill her."

The swordmaster cast a concerned look at the callous statement.

Kyopp, carried Zaad into the tunnel and set the panting EEtah gently on the floor. Out in the main room, all heard the creature shriek again as it climbed out from under the pile of rocks.

The passageway was rocked again, showering them with dust. Mal gave Alto a desperate stare. "Listen Bladeslinger, it's held by magic and unless you got any fucking magic, we gotta do something!"

Both gazed at her captured foot, then back up at each other.

"You know what you have do!" she said eyeing his blades.

The swordmaster wavered upon hearing Mal's conclusion, searching his companions worried expressions.

"We'd best do something," Cha-Rod advised from the tunnel opening. "That thing just broke free."

"None if it will mean anything if we're buried here," Kyopp said as another tremor rocked the cavern. "This whole place is coming down!"

As Alto reluctantly drew his short sword, the shadow of an idea surfaced. "Kyopp, I need that!" he abruptly said, pointing to the orange wand laying a few feet outside the shaft.

The Do-Tarr nodded and raced out into the crumbling room. He grabbed the wand and made it back as a whole section of wall collapsed burying the tunnel entrance.

Taking the rod, he placed it against the blade of the etheria short sword. Pausing one more time, he scrutinized his lover's resolute stare.

"Will you fucking do it?!" she ordered, as the sound of the creature smashing at the clogged entrance was combined with another rumble and falling rocks.

Alto kept staring at her captured foot then swallowed hard.

"Alto," Mal said, her voice softened. "It's the only way. Do it."

With a quick fluid motion, the swordmaster severed her foot at the ankle. The orange wand glowed as the blade sliced through the boot cauterizing the wound. Mal grimaced but didn't cry out.

Alto lingered for a moment staring at Mal's severed foot. When he checked back up, the Spice Rat was gazing at him with a pained but understanding presence. Reaching out she touched his cheek.

"It was the only way."

The creature had now partially opened up the tunnel entrance and was attempting to get to them. Several undulating tentacles lunged at them as it's putrefied, malleable body was slithering through the restricted opening. The area shook again and the top of the channel opening caved in on the advancing beast.

"We must go!" Kyopp proclaimed, as he picked up the wounded Spice Rat.

All but Mal briefly fixed their attention back on the tunnel entrance as the creature screeched and peeled rocks off its battered frame. The Spice Rat leered at the incoherent Rayth and scowled.

Taking advantage of the distraction, Mal quickly reached over and snatched Alto's long knife from its sheath. In a single motion, she brought the blade viciously onto the top of Fia's skull splitting it in two.

Blood erupted along the wall where she sat, but the Rayth betrayed no emotion or pain as her prattling finally stopped.

Alto wrenched around and stared in shock at Mal in Kyopp's arms. Her hand was still clutching the blade which was now buried all the way down into Fia's neck. Reaching over he placed his hand on hers. She slowly pulled her hand back and Alto retrieved his knife in stunned silence.

Mal defiantly stared into Alto's astonished face. "I told you I was going to fucking kill her."

The creature had now freed itself and was moving rubble away from the entrance. A few yards beyond their position the tunnel was starting to collapse.

"We need to go now!" Kyopp said anxiously as he stared at the rapidly crumbling sewer. "Follow me, I've had some experience with tunnels."

As he did every morning since his advancement to Sectary, Natuna walked the chains at the lifting of the Kan. The young human stared upward at the mountain peaks and marveled at the massive chains connecting them.

When he was first assigned the task, he would fantasize about walking on a tight wire in a carnival. One foot would be carefully placed in front of the other, the slightest misstep meant falling to his doom.

In reality, each individual link was three feet wide and ten feet long. Most were overgrown with vegetation which, when still damp with Kan dew, felt good on the bottoms of his feet.

Glancing over the edge to the valley floor hundreds of feet below, he chuckled at his former immaturity. This was a serious task, requiring diligence and perception. Each chain was to be inspected daily as it had been for thousands of grands. Any in need of repair were to be reported to brother Arweinyd the monk in charge. Natuna still didn't know what the chains that stretched between the mountain peaks were for. He dreamed about the day when he reached the position of full monk and the explanation was revealed to him.

When the young monk in training arrived where the link entered the rocky cliff, two birds were fighting. The brightly colored fowl squawked loudly as they fluttered aggressively toward each other kicking up the foliage.

Shooing them away Natuna noticed something strange where the birds had disturbed the vegetation. It was about a foot long and it was nestled up against the side of the chain.

Inspecting it closer the young man noticed it was extremely hard and covered in a white paste. Moving more of the branches, he discovered another on the other side of the link.

He couldn't discern how long they had been there, but someone obviously placed, then concealed them.

It's heavy, he thought, as he carefully picked one up. Brother Arweinyd would need to see this immediately.

Mal opened her eyes and the room slowly came into focus. She was lying in a comfortable divan covered by a sheet.

Alto was seated by her head and Kyopp in human form stood by the foot of the bed.

"Where?" she said groggily.

"Clerria House," Alto said in a calm steady voice. "Kyopp carried you here. You slept through the Kan."

"All I remember is you getting me out before everything collapsed," she said to the Do-Tarr.

Kyopp smiled. A lock of short brown hair swept across his golden skinned youthful features. "You passed out as I took to the rooftops."

A moment of realization swept over the Spice Rat and her gaze darted to her feet. There was only one lump under the sheets.

She sighed in resignation. "I was hoping it was all a bad dream."

Alto's disposition turned maudlin and he sadly shook his head "no."

"Quit beating yourself up," she gently said. "You did what you had to do. I guess the question is, how am I going to do anything with just one foot?"

"You should be up and about by midday," Kyopp optimistically proclaimed.

The Spice Rat appeared skeptical. "Really?"

The Do-Tarr excitedly shuffled his feet and beamed. "Mora and I made a deal with the Clerria Marassa."

"Deal?"

Alto reached over and gently touched her hand.

"They're making you a rubber foot," he said softly. "The Clerria measured your remaining one shortly after arriving. They also treated our wounds. Cul-Ta are not the cleanest of animals and they were worried about infection."

"Yes," Kyopp chimed in enthusiastically. "They claim once you get used to it you won't even know the difference."

"How fucking expensive was that?" Mal said sitting up with her back to the headboard.

Alto fluffed the pillow behind her. "Clerria don't accept money. Their school of medicine is part of the university."

"I thought you said you made a deal?"

"I agreed to trade your spore from Nocturn," Alto said somberly.

Mal sat forward and angrily glared at her lover. "My spore?!"

The swordmaster shrugged. "Spore for a foot, I thought it a good trade."

"You traded my fucking spore?!"

"That wasn't all," Kyopp said in a less gleeful tone.

"What?!"

The young man gave an embarrassed smirk. "I had to agree to give the medical school my body upon my demise."

"You did what?"

"Apparently the university is interested in my race."

Mal grunted as she sat back. "Fine!"

"Now," Alto said, adjusting Defari in his sash. "I must go, you get better."

"Wait! Where the fuck are you going?"

"Demetrius is taking a group of us over to a place called the Valley of Chains," the swordmaster explained. "It's up in the mountains. Stryder escaped and Captain Okawa is certain that's his destination."

The Spice Rat started to get up. "I'm coming."

Alto rested his hand on her shoulder. "You need to rest and get your new foot before you go anywhere. Kyopp will stay with you. Then you two need to concentrate on setting off the turine's emergency signal. I've got a score to settle with Si Aramos."

Mal begrudgingly sat back. "The quartermasters are in charge of the turines. I doubt if they're gonna be very receptive to me."

"Perhaps the Captain's Guild can help?" Alto suggested. "Either way, I must go."

Leaning over he cupped her chin and tenderly kissed her. "I shall return."

"My fucking spore…" she said in a low mumble of protest as he went to leave.

The swordmaster winked. "My love, pouting does not become you."

Midmorning on the northern docks of the high holy city of Zor is a hectic time for most of the races that call it home. Any of those having business with the EEtah race must inevitably go through House Nur.

The massive double doors situated below the high double shark fin arch is the way land sentients must enter the temple of this powerful company of females. On any day a progression of inhabitants can be observed bidding admittance. For those who abide in the water, access is conducted differently.

Rising from the Shallow Sea, six Otick all wearing ooDs, made a regal progression up the wide ramp. Three led the way, carrying themselves with an air of authority.

Directly behind, a single Otick bore a large sack. He was flanked by two obvious guards. Their solid black eyes darted about in menacing anticipation.

Standing solemnly on the ramp were three orange-robed EEtah's of House Nur.

When they reached the top of the incline, all parties bowed to each other. The Otick representative of House Awa stepped forward.

"Moret Awit," he said formally as he gave another short bow. "We the representatives of the Shelled Triad, thank you for granting us an audience."

The EEtah in the center nodded and gave a slight smile at the proper, formal address.

"We come united to seek your people's aid," he continued.

The Moret Awit extended her hands. "How can the sisters of House Nur assist our friends the Otick?"

"We seek your strength for the coming darkness," the Awa representative said soberly.

"What do you seek and what do you offer?"

"We seek the EEtahs of Dakor Sunal."

The high ranking EEtah paused. Dakor Sunal were shock troops, made up of the largest, most aggressive males of their race.

"How many?"

The Otick stared upward at the female EEtah. "All of them."

This request set both priestesses on either side of the Moret chattering softly in their staccato language.

Raising her hand for silence, the queen's political aide quizzically assessed the crab's intentions.

The lead Otick continued. "We would also ask for fifty of Zorod Sunal to assist us in protection of the Golden One and his temple."

The Moret approved the second appeal. "And what would you give for such a request?"

The Awa representative motioned over his shoulder. The warrior bearing the large sack marched up and placed the bag between the Oticks and EEtahs, then returned.

"We offer one thousand Veros pearls," the Otick said as he opened the bag for their inspection.

Guttural chatter among the EEtahs erupted again, silenced by a single raise of the Moret's hand.

"This is very generous!" she said admiring the most coveted pearls in the Annigan. Any one of the glittering white orbs contained the ability to hold a magical charge.

The Awa Otick's became grim. "How much would *you* pay to protect your family, clan and very way of life. When the darkness and its allies descended on us long ago, we were caught by surprise. That will not happen again."

With the early Moonless in Immor-Onn, a sudden calm brought welcome relief from the usual blustery winter winds. On the streets, citizens took advantage of the calm weather milling about on the usually empty avenues.

The walk from Queen Shula's royal palace to the diplomatic quarters was thankfully short as Ma-Tah and No-Le navigated the unexpected crowds.

"State dinners are tedious but necessary," the Tiikeri nonchalantly complained to his mongrel seneschal directly behind.

No-Le knew better than to respond. She had been with the Tiikeri almost all her young life and knew her place in the political game.

Coming up on the diplomatic compound, the EEtah marine guard saluted and allowed them to pass. As the Tiikeri moved inside the gate, he felt the hint of a breeze barely ruffle his fur. Veering left toward the lesser dignitaries' quarters the finance minister scowled.

"These accommodations are little better than a hovel," he said in a voice dripping with elitist distain. "Still, we are thankfully across the compound from that boor Jo-Rakk. Ambassador, huh…ah, here we are."

Slipping past her master, No-Le opened the door for him. As the Tiikeri proceeded through the doorway the wind picked up one more time then quickly died.

Once inside, the mongrel tapped on a small light by the door. Ma-Tah moved to the center of the room and stood expectantly. The dutiful seneschal came up behind her master to assist in removing his robe.

A scraping sound on the wall to their right caused both to freeze. The corner of the room was dark and the two mawls barely perceived only the most nebulous of forms.

With a tap, an orange gem in the wall glowed, revealing Kai with dagger in hand. The stark illumination made her features deep and menacing.

"Hello minister," the one-armed woman said as she deftly twirled her dagger and sheathed it. "I trust you're having a pleasant Moonless?"

Ma-Tah sputtered in shock as No-Le advanced in front of her master and potential danger.

"Who are you?!" the Tiikeri bellowed. "How did you get in here?! These are private quarters!"

"So many questions," Kai said with a shake of her head. "Come to think of it, I've got a few questions."

The assassin casually pointed over her shoulder at the two runes she had just carved in the wall. "Any of that look familiar?"

As the Tiikeri took in the X and I crudely scrawled in the stone, his demeanor changed from shocked to enraged.

"I refuse to be interrogated by an intruder!" Ma-Tah said with a sneer.

No-Le drew her knife and slowly advanced toward Kai.

"These runes are from Nocturn," Kai said, ignoring the mongrel's approach.

Ma-Tah's whiskers twitched in rage. "Is that so? I'm afraid I can't help you. Perhaps you can ask ambassador Jo-Rakk. He too is from Nocturn."

Kai's stare was resolute. "I did. The ambassador and I are friends."

For the first time the priestess of Orad detected a concerned pause in the white tiger.

"He said those were the runes used by a dangerous religious cult in the Land of Mists." Kai paused for effect. "Numerologists, he said."

Ma-Tah's concern reverted to a contemptuous leer as Kai continued. "So, we've got numerology and finance. You can understand why I wanted to talk to you."

"I understand nothing," the Tiikeri howled. "Now leave!"

"Let me help you out," Kai said in a confident voice. "We found these runes all over the walls at a murder scene, then on a financial proposal from you to the queen."

Ma-Tah puffed up in indignation. "Are you accusing me?!"

"I'm asking you a question."

"You have neither the right nor the rank to ask me anything," Ma-Tah declared. "No-Le, remove her!"

As the mongrel closed in, dagger at the ready, the stump of Kai's left arm began to emit blue sparks. Pointing it at the approaching mongrel a shimmering blue sword erupted, impaling the mawl.

No-Le froze with a stunned expression as she dropped her knife. Torrents of blood soaked the front of her tunic as she wobbled helplessly, held in place by the ghostly blade.

In a flash, the otherworldly weapon disappeared and a stunned Ma-Tah watched as his devoted seneschal toppled to the floor, dead.

Kai never broke her stare at the Tiikeri. "Your work here is done minister. Leave my city now and take your unwelcome practices with you."

Unable to speak the Tiikeri finance minister continued to stare at his dead servant.

"I won't tell you again," Kai said threateningly as she lifted her hand and pointed at the nearby window.

With a sudden howl, the wind blew the window open. The icy gust coursed through the apartment blowing papers and unsecured items around the room.

Ma-Tah spun glancing at the wind-driven chaos then back to the mysterious intruder.

She was gone.

The road to the summit of Mount Goya and the Avion City of Darmont perched high atop it, is well guarded. Carefully orchestrated treaties by House Pyre with communities along the route ensured security.

First is the bridge city of Quantara Keep, run by Prince Serkel and his personal army the Jomake. It is the only access over the Quantara ravine. Further up the mountain's only road, lies the Azorith Monastery and the mysterious monks who tend to the Valley of Chains.

Recently however, both of these communities' effectiveness had been considerably reduced with the invention of the airship.

"There it is," Okawa said pointing out the windshield as the *Drakin* banked toward the eastern face of Mount Goya.

The monastery was a three-tiered structure, built into the side of the mountain. The facade was surrounded by a high wall which completely cut off the wide road up the mountain. Two wide openings on either side of the barrier allowed travel, but the closed gates indicated passage was restricted.

Along the slope below the monastery compound, was an elaborate terraced garden. It was situated above one of the massive chains jutting from the mountainside.

"Obviously they were not joking when they named this valley," Alto said as he glared quizzically at the massive black chains overgrown with vegetation. "What might they possibly be for?"

"You sure got me," Demetrius said as he maneuvered the airship closer. "And what's with the makeshift hamlet?"

All peered at the small crudely thrown together community of ramshackle wooden structures, lean-tos, and tents. It sat fifty yards from the monastery walls on a wide spot in the road.

"Wannabes," Okawa said simply.

"How about I land us over between the walls and that shanty town?" Demetrius asked, casting a side glance at the Valdurian agent.

Staring forward, she wordlessly approved his choice and grinned at the lack of ego in the veteran pilot. *He's a keeper.*

The *Drakin* set down gently on the road between the two communities. When the ramp dropped, the howling gusts whipped at their clothing and everything not secured in the cabin.

"Okay, this is where you get out," Demetrius announced over the wind. "Make it quick before my stuff ends up scattered all over the mountain!"

Zaad grumbled as he grabbed Bowbreaker and Cha-Rod used his cane to help him stand.

"Human monks," the Bailian said as he peeked curiously out the hatch. "This should be something."

Alto and Zaad followed the Bojo-Vat master out of the ship with Okawa in the rear.

"Hey!" Demetrius called out over the howling flurries. "You make sure you take care of yourself."

The Valdurian blushed slightly and gave a shy grin. Without a word she slipped out onto the ramp.

As the craft lifted off everyone took in the bleak and windswept terrain.

Alto noted the mood of the inhabitants in the hamlet. They were angry and uncomfortable in their surroundings.

"If these are the hopefuls, I seriously doubt they will be chosen," the swordmaster said to Cha-Rod.

The Bailian snickered in agreement and the group proceeded to the monastery walls. Standing on either side of the road, slightly in front of the gate, were a group of a dozen men and women. They stared patiently at the archway, apparently oblivious to everything.

"These might just stand a chance," the Bojo-Vat master said to Alto as they passed the field of aspirants.

"Amazing how admittance to a martial discipline is strikingly similar despite the culture," Alto noted.

Cha-Rod appeared to reminisce briefly. "Indeed."

Coming up to the slatted wooden barrier, it slowly opened before any had the chance to knock. An older man dressed in bright yellow and orange robes stepped out from the threshold. His unkept beard flowed in the breeze. On top of his head long dreadlocks were coiled tightly so as to not fly about. His face was colorfully decorated with geometric lines and patterns. Running vertically down his forehead was a thick red stripe. The three others behind him appeared similar but had no red stripe.

"Do you seek passage?" he asked in a friendly tone.

"We seek an audience with your master," Okawa said in a firm but friendly tone.

Still retaining his smile, the lead monk assessed the crowd assembled at the gate then returned his attention to the group.

"The master is not seeing anyone at this time," he said in a pleasant, lyrical voice. He then brought his attention onto the gathering of potential students standing indifferent to the icy whistling wind. "You may all go."

For three of the dozen people in the crowd, the statement acted like a dousing of cold water. Their concentration faltered and they started to slouch back to the shanty town with heads lowered in disappointment.

Alto felt his shoulders tense at the monk's statement. They didn't have time for master-student initiation games.

Ignoring everyone, the monks filed ceremoniously back in the gate.

"We know about the crystals in the valley," Okawa proclaimed as the lead monk was about to enter.

Pausing under the threshold, he stared back at the brash female. "Wait here."

Mal was limping slightly as she made her way up the wide steps of the Zorian Forum.

"Looks like you're getting the hang of it," Kyopp said from beside her. "How does it feel?"

"Okay I guess," the Spice Rat shrugged. "I mean, it's the new normal for me so... I can tell you; this thing is Lurdian Rubber and it's making my fucking stump sweat like someone who's got a date with the noose."

"I really love you humans' colorful expressions!" the Do-Tarr beamed. "So, captain, what's the plan?"

Mal glanced over at the animated young human walking beside her and smirked.

"I know a guy," she said as they reached the plaza in front of the main entrance.

In the harbor the Grand Turine rang four bells. The Spice Rat paused and acknowledged the alarm.

"And we're running out of time," she added as she started off again at a brisk pace.

The glamoured Do-Tarr easily kept stride with the determined Mal. "So, we're on our way to see your *guy*. How are you so sure he'll even talk to you?"

"He wants to fuck me," she said staring down the hall.

Julan de Arno stared intently at the board covering the wall and absentmindedly cupped his chin.

The giant map keeping the man entranced was a highly accurate closeup of the Goyan Islands, Amarenia and the western Twilight Lands. Filling the map's considerable oceanic areas were scores of multi-colored pins. Each represented a ship's last reported location.

"So, how do you like desk duty?" Mal said from the doorway as she took in his six-foot frame and rugged good looks.

The Calden naval officer froze and he slowly nodded with a smile of recognition.

"Well hello, Maluria," he said as he hungrily took in her frame. "You're looking especially fetching."

"Right back at ya," the Spice Rat said flirtatiously as she entered his office.

Julan's suspicious gaze fell upon Kyopp as he followed her in.

"Are we collecting pretty boys now?"

The touch of jealousy in her friend's voice made Mal chuckle. "This is Kyopp. He's from Nocturn. Trust me, he really doesn't look like this."

Julan nodded reluctantly. "So, to what do I owe the pleasure of this visit. Surely you didn't come to join the hallowed ranks of the Captains Guild?"

"Not hardly," Mal said sauntering over to him. "Jul, there's gonna be some serious shit happening here very soon."

The senior naval officer ran his hand across the stubble on the top of his head and exhaled noisily. Mal was never prone to drama or exaggeration.

"I'm listening?"

The Spice Rat took a deep breath. "Okay, the when is going to be within the next cycle or two, so there's not much time."

The logistics commander of the Captain's Guild stared expectantly at the airship captain.

"As far as the what is concerned, you gotta trust me," Mal prefaced. "There's gonna be an eclipse soon."

"A what?"

"An eclipse. The moon blocks out the sun."

Julan leaned back skeptically. "And how does that happen?"

Mal waved her hands in front of her. "How the fuck do I know Jul?!"

Thinking he was now the brunt of a joke, the Calden commander's demeanor changed to one of amused placation.

"I'm not kidding Jul!" Mal said defiantly. "And the eclipse, that's not the worst of it."

"Oh?"

"It's gonna be dark here for a few cycles. That means things from the dark side of the Annigan can now come over here to play. It's not going to be pretty!"

Julan was about to make a quip when Kyopp interrupted him.

"It's happened before."

Julan's gaze fell on the handsome young man with blonde hair and golden skin.

"Never heard of it," he said in a flat unconvinced tone.

"My dear fellow," Kyopp said gesturing adamantly. "The last time it occurred your race didn't even exist."

"So, what do you want from me?" he asked bringing his attention back to Mal.

The Spice Rat bounced nervously on her heels. "We may need to activate the Grand Turine's emergency beacon."

Julan suddenly paused. "That will set off every turine across the entire Goyan Islands!" he said in astonishment.

Mal leaned into her surprised friend. "That's the point!"

Julan gave Kyopp a frustrated glance. "She said you were from Nocturn. You can't do anything about this?"

"In all matters not dealing with the hive, the Do-Tarr are neutral. My people had nothing to do with the last invasion."

"Invasion huh?" came the unconvinced reply.

Mal exhaled in frustration. "Show him."

A shimmering wave flashed in front of the human. When it passed, the Do-Tarr king in his mantis form stood in his place.

Julan leaned back in shock as he took in the strange creature.

The shimmering reappeared and the handsome young man once again stood facing him.

With mouth agape, Julan stared back at Mal.

The Spice Rat's voice was haunting. "The shit I've seen…"

Julan held up his hands in surrender. "Okay, okay, you win!"

"Look, if the eclipse is all bullshit it won't matter," Mal paused. "But if it's not, at least people can be on guard."

The superior of the Captain's Guild paused, deep in thought.

"I can't officially help you," he said in a cold administrative tone.

Mal's eyes narrowed, "Officially?"

"The Quartermasters Guild is in charge of the turines," Julan said in a defeated cadence. "There's really nothing I can *officially* do for you."

"Yeah, well I'm sure the quartermasters would just love for me to waltz into their arms," Mal said as she watched Julan casually walk over to his desk in the far corner. Pulling out a sheet of paper from a drawer, he scribbled furiously, folded and palmed the document.

With a confident swagger he halted uncomfortably close to Mal.

"It was so good of you to drop by," he said loudly. "How about a hug?"

Mal recoiled in confusion. "Huh?"

"A hug," he said opening his arms. The Calden leader smirked at her perplexed stare. "Trust me," he mouthed.

Hesitantly the Spice Rat opened her arms and leaned forward.

As she fell into his embrace, she fought a wave of awkwardness at her natural attraction to the man.

Immediately his mouth went to her ear. "I'm going to grab your ass," he whispered.

"If you grab my ass, I'm gonna slug the shit outta you!"

"I know."

"What?"

"I'm gonna grab your ass and you're gonna slap me...like you mean it."

"Oh, I'll mean it!"

True to his word Julan pulled her in close and his hands roughly cupped Mall's butt.

But she felt it. His right hand slipped something inside her left back pocket.

"Don't do anything with it until you're well away from here," he whispered. "Now give it to me."

Mal instantly stepped back and delivered a punishing open-handed blow to the side of his face.

"Fucker!" she yelled before she and Kyopp stormed out of the room followed by Julan's mocking laughter.

As stunned guild workers stared at the apparent drama, human and Do-Tarr quickly left the Captains Guild headquarters and pushed through the wide busy hall.

"I adore court intrigue!" Kyopp gushed.

"You chose to exclude yourself from Do-Tarr intrigue," Mal said sarcastically as they made their way around a small group of Piceans engaged in a heated debate.

The young man pouted slightly as he weighed her statement. "I guess human drama is much more interesting, and I won't get my head bitten off."

"Don't be too sure of that," Mal said as she stopped at a main intersection.

As the glamoured Do-Tarr paused, a realization crossed his consciousness. Mal was right, this chosen path might very well get him killed too.

"While we're here, I think I want to drop in on an old friend," she said. Taking a sharp right, she led the duo to the office of Joc' Valdur.

Zekoff had always considered the Aramos ambassador to Zor a pudgy, whiney little prick. Now, as he sat across his desk witnessing him stressfully play with his eyebrow, he was more sure of it than ever.

"I'm afraid my brother has disappeared on us," Bartol Aramos said in a nasally voice. "I've not seen him since he left for the Twilight Lands over a quinte ago."

The colonel of the Zorian Guards slumped back in his chair. "No contact?"

"None I'm afraid. If I may ask, why do the Zorian Guards want my brother?"

"Quite frankly ambassador, murder and blood rituals."

Bartol reeled in astonishment. "I'm sorry, what?!"

A grim frown played at the corners of Zekoff"'s mouth. "Were you aware he was over in Nocturn?"

"Why, no!"

The old colonel's tone was cold and factual. "He got involved with something over there and now it's got ahold of him."

Bartol sat staring silently. Zekoff saw his mind fast at work.

"Put quite simply, your brother is possessed. Whatever has him is quite dark."

Bartol went back to uneasily petting his eyebrow. "I'm not sure how his basic dark nature could be surpassed."

"Rest assured, it has."

Bartol's appearance betrayed genuine concern.

"I'm sorry I can't be of any more help colonel," the ambassador said sincerely.

The colonel sighed and stood. "I trust you will contact me if anything changes?"

Standing, Bartol offered his hand. "Of course, of course."

With a nod of thanks, the commander of the Zorian Guards was gone.

The Aramos ambassador sat for a while, stroking his eyebrow while staring off into space. He smiled at the thought of his troublesome brother going rogue. This was going to make things easier, for all his plans.

Casually reaching to his right he flipped a small lever on his desk. A young male aide promptly appeared. His attentive expression was fixed on his boss.

"I need you to locate Peligro de Aris. He's probably in Rophan," he said authoritatively. "Tell no one and instruct Si Peligro to do the same."

The aide bowed and swiftly left.

Hopefully we can nip things in the bud. If the Zorian Guards don't get him, Peligro will.

As the monk opened the double doors to the monastery, all recoiled slightly from the pungent odor of incense.

The room was long and narrow with deep alcoves carved into the stone walls on either side. Running the length of the room, situated between each of the openings was an obsidian pillar. They led to a riser at the far end of the chamber.

The wall behind the riser, as well as the pillars themselves were covered in strange flowing glyphs.

Several monks stood beside the platform watching the group as they approached. Directly in the center of the raised platform, seated cross-legged, levitating a foot above the surface, was Azorith Master Vorel.

His appearance was equally as disheveled as the others. He wore his thick rope-like dreadlocks loose. They cascaded around his body outlining his painted features.

Resting in the forward left corner, Okawa caught sight of an exploding gem.

Everyone stopped at a respectful distance and Okawa took a step forward. "Master Vorel, thank you for granting us an audience."

The old monk lifted a frail, boney arm and bid them closer.

"You have news about these mysterious objects we found in our valley?"

"Yes, Master Vorel," the Valdurian agent began as her attention drifted from the gem to the master. "We know who put them there and what they do. We just don't know why."

"Tell us."

"A man named Stryder Aramos placed them there. He is under the influence of a malicious force from Nocturn. We also know that when the pasty coating is removed the gem beneath it explodes and burns."

All attention in the room focused on the gem.

"Unfortunately, we're not sure why he chose your valley."

Okawa's question caused the junior monks to trade concerned glances.

Vorel pointed to the crystal. "These were placed beside the valley's holy bonds. If they do what you say, his intention is clear."

The master slowly lowered himself to the floor then stood. "He seeks to destroy the holy bonds and release the etheria field below the valley's surface."

"The moon!" Okawa blurted out.

"I don't understand," Alto said, finally entering the conversation.

"Don't you see?" The Valdurian said, excited that the last piece had fallen into place. "The explosive gem is covered in a moonstone paste. It will dissolve under moonlight. The eclipse!"

"A fuse," Cha-Rod said in amazement.

"So why is an etheria field popping up bad?" Zaad said in confusion.

Vorel descended from the riser. "We are the four-hundredth enclave of the Azorith charged with maintaining the holy bonds and keeping the valley closed to the monoliths of Nocturn."

"The Black Mural," Alto said in a hushed tone. "That kind of incursion from Nocturn may be the very thing to tip the balance and get it to fall."

"Then what are the Otick massing for?" Zaad asked, his voice still betraying bewilderment.

"The diversion," Okawa said with ominous confidence.

Cha-Rod tapped his can resolutely on the floor. "We've got to get those gems away from the chains before the darkness sets in."

How does one cope, after witnessing an event so cataclysmic, that it challenges everything you have ever known about your world and yourself?

The answer for most of the good folks of the high holy city of Zor, as well as across Lumina, was panic.

The Kan fog was rising from the shallow sea. It had already enveloped the outer docks in its smoky, translucent haze. At the same time, directly overhead, the eclipsing moon carved its first sliver from the sun.

The sudden change in light caused those in the streets to gape about in confusion. When they finally gazed upward a collective gasp echoed down the boulevards.

By the time Mal and Kyopp made it out onto the main road through town the crowd was alive with fearful chatter as more and more of their luminary orb slipped into gradual darkness.

"Fuck, I guess they were right," Mal said in a foreboding tone. "The sun's almost a quarter covered. We better get our asses out to that turine."

"No one is going to sail in that fog," Kyopp said. "Besides…"

Mal suddenly stopped. "Fuck! Wait a moment!" Patting her back pocket, she pulled out the folded paper. "With all this eclipse shit going on I almost forgot."

The Spice Rat studied the paper as panicked people swarmed past the duo. She nodded in satisfaction with a wary grin.

"Let's get to the air station," she said before starting off.

"Captain, what is it?"

Keeping her attention on quickly navigating the crowd. She handed the paper to Kyopp. "It's a drawing of the location of the emergency signal on the Grand Turine. We need an airship quick!"

The Do-Tarr studied the paper. "Captain, the *Haraka* may not be ready for flight."

"We're getting an airship Kyopp," Mal said resolutely. "At this point I'm not fucking concerned with whose."

The four student monks' deportment changed from stony to awestruck when the moon began to paint the sun in a slow curtain of darkness. Their attention darted about apprehensively with every gradual degree of fading light.

"We're at half eclipse," Okawa said spurring her lizard mount. "We gotta move!"

The large reptile hissed in defiance as it reluctantly picked up speed.

The five lizards and their riders slipped from the valley floor up the far side of the basin. Farther north, Alto led another mounted party of four. Zaad and Cha-Rod led their parties by foot along the valley's near side.

The Valdurian agent marveled at the size of the chain as they approached. Underneath the hanging vegetation she now got a clear view and could scrutinize the massive obsidian links.

At a steep embankment the group stopped. Thirty feet above them the link disappeared into the solid granite of the mountainside.

"There's one," she said pointing to a white cylinder tucked into the vegetation.

"Over here too," one of the monks said pointing to the other side of the chain.

Without waiting for direction, two nimbly shimmied up the rocks while the other stood directly below.

"Be careful with those things," Okawa warned as she slid out of the saddle.

The monk on the far side reached his first. Brushing back the vegetation he gingerly picked it up. The monk on the ground indicated he was ready and extended his hands to catch it.

As the monk above let go of the crystal, the rocks beneath his foot gave way. He quickly regained his footing, but the gem didn't drop cleanly.

Bouncing off the cliff wall several areas of the white paste were chipped away. The cylinder was immediately sparking as it tumbled to the ground.

Okawa knew what was about to happen. Without taking time to shout a warning the Valdurian dove at the monk on the ground. She tackled him out of the way as the crystal bomb struck where he had been standing.

It bounced and came to rest twenty feet away where it burst into a shower of fire.

Okawa and the monk exchanged relieved glances then got up.

Up where the chain met the rocks the other monk had made it to his crystal. All were staring at the near fatal mishap and the still burning gem.

Okawa focused upward at the monk. "Okay, now you know what these things can do. Be careful!"

The light was fading rapidly through the thickening fog. Mal and Kyopp made their way around panicked citizens as they dashed for the relative safety of nearby buildings.

"We're not gonna make it at this pace," Mal yelled over the screams of terrified sentients.

"This way," Kyopp said indicating the side of a nearby building.

Slipping inside an adjacent alley, waves of opaque air streamed in front of the handsome young human revealing his insect form.

"Hop on," he said motioning to his back. "Then hold on."

Mal did as instructed, wrapping her arms around his humanoid torso. In a flash the Do-Tarr scrambled up the wall to rooftop level.

Below, on the streets, already frightened people pointed and cried out at the huge insect running along the walls with a human in tow.

No shit, hold on! Mal thought, tightening her grip on the Do-Tarr's torso as he skimmed effortlessly along the city's buildings.

They made it across two structures with the Do-Tarr nimbly leaping between them when Mal heard the distinct sound of impact on the wall below them.

"The fucking city guards are shooting at us!" Mal said tensely.

"They are unaccustomed to seeing my kind," Kyopp said as another volley of crossbow bolts thudded against the wall right behind them.

"Time to leave our enthusiastic defenders behind," the Do-Tarr said casually as he leapt onto the rooftop and out of range.

Hopping between multiple buildings they arrived at the Shimol Plat. Both barely made out the hulking monolith of the air station through the fog. Once below the opening it was a quick climb up to the wide entrance.

As Mal expected, all airships were secured in their slips for the Kan. As the Spice Rat jumped off his back, Kyopp resumed to his human form and the two raced across the flight deck.

"I sure hope the *Haraka's* ready to fly!" Mal said as they entered the commercial hangar.

"You there!" came a stern voice from their right. "Halt!"

"Perfect," Mal huffed. "Just what we need. The locals!"

Ignoring the command, they picked up the pace, keeping slightly ahead of the marine security patrol's heavy footfalls.

Mal's heart sank when they came to a stop in front of the *Haraka*. The rear engine hatch was lifted and two maintenance workers were peering inside under the illumination of a bright orange light.

The marines caught up almost immediately.

"I told you to halt!" a scowling human said with short sword drawn.

"What are you doing here?" the other tersely asked as he pointed his crossbow.

Mal took a deep breath. "We're here on critical, personal business of Joc' Valdur!"

The two guards regarded them skeptically, but slightly lowered their weapons. By now the EEtah sergeant had caught up with them. He did not appear happy.

"When my men give an order, you best comply!" he growled.

"There's no time," Mal said taking on an urgent tone. "We need an airship now!"

This caused the EEtah to laugh. "Yeah and I'd like a million secors. I'm placing you under arrest. You can tell your story to my lieutenant."

"Sergeant, we don't have that kind of time," Mal pleaded.

"She did say she was acting for ambassador Valdur," said one of the marines.

"Is that so?" the EEtah said with an unconvinced sneer. "Where are your orders?"

Look sergeant," Mal growled in frustration.

"No, you look!" the sergeant barked.

His next statement was cut short by the *Drakin* skimming over to them. It silently cruised a foot above the deck then settled.

When the side hatch dropped Demetrius, adorned with his round blue spectacles appeared smiling.

"Anybody need a ride?" he said in a voice way too chipper for Mal's liking.

Now the angry EEtah turned his embattled bewilderment toward the pilot.

"You can't fly in the Kan! I don't care if they did give you unrestricted clearance. Besides there's something strange going on out there."

"You let me worry about that my scaly friend," he said touching the rim of his glasses. "Right now, my instructions come straight from the top. These two get our full cooperation."

The marines hesitated for a moment before begrudgingly stepping aside.

Once inside, the gifted young pilot lifted off and slid out the main access way of Valdurian Air Station Three.

The moon now covered three quarters of the sun and visibility was worsening. Demetrius casually lowered the orange lens and gazed over at Mal. "Where to?"

"This is a short hop then a wait-on," Mal said hurriedly. "Get us to the Grand Turine in the harbor."

Demetrius peered quizzically at the Spice Rat.

"Now!" Mal emphatically said.

"Yes ma'am," Demetrius said banking the craft toward the harbor. "Geez, straight from the top. What do you have on this guy?"

General Onse had never encountered dark waters before. He felt no fear however. The Golden Avatar's aura was with them. It comforted and encouraged. It sanctified this engagement.

Blessed be the Golden One, he said to himself.

Behind the junior general were five hundred Otick of House Awa. They stood on the western outskirts of the sacred oyster bed between the Tellasian and Zerk Atoll island chains. Five hundred more guarded the eastern border. On either flank, towering EEtahs of Dakor Sunal, were ready for a fight and barely able to restrain themselves. Around the temple of the Golden Avatar, the EEtah's of Zorod Sunal stood guard.

Onse was confident that the two other houses of the Shelled Triad also stood ready to defend their beds.

The darkness will not prevail!

As his eyes adjusted to the dim lighting of passing schools of bioluminescent fish, he saw them.

Massive rows of fish heads were rising from the reef in the distance. He saw the outlines of snapping jaws and long needle-like teeth.

So it begins, he thought as he started clicking his claws.

Soon he was joined by the forces behind him as the rhythmic clacking of Otick claws echoed through the waters of the Shallow Sea.

The sun was little more than a sliver of light directly above. Its weakened rays were barely able to penetrate the thick fog which enveloped the valley.

Zaad was impressed with the student monks. They moved quickly, obeyed orders and worked efficiently at removing the crystalline bombs from two of the chains.

Getting to the third and final tether was proving more difficult. It was situated above a small grotto and a hamlet had been established in the narrow clearing.

As they moved closer the EEtah spotted a dozen wooden structures with people milling about. When they reached the outskirts of the village, twenty men and women confronted them. Each held a sharp farming implement like weapons. Recently carved into each of their foreheads was the all too familiar X and I. The humans grimaced threateningly as they approached.

Behind the mob, Zaad noticed the same binary fields scrawled on the walls of the buildings.

Behind the EEtah, the monks assumed fighting stances.

"So, you've decided to join me again," Stryder's voice rose above the commotion. "Very good. I extend to you one last chance. Embrace my lord and receive his mark or perish."

As he finished his proposal, Orrk ambled up to his side from the rear of the mob.

"There's only one mark I'm interested in making," Zaad said as he drew Bowbreaker and grimaced at the half-EEtah.

With a furious cry the villagers charged.

Zaad motioned to two of the monks. "Get those gems! You two, with me!"

Bellowing loudly the EEtah charged the wave of villagers knocking them aside on his way to Orrk. The two monks behind him took on the possessed farmers with various blocks, punches and kicks.

Zaad had broken through the mob and was now barreling toward the ironmark, sword raised. Retreating several paces Stryder raised his hand and several fields of runes on the side of the nearest building glowed bright blue.

Suddenly, Zaad felt his extremities begin to tingle. His charge slowed to a snail's pace no matter how much he struggled.

Orrk took advantage of his master's enchantment and rushed the slow moving EEtah with a savage grin and engorged erection.

Zaad swung Bowbreaker with all his might but the long heavy blade arced lazily in the murky air.

Taking advantage of his longer legs and magically slowed opponent, Orrk easily danced inside the swinging blade. With a hammer strike to his sword arm Orrk delivered a punishing blow which wrenched Bowbreaker from the man-shark's grasp.

Orrk's next blow was to the EEtahs midsection which doubled him over bringing his face within inches of the ironmark's rampant organ.

"Get a good look at it," Orrk said with a sneer. "It'll be fucking you soon enough!"

Zaad lurched forward as fast as possible toward the gloating half-EEtah. Opening his mouth wide, he wrapped his jaws around and chomped into the erect fourteen inches of flesh before him.

Orrk screamed as Zaad's powerful jaws and razor-sharp teeth severed the massive penis at its base.

Behind him, the two monks were making short work of the untrained farmers. They broke bones and knocked the villagers unconscious as they punched and kicked.

Two of the monks had shimmied up the cliff and were attempting to get to the gems when Stryder glanced up and brought the focus of the glowing runes on them. The effect was the same as with the EEtah, their pace slowed to a crawl.

Orrk was now on his knees screaming in agony. His hands covered his severed groin area as blood rushed through his fingers.

Zaad spat out the now flaccid but still formidable penis into his hand. Leaping on the wounded ironmark, he pinned him to the ground and started beating him about the head with his own cock.

Stryder had now completely disappeared into the village. From inside the huts, a swarm of unarmed children now charged. Their tiny possessed yowls were accompanied by rage. Their foreheads all contained the same marks as their parents.

The wave of children swept over Zaad who continued to pummel Orrk. They climbed on the EEtah's back and peppered him with ineffective blows. Zaad was now in the beginnings of a blood frenzy and easily swept away the nuisance.

Suddenly, from up above, showers of sparks erupted, followed by a handful of explosions. The monks screamed and fell by the cliff base totally engulfed in flames.

A few more blasts jolted the cliff, followed by the sound of cracking rock. Zaad peeked up to see the giant chain above begin to swing wildly.

Abandoning his attack, Zaad dove to the side as the sound of blasting rock preceded a shower of boulders peppering the area. With a giant crash, the chain broke loose from the side of the mountain and plunged to the ground with a thunderous roar.

The monks, villagers and attacking children as well as his castrated opponent all disappeared, crushed under the giant links.

Zaad lay on his back trying to catch his breath in the choking dust. From under the ground where he lay, the EEtah felt the terrain start to rumble.

Groaning the EEtah slowly got to his feet. The entire village and surrounding area were crushed. Searching the devastation, he didn't see any sign of Stryder.

The rumblings were growing louder and the entire clearing was starting to quake.

Regaining his wits, Zaad picked up Bowbreaker and ran back in the direction he had come. Stopping at what he felt was a safe distance, he took in the devastation.

The giant black chain and the rubble surrounding it was now pushed aside as an enormous fissure had opened. Protruding out of the cleft, a lone pillar of purple azurite etheria crystal had broken the surface.

The EEtah leaned on his sword as he caught his breath. Watching the lone crystal column slowly rise to a height of thirty feet, he couldn't help but wonder if he failed his mission by allowing only a single crystal to escape, instead of the whole field below, and if so, what would it mean?

While it's true the Otick race does not grasp the concept of fear, pragmatism abounds.

General Onse focused out onto the floor of the Shallow Sea as far as the light would allow. He was overwhelmed by the sheer size of the force that now assaulted them.

As he and his companions hacked at the first wave of unarmed berserkers another frenzied wave clamored for their chance to swarm the defenders.

Coming into view from out of the darkness were wave after wave of trident wielders.

This is no undisciplined mob, he pondered as he slashed and stabbed at three more. *Those ranged weapons are more to keep us at bay. Why?*

His question was answered as the last berserkers stormed through the Otick lines and charged for the shore.

Onse now prepared to engage the first group of Gar-Kals armed with tridents when he saw what followed. Marching from the gloom, an army of the same dreaded monstrosities with pickaxes steadily advanced.

The Otick general gasped. *They're going to destroy the holy oyster beds*!

As Onse engaged the first trident attacker, he noted along the line that all of his kind struggled with the rapidly thrusting ranged weapon. Deadly sparring matches consumed the center of the defender's positions as each of his brethren was now dealing with two or three attackers. For every Otick killed they took at least four or five Gar-Kal with them. The general recognized however that even at this kill rate the sheer numbers were against them.

Their EEtah allies on the flanks were having no such difficulties. The EEtahs of Dakor Sunal were all around fifteen feet tall. The fish creatures with mere ten-foot polearms were rent apart under the shock troops' blood fury.

Three tridents now assaulted Onse. As he sank his claw into one of his attackers, he felt a searing pain. One of his stabbing arms had been caught in the trident's tines. With a sadistic hiss the Gar-Kal twisted the weapon, breaking off the limb and sending a stream of blood billowing out into the water.

With the enemy's weapon caught, Onse easily drove his claw into the fish creature's skull before having to deal with two more who replaced him. Now fighting intense pain and a creeping sense of futility, Onse was too consumed to notice the axe wielders flowing into the beds past the fighting.

All heard the sickening cracks of shells being pierced.

Pragmatism made the young Otick general realize they were being overrun. The absence of fear would make him stay and fight until the end.

From a strategic three-story rooftop just off the northern docks of Zor two men stared at the dimly illuminated beach.

Joc' Valdur flipped an orange lens over the end of his extended spyglass. "Here they come."

The Valdurian ambassador stared in dazed silence as hundreds of heat signatures came pouring out of the surf and onto the beach. On cue, a hail of arrows rained down from the adjacent rooftops and the opening of Air Station Three on the attacking force. Scores of Gar-Kal immediately dropped as the deadly missiles found their mark. They were instantly replaced and trampled by the unrelenting throng who now charged for the opening to the temple of the Golden Avatar.

Joc' continued to watch through the fog. The large glowing forms of the EEtahs guarding the entrance were just now engaging the overpowering force.

"Looks like the EEtahs are holding their own." Joc' said as he lowered the glass and handed it to captain Rafel.

The Zorian spymaster curiously examined the device before putting it up to his eye. He sighed in dismay as he saw the slimy aquatic beasts still pouring onto the beach.

"Yes, but I'm afraid we're being overrun," Rafel grimly added. "This could easily be a slaughter. We've got no way to warn anyone."

Joc' took back the glass and noted a flash of motion out of the entrance to the air station. "I wouldn't be so sure of that."

As the *Drakin* shot into the fog-draped skies, Demetrius casually down through his orange lens glasses.

Mal peered over curiously from the next seat. "You can actually see all that shit out there with those?"

Demetrius gave a satisfied smile as he performed a steep bank propelling the ship into the harbor at a high rate of speed, "Yep, courtesy of the good folks over at House Valdur."

Mal gave an appreciative nod as she inspected them. "I gotta get me a pair of those!"

Demetrius did a low sweep across the water descending on the time-keeping device in the center of the harbor. "Well, you know who to talk too...what the!"

Mal immediately went on guard. "What?!"

Demetrius pulled the *Drakin* in a tight circle around the Turine ten feet over the water. "That water's hot!"

"What?"

"Under the water, there's a lot of activity!"

"You can see under water with those things?"

"Not really. The orange lenses pick up heat."

Mal peered out into the dense fog then back to the pilot. "Now I really gotta get me a pair!"

The airship continued circling the turine. To their left the curved sides of the great tidal clock slid by. The right side of the windshield was obscured in impenetrable fog.

Demetrius was locked in concentration on the wheel as he navigated the nearby wall. "Mal I'm serious! There's something big going on under the surface."

The *Drakin* rounded the turine and was now facing the Zorian harbor. Demetrius gasped loudly. "And on the beach! This is an invasion!"

Mal looked over at Kyopp. "Can you get me onto that thing?"

The glamoured Do-Tarr was twitching with excitement. A wave obscured the human revealing the Do-Tarr when it passed. "If you can hold on."

Mal pulled the crudely drawn map out of her pocket and consulted it. "There's a maintenance walkway about five feet above the water. By this drawing the access hatch should be coming up any time now."

Demetrius slowed and lowered the craft. Sure enough, circling the turine was a narrow walkway. A single hatch, large enough for an average-sized human to access soon appeared. Below the ledge, all took note of the churning water of the Shallow Sea.

Mal sighed deeply. "Alright, you ready?"

The Do-Tarr pulled his hammer and laughed exuberantly, "Yes, captain!"

The Spice Rat gave an amused smirk. "Yeah I know, you love saying that."

Sliding onto Kyopp's back she gave the pilot the thumbs up and Demetrius reached for a lever on his left.

The hatch dropped and Mal gasped as she and Kyopp were inundated by a blast of cool, saturated air. Both now clearly perceived an upheaval coming from under the turbulent water a narrow distance below them.

The Do-Tarr took in a deep breath. "Refreshing, isn't it?!"

Without waiting for a reply, the humanoid mantis bounded out the doorway and into the fog.

Kyopp landed on the ledge with a loud thud which challenged Mal's grip on his torso.

"Sorry captain," he said in a slightly embarrassed tone. "The surface wasn't what I expected."

Now used to his surroundings the sure-footed Kyopp shimmied over to the door and Mal carefully climbed onto the ledge.

A gust of wind suddenly rocked the *Drakin* and caused Mal to reach out and grab Kyopp's arm. Demetrius moved the airship away from the structure and hovered.

Once confident the wind had passed the Spice Rat made her way cautiously on the slippery, narrow walkway.

The door, as well as the entire turine was made of ukko wood. On the left side of the small door was a short ukko latch.

Mal attempted to move the stubborn lever. "Fuck! Locked!"

Kyopp stepped past the frustrated Spice Rat. "It only makes sense."

"Now you're starting to sound like Alto."

The Do-Tarr placed the head of his hammer against the upright lever. "There are much worse people to sound like. You are fortunate to have Mora."

Mal's heart sank for an instant at the thought of Alto leaving then scoffed in protest. "That fucking thing is ukko wood. Your hammer is only going to bounce off."

Kyopp stared confidently at Mal as he slowly applied pressure. "Ukko wood is mirrored in Nocturn with the etheria crystal, Ukkonite which my people mine. They both repel forceful, rapidly advancing objects."

Kyopp strained a bit as he kept increasing the pressure. "However, slow advances are able to get through their natural properties…"

The click of the latch falling interrupted the Do-Tarr's lecture and he gave an accomplished grin.

As the door popped ajar Mal's feeling of satisfaction was disrupted by the sound of wet slapping on wood. Eight Gar-Kal were climbing up the side of the tidal clock directly at them.

Kyopp readied his hammer. "I'll hold them, get in there and find that alarm."

No matter the number of fallen foes littered around him, with every sound of pickaxe falling on shell, Onse knew his great house was dying. Every enemy vanquished by him and his comrades was replaced by two more. They flowed out of the gloom in an unending wave, united in a solitary purpose: destruction.

This was the general's first large battle and the smell of blood in the water was almost overwhelming. It billowed up from the corpses on the sea floor. It flowed outward with each body pierced and limb severed so that the water itself was becoming murky and cloying. His arms felt like weights were tied to them and his breath was ragged as he fought to push the tainted water across his gills.

Duty and determination drove the Otick warrior to keep fighting even though wounded. It was the tip of a trident piercing under his right armpit which caused him to break off his attack.

As searing pain racked his body, he spun to see his attacker being impaled from behind by an EEtah's sword. His vision was becoming cloudy and he realized the blood he was now smelling in the water around him was his.

If the Golden One wills it, let this be my last stand! Onse defiantly reflected as he toppled over to the sandy bottom with his assailants falling dead on top of him.

Mal ducked and quickly slipped through the now open hatch. She attempted to close the door but found Kyopp had broken the latch.

Quickly abandoning the idea, the Spice Rat appreciatively took in the elaborate mechanics. She had never seen the inner workings of a turine, and this was one of the largest, most elaborate.

She was standing on a wide catwalk with a railing which stretched the entire circumference of the open structure. Up above was filled with wide beams which supported elaborate gears and pulleys. These were attached to bells and chimes of different sizes. All were connected to a long thick white rope which draped down the exact center of the turine.

Mal immediately recognized the cord as Darian silk.

At the base of the rope, floating in the waters of the bay, was an enormous buoy. A short distance away was a panel with various levers, dials and wheels.

"No wonder they need a fucking artificer to run these things," she said trotting over to the control board.

Out the open door Mal heard the clash of Kyopp engaging with the Gar-Kal.

When the fish creatures hopped onto the ledge the Do-Tarr king scrambled above the doorway and awaited the inevitable.

"I don't know which lever!" Mal's voice echoed out of the hatch.

Kyopp watched the Gar-Kal cautiously fan out across the surface toward him hissing and snapping as they edged closer.

"Pull them all," he said in a flippant tone. "I don't think it will make things any worse."

Throwing her hands up in frustration, the Spice Rat started systematically manipulating every control device.

The Gar-Kal lunged at Kyopp from their surrounding positions on the turine's side.

The Do-Tarr stood up on the vertical wall. His advantage was obvious; he had four feet to hold onto the slick perpendicular surface, leaving both his hands free. The climbing fish had only a single claw and a bite if they were able get close enough.

Kyopp lifted his hammer high above his head. "I just adore a party!"

Swinging the hammer from side to side the nimble Do-Tarr danced among the clinging Gar-Kal pulping a fish head with each swing and utterance.

"THANK, YOU, FOR, PLAYING, WITH, ME!"

He stopped and smiled widely at the remaining two. They stared up past him with surprised expressions.

Hearing the now familiar wet slapping sounds the Do-Tarr spun and saw six more crawling over the curved top of the turine. Two jumped at him before he could react. They both tackled Kyopp biting and scratching, plunging all into the turbulent waters below.

Mal was growing concerned. None of the controls seemed to be doing anything and she no longer heard any scuffling outside on the hull.

Halfway down the panel a small red lever sent all the bells and chimes in motion clambering furiously. The noise was deafening, and the Spice Rat covered her ears and made for the exit.

Two Gar-Kal met her at the door as she was about to leave. Reeling back in surprise she drew her sword and ran through one who was unarmed. The second one was equipped with a trident and it lunged at her.

Mal jumped to the side of the door but she felt her shirt rip and a searing pain across her waist as one of the barbs raked her stomach. Reaching out, she grabbed the exposed weapon right below the tip and braced it against the door jam. She then yanked it forward pulling the stunned fish partially into the room. With an overhead swing of her blade she severed both of the Gar-Kal's arms. It howled in agony. Blood erupted from the stumps as she kicked it backwards from the landing and into the water.

Crossing out onto the narrow platform, Mal quickly searched for her friend. "Kyopp!"

She heard no reply, only the ominous hissing of Gar-Kal as they climbed toward her from above and below. Dancing dangerously close to the edge of the walkway she sliced one's skull in two as it attempted to climb up beside her. Then, waving her sword in the air summoned Demetrius.

As the *Drakin* swung in close for a pickup, three Gar-Kal jumped at the craft and grabbed onto the landing skid. The airship swayed wildly with the excess weight on one side. In a rapid rocking maneuver, Demetrius shook the beasts loose.

Two were almost upon the Spice Rat when she sheathed her sword and jumped. She grabbed a landing skid and held on as the airship began to pull away.

Suddenly, Mal felt a massive tug on her legs that almost made her lose her grip. Two of them had grabbed onto her. She felt their claws digging in but her screams of shock and pain were drowned out by the cacophony of alarm bells and chimes echoing from one end of the bay to the other.

With her free leg she kicked downward with all her strength at the two assailants. Her heel found the forehead of one. It howled in agony and let go. The other reached up and grabbed onto the attacking foot. With a drooling snarl it wrenched the boot into its mouth and took a bite.

Mal yanked her leg back hard and the boot, prosthetic foot, and Gar-Kal plummeted into the churning water of the bay.

When they were safely away, Demetrius set the craft to hover and helped her in. "You did it!"

"Where's Kyopp?" Mal asked as she fought to catch her breath. Staring back at the besieged turine she caught sight of Gar-Kal crawling all across its surface.

The pilot's expression went morose. "They jumped him and pulled him into the water."

"What?!" Mal screeched as she peered into the bay.

"I'm pretty sure Do-Tarr can't swim," Demetrius said sadly. "And, there were so many of them."

"Let's circle around, maybe we can find him!"

Demetrius' lower lip trembled slightly. "Mal, he didn't make it. Now come on, you're bleeding."

Mal slumped back against the side of the craft and sighed. "Never mind that. Get us the fuck out of here."

Demetrius got back in his pilot's seat and maneuvered the *Drakin* toward the air station. Mal winced in pain as she gingerly removed her torn shirt and started ripping it into strips. Applying them to her wounds she mournfully stared at the water below.

In the distance, she could hear turines resonating all down the coast.

Between the darkness and the fog, there was no way to get a real assessment of the beach littered with fish bodies.

The darkness was not an issue for the Gar-Kal who continued to stream onto the shore. They were used to navigating about in dark, deep waters. It was the Kan fog that had them tripping over the carcasses of their dead comrades who now acted as obstacles.

Kaza of Zorod Sunal couldn't see either and when the turine in the harbor's alarm started sounding there was little else for his ears to detect. As for him and his brothers in arms, the Kan fog was a daily event. It was the darkness that had the twelve-foot EEtah on edge. He knew that on either side of him, at exactly sword length, another Sunal fighter was standing. Together they formed a concentrated line of might which separated the city of Zor and the Otick temple from anything that might try to assault. The bodies of the fallen enemy around him were proof of that.

Humans are good archers, Kaza thought, as he became aware of another volley of arrows streaking across the sky aiming for the shoreline. Another sound crept through the persistent ringing as a new wave of fish monsters bumbled their way toward him, hampered by the inhospitable atmosphere.

As they closed in, the EEtah swung his sword in broad circles in front of him. "Here comes more!"

To his left, he heard several comrades reply over the alarms filling the air. Even harder to detect was the following whooshing sounds of their blades added to his.

Kaza had only an instant to realize there was no response to his right before a line of Gar-Kal appeared.

Two died immediately when they blindly charged into the EEtah's swinging blade. As three more jumped on him they bit down as he caught motion to his right, in the dark and fog.

The line had been breached!

Rafel rebounded from his sullen stare and gasped as the Grand Turine's emergency beacon resounded into the dark. The cacophony of rapidly ringing bells and chimes echoed from the harbor outward. The spymaster followed the chain reaction along the coast as turines from the small trading ports on cue, started ringing furiously.

"They're all going off," he said with a touch of hope in his voice.

Joc' Valdur lowered the enhanced spyglass, his brow furrowed. "Perhaps, but they've breeched the EEtah's line and are entering the Temple of the Golden Avatar."

"By the gods!" Rafel blurted out.

Joc' casually brought the glass back up. "It appears the gods have abandoned us right now."

The sound of battle was now only faintly heard as it filtered up through the fog overwhelmed by the blaring alarm.

"It's a mess down there," Joc' reported sweeping his spyglass all around the entire area.

The Valdurian ambassador was thankfully inspecting the beach away from the EEtah position when the recently invaded cave entrance suddenly erupted in golden light. The massive beam of radiance filled the cave. It streamed outward, burning away the fog and bathing the entire beach and shoreline in brilliant luminosity.

All could now see the carnage which littered the beach. Arrow shafts as thick as porcupine quills lined the shore. Dead Gar-Kal bodies, sometimes up to three deep, carpeted the sand. Of the original fifty EEtah guards, only a dozen remained fighting.

Both humans stared on helplessly taking in the still dynamic battle. The EEtahs were hopelessly outnumbered but the human archers from the roofs had prevented any of the fish creatures from entering the city.

As the light became brighter from the cave mouth, the intensity of the fighting immediately began to wane. Combatants on the beach closest to the temple entrance actually stopped and stared.

Rafel shook his head in quizzical relief. "What in the name of the gods?"

Joc' held up his hand. "Do you hear that?"

Rafel concentrated, attempting to block out the piercing alarm. His gaze now appeared even more perplexed. "Is that, singing?"

The brazier in the center of the room glowed warmly. Beside it, a dozen children sat eating as one after the other recounted the happenings of their day on the streets of Immor-Onn. Storytime, as well as its originator, had returned to the Whispering Zephyr. Now the daily event was held in their very own newly built room in the rear of the pub.

"Where did you say the guards found the man's body?" Kai asked the young man named Broten who was shoveling porridge in his mouth from a wooden bowl.

He paused briefly to swallow the last mouthful. "On the far north end of town. I saw it hanging in the windchimes above the street."

"Did you know who he was?"

"I seen him sometimes. I think he worked the farms," Broten said before taking another bite.

"Wow, hanging?" Kai gently prodded.

Broten stopped again and waved his spoon. "Yeah, it was weird. There wasn't any blood left in him, but there wasn't any on the street. He also had big chunks taken out of his neck and upper body."

This revelation sent the rest of the children chattering nervously.

"No blood huh?"

"Yeah it was strange. The guards that took him down seemed really scared."

Kai sighed in recognition. She hoped she was wrong, but it sounded like a classic Ash-Ta kill.

Drucilla must be around somewhere.

"Thank you Broten," she said smiling as the boy resumed eating. "Now anyone else?"

Before any were able to raise their hands, the rear door flew open allowing cold gusts of wind to sweep into the room. A young girl of no more than thirteen, with a tattered blue dress came rushing through the door. She was out of breath and she appeared terrified.

All eyes were fixed on the young lady as she gulped for air and looked pleadingly at Kai. "He took Sied and Pala!"

A cry of alarm spread among the group of youths.

Kai stood and the girl rushed over into her arms.

"I was so scared, he…"

"Who?" Kai said softly.

"The white tiger man," she sobbed. "He, he said to tell you that, accounts must be balanced."

The children were now out of their seats, crowding and comforting one of their own.

"Where did this happen?" Kai softly but firmly probed.

"Over by the available regions," came the trembling reply.

Kai became grim. "Alright, all of you, fan out in and around the available regions. We've got to find them."

The street children abandoned their meal and quickly bolted for the door. Reaching out and touching her arm, Kai halted a young woman of about her same size and build with long brown hair. "You stay with me Geea."

The door opened once again, and a line of children poured out into the cold windswept streets of Immor-Onn.

The stream of golden light was becoming brighter as it reached the mouth of the cave. The rhythmic sound was also increasing with the illumination.

"I think that is singing," Joc' Valdur affirmed. "It's just not very good."

Both humans stared from their rooftop perch in wonder as six Gar-Kal marched out onto the sand. Above their heads they reverently carried the large open shell of the Golden Avatar. All of the aquatic beings had shed their sinister demeanor and were indeed attempting to vocalize the avatar's song.

"I don't believe it!" Rafel gasped. "The avatar never leaves the temple!"

The golden orb in the shell was doing more than giving off light. As the Gar-Kal marched atop the blood-stained sand, the avatar was slowly dissolving into the surrounding air. Golden radiance coursed outward in all directions bathing all on the embattled beach.

When the radiant waves descended on the fighting, the Gar-Kal ceased their attacks. At first, they appeared confused. However, when the avatar's procession passed them, the beams of light passed through their bodies, stunning the combatants. Dropping their weapons, they all fell into the growing procession and began mimicking the avatar's song. Even the EEtahs were immediately lulled out of their combat frenzies and ceased hostilities.

Slowly the parade stretched across the beach. With each group of combatants passed, their trudging ranks swelled as the Gar-Kal stopped fighting and meekly joined their comrades. Finally, the trek of singing fish entered the water.

When the avatar submerged below the waters of the Shallow Sea, darkness gradually descended on the shore.

"I would say, 'Now I've seen everything,'" Rafel muttered as he watched the bay waters just offshore glow. "But the way things have been of late. I'm sure that statement would prove me a liar."

Despite the muddle of searing pain Onse heard the song of the Golden One. The familiar melody drifted through the blood-saturated water and was accompanied by hideously shrill voices attempting to emulate it.

When the Otick general fully regained consciousness he realized that there were three dead fish bodies draped over his, pinning him to the sea floor. From his limited perspective he gazed at the carnage littering the sandy bottom. Bodies of Otick, Gar-Kal and EEtah were strewn about where the throes of combat had deposited them.

All about, the fighting still raged in smaller pockets, but at least there were no more of the enemy streaming in from the depths. Onse still heard the sickening cracking sound of axes destroying oyster shells.

Coming from the direction of the shoreline he recognized the bright golden light moving toward him. The singing was drawing closer too.

Shifting under the weight of the bodies, the Otick general discovered his right claw arm paralyzed. His left second stabbing arm was completely severed almost to the base but the wound had mysteriously cauterized. Other than that, he seemed functional, just awash in agony. Slowly, he untangled the corpses that had him trapped on the sandy bottom.

By the time he freed himself and sat up, the visibility in the water was that of daylight and the blood was gone.

As the Gar-Kal carried the avatar along the bottom of the Shallow Sea, the fighting and swinging of the pickaxes stopped the moment they passed. All stared at the golden orb dissolving into the water around them enveloping everything in its wake.

In its shell, the Golden One was all but gone, disappearing before the general's very eyes as it cast its calming rays on the embattled seabed. When the procession reached the end of the almost totally destroyed oyster beds, the Golden Avatar had completely vanished, and darkness slowly engulfed the bottom of the Shallow Sea.

Blessed be the Golden One, Onse meditated. *It sacrificed itself for us.*

The six Gar-Kal halted and reverently set down the now empty shell. They stared at it briefly before resuming the avatar's song on their own. Then, with a flutter of their webbed feet, swam off into the gloom. The remaining fish army picked up the song and followed their leaders.

All throughout the aquatic battlefield, the stunned Otick and EEtahs still on their feet marveled as the greatly reduced army of Nocturn peacefully trailed out of sight, this time to the east, singing as they went. Their chorus echoed through the dark water and eventually faded away.

Onse knew where they were bound. They had been touched by the Golden Avatar and had been transformed. No longer agents of the darkness they were swimming to Immor-Onn to serve the Fifth Avatar.

Above the streets of Immor-Onn the windchimes went from melodic to symphonic when the Fifth Avatar picked up the Golden One's final song.

It is done
The battle won
I did what I must do
My children are safe
The balance restored
I now return the song to you

All throughout the covered thoroughfares, citizens stared up in wonder as the chimes echoed the news that the fifth was now the sole pearl avatar in the Annigan.

Ma-Tah cursed the chimes. They made his head ache. The noise also interfered with his spell writing ability.

The body of Sied sat propped up in a far corner of the bare room. The young man stared emptily into space. His throat had been cut and blood soaked the front of his shirt. His life blood was also scrawled into several lines of hastily drawn sacred numbers.

In the middle of the room, toward the rear, a bound weeping Pala knelt.

"Hush child," the white tiger said in a deep soothing voice as he stroked her hair. "It will all be over soon."

From across the room a gust of wind blew the door open. The Tiikeri hefted the crossbow in one hand and smiled.

When a cowled, one-armed figure appeared in the doorway Ma-Tah pointed the weapon directly at the sobbing young woman. "What took you so long? I left a trail easy enough for a blind mongrel to follow."

The figure remained silent as it slowly approached.

"In my culture we have a saying," the Tiikeri nonchalantly said as he kept a wary leer on the advancing figure. "To truly appreciate the taste of vengeance, it is best served late. Unfortunately, in this instance, there is no time for tradition. So, here we are."

He pressed the tip of the bolt to the center of Pala's back when the figure reached twenty feet away. "That's quite close enough."

The figure halted but still remained silent.

"So, your life for hers?" Ma-Tah posed. "What do you say?"

Slowly the figure raised its single arm and pulled back the cowl. "Your magic writing has no power here."

The voice, it was different! The face was not Kai's but a young girl with long brown hair. From under her cowl the Tiikeri now spotted her other arm hidden behind her back.

Ma-Tah sputtered in sudden confusion. For the briefest instant he sensed sudden movement above and behind him.

It was immediately after the quick, searing pain at the base of his neck when the Tiikeri toppled to the ground, awake but paralyzed. He then heard the visceral sucking sound of something being extracted from his flesh but felt nothing.

Lying helplessly on his side all the man-tiger could do was watch as Kai casually walked in front of him. In a graceful motion she sat cross-legged by his face. In her hand she was twirling a thin foot-long cross between a needle and spike.

Sighing, Kai glanced at the weapon in her hand. "This is a taisan. You should feel honored. We usually reserve this for taking out EEtahs."

Ma-Tah tried to speak but all that managed to escape was a series of growling gurgles.

The assassin and priestess of Orad leaned forward and gave the dying Tiikeri a solemn stare. "She comes as the wind and takes whom she wishes. Her name is Orad and she is death."

Kai kept her tone slow and metered. "Seeing how you'll be meeting him soon, I've got a message, from my boss to yours. Leave my children and my city alone."

Lost in thought, a nude Alto stood in front of the room's window at the Demon's Gate Inn gazing out at the dark, nearly vacant, fog-shrouded streets.

"How long?" Mal said slipping up behind him and putting her arms around his waist. She snuggled in close, pressing her bare body against his.

"Huh?" he said softly breaking out of his self-imposed trance. "The eclipse?"

"Uh huh."

Reaching back, he ran his hands back to her waist, pulling her in closer. "Zau says we've got another cycle of darkness."

Mal sighed. "Not much time."

Alto turned and took her in his arms. The kiss was soft and passionate.

"I will always have time for you my love," he crooned, as they slowly separated. "Even though I sail for Makatooa with the sun, know this: There will always be a place for you in my heart, my home and my bed."

The Spice Rat's eyes misted over. She grabbed the sides of his head and pulled him in for a hard, passionate kiss.

As they gradually leaned back, Mal reached out and playfully punched him in the chest. "Yeah, while I'm gone, try and keep the whores to a minimum."

Alto chuckled. "I would ask the same while out seeking your fortune."

Placing her arms on his shoulders Mal gave a wicked grin. "So, I've only got you for one more cycle. Well, I don't think we're gonna see much outside this room."

The swordmaster appeared thoughtful. "What about food? We've already been in here awhile. I'm getting a bit hungry."

"Easy. I'll get them to bring food and drink to us."

Alto's presence erupted in amused surprise. "They do that?"

Mal gave a confident smirk. "Are you fucking kidding? We just pulled everybody's ass out of the fire...*again*! They can come up with a little room service."

The throne was damn uncomfortable. It was hard, flat and ugly. Shom Eldor vowed to himself to replace it as soon as possible.

It's no wonder father never spent much time in here, he thought.

Right now, before him, one of the leading fish merchants in the city of Rophan was pleading his case.

Shom sighed heavily. "My good man, it's only been two cycles since the darkness passed! We all share the same burden of revenue lost during that time. My suggestion, is to quit whining and get back to work!"

The city elder's poise wavered at the thought of displeasing the new king so soon in his reign.

"Yes, my sovereign," he acquiesced as he bowed and swiftly backed out of the throne room.

Shom slumped back and rested his forehead in his hand. It had been a long two cycles and his schedule was still full.

"Shall I call in the next audience sire?" came a youthful voice from beside him.

Shom nodded wearily without lifting his head. "Send them in."

The young aide waved his hand at the guard by the door and he opened it.

A tall woman with shoulder-length brown hair, thigh-high boots and a short-waist coat entered. She involuntarily checked the short sword at her side as she stared about in awe at the high ceiling and opulent furnishings.

Shom finally looked up and a cleaver, satisfied smile crossed his face. "And pray tell what House Eldor can do for you my dear?"

Attina froze, then gaped unbelievingly at the source of the familiar voice.

"SHOM!" she squealed in delight as she bolted toward the throne.

The palace guards tensed for an instant but relaxed when they saw their new king rushing down the stairs of his riser.

The colliding embrace rocked the smaller Shom and she swept him up into a long deep kiss.

Stepping back the hill sister blushed slightly as she smoothed her jacket. "I'm sorry Your Majesty, that was inappropriate."

Shom's grin became lecherous. "I'm the one who decides what's inappropriate around here."

Attina blushed again. "Yes, but, how? I mean, I was only told to report here for a sensitive mission."

"After that little agricultural incident last grand, your queen has become quite beholden to me and my friends. I requested you be assigned as my seneschal. Now come, I'll personally show you to your quarters."

"I wouldn't want to take you away from your duties sire," she modestly said with a sly grin.

Shom glanced at the guards and his aides feigning indifference. "Nonsense. My people love me!"

Attina's demeanor was skeptical. "You want to talk about the dozen or so hanging in the square."

Shom shrugged. "Father's inner circle. Eventually they would have only caused trouble."

The hill sister placed her hands on her hips and shook her head in amusement. "This is either going to be the best assignment of my life, or my last."

Eldorian sovereign Shom Eldor placed his forefinger under Attina's chin. "Or both. Tell me, would you have it any other way?"

When Stryder Aramos caught the smell of cooking beef, he knew the soles of his boots were slowly burning. Sweat poured off him stinging the newly carved fields of sacred numbers on his legs, chest and back.

The Tiikeri empire had been most accommodating upon his return to the Land of Mists. The mongrel guide they had secured for the journey was of course killed the moment he reached the cavern entrance. Witnesses and loose tongues were a liability and he didn't want his Tiikeri hosts to know he was visiting their ancient enemy.

Now in the sweltering heat and dim illumination, he waited.

The tunnels below the eastern Land of Mists were connected with Mount Natal and the infamous Fire Hive.

An ominous rumble reverberated in the shaft ahead and the temperature rose considerably.

They were coming.

Closing his eyes briefly a set of numbers on Stryder's neck began to glow with a faint blue light.

When he opened them again, he took a deep breath and readied himself. He had confidence in his god and his abilities, but the Na-Kab were never to be taken lightly.

GLOSSARY

Spoiler warning: The following is a master glossary for all the books in this series. Reading beyond a specific word or phrase searches could result in spoilers.

Adad Sunal – EEtah war collage belonging to House Bran, specializing in conducting internal security for House Bran.

Agress – A green Etheria Crystal with red striations which opens and closes doors, windows and hatches, negating any locks but not traps or wards.

Aiken – Semi-sentient clouds sent out across the Annigan from Mount Ghas-Tor, recording everything they witness on the ground and in the air. They are indistinguishable from other clouds against the backdrop of a blue sky. Aiken constantly send visuals back to the mountain, but recent images remain in their limited memory. Those possessing psychic abilities can access their recent memories by flying through and communing with them.

Akina – Humanoid fox creatures native to the Barrens in the Twilight Lands. Often sly and excellent thieves.

Amarenian – Female human race formerly noted for their hatred and slavery of men and piracy.

Angona – Roasted eel on a stick. Sold from vendors' carts all over the City of Immor-Onn.

Annigan – The name of the world which is the setting for the various stories in the Tales of the Annigan Cycle. It includes the two hemispheres of Lumina and Nocturn separated by the Twilight Lands.

Anointed Sister – The title for the Amarenian Queen.

Aquamarine – Pale blue Etheria Crystal which reveals something's true nature.

Ara-Fel Party – Political party of Amarenian farmers.

Arapa Fish – A large fish native to the back waters and tributaries of the Otoman River. Their tough scaly skin is coveted among the Dreeat as armor. The scales by themselves are so abrasive they are also sold as nails.

Ash-Ta – Avion term (winged monster) for the widespread colonies of humanoid bats inhabiting the rocky crags stretching across of the Spine of the World. Avion scholars record six tribes: the Molossi, Acero, Chiro, Ptero, Diaemus and Desmodus. The Ash-Ta allied with the Tiikeri due to their shared enemy, the Do-Tarr.

Astute Sister – Amarenian title for high level politician.

Aur-Quaz – Iridescent Etheria Crystal stimulating energy.

Available Regions – Uninhabited areas of Immor-Onn waiting for the residents displaced by the recent Black Pearl Revolution to return and inhabit.

Avion –Proud sentient rulers of Lumina's sky. Incredibly beautiful and graceful to behold and unabashedly elitist, especially towards their distant cousins, the Humans. Avions refuse to wear any armor and yet have led the way in almost every major war fought. Their scholars contributed a great deal to the knowledge of Lumina. Their four Great Houses occupy the airspace and mountain tops of the Goyan Islands.

Avion Great Houses:

House Azar - Avion House inhabiting the City of Mitar, on the Island of Dal, in the Tellasian chain, ruled by Queen Averin. Their territories include the skies over the Tellasian Chain, Otomoria, Zer-Tal Twins, and the Zerk Atoll. They are known for their healing Clerics of Neami and their beautiful music.

House Eacher - Avion House inhabiting the Island of Wou, City of Picon & surrounding airspace. Ruled by King Sindil.

House Solas – Smallest of all the Avion houses. They inhabit the city of Adean on the Island of Temil in the Outer Zerians and control the surrounding airspace.

House Pyre - Eldest, largest, and most powerful of all the Avion Houses. They inhabit the skies above the Island of Goya. Their city stronghold, Darmont Keep, sits on the north face of volcanic Mount Goya. Unlike the other Avion Houses who utilize Air Magic, they mastered Fire Magic drawing their power from the volcano.

Awal – First of the ten Quinte Grand Cycle, Spring.

Azurite – Purple Etheria Crystal which connects to the Middle realms.

Bailian – Predominate race of the western Twilight Lands. Descended from the Piceans, they are a beautiful humanoid race with pale blue skin and large eyes.

Banja – The seventy-seven Amarenian noble families, eleven for each of the various seven provinces called Dors.

Banok Atoll – Island ring in the Southeastern Ocean of Lumina housing one of the largest permanent Flavian portals. Its psionic ripples extend out hundreds of miles and affect the entire southeastern Deep Ocean of Lumina.

Banok Run – The final test for admittance to the elite Brightstar Sailors where they must navigate a tight circle around the turbulent seas surrounding the Banok Atoll without being pulled into its giant Flavian portal.

Bespoke Lords – Members of prominent families who have Bespoke Names and serve as advisors to the sovereign in a respective noble human house in the Goyan Islands.

Bespoke Names – Honorary family names only bestowed by a Goyan Island governor or higher as reward for exemplary service to the crown.

Black Mural – A magical record of the Annigan located deep in the Rod-Ema Trench in the Ocean Deep of Nocturn. It slowly grows in size as it records every act of imbalance on the planet. If it grows too large, it will penetrate into the planet's core, killing all life and allowing it to start anew.

Black Talon – Special forces of the Aramos Army, the Fosvara Guard.

Boustian Mage – Bards who perform magic by singing, playing music and storytelling, found predominantly in the larger cities of the Goyodian Chain of islands.

Brightstar – Elite sailors of House Calden qualified to sail the Deep Oceans and the storm-tossed seas of the Twilight Lands. Captains in the Calden Navy must be Brightstar qualified. Brightstar only allows acceptance to their ranks upon completion of the treacherous Innaca or Banok Runs.

Brom – Horse size dragonflies inhabiting the steep southern foothills of the Amaren Mountains.

Calcite – Clear Etheria Crystal which aids in navigation.

Caldani – Privateers hired by Human House Calden to patrol their waters.

Calden Intelligencer Service – House Calden's elite spy agency and secret police. They draw recruits mostly from the Calden Maritime Legion.

Calden Maritime Legion – Marines for House Calden

Calisma – Main library in the University of Marassa.

Cali – Branch libraries and scriptoriums in the five Human capital cities in the Goyodian Island Chain.

Carbana – Chewing tobacco rolled into a tight tube.

Cavernite – A pale green Etheria Crystal with pink striations that can increase the physical dimensions of the interior of any structure it is placed within. The size increase depends on the amount of Cavernite used and the level of PSI used to power it. Without a constant supply of PSI power, the dimensions revert back to their original size. Often used with an Obsidian PSI battery backup.

Centi Elipse – Called a Centi for short. Unit of time in the Goyan Islands equaling a minute.

Celot – Amarenian term for a priestess.

Cevot – Large sentient spider creatures known for their silk, inhabiting the Os-Oni Mountains of the Twilight Lands.

Ched – Seventh of the ten Quinte Grand Cycle, Autumn.

Chanakans – An ancient race of sentient octopoids dwelling in vast underwater cities in the Ocean Deep of Nocturn. They worship the ancient ones of the abyss and practice a powerful water magic.

Cluster – The name for ten cycles, the Annigan's version of a week. There are five clusters to a Quinte (month).

Cobalcite – Deep pink Etheria Crystal used for healing.

Code of Tisina – Mobster code of silence in the City of Zor. Because of Zor's zero tolerance for organized crime, the various independent criminals adopted a "no cooperation" rule with city officials. The slightest violation of this code is punishable by death.

Common – The Common Tongue, a spoken only language used mostly by humans and those in business with them.

Cocoonessa – Cocoon city of the Tinian Moth people on Mount Natal in the Land of Mists. Also called the Silk City.

Corporal Reach, The –The prime material plain of the middle realms where the Annigan resides.

Coxeter – Both the language and magic system of the Tinian race based on a complex form of three-dimensional geometry. The written language is made up of cryptic mathematical notations using lines and dots. Tinian minds perceive all math as the three-dimensional mapping, best displayed in their silk weavings of intricate geometric patterns. When combined with Etheria Crystals, these patterns can be used to perform spells.

Croquis – Magitech mapping devise projecting a scalable three-dimensional holographic image of a desired location, including the other planes of the multiverse.

Cub Prince – A rare black tiger heir to the throne of the Tiikeri Empire. Once every generation, the Tiikeri king must breed an heir. All prominent Tiikeri families offer their most eligible daughters for breeding, but only one will conceive of a black tiger. All other cubs produced from this royal union are killed at birth. They move the complete family of the female who gives birth to the Cub Prince into the palace and considered them nobility. They immediately begin grooming the Cub Prince for the throne, and, when he comes of age, he must kill his father to take it.

Cul-Ta – Humanoid rat creatures found in almost every City in Lumina.

Cycle – Time period equivalent to a day.

Dag – Amarenian term for a common slave. A derogatory slang word for a male.

Darek Witch – Amarenian earth shamans acting as midwives and performing other shamanistic duties.

Darian Silk – High quality silk spun by the Cevot Spiders traded to the On'Dara.

Darwan – A cross between the Balians and the Fudomi, this race is the most prolific humanoid native to the Barrens. They situate their villages around Ghorn temples and must pay tribute to the Onay hordes of the region. Villages close to the borders of the hordes remain under constant threat. Darwans raise a herd animal called the Ng'Ombe which provides the major staple food in the Barrens.

Dasam – Tenth of the ten Quinte Grand Cycle, Winter.

Deci – Time unit equivalent to one hour.

Derde – Third of the ten Quinte Grand Cycle, Spring.

Diamond – Clear Etheria Crystal which transfers power.

Doggin – Derogatory term used for slave dock workers in the city of Aris.

Dolin – Etheria gem hunters, mostly of the Gila race, traveling the Barrens in small caravans and harvesting raw Etheria Crystals to sell to the Zadim lapidaries of the Oasis in the Dark Waste Desert.

Dor – Title of the seven various provinces in Amarenia. Taia-Dor, Denat-Dor, Mivira-Dor, Amoso-Dor, Kinning-Dor, Rackam-Dor, Durik-Dor.

Do-Tarr – Sentient, hive-minded mantid creatures from the Land of Mists in Nocturn. They comprise two large hives in the north and south with precise subterranean tunnels connecting them. They are expert builders and remain neutral in all forms of politics.

Dreamer in the Lake – Demi-God of the Os'Tor Forest and a Harbinger of Balance. She rests at the bottom of a large lake encased in mud and manifests herself on the lake's surface as a multicolored lotus. Her accolades, sentients from every race, sleep around the lake's shore, sending their ethereal bodies out into people's dreams and guiding them.

Dreeat – Humanoid crocodilians inhabiting the end of the western fork of the Otoman River in Otomoria. They grow sugar cane and make magical healing candies from it. They harvest river fish as a major part of their diet. For thousands of grands, ever since the arrival Human race, the Human families have tried to eradicate them.

Dronning Mare – Female horse chosen to breed with the On'Dara chief.

EEtah – Large, powerful and aggressive sentient humanoid shark creatures trained in martial schools known as Sunals to become the professional warriors of Lumina. After their egg birth in the hatcheries and their first year in the nursery, they are sorted into one of the various Sunals of their House. Females enter House Nur and the males go through a highly competitive Sunal scouting and recruiting process with the nursery's called the Garess. Sunals hire out bodyguards, sentries, mercenaries and virtually anything martial. This, along with weapon manufacturing and sales, provides the main revenue stream for the great houses.

EEtah Great Houses:

House Nur – This Noble house is female only. Co-ruled by a secular Queen Mother and spiritual High Priestess.
Temple of Drulain headquartered in the High Holy City of Zor.
Specialty: Scribes, Clerics, Healers, Politics, Domestics.

House Crom – Three Sunals in the Tellasian Chain.
Sedar Sunal on Roe Island. Specialty: Bodyguard.
Boril Sunal on Uma Island. Specialty: Crom Internal Security.
Zorod Sunal on Tel Island. Specialty: Castle and Town Defense.

House Bran – Four Sunals in the Goyodian Chain.

Garf Sunal on Quell Island. Specialty: Long term inland duty.

Tukk Sunal on Mobis Island. Specialty: Shipboard Security.

Adad Sunal on Creos Island. Specialty: Bran Internal Security.

Farak Sunal on Roust Island. Specialty: Bounty Hunter, Vengeance.

House Zed – Three Sunals in the Wouvian Islands.

Dakor Sunal on Owling Island. Specialty: Shock Troops.

Jut Sunal on Tor Island. Specialty: Zed Internal Security.

Morrak Sunal on Billow Island. Specialty: Police, Executioners.

Elipse – A unit of time equaling a second.

Ellie – Slang and abbreviation for an Ellipse.

Esteemed Sister – Amarenian title for Ambassador.

Etheria Crystal – Crystals containing magical properties mostly found in crystal trees in the Barrens of the Twilight Lands. Residents of the Dark Waste Desert harvest and process the oases' crystals. These crystals provide the primary form of magic in Nocturn.

Flavian Portals – Portals through space making different points in the Annigan instantaneously accessible by passing through the inter-dimensional Middle Realms. Each portal is different. There are several large, fixed portals on both Lumina and Nocturn and hundreds of smaller dedicated Flavians. Certain animals, intoxicants and magical items can open smaller portals.

Frozen Sea – The vast expanse of ice flows covering the majority of Nocturn and the largest centrally occupied area in all of Annigan. The ice ranges from a slushy mixture with icebergs near the land masses to several hundred feet thick in the eastern areas.

Forsvara Guards – A rank-and-file foot soldier army of House Aramos.

Fudomi – Sentient humanoid ram creatures inhabiting the western Os-Oni Mountains of the Twilight Lands. They steal and sell the Cevot Spider broods' silk and eggs, which they consider a delicacy.

Galeb – Sea Gulls with a psychic connection to a handler. They are used to transport messages across Lumina.

Garf Sunal – EEtah War college belonging to House Bran. Their specialty is long term inland duty.

Gar-Kal – Fish head humanoids living on the ocean floor of Nocturn. They are of low intelligence and aggressive.

Geta – Amarenian title for a master at a skill or craft, especially if they teach it.

Ghas-Tor – This is the tallest peak on the Annigan. It reaches upward 32,000 feet in the Os'Ani Mountain range of the Twilight Lands. More than a mountain, it is a sentient being and the epicenter of Air Magic in the world.

Ghorn – Necromancers of the Barrens in Twilight Lands.

Ghost Suit – A gray, skintight jump suit used mostly by Valdurian forces to blend into the Kan fog.

Ghosts of the Kan – Mariner's term for Rayth raiders. Due to their ghost white chalk covering their bodies and acting as camouflage when they attack during the Kan fog.

Gila – The main sentient race populating the Dark Waste. Hybrids comprising Bailian pilgrims and a now long-gone sentient lizard native to the region. They are an advanced race occupying the three large oases of the desert.

Golden One, The – Otick term for the Golden Avatar.

Goy-Ardia – Goyan fire mages trained at the University of Marassa.

Goyan Calendar – Method of time keeping found only in the Goyan Islands. It consists of a Grand Cycle (year) which is comprised of ten Quinte (months) named; Awal, Teine, Derde, Kvara, Peto, Sesto, Ched, Merve, Tisa and Dasam. Each Quinte is divided into fifty Cycles (days) with each cycle being divided into fifty Deci (hours) twenty-five in sunlight and twenty-five in Kan. Ten cycles equal a Cluster (week) with five Clusters per Quinte.

Goyan Rise – A 300-mile-wide sea mount in central Lumina acting as the floor of the Shallow Sea. Its volcanic vents fuel the volcano of Mount Goya.

Grand – Short for Grand Cycle. Unit of time equivalent to a year.

Grass Eater – Singa insult

Gustare' – Amarenian bath house and tavern.

Hackney – Etheria driven floating carriages found throughout the major cities of Lumina.

Hand of the Wind – The Assassin's Guild of Annigan. All members worship Orad, goddess of death. The upper levels are clerics of Orad.

Hakim – A judge in the High Holy City of Zor.

Harbingers of Balance – Sentient creatures of all types called to a secret society monitoring the balance of the Annigan and warning when something upsets it.

Hasteen – City of the Dreeat crocodile people.

Hill Sister – Hermaphroditic warriors inhabiting the northern foothills of the Amaren Mountains in Amarenia. Though they possess both male and female sex organs, they cannot procreate. Popular with Amarenian nobility as seneschal/bodyguards partly because they can have sex with them and not violate their "no man" pledge.

Hoon – Word used in Zor to denote a pimp or the manager of a brothel.

Howlite – Gray Etheria Crystal used for glamour, disguise and polymorphing.

Humans – The Human race descended from the Avion race. In 5070 PA, the rebellious Avions which joined Xandar the Mad's doomed Great Kraken Incursion had their wings severed as punishment before being banished and scattered to the Goyodian Chain. 171 years later the Seventh Avatar sang the "Song of Rebirth" evolving them into a separate race. They formed their Great Houses, spreading out across the Goyan Island Chain and beyond the Shallow Sea.

Human Great Houses:

House Aramos –The largest and wealthiest of the great human families directly descended from the First Men. The capital city of Aris is located on the Island of Vakai in the Goyodian Chain of Islands in the Northern Shallow Sea. They control banking and finance in Lumina and constantly hatch Machiavellian plots to expand their power over the other houses.

House Calden – This great house controls the seas with the largest military and commercial fleets. Their Capital City of Nader is on the Island of Tarla in the Goyodian Chain, but they command the island chain of the Zerk Atoll where their sailors are trained.

House Eldor – This great house controls virtually all the agricultural islands of the eastern Goyan Islands. Their Capital City of Rophan is on the Island of Tolle in the Goyodian Chain of Islands in the Northern Shallow Sea.

House Valdur – This house is known for their incestuous practices to keep the family bloodline pure. Their capital city of Dryden is on the Island of Atar in The Goyodian Chain of Islands in the Northern Shallow Sea. All but destroyed in a surprise invasion by House Eldor called the Unification War, only the discovery of lighter than air travel and a fleet of war balloons saved their home island. They lost the rest of their agricultural lands to Eldor. Their entire culture revolves around their powerful air guild, the Valdurian Air Service.

House Whitmar – This family runs the organized and sanctioned slave trade on Lumina from the City of Nier on the northern Goya coast. Their Capital City of Brinstan is located on the Island of Umin in the Goyodian Chain in the Northern Shallow Sea.

Immor-Onn – Large city known as "the Shining Jewel of the East" located on the western coast of the Twilight Lands. Home of the Bailian Empire.

Idonian Philosophy – The Avion prejudice that Humans are a scourge which should be wiped out. The driving belief of the Idonian Cabal of Avion House Pyre and Solas.

Innaca Deep – Giant whirlpool in the Northwestern Ocean of Lumina housing one of the largest Flavian portals. Its psionic ripples extend out hundreds of miles.

Innaca Run – The final test for admittance to the elite Brightstar Sailors where they must navigate a tight circle around the turbulent seas surrounding the Innaca Atoll without being pulled into its giant Flavian portal.

Ironmark – Brutal enforcers of the Quartermasters in the Goyan Islands of Lumina. Each island chain has their own Ironmark specializing in their own unique form of torture.

Itori – Insect Shamans found throughout the agricultural western Goyan Islands. Although they control mostly locusts, they can command any insect and are immune to all insect venoms and stings.

Jangwa – Elite desert commandos defending the outer parameter of the two civilized oases in the Dark Waste Desert. Capable of traveling under the sand and rapidly over the surface of the desert, they make frequent scouting missions to the untamed Qua-Raman Oasis and the Buried City of Nof-Saloom.

Kaefom – Traditional Amarenian breeding ritual overseen by the Darek Witches.

Kan – Period of the day in the Goyan Islands when the thick sea fog rises blotting out the sun, used mostly for sleep. It is an effect caused by geothermal activities only found in the Goyan Islands and Shallow Sea.

Kel – Flying lizards bred and tended by Avions for food and as beasts of burden.

Kharry Institute – Tiikeri medical facility located outside the Tiikeri capital city of Hai-Darr and run by the brilliant and ruthless Dr. Met-Ge, specializing in crossbreeding Mawl races to produce Mongrels for specific duties. The Institute created Cheepas and the Ves-Lari.

Kinjuto Dominator – Sex mage using BDSM techniques.

Konaleeta – Called the Island of the Lost. The entire island is caught in a permanent Flavian Loop. It bounces around from location to location across any of the planes of the Middle Realms, never staying in anyone place for very long.

Kusars – Mawl bandits from the Dasos region in the Land of Mists.

Kvara – Fourth of the ten Quinte Grand Cycle, Summer.

Ky-Awat – Sentient rat creatures of the Dark Waste Desert. They have bred them up from the Cul-Ta and are larger and more aggressive, but no smarter. Various factions use them as cannon fodder. They breed quickly and are plentiful, especially around the three main oases.

Land of Mists – The largest land mass in Nocturn. So named because the mixture of cold temperatures in the air combined with the warmth of the ground results in a uniform constant low hanging fog over the entire continent. Three distinct landscapes cover the surface of the land, separated by the Kel-Raku Mountain range and dimly illuminated by bioluminescence, outcroppings of Etheria Crystals and the moon and stars. The thick rainforest of Arboro lies to the north, and the vast savannah of Rovina runs to the south. They're connected by the Bor-Kaa Pass. The dense jungles and swamps of Dasos lie to the east.

Landagar Group – Research and Development Division of the Valdurian Air Service located in the balloon city of Landagar high in the mountain peaks of the Valdurian home island of Atar.

Larimar – The "Talking Stone," a milky white Etheria Crystal with blue striations, used for psychic communication between parties within proximity of the gem.

Learned Sister – The title given to Amarenian teachers, scribes & academics.

Legates – Suicide messengers hired through House Whitmar. Candidates are usually elderly or terminally ill. Upon their death, House Whitmar agrees to care for their surviving family for their remaining lifetimes.

Lor-Danta Oasis – The eastern most major oasis in the Dark Waste Desert. The large Obsidian field stretching from its shore contains six Tanum Charts of the skies used by the Arron-Nin Astrologers dwelling there.

Lumina – The hemisphere of the world in constant sunlight.

Luna – Term for the lunar cycle used by every culture in the Annigan except the humans in the Goyan Islands, who cannot see the moon.

Luroh – Bolo/sash weapon used by the Mahilia. The sash contains the person's rank and record. The two metal balls at either end become an effective weapon when twirled.

Magitech – The fusion of magic and technology. Mostly referring to the use of Etheria Crystals and specific mechanical items. i.e., Airship engines.

Mahilia – City guards in Mostar, the capital of Amarenia.

Makari – Inter-dimensional race of sentient spiders from the Pasture Plain of the Middle Realms. They seeded the Cevot race in the Os'Tor Mountains in the Land of Mists. The males resemble hairy wolf spiders, the females resemble black widows. The females have been known to allure any male of any race. They compulsively kill after sex.

Malachite – Light green Etheria Crystal, absorbs energy.

Marassa – A professor at the University of Marassa.

Masha – Amarenian for master.

Maudo Grass – Tall grass with a bright blue flowering tuft growing in the Land of Mists. The flowers are a favorite intoxicant for Mawls and especially coveted by the Tiikeri.

Mawl – Overall name for the humanoid cat races of the Land of Mists. It is also the term used for the common language they share.

Medikua – Medical officer aboard Calden naval vessels.

Merve – Eighth of the ten Quinte Grand Cycle, Autumn.

Middle Realms – Constantly shifting inter-dimensional plane between worlds. Sometimes referred to as the Fairy or Dream Realms.

Mongrel – The product of cross breeding between the Mawl races found all over the Land of Mists. Pure breeds mostly shun them and the Tiikeri use them for slave labor.

Moonfall – Period of the cycle when Nocturn's main illuminating body, the moon, dips below the horizon issuing in the Moonless

Moonless – The "night" period of the cycle when Nocturn's main illuminating body, the moon, orbits around to the Lumina side of the Annigan.

Mora – Term used for teacher or master in the Whovian Sword Schools of Rohina Takki.

Morasian Puff Boy – Male prostitute from the Port City of Moras on Goya's west coast. Known for their distinctly feminine demeanor.

Mostas – Capital City of the Amarenian Empire on the western shore of Amarenia.

Najuka – Amarenian emasculation ritual performed on all males except those used for breeding purposes in the Kaefom Ritual.

Na-Kab – One of the three insectoid groups originating from below the Land of Mists. They occupied the easternmost hive closest to Mount Natal. Their exoskeleton is made up of fire magic. Their tail has a penis shaped stinger capable of impregnating any living thing they sting.

Namesake – Term used for spouse when they share a bespoke last name.

Narrows, The – Remnants of an old iron mine forming the slums of the Hidden City of Toriss in Otomoria.

Nocturn – The hemisphere of the world in constant night

Nolton Boat – Ships made of Ukko wood in a secret shipyard on the Island of Zer, mostly used by Brightstar sailors. Hovering less than an inch above the water, their Ukko rudder guides and propels. The specific construction of the hull makes the boat unsinkable.

Noma – Poison from the Noma Viper.

Nurian Edicts – EEtah rules of conduct set down by House Nur forming the basis for all Sunal laws. The various Sunals add their own individual laws to this baseline.

Nyanja – Large seahorses ridden as sea cavalry by the Calden Navy.

Obsidian – Black Etheria Crystal storing psychic energy.

Ocean Deep – Name referring to any of the deep oceans of Lumina or Nocturn.

Ol'daEE – Person able to cast spells while having sex under the influence of Oldust.

Oldust – Hallucinogenic powder derived from the spores of the rare Impia Mushroom, increasing magical abilities and is essential for individual travel to the Middle Realms.

Onay – Humanoid wolf men of the Barrens, banding their various packs together in three distinct hordes.

On'Dara – Sentient horse creatures living on the Plains of Taka-Vir in the southeastern Twilight Lands. They raise and train horses, trading them for silk with the Cevot Spiders and selling them to the rest of the Annigan.

ooD – Shell worn on the back of the male Otick warriors as armor. They mark the warrior's rank and house on the outside of the shell and inscribe a record of their deeds on the inside. They place the ooD over the entrance to their homes in the sand.

Oracle of the River – Demi-God who dwells in the cypress swamp at the end of the western fork of the Otoman River for thousands of grands. It appears as a partially submerged giant catfish with its many whiskers sunken into the water. These whiskers perceive anything happening in, on, or around the waterway.

Orad – Air goddess of death and predominate deity of the assassin's guild, the Hand of the Wind. Her creed: *She comes as the wind. And takes whom she wishes. Her name is Orad. And she is death.*

Orad Dex – Initiates to the Orad priesthood. Street/entry level assassins.

Orad Con – (Taker of the Divine Wind) These are full priests of Orad. Their special skills are the Kiss of Death, the Poison Breath and the Phantom Dagger.

Orad Sto – (Giver of the Divine Wind) High priests of Orad who can also restore life.

Otick – Humanoid crab people inhabiting the Shallow Sea. Among the first sentient creatures to rise from the ocean floor they evolved into a proud, deeply spiritual and noble race. Goya's volcanic warmed waters provide home to the Otick's prolific oyster beds littering the floor of the Shallow Sea. From these beds arose the five great Pearl Avatars, creation gods whose songs brought life and sentience to Lumina. Otick society is divided into a highly structured caste system: Worker Class, Warrior Class and Mother Class, and organized into two main categories: domestic and military. The Shelled Triad, the three Otick Great Houses, tend their own oyster beds and compete for the birthplace of the next Avatar.

Otick Great Houses:

House Awa – Home of the last two avatars. Located in the Tellasian Chain, in the capital city of Hidet on the Island of Zod. Mother Class specialization.

House Pewa – Located in the Goyodian Chain, in the capital city of Oniack, on the Island of Zak. Worker Class specialization.

House Sensu – Located in the Otoman Group, in the capital city of Sunico, on the Island of Lakia. Warrior Class specialization.

Otomoria – Large Island continent in the western Goyan Islands. The main grain producing agricultural island.

Outer Clan EEtah – Humanoid shark creatures smaller in stature than regular EEtahs and cast out from the three great EEtah Houses hatcheries. The survivors band together into loose clans, contracting themselves out as deck hands or recently volunteering in the Valdurian Marines.

Padi – Regional demi-god of water worshiped in and around the High Holy City of Zor, associated with the peace and calming effect of water and represented by a calm pond.

Palu EEtah – Rare hammerhead EEtahs. They are as big as the Outer Clan EEtah but extremely intelligent. They tend to be reclusive loners.

Pappia – Members of the child street gangs of the Hidden City of Toriss in the slum section of The Narrows.

Pa-Waga – Lawful evil god of greed worshiped mostly by the Tiikeri. Its clerics practice binary blood rune magic comprised of the letters "X" and "I."

Peace Babies – Children born of a union between any of the five major Human noble houses.

Peto – Fifth of the ten Quinte Grand Cycle, Summer.

Piceans – Humanoid fish people of Lumina. Capable of breathing above and below the water and impervious to the ocean's depths. They have gill flaps large enough to fold over their ears and when the vocal sound waves pass through the membrane, it translates it. This makes them valuable translators in the seaports of the Goyan Islands.

Piety Watch – Militant, religious police faction of the Pa-Waga church. They arrest anyone caught begging, idle, or not being productive. Minor offences are punished by a beating with thin cane rods. They wear red shirts under black capes with high pointed collars resembling cat ears.

Pisar – Bailian title for a scholar.

Pomaku – Humanoid leopard people (Mawl) native to the Arboro region in the Land of Mists, Nocturn.

Protocol 13 – EEtah House Nur code phrase requesting a meeting between an intelligence asset and their handler.

Qua-Raman Oasis – An oasis in the central Dark Waste Desert. Due to its location just south of the Tur-Qua Pass, it serves as a major trading post for gems harvested in The Barrens to the north.

Quartermaster – Collector of taxes and tariffs in the Goyan Islands who use the Ironmark to enforce their rule.

Queen's Envoy Service, The – The Amarenian Empire's spy service and member of the Society of Whispers.

Quinte – Time period equivalent to a month.

Ramu – A gambling dismemberment game banned everywhere in Lumina, except the Free City of Tannimore.

Rayth – Pirate faction of the Amarenian people in open revolt and attempting to form their own nation.

Rod-Ema Trench – Massive abysmal fissure running along the equator in the western ocean floor in Nocturn. At its head is the Agar Goyot and the Black Mural is found on its north wall dipping into the ocean depths.

Rohina Takii – Sword school originating on the Island of Wou. Known for its strike while drawing technique.

Sardor – Amarenian title for a female warlord.

Salar Winds – Turbulent winds surrounding the peak of Mount Goya which must be navigated to enter the Avion City of Darmont on the mountain's northwestern face. Avion term of exasperation, "By the mighty Winds of Salar!"

Secor – Street name for the Imperial Gold Ingot equivalent to ten struck gold coins.

Sesto – Sixth of the ten Quinte Grand Cycle, Autumn.

Shallow Sea – The body of water surrounding the greater Goyan Islands covering the Goyan Rise. The depth is no more than thirty feet deep at its lowest point.

Si – The term for "mister" in the Common Tongue spoken in the Goyan Islands.

Sikari – Female Singa hunter/killer squads, traveling in groups of two or more. They arm themselves with crossed bandoleros covering their chests and filled with sickle shaped throwing blades.

Silent Partner – Seven cabals of organized crime families in the Goyan Islands.

Simikort – Round engraved coin acting as an Amarenian noble's calling card.

Singa – Humanoid lion people (Mawl) inhabiting the southern Rovina area of the land of Mists.

Skirting the Upwinds – Dangerous maneuver practiced by few airship pilots. It involves taking the airship up to the edge of the atmosphere and then plummeting down to your destination. Allowing long-distance travel in a short period.

Society of Whispers – The general intelligence cooperative of the five Human noble houses, the Zorian Spymaster, the Calden Intelligencer Service, Suusho, and the Queen's Envoy Service.

Spice Rat – Smugglers operating in the Spice Islands chains (Zerian Reef Chain and Outer Zerians) and occasionally in the entire western side of the Goyan Islands.

Spooks – Street term for spies and operatives in the Society of Whispers.

Strasta – Ancient prophet in the folklore of the Cevot spider people of the Os-Ani Mountains.

Sunal – EEtah war college specializing in martial skills.

Suusho – The Bailian Empire's spy service and member of the Society of Whispers.

Szoldos Mercenaries – One of several small private armies for hire on the Goyan continent.

Taking it Upstairs – Airship slang for skirting upwinds

Tanum Charts – Six maps of Nocturn's night sky. The Arron-Nin Astrologers use them for divination and sometimes the opening of Flavian portals.

Teine – Second of the ten Quinte Grand Cycle, Spring.

Ten/Fifty— Cliché phrase in the Goyan Islands referring to the ten cycles (days) in the cluster (week) and fifty decis (hours) of the cycle (day). The equivalent of 24/7.

Tenable Sister—Title given to Amarenian lawyers.

Tiikeri – Sentient humanoid Tiger creatures of the Dasos region in the eastern Land of Mists.

Tisa – Ninth of the ten Quinte Grand Cycle, Winter.

Trinilic – Orange Etheria Crystal, fire magic connection.

Turine – Tidal clocks used in the Goyan Islands.

Twilight Lands – Area between Lumina and Nocturn in constant state of Twilight. Due to converging hot and cold air masses its weather remains perpetually stormy.

Ukkonite – Bronze Etheria Crystal with natural repellant properties. It is the crystal equivalent to Ukko wood found only in Nocturn.

Ukko Wood – Magical wood from the World Tree, harvested only on the Island of Zer in the eastern Goyan Islands. Its natural repellant properties are used in shields, weapons, Brightstar Nolton Boats and used as currency.

Ulana – Chaotic evil sea goddess worshiped by a small sect of Amarenian Rayth in the province of Durik-Dor

Unification War – Conflict started by House Eldor in 2 P.A. against the eastern agricultural islands of House Valdur. It ended as quickly as it began when House Aramos forced them to the negotiating table by threatening to freeze both houses' accounts in the Imperial Bank.

Valorous Sister – Amarenian title for heroic acts which affected the realm.

Vedette – Small fast Nolton Boats crewed by a single ex-Brightstar sailor and used for fast, anonymous travel around the oceans of Lumina.

Velocomite – Pale blue Etheria Crystal with red bands, increases or decreases an object's speed travelling.

Veros Pearls – Highest quality pearl cultivated in the Otick oyster beds. They are capable of holding a magical charge.

Ves-Lari – Mawl mongrels bred by the Tiikeri for rowing and poling. They are a combination of Pomaku (leopard) and Duma (Cheetah). Crews can pole or row for hundreds of miles at a time without stopping.

Vurr Carts – Carts used by the Vurr Clerics to collect the City of Zor's dead and garbage. There are two types: stationary carts situated on every major street where citizens can deposit their waste and roving carts mostly dealing with collecting the bodies of the dead.

Vurr Clerics – Accolades of the Free God Vurr serving as waste disposal in the City of Zor. Once maintaining constantly pyres burning everything from corpses to ordinary refuse. The city upgraded the pyres to full crematoriums. Vurr clerics smell of smoke and generally work nude, wearing only a simple cloak.

Wraith – Deep cover agents for House Aramos drawn from the elite Black Talons unit.

Yagur – Humanoid jaguars (Mawl) from the Arboro region of the Land of Mists. They are seers, healers and shamans, serving all the various Mawl races.

Yudon – Harpoon with a rifled the shaft for throwing accuracy. The standard weapon of every Sunal EEtah.

Yupik – a.k.a. the Ice Clans, one hundred and sixty-five clans divided into three major groups. The nomadic wanderers of the Western Flows compete for resources while the Ash-Ta constantly hunt them as prey. The largest group inhabits the vast Eastern Flows with semi-permanent settlements surrounding the Ice City of Mos-Agar'.

Zadim – Lapidaries operating in the Dark Waste Desert.

Zerian Rangers – Woodsmen fighters belonging to any of nine different clans occupying the forests of the Island continent of Zer in the Goyan Islands.

Zoldak Group – A private mercenary army comprised of former Black Talons of House Aramos.

Zorian Monetary Council – A ruling body founded in 3850 P.A. controlling all banking in the High Holy City of Zor. The council coordinates with the Calden Commodities exchange to regulate the exchange of money, goods and services, and uses the Quartermasters Guild for the collection of taxes and tariffs.

R.W. Marcus

MAPS

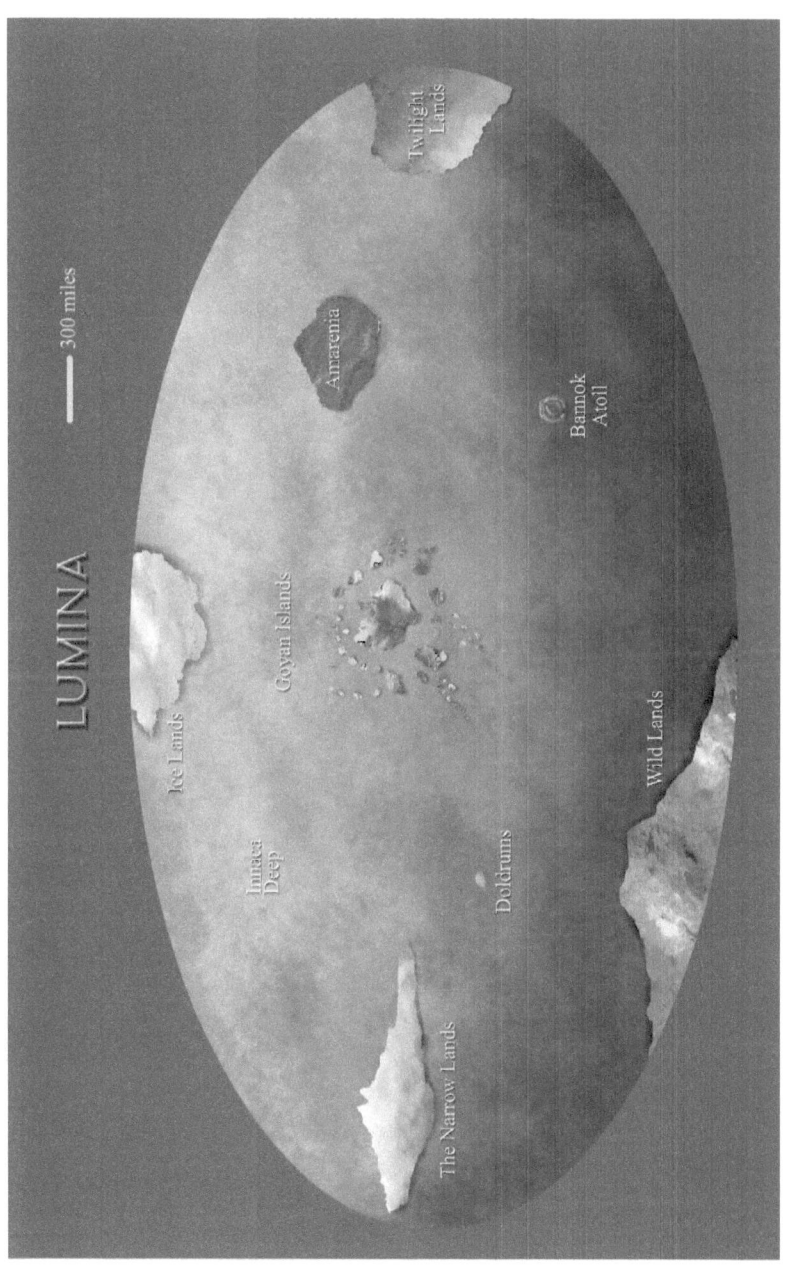

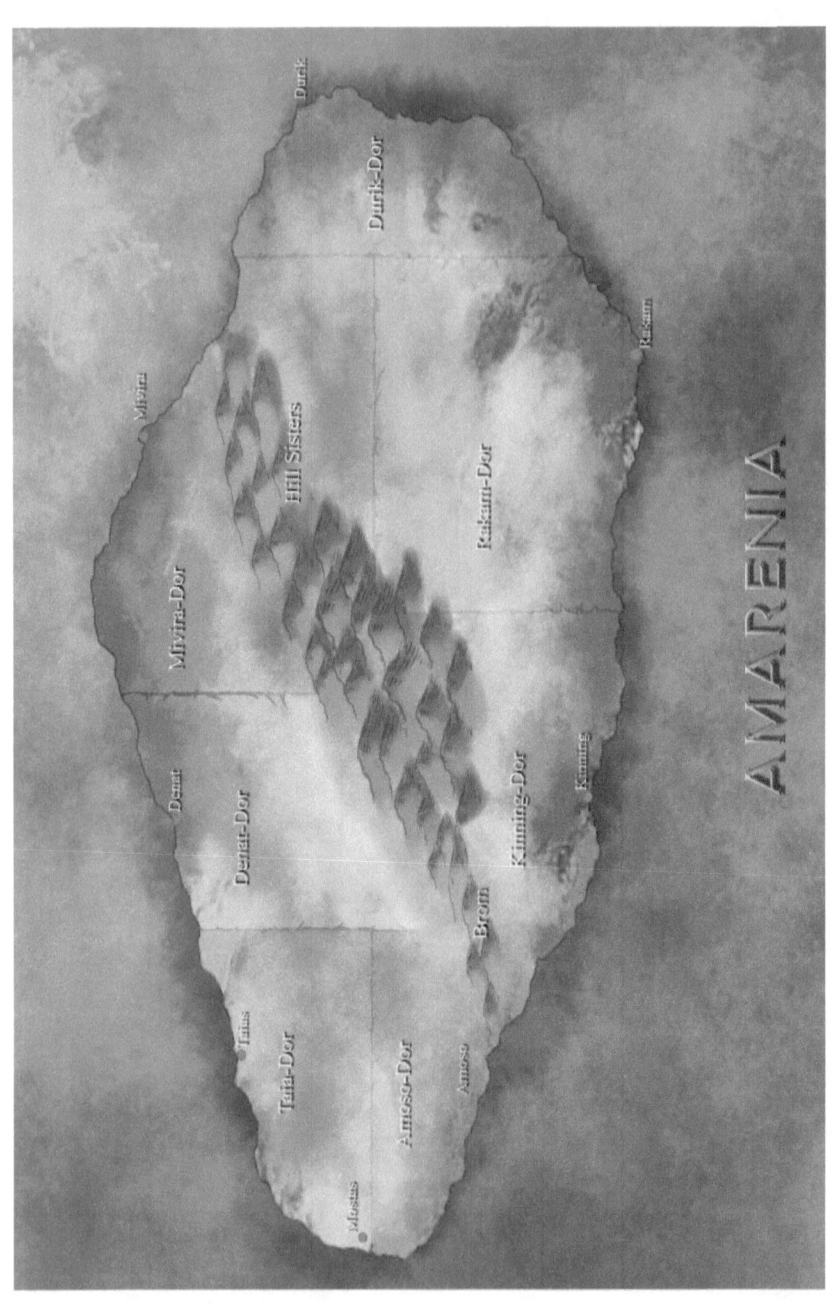

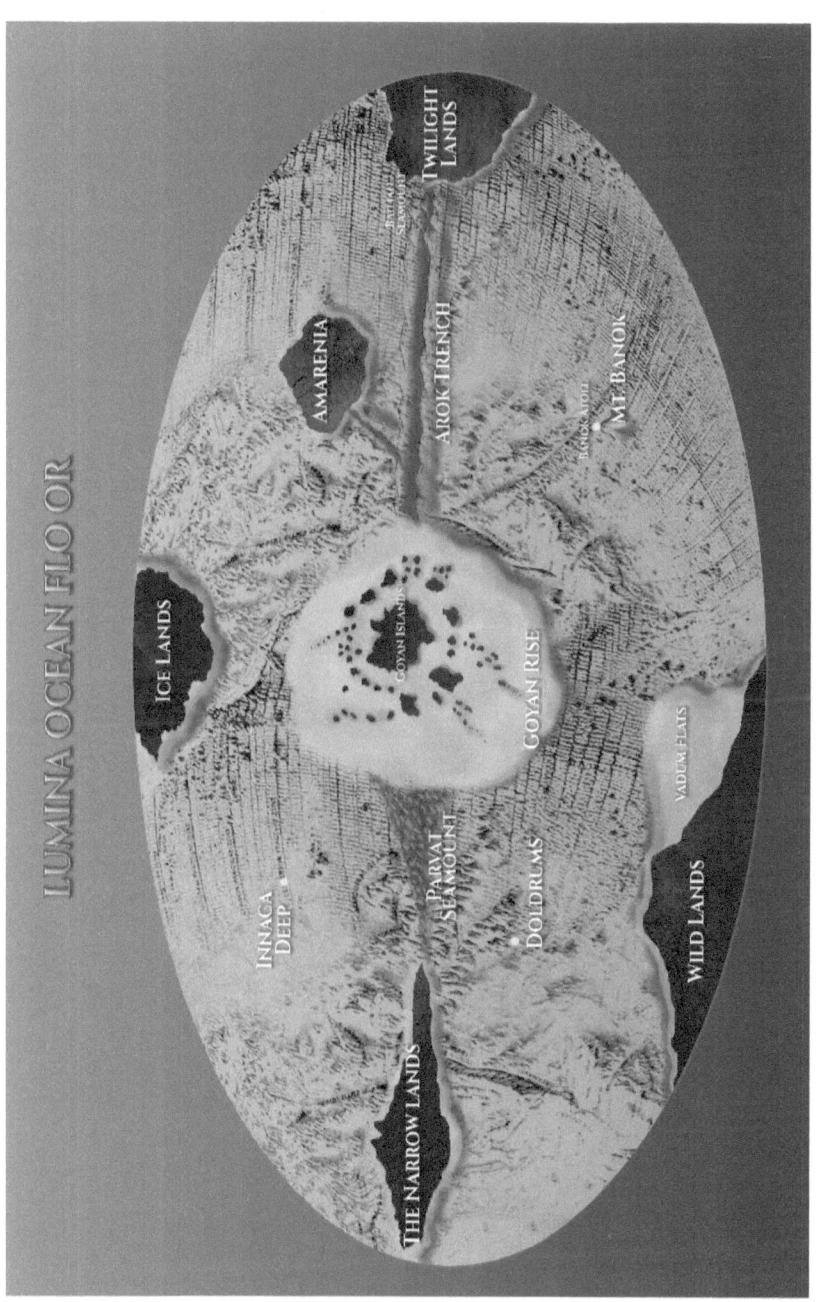

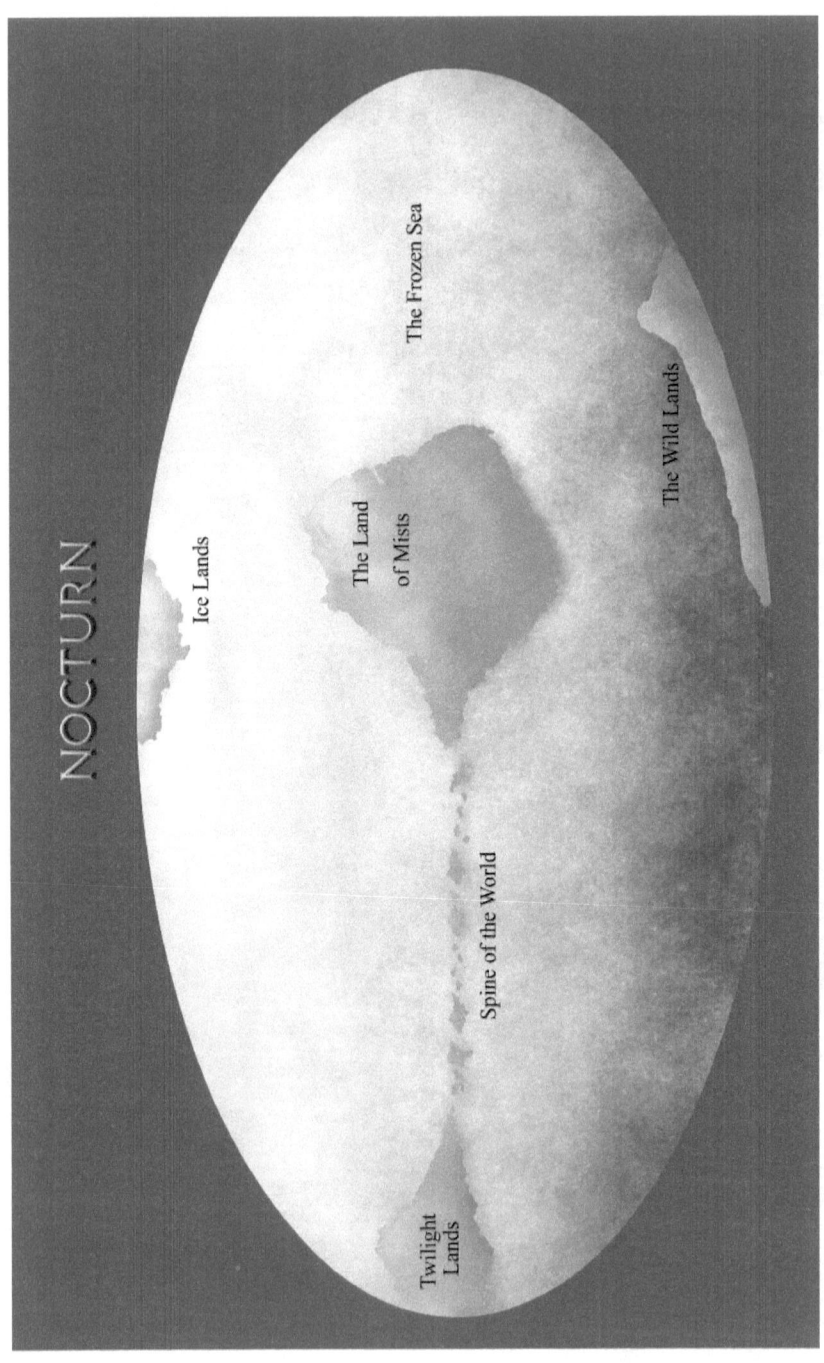

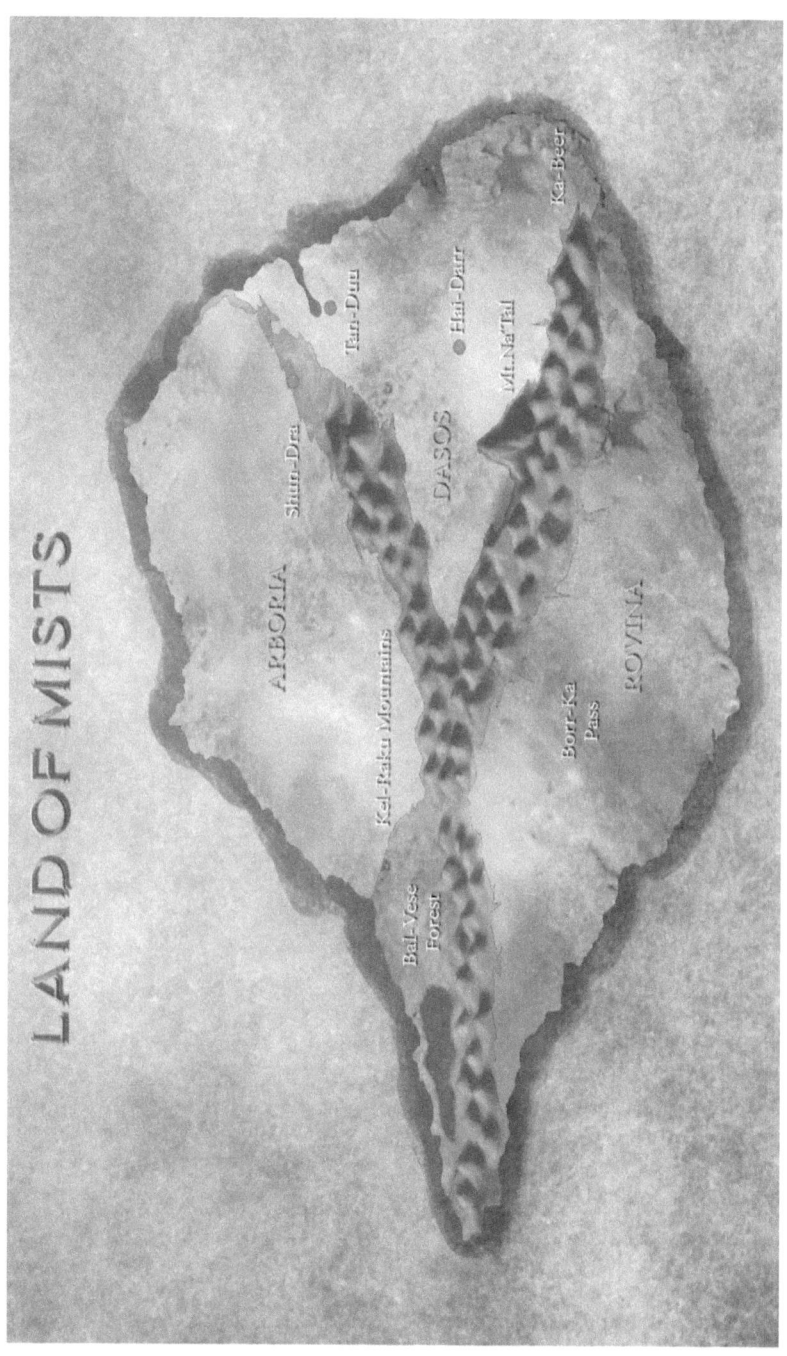

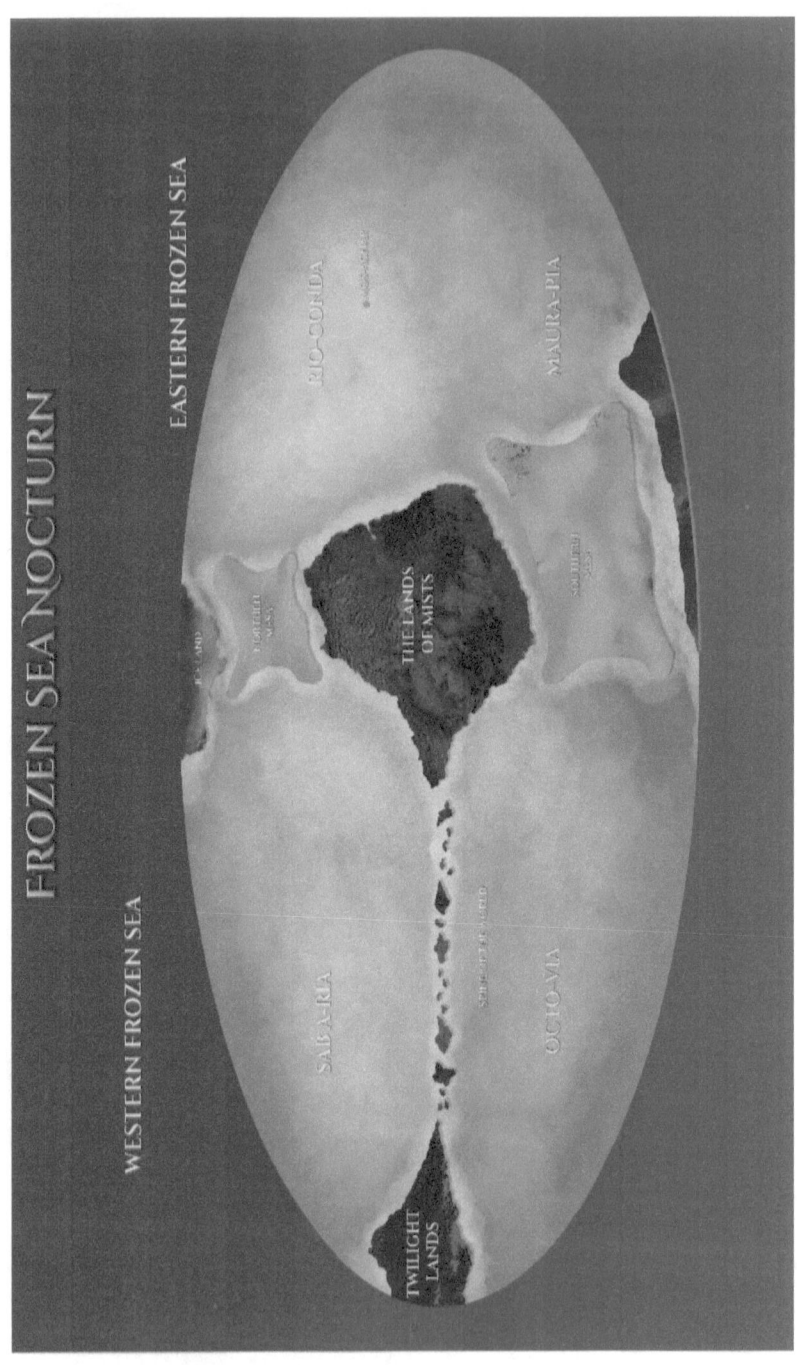

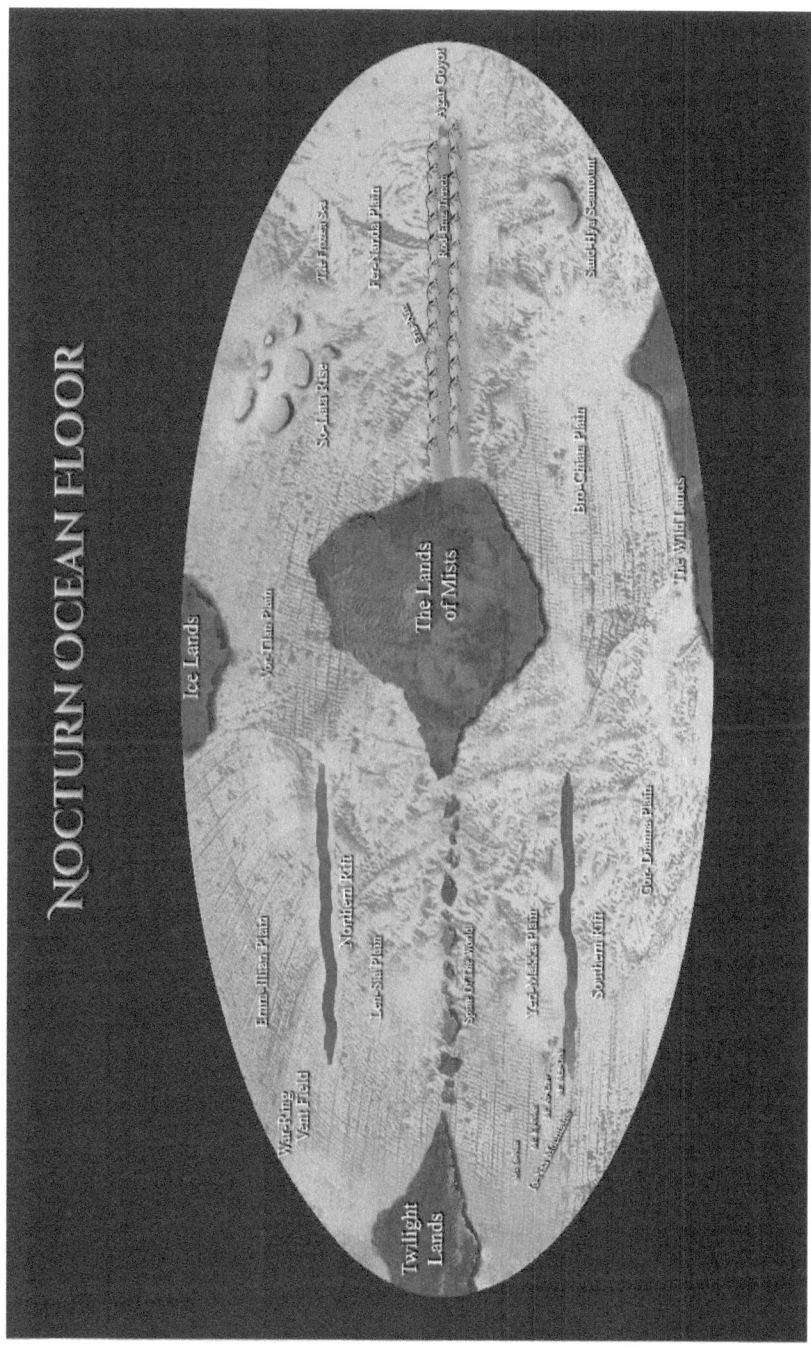

ABOUT THE AUTHOR

R.W. Marcus spent most of his life selling books. Along the way he managed to become a Falconer, 2nd Dan Black Belt in Yoshukai Karate, Freemason, Freelance Photographer, Ad Copywriter and WMNF Radio Disc Jockey. Marcus' radio commercials and freelance photography won numerous awards, including Best of Shows and Best of the Bay Addy Awards for work with Creative Keys and Laughing Bird Productions. R.W. Marcus was also Founder and Creative Director of United Game Masters, where he cowrote the UGM Universal Gaming System which he used to create and playtest a role-playing game based in the world of the Annigan Cycle. He formally held the title of Director of Incunabula at Griffon's Medieval Manuscripts, where he penned his first nonfiction title, *The Ship of Fools to 1500*, which Amazon called "an authoritative guide to one of the most popular works of secular writing." Now retired, he has created a new genre of fiction - Pulp Fantasy Noir - to exorcise the darker side of his good nature.

CONNECT
WEBSITE: https://AnniganCycle.com
FACEBOOK: https://www.facebook.com/noirrwmarcus/
TWITTER: @NoirRWMarcus
EMAIL: RWMarcus@yahoo.com

AGENTS of the VOID
TALES OF THE ANNIGAN CYCLE
BOOK FOUR
AVAILABLE FROM LAUGHING BIRD PUBLISHING

www.ingramcontent.com/pod-product-compliance
Lightning Source LLC
Chambersburg PA
CBHW021118260626
47169CB00005B/1331